# The Grey Wolf

LOUISE PENNY

# THE GREY WOLF

MINOTAUR BOOKS

NEW YORK

First published in the United States by Minotaur Books,
an imprint of St. Martin's Publishing Group

www.minotaurbooks.com

Endpaper art by MaryAnna Coleman / www.maryannacolemandesign.com

Excerpts from "Up" and "Sekhmet" from *Morning in the Burned House* by Margaret
Atwood. In the US: Copyright © 1995 by Margaret Atwood. Reprinted by permission of
HarperCollins Publishers. In Canada: Copyright © O. W. Toad. Reprinted by permission
of McClelland & Stewart, a division of Penguin Random House Canada Limited.

Library of Congress Cataloging-in-Publication Data

Names: Penny, Louise, author.
Title: The grey wolf / Louise Penny.
Description: First edition. | New York : Minotaur Books, 2024. | Series:
    Chief Inspector Gamache novel ; 19
Identifiers: LCCN 2024019335 | ISBN 9781250328137 (hardcover) |
    ISBN 9781250374417 (signed edition) | ISBN 9781250328144 (ebook)
Subjects: LCGFT: Detective and mystery fiction. | Novels.
Classification: LCC PR9199.4.P464 G75 2024 | DDC 813/.6—dc23/eng/20240429
LC record available at https://lccn.loc.gov/2024019335https://lccn.loc.gov/2024019335

Our books may be purchased in bulk for promotional, educational, or business use. Please
contact your local bookseller or the Macmillan Corporate and Premium Sales Department at
1-800-221-7945, extension 5442, or by email at MacmillanSpecialMarkets@macmillan.com.

First Edition: 2024

This edition was printed by Bertelsmann Printing Group

10  9  8  7  6  5  4  3  2  1

*For Rocky and Steve, forever in my heart*

# THE GREY WOLF

# CHAPTER 1

The phone rang. Again.

It was the fourth time in eight minutes.

All from the same number. All ignored by the head of homicide for the Sûreté du Québec. In the hopes it would go away.

But like most things ignored, it just got worse.

The first peal had interrupted the peace of the Gamaches' back garden this Sunday morning in mid-August, in the Québec village of Three Pines. It broke into Armand's thoughts as he sat on the field-stone terrasse, absently brushing croissant flakes from his shirt and sipping strong, smooth café au lait.

While Reine-Marie read the paper, his section lay folded and warming and gathering crumbs on his lap. He tilted his head back slightly to the sun, taking a deep breath of the late-summer air. Then he contemplated the bobbing black-eyed Susans and the morning glories and sweet pea and purple Jackmanii Superba clematis climbing the fence that separated them from the mad poet next door.

It was a lovely, though ineffective, barrier. Barbed wire would have to be added.

Actually, the duck was the menace. Thank God Rosa seemed to have forgotten that she could fly. Or, more likely, she simply chose not to.

Paper read, or ignored, and mugs in hand, they strolled down the long dew-glistening lawn, past the huge maple with the swing for the grandchildren, pausing now and then to examine the perennial beds, until they reached the point where their property ended and the rest of the world began.

This was the Gamaches' Sunday ritual. In lives so unpredictable, they found sanctuary in certainty. Even if just for a moment.

Life was, after all, made up of tiny choices. Like a pointillist painting, no one dot, no one choice, defined it. But together? There emerged a picture. A life.

Where to live, where to sit. What to eat, to drink, to wear. Whether to cut the grass or let it become meadow. What to say and, perhaps more important, what not to say.

What job to take. What calling.

What call.

Returning to the sun-trap that was the stone terrace, he stretched out his legs, leaned back, closed his eyes, and Armand Gamache thought of . . . nothing. His mind a welcome blank.

So much peace. So much to break.

When that first call came through, Armand had reached for the phone, with every intention of answering. It was, after all, his private number. Only friends and family had it.

But his finger stopped on its way to swiping the screen.

Then he slowly replaced the phone on the table, narrowed his eyes, and as the ringing continued, he stared ahead. No longer seeing the garden. No longer hearing the birds or the cicadas, which managed to be both intrusive and comforting.

All were consumed by the ringing, ringing. As was he.

Reine-Marie lowered the newspaper slightly. Just enough to look at her husband, then down at the phone. She could not see the number, but she could see the creases forming at the corners of Armand's eyes and mouth.

Now in his late fifties, his clean-shaven face was lined and weathered. From decades spent kneeling in snowy fields, in forests, and on the rocky shores of turbulent lakes, on sunbaked pavements. Staring down at a corpse.

As the head of homicide for the Sûreté du Québec, Armand

Gamache had seen more than his share of death. Violent, brutal, devastating death. Unnatural death.

Which was why, to balance the details of an autopsy, he sought the bumble of bees and racket of crickets. To offset a report from one of his agents into a murder, he listened to the wind through the forest, and smelled the musky scent of autumn leaves. They were his balm. His calm.

It was why home and family and a peaceful Sunday in a garden meant so much. To him. To them.

His hair was wavy and now mostly grey. It curled around his ears and at his collar. *He needs a trim*, Reine-Marie thought.

He was tall, over six feet, sturdily built, and far more likely to be mistaken, by anyone who met him casually, for a professor of arcane history than for a man who hunted killers.

And still the ringing continued. And the creases on his face deepened into crevices.

He could have, she knew, declined the call. But he didn't. He could have shut off the phone. But he didn't. Instead, he allowed it to ring. And ring. As he stared into the distance.

Finally, it stopped.

"Wrong number?" she asked.

He looked at her. "*Non.* Wrong person."

Who must have, he thought, called by mistake. Easily done. He'd done it himself.

Yes. It was only that. A mistake. This call was not intended for him.

Reine-Marie raised her brows but left it at that.

And then he smiled at her. And as he did, the furrows deepened. And she was reminded that while some of the lines down his face were certainly caused by pain and sorrow, stress and grief, by far the deepest impressions were made by just this. Smiling. Like lines on a map, these chartered the longitude and latitude, the journey of a man who had found happiness.

Though there was the deep scar at his temple, which cut across the other lines.

Silence once again descended on the garden. After a tense few moments, they raised their sections of the weekend paper and went back to reading.

Three Pines was not on any map and was only ever found by people who had lost their way. They'd crest the hill and stop, looking in wonderment across the top of the forest, to the Green Mountains of Vermont beyond the borders of Québec. Then, dropping their eyes, they would see something even more unexpected.

There, in the middle of nowhere, fieldstone and clapboard homes and rose-brick shops circled a village green. People would be out walking their dogs, or working in their gardens, or sitting on the bench on the green. Chatting. In at least one case, to herself.

In the center, three immense pine trees towered skyward. Like a beacon. A signal.

A sign.

*You are home and you are safe.*

Those who chose to stay—and not everyone did, though all were welcome—soon realized that the village was not impervious to the passage of time, or tragedy, any more than any community.

It was a haven, not a hiding place.

What Three Pines offered was comfort in an ever-changing world. It offered a place at the table, it offered company and acceptance. And croissants.

It offered a hand to hold.

Three Pines was where the head of homicide for the Sûreté du Québec and his librarian wife had chosen to live. To make a home. Not to escape from the horrors of the world, but to heal from them.

But the world had found them, that Sunday morning. As the Gamaches sat peacefully in their back garden. The ringing, ringing, ringing had begun again. And again Armand ignored it.

The peal now mixed in, perversely, with the ringing of the church bell.

St. Thomas's was calling the faithful.

And something else entirely was calling Armand Gamache.

"Answer the fucking phone!" A handful of compost, or dirt, or . . . was lobbed over the fence.

4

And still the phone rang. Then abruptly stopped mid-ring. Making the sudden silence almost as jarring as the sound.

When, a few minutes later, it rang for the third time, Reine-Marie lowered the weekend paper completely and looked first at the phone, then at her husband.

"For God's sake, Armand, who is it? Is it work?" Though she knew it could not be. He'd have answered.

After a brief hesitation, he held the phone up for her to see. There was no name, but she recognized the first few digits. A government number. Federal, not provincial. Though she had no idea whose number it was, it was clear that her husband knew who was calling. And calling. Knew who he was ignoring.

"Do you want me to answer?"

"*Non.*" He drew the phone to him, as though to protect her from it. He felt the vibration against his chest and moved it away.

The caller was already in his head, he sure didn't want them burrowing into his heart.

At that moment the ringing stopped, and he replaced the phone on the table.

The peace of their Sunday lay in shards around them. Even the quiet wasn't calming. It seemed merely a prelude to what they both knew was coming.

A few minutes later, it arrived, and when it did, Armand's patience broke. Grabbing the phone, he gave the screen a vicious swipe and stood up.

He listened for a few moments before saying, "Go to hell."

Then, as Reine-Marie stared in shock, he hung up. She'd never heard him speak to anyone like that. She was sure in his professional life it was sometimes necessary, but here? In their backyard?

"Tell me," she said when he turned back to her, his knuckles white where he gripped the phone.

And he did.

Reine-Marie listened, then let out a long exhale. Now she understood why he'd refused to answer the calls.

"What did she want?"

"To meet."

"Why?"

"I don't know. I didn't ask."

"I can't believe she'd contact you," said Reine-Marie. "After what happened last time."

They waited for another call, but none came. The next hour was spent apparently at ease, but their shoulders had inched up, and Reine-Marie had had to read the same book review several times before finally giving up.

"Let's go to the bistro," she said, hauling herself out of the chair. "We need a distraction."

"You might need a distraction," he said, getting up too. "I need a pain au chocolat."

She laughed and saw him smile. But the creases that appeared were from worry, not amusement.

# CHAPTER 2

—

W hat was that about?" asked Ruth, joining them on the back patio of the bistro, in the shade of the tall maples.

"What do you mean?" asked Myrna.

"The phone calls." The old poet jabbed a crooked finger at the Gamaches. "The racket went on all morning. I almost called the cops."

"You do know that Armand is the police," said Clara, brushing a hand through her wild hair and looking surprised when a licorice all-sort fell out.

No one else was surprised.

She ate it.

"Don't tell me you believe that bullshit?" said Ruth. "Like Clouseau here could possibly be a senior officer with the Sûreté. Next you'll be saying the library is a bookstore, and these two are married." She pointed to Olivier and Gabri. "Like that's even possible."

"Hag," muttered Gabri, putting a pain au chocolat in front of Armand and dragging a chair over to join them.

"Fag," muttered Ruth, sliding the plate over and sticking a bony finger into the middle of the pastry, as though it were a country and her finger a flag.

Armand sighed, then smiled when Olivier placed a second pastry in front of him. "*Merci, patron.*"

Then noticed Ruth was staring at him, expecting an answer.

Ruth Zardo. The poet. The laureate. Who from her ramshackle home in this little lost village managed to see things others did not.

*Now here's a good one:*
*you're lying on your deathbed.*
*You have one hour to live.*
*Who is it, exactly, you have needed*
*all these years to forgive?*

She was one of Armand's favorite poets, if not favorite people. Though he had to admit, she was close there too.

"So who was on the phone?"

"It was no one."

Myrna Landers, the owner of the bookshop, sat beside her best friend, the painter Clara Morrow. Olivier and Gabri, the owners of the bistro, had joined them.

"Jesus, you must really hate it when no one calls," said Ruth. "Four times in a row. The way you shouted." She looked knowingly at the others. "At no one."

Now they all, as though choreographed, tilted their heads and looked at him.

*Really?* Myrna thought. *Armand was shouting?*

Like everyone else, she'd seen him on the news being hammered by reporters, fielding accusations of incompetence, corruption. One blogger in particular, a young woman, really had it in for him.

But Chief Inspector Gamache kept his head, his answers measured and thoughtful.

She could not image Armand actually shouting.

What would provoke that? Who would provoke that?

Myrna Landers knew the Gamaches well. They'd often wander into her bookstore to browse, pulling new and used books from the shelves and glancing through them until something caught their interest. But sometimes Armand would come by on his own. On snowy winter days they'd sit by the woodstove, sip strong tea, and share confidences.

He'd tell her what it was like to crawl into sick minds, moving ever deeper into dark caverns until he had the answers he needed. Until he had a killer.

And she'd tell him what it had been like to be Dr. Landers, a senior psychologist specializing in criminal behavior. Until one day she'd wandered too deep into a mind, into a cave, and gotten lost. She needed to find her way back to the sunshine. To a world where goodness existed.

She'd quit her job, packed up her small car, and left the city, without a particular destination in mind. Just, away.

Stopping in the unexpected village for a break, she went into the bistro, had a café and a croissant, discovered the shop next door was for rent, as was the loft above, and Myrna Landers never left.

She had found her quiet place in the bright sunshine. And Dr. Landers became Myrna.

Then one day the head of homicide for the Sûreté du Québec and his wife bought the rambling old home across the village green. He'd wandered into her shop, sat down, and Chief Inspector Gamache became Armand.

The only difference, and she knew it was huge, was that while she was out of those caves, he was still in them.

Who had been on the other end of the phone that morning? And what had that person said, what had they wanted, that pushed this steady man so far off balance he found himself shouting in his peaceful garden on a bright Sunday morning?

For his part, Armand knew he'd let his rage overpower his reason. It didn't happen often; he'd worked hard to disarm those triggers, ones that could, in his job, have catastrophic consequences. He'd seen it often enough with colleagues.

Unresolved rage and a loaded gun were a very bad combination.

He got angry more often than most knew. You could not look at the body of a murdered child and not be enraged. But anger clouded judgment. It became another problem, not a solution.

Though Armand Gamache was honest enough with himself to know that he had his own caverns, his own sinkholes. One in particular. And he'd fallen into it that morning. Pushed over the edge by a reasonable voice many, many miles away, with a simple request.

To meet.

To steady himself now, he took a bite of the soft, still-warm pastry, oozing dark chocolate. As a further balm, he looked across the patio to the Rivière Bella Bella, its fresh mountain water rushing by, catching the sun and gleaming golden. It was calming. Meditative.

His heart slowed and his shoulders dropped.

*Was it a mistake to answer that call?*

Why hadn't he turned off the phone after the first ring? Why hadn't he moved the phone into the study and shut the doors between it and them?

He knew why. Because he always had intended to answer. Because he had to know.

Because knowledge really was power. Where some cops thought of their guns as their weapon, Chief Inspector Gamache knew the only real weapon, and protection, was knowledge.

And yet, and yet . . .

And yet he'd stopped short of getting all the information. He'd run away. Refused to meet. Refused to find out what the person wanted. He'd hung up not because he was angry, but because he was afraid.

Just then, his phone rang again.

# CHAPTER 3

⁓

At the first ring, Reine-Marie's hand jerked and the blue-and-white plate she was holding fell, shattering on the fieldstone terrace.

Then her own phone began ringing too. She looked at Armand, and Armand looked at her.

Was it possible, he thought, his mind racing. Had the caller, infuriated by his response, decided to change tactics and go after Reine-Marie?

He half expected all their phones to start ringing. A cacophony, a scream. An attack.

He had to stop this. He had to answer.

As he swiped accept, he stood up and walked to the grassy verge of the river. Reine-Marie's phone stopped ringing. She too had answered.

"What do you want?" he demanded.

"Chief Inspector Gamache?"

"*Oui.*"

"This is the alarm company. A sensor has gone off at your home in Montréal. Would you like me to send a car?"

Armand felt a wave of relief, and a slight hysteria bubble up. "*Un instant, s'il vous plaît.*" He turned to Reine-Marie. "The alarm?"

"*Oui.*" She too was relieved. "It's the front door?" she said into her phone. "It's faulty. This has happened before."

"Have the motion sensors been activated?" Armand asked, returning to his call.

"*Non.* Nothing. No one actually entered your home. It appears to be another false alarm. I'm guessing you're not there."

"No. Don't bother sending a car. I'll have someone drop by and check."

"If you're sure, Chief Inspector."

"I am, *merci.*"

"I'll turn off the alarm," said the young man. "But you really should have it fixed."

Are you kidding me?" the familiar voice said. "Again?"

"We all need a hobby, *mon vieux,*" said Armand.

He was talking to Jean-Guy Beauvoir, his second-in-command and son-in-law.

Annie and Jean-Guy lived close to the Gamaches' pied-à-terre in the Outremont *quartier* of Montréal. Though the young couple and their two children lived in the less swanky Mile End neighborhood.

"I'll walk over with Honoré, but I should warn you, Armand, whoever broke in might've stolen all your cookies."

"What cookies?"

A few minutes later Jean-Guy called from their apartment.

"All clear. No break-in. But can you please get it fixed?"

He was standing at the open doorway to the Gamaches' small apartment, the one they'd bought when they'd sold the family home and moved to Three Pines. This was a pied-à-terre, for when they had to stay in the city for work, or just a nice weekend in Montréal.

Over the years Chief Inspector Gamache had, inadvertently, become the public face of Québec's provincial police. The Sûreté. Whose motto was *Service, Intégrité, Justice.*

But a motto and reality were two different things. Gamache knew that the vast majority of the agents and inspectors, the chief inspectors and detachment commanders, did believe in service, integrity, and justice. But there remained pockets of corruption. And not just in the Sûreté.

With that thought came the memory of the phone call that morning.

From a government number. From a person he knew to be corrupt, though he could not prove it. Someone whose power and influence had only grown over the years and was now almost limitless.

"Armand?"

Jean-Guy's voice on the phone brought him back to the matter at hand. The annoying false alarms.

"*Désolé*," said Armand. "I was distracted." Which was true. He was now staring at Rosa. The duck had planted her beak in his pain au chocolat.

"I must warn you, I think the mice have gotten into your stash of chocolate chips you hide from Reine-Marie."

"I do nothing of the sort."

"Oh, good. Then you won't miss them."

"Terrible man," Armand mumbled, and heard Jean-Guy laugh as he hung up. Then, turning to Reine-Marie, he said, "Want to go into Montréal? Spend the night. Maybe see if Vivienne and Marcel can join us for dinner."

The LaPierres were the Gamaches' best friends in Montréal. Had been since the day Daniel broke his leg, and Dr. LaPierre had run across avenue Querbes to help the screaming child and the distraught parents.

That had been twenty-five years earlier.

"I'll call, see if they can meet us at Leméac," said Reine-Marie.

The restaurant was around the corner from their home. She could already taste her truffle oil salmon tartare, while Armand and Marcel would have their usual moules frites.

Vivienne, a marine biologist, preferred the creamy mushroom risotto, with slabs of aged Parmesan. She and Reine-Marie would have Pinot Noir while the men would order beers.

The decision was easy, the calls made, the dinner arranged.

Before leaving, they stopped at Monsieur Béliveau's General Store. For cookies.

As they walked to their car, they passed a man heading toward the bistro. A stranger. Slender, elderly. In a suit that didn't quite fit, and a tie too wide for the fashion of the day.

A few paces on, Armand glanced back and saw the man had also paused, to look at him. Their eyes met, briefly, before both turned away.

The man seemed vaguely familiar. He must, Armand thought, be staying at the B&B. Reaching for the handle of the car door, he looked back again, but the man had already entered the bistro.

The slightly odd thing, thought Armand as they drove out of the village, was that he had a warm feeling about the man. If he did know him, it was a pleasant memory.

# CHAPTER 4

⁓

The strange things began happening the next morning when Armand arrived at work.

The evening before, when he and Reine-Marie were heading out to Leméac, it had begun to rain. He looked for his light summer coat, then realized he must have left it in Three Pines, though he couldn't remember seeing it there.

The LaPierres were already at the restaurant, and the couples spent an enjoyable evening catching up on family, on careers, on this and that. Vivienne was heading to the Arctic, to check out the polar ice melt. Marcel was going with her this time. They invited the Gamaches, who were sorely tempted and talked about it all the way home.

By the time they left Leméac, the drizzle had stopped, and Armand and Reine-Marie strolled arm in arm, pausing to look in shop windows along avenue Laurier. Turning up the side street, they glanced into lit windows of apartments, converted from what were once mansions.

They finally arrived at their own small walk-up with its flight of outside stairs, high ceilings, intricate moldings, and ornamental fireplace.

This place reminded them of their first home together, though that one was even tinier, and rented. Buying a place had seemed an impossibility. Armand was just starting out at the Sûreté, and Reine-Marie was a young librarian dreaming of one day working for the Bibliothèque et Archives nationales du Québec. Never thinking that one day she would be the senior archivist and Armand would be head of homicide.

*Je me souviens*, thought Armand as he climbed the stairs. I remember. The motto of Québec was not wrong.

Thankfully the faulty sensor did not play up again that night, and their phones remained silent. All seemed right with the world. Until the next morning, when the package arrived.

The day started predictably enough.

After coffee and croissants in the kitchen together, Reine-Marie went off to the archives to do some research, while Armand headed into his office at Sûreté headquarters. It was Monday morning, and there was the weekly meeting with his boss and other department heads to go over the cases still active, those concluded, and those about to go to trial.

He'd already met informally with his counterpart, Evelyn Tardiff, in Organized Crime. He wanted her thoughts on two murders his team was investigating, what he believed were mob-related executions. One in the Saguenay region, and another on the windswept Les Îles de la Madeleine.

Organized crime in Québec went back generations, to Prohibition, when the mob ran booze across the border. And still did. But now it also ran billions of dollars in drugs and arms. It had, in the intervening years, grown into a monster with connections to the East Coast mafia, the Big Five families. So deep were the mafia's roots in construction, trucking, garbage collection, even the cheese industry, all sorts of "legitimate" businesses, that the Sûreté had formed a special unit to investigate it.

What troubled Gamache about the cases in both regions outside Montréal was that the victims had no apparent connection to the drug trade, or prostitution, or, or, or. The woman in the Saguenay had worked for Canada Post. The man on the Magdalen Islands was a teacher on the cusp of retirement. Both appeared to be leading perfectly ordinary, peaceful lives.

Until they were trussed up and shot in the back of the head. Within a day of each other.

"What do you think, Evelyn?"

She removed her glasses and reached for her mug of coffee. "They must have seen something that got them killed."

"Both of them? One day apart?"

Tardiff studied her counterpart in homicide. "Are you suggesting the two are related? They're thousands of kilometers apart, have no connection to each other and no record of criminal activity."

"True. And yet . . ."

"And yet you think the killings aren't just related," said Tardiff, looking at the photographs, "but mob-related." To give her credit, thought Gamache, her tone held no sarcasm or even cynicism.

"They look like executions to me," he said. "Hits. Don't they to you?" He waited for her response, but when none came, he said, "Something must be stirring. Have you heard anything?"

She shook her head. "It's been quiet since old man Moretti died and the son took over the family. We were expecting a war, but the transition has been smooth. This new generation of mobster is more polished. Less interested in violence and more interested in profit. A turf war benefits no one."

Except the winner, thought Gamache. But even then, so much damage was done to everyone involved it took years to recover.

While what Chief Inspector Tardiff said was true, they both were old enough and experienced enough to know that "polish" was superficial. This new generation of mobster might appear more refined, but underneath? They were at least as ruthless, literally cutthroat, as their fathers and grandfathers.

These were not, as his granddaughter Florence would say in typical understatement, nice people.

Gamache knew something else. There was an informant high up in the Montréal mafia. A very "not nice" person. A necessary evil.

Very few knew this person's identity. Armand was not one of them, but the woman across from him was. What he did know was that this was not a brave individual, quietly working to bring down the Moretti organization. No, this was a scheming, manipulative, detestable opportunist. Working to his or her own ends.

So far, the information had proven valuable, but one day, Gamache knew, it would not. One day, when it suited them, this person would lead them into a trap.

When he'd knelt beside the recently executed woman and man, who'd had absolutely no reason to be murdered that he could see, Armand had had a prickling sense that day was approaching.

Tardiff was right, though. Things were relatively quiet. But far from feeling that a monster had gone to sleep, it felt to Armand like it was resting, watching, gathering strength. The silence wasn't slumber, it was a deep breath. Held.

And those murders he was investigating? They were the prelude, the short, sharp gasps before the scream.

Evelyn Tardiff tapped the dossiers with her glasses. "You really believe these were hits, Armand?" At his nod, she sat back, crossed her legs, and looked out the window at the skyline of Montréal. Then her gaze returned to her colleague. "I'll see what I can find out."

"*Bon, merci.*"

It occurred to him that these executions might not be news to Evelyn Tardiff. Like him, she had her secrets. Closely guarded and dangerous if allowed to escape.

One day soon it would be a good idea to sit down quietly together and bring those secrets out into the relative open. But that carried risks. While he trusted Tardiff, he knew that there were elements within the Sûreté. Old ones, planted years ago. Who bided their time.

The *quid* to their *pro quo* informant. The mafia's own, mafia-owned, senior Sûreté officers. And they wouldn't be alone.

There'd be prosecutors and judges, politicians and lobbyists. Journalists.

Gamache had no proof of this, it was just common sense. The mob had untold wealth, weapons, no conscience, a thirst for power, and a need for protection. They could buy almost anyone they wanted, and did.

Were those executions the first putrid whiff of the storm to come?

But if so, it still begged the question, why were those two victims the harbinger? Why would anyone, never mind the mob, need them dead?

He checked his watch and got up. "We're going to be late."

"Oh, no," said Chief Inspector Tardiff, and Gamache gave a grunt of amusement and commiseration.

These Monday morning meetings of department heads could be tedious, especially when Chief Inspector Goudreau of the Highways division felt slighted and decided to take up more time than was allotted him.

Which was most Monday mornings.

Armand sat at the long table, his dossier closed in front of him, and listened. Where others looked bored, or glanced out the window, or surreptitiously checked their phones, he forced himself to pay attention. Though he struggled to pay close attention, or any, to the head of the Highways division. He found his mind wandering to Goudreau's tie. It was a warm orange. Was "amber" more the word? He liked it and thought he might go to Ogilvy's later and see . . .

Goudreau had just finished droning on about how many perforated lines per kilometer were ideal, and the Chief Super was turning to the next report, when Goudreau began again.

There was an audible moan in the room.

*Maybe get a new summer coat . . .*

Gamache all but shook himself out of his reverie.

Goudreau was now trying to justify cutting back on inspectors at weigh stations, citing statistics that showed truckers were, for the most part, complying with the laws.

"Could that be," the Chief Superintendent asked, wearily, "because of the lack of inspections? You're simply not catching them?"

Gamache lowered his head and pretended to consult his report, to mask his smile. By now most of the senior officers were wondering if the windows opened and they could jump.

"It's because of the hard work my department does," said the perpetually wounded officer. "Truckers don't dare try to get away with anything. They know they'll be caught."

"Yes, but if . . . ," began the Chief Superintendent, then stopped herself. "Let's discuss this after the meeting."

When Gamache returned to his office, he found Isabelle Lacoste waiting. In her mid-thirties, married with two small children, she'd worked for Gamache for ten years, ever since he'd hired the young agent on the day her former chief was about to fire her. For being "soft."

But then, Armand Gamache himself was often accused of being "soft." Because he cared. Because he knew the value not just of facts but of feelings. Because he preferred listening to intimidating. Because he wanted to understand.

Lacoste had risen swiftly through the ranks and was now his co-second-in-command, a position shared with Jean-Guy Beauvoir.

"Wait, *patron*," she said, barring his way into his office and pointing to his desk.

A parcel, wrapped in newspaper and tied with string, sat there.

"It's not a bomb," she said.

He turned to her, somewhat amused that she'd have to say it. If it was, he'd have hoped they wouldn't place it on his desk.

"And why are we standing here?" he asked.

"The fellow who dropped it at reception pretty much ran away. No note, but someone's printed your name and written, *This might interest you.*"

The two of them stood on the threshold and considered the package.

"Fingerprints?"

"*Non.* We've also had it checked for toxic materials. Clean."

"Stay here." He walked in and noticed that she was right beside him.

It hadn't exactly been an order, but still . . .

He bent over to examine the package. Sure enough, written in block letter in felt pen was: *Chief Inspector Gamache. This might interest you.*

He straightened up as his mind went over the possibilities. The cases still open. The deaths, the murders, they were investigating.

Could this be evidence someone had sent anonymously? People often did. Wanting the killers caught, but not wanting to be involved.

It was wrapped in *Le Journal de Montréal* newspaper, the most popular daily, so that was no help. It was from an old weekend edition. The food and wine section.

It did not appear to carry an implied threat. Not the obits. Not the reports on crimes. Just recipes and restaurant reviews. His name had been printed on top of instructions for a cocktail called the Last Word.

"Security is sending me the footage from reception," said Lacoste.

"Good." Gamache reached into his desk and brought out sealed packages containing sterile gloves. Tossing a pack to Lacoste, he put on a pair, then cut the string and carefully placed each strand aside.

He had to admit to some concern about what might be inside. He was thinking of the murders in Chicoutimi and on Les Îles de la Madeleine, and whether the executions and the appearance of this package could be connected.

There was no seepage. No smell. But . . .

More agents crowded into the office and watched.

Just then, Beauvoir appeared and pushed his way to the front.

"Are you all here to see if I still know how to collect evidence?" asked the Chief Inspector. "Go back to your work, please."

He knew they were there out of concern for him. In case this was more threatening than it appeared. And if it was, he wanted them well away.

That left Lacoste, Beauvoir. And himself.

He carefully peeled back the layers of newspaper, page after page, until he got to the last layer. He paused, looked at the others, whose faces were tense, their focus complete. Then he drew the final page aside and stared down at what was revealed.

He tilted his head, his brows drawn together in puzzlement.

The Chief Inspector had a pretty well-developed imagination, but even he had not imagined this.

"What is it?" asked Lacoste, stepping forward, as did Beauvoir.

There, on Gamache's desk, was a summer jacket. Stone-colored and neatly folded, with a red stain on the chest.

He reached out, but instead of picking up the coat, Gamache picked up his phone.

"Reine-Marie, are you at home?"

"*Non.* I'm still at the archives. Why? Is something wrong?"

"I'm not sure. Don't go home just yet."

"Why? What's happened?"

"Please, just stay away until you hear from me."

Reine-Marie was about to agree, but found herself holding a dead phone. He'd already hung up.

"*Patron,*" said Jean-Guy. "What is it?"

"This's my coat."

"Yours?" said Lacoste. "Are you sure?"

"I recognize the stain from Florence's strawberry ice cream."

He'd meant to throw the coat into the wash but had forgotten.

Lacoste was smiling with relief. "Well, that's good news. We don't have to blow it up. You must've left it in a restaurant or shop, and someone dropped it off." But even as she spoke, she took in his grim expression. "What is it?"

"I didn't leave it anywhere." Gamache continued to stare at the coat. The one he'd looked for the night before. "It was in our apartment."

"Then how did it get here?" Lacoste asked, but Beauvoir had a sick feeling that he knew the answer.

"*Tabernak.* The alarm," he said.

"*Oui.*"

Beauvoir got on his phone and asked the Montréal police to send a squad car to the apartment. "And wait outside. We'll be there soon. *Merci.*"

"What alarm?" asked Lacoste.

"Yesterday. At our apartment in the city. We thought it was a broken sensor or a door that was jiggling in a draft, setting off a false alarm."

"It wasn't?"

Instead of answering, Armand was staring down at his coat. "I looked for this last night and couldn't find it."

Now it was here. On his desk. In his office. At the Sûreté. *This might interest you.*

And it did.

"Wait a minute," said Isabelle. "You're saying someone broke in and took the coat? Nothing else?"

"I checked," Jean-Guy explained. "Nothing was disturbed. The door was still locked."

"But—" began Lacoste.

"Why take just this?" said Gamache. "I don't know."

"And why return it?" said Beauvoir, not expecting an answer and not getting one.

Gamache picked up the coat and let it unfold, half expecting something nasty to fall out. But nothing did.

It was only when he went through the pockets that he found the note.

*Please, I need to speak to you. Meet me today. Four o'clock at Open Da Night. I'm sorry. I didn't know it was your home.*

He handed it to Beauvoir, who stumbled, "What . . . ? Why . . . ? Wha . . . ?"

". . . does it mean?" The Chief had the same question.

"Maybe it means exactly what it says," said Lacoste. "Whoever broke in didn't realize the place belongs to the head of homicide for the Sûreté. When he did, he got scared and sent it back."

"And asked to meet?" said Beauvoir. He studied Gamache. "You're not thinking of going?"

"I'm not thinking anything yet." He was going through the other pockets. In the small inside one, he found another piece of paper. It was folded up and thicker than the first.

"What does it say?" asked Lacoste, as they crowded around.

*Fennel, thyme, sage, mace, nutmeg . . .* It went on.

"Yours?" asked Lacoste.

"*Non.* And not Reine-Marie's." He knew her handwriting.

"They're herbs," Isabelle said. "A recipe? Maybe a shopping list?"

"Or a planting list?" asked Beauvoir. "For an herb garden?"

It was possible Myrna or Clara or one of their other neighbors had drawn up this list. But if they had, they hadn't handed it to him, so how did it get into a pocket he never used? Hadn't even known was there.

And while some of the herbs were common—sage and thyme, for instance—others were obscure. Not ones they were likely to use or plant. And some were spices.

Gamache turned it over. On the back was written one word. *Water.*

"A reminder to water the plants?" asked Isabelle.

"Maybe." Gamache held the paper up to the light. Nothing.

"It's torn." Lacoste pointed to the bottom of the page. "Incomplete."

It was true. The paper was slightly feathered at the bottom.

At the tear, two words could just be made out.

"*Angelica,*" Gamache read. "And this other seems to be *Stems.* What's that?"

"No idea," said Lacoste.

He took a photo of both notes, then handed them to Lacoste. "I'm going home."

"I'll get everything to the lab."

"Good. When they've been tested and photographed, bring the notes back to me."

"I'll get the Scene of Crime team to your place," said Beauvoir.

They made for the door. "And get that surveillance video. I want to know who dropped this off."

# CHAPTER 5

⁓

"So, it was a break-in, sir?" asked the young Montréal officer who'd been dispatched.

"Yes. It seems so."

They were standing outside on the landing, looking at the closed door to the apartment.

"And the place was still locked when you arrived?" She looked at Beauvoir, who nodded. "And the only thing taken was a coat?"

"*Oui*," said Gamache. The Montréal cop was looking at him, perplexed. He knew how this sounded. And it was about to get worse. "But it was returned this morning."

"*Pardon?*"

Gamache repeated it. Even to his own ears it sounded ridiculous. If he hadn't been who he was, no one would pay any attention to him, or this supposed crime. They'd dismiss him as a crank. And, to be honest, it looked like she was about to.

"I'm not sure what you want from me, sir."

It was clear, by her wide eyes and nerves, that she knew who this man was. The scar on his forehead, by his temple, would tell her, if nothing else did.

She'd heard many things about Chief Inspector Gamache. What she hadn't heard was that he was nuts. This was new.

"My people will investigate," said Gamache. "I just need you to write a report and say no further action by the Montréal police is expected or required."

"Okay." Still perplexed, she left.

As she made her way down the outside stairs, the Scene of Crime team from the Sûreté made its way up.

Once they'd finished with the door, and confirmed it hadn't been forced, Armand and Jean-Guy stepped in and quickly went through the apartment, to make extra sure nothing else had been removed or added.

It didn't take long. The place was small, but bright and cheerful, with a comfortable sofa and armchairs. Oriental rugs were scattered on the wood floors, and the bookcases were stuffed with hardcovers and paperbacks. Framed photographs of family and friends stood on the mantelpiece, including one of Armand's godfather, Stephen Horowitz, who was now living with a niece in Ottawa.

"Where was the coat, *patron*?" asked the head of the SoC unit.

Gamache pointed to a row of brass hooks by the front door where a woman's coat hung.

It interested the Sûreté officers to see that the home that the prominent Chief Inspector shared with his wife was so modest. Most knew this was simply a pied-à-terre, that Gamache's real home was south of Montréal in Québec's Eastern Townships. Still, this apartment was smaller than they'd have expected the senior officer to have.

Jean-Guy stood in the middle of the living room and tried to work it out.

The door opened away from the hooks, so the thief only had to reach in and grab the coat. There was no "break," and barely an "enter."

So why go into a home and then take nothing except some dirty old coat?

And why give it back? Even if, as the note said, the thief hadn't immediately realized he'd just broken into the home of not just a senior Sûreté officer, but Chief Inspector Gamache, wouldn't it have been prudent to just throw the jacket away?

And why ask to meet? If he wanted that, why not just ask for an appointment?

Armand had called Reine-Marie and let her know she could come home. She arrived a few minutes later.

"What's going on?"

"Let's go into the kitchen."

They sat at the table by the window and, with the sun streaming in, Armand explained. When he finished, she stared at him for a moment or two before finally speaking.

"So, someone did break in yesterday?"

He nodded.

"And took just your coat?"

Nod.

"Why?"

"I don't know."

"But you think there's more to it than a simple break-in."

"I don't know. I'm just being careful." Reine-Marie looked through the door at the activity in their small apartment. This went beyond careful.

"There's more," she said. She'd thrown it out there in the hopes he'd shake his head and reassure her. But she'd known, she could read his face.

He brought the photos up on his phone and showed her the notes. "I found these in the pockets of the jacket. Do they look familiar?"

He'd thrown it out there, in the hopes she'd nod and reassure him. But he'd known. And now he could read her face as the lines between her eyes deepened.

"Why would he want to meet you?"

He shook his head.

"You're not going, are you?"

"I haven't thought that far ahead." He pointed out the second note. "What do you make of that?"

"Looks like a shopping list, or ingredients for a recipe, but there aren't any measurements."

"An herb garden maybe?" he suggested. "Could Myrna or someone else have given this to you?"

"Not any writing I recognize, and I haven't asked for advice on planting an herb garden. Besides, there are a couple of spices mentioned. There's no way we're growing nutmeg in Three Pines."

Armand wondered fleetingly how one would grow nutmeg. It was a nut, no? That you grated? There were enough nuts in the village, at least one of them grating, but not of the same sort.

"And why would it be in the coat you keep in Montréal? What do you think, Armand?"

He took a deep breath. "I think what you think, what any rational person would. That this is very odd behavior. That someone wants my attention. But"—he smiled at her—"it's not a threat. If this person had something nasty in mind, they would not have sent a note politely asking to see me."

But still . . .

She looked again at the note. "Doesn't it strike you as odd?"

"Yes, I just said that."

"No, not the note itself, but where he's asked to meet you."

"It's a well-known café in the area."

"True, but still. Open Da Night? Does he know you better than you realize?"

He smiled. Trust Reine-Marie to pick up on something few others would know. Except him. And, perhaps, the thief. Which was, he had to admit, disconcerting. It wasn't just a local café, it was one Armand and Reine-Marie had visited often. And the man had used its nickname, known only to locals.

"How do you feel about going back to Three Pines?" he asked.

Now it was her turn to smile. It was put as a question but was really a request.

"Happy to. Will you join me there tonight?"

"That's my plan." Though, she heard in his voice, far from a certainty.

When Reine-Marie left, Armand made a call, then joined Beauvoir outside the front door.

"It looks like whoever did this must've had a key," said Gamache.

"I agree," said Jean-Guy. "But how could they?"

Gamache shook his head. "I've arranged to have the lock changed.

Though I doubt there'll be more trouble. I think whoever it was got what they came for."

"What? The coat?" asked Beauvoir.

"My attention."

"There's something else odd about the break-in," said Beauvoir. "What thief that you know does it in broad daylight? On a Sunday, when neighbors are around? I'll have the team go door-to-door to see if anyone saw anything. What time did the alarm go off?"

Gamache checked his phone. "We got the call at eleven forty-six yesterday morning."

Beauvoir passed the information along to the senior investigator.

"There's a message from Isabelle," said Gamache. "The surveillance video from Sûreté reception has come through."

He and Beauvoir sat at the kitchen table and brought up the link.

They watched as a slender young man entered the Sûreté building holding the now familiar package to his chest. The time-code generator said 8:37 that morning.

Beauvoir hit pause and went forward slowly, trying to get a look at his face. But the young man kept his head down and managed to avoid a direct shot from the cameras. Still, it was possible to get a sense of him. Longish, scraggly dark hair. Clean-shaven, lithe. He wore sweatpants and a T-shirt. No piercings or tattoos that they could see.

"Does he seem familiar to you?"

"*Non*," said Gamache.

"He's monumentally foolish. He must know he'll be on all sorts of cameras."

"And yet he's managing to avoid having his face clearly seen." Not easily done. Without help.

The locksmith arrived, and as he worked, Armand stood at the front door and looked into the apartment. The door opened directly into the living room. From there, what would the intruder have seen?

Comfortable furniture, shelves crammed with books, stacks of magazines waiting to be read. Crayons and coloring books for the grandchildren. Chewed-up, mangy dog toys. Hanging on the walls were original framed posters from Expo 67 and various concerts and festivals.

And there were photographs. Of children and grandchildren. Black-and-white wedding photos of Armand's and Reine-Marie's parents. There was one of Armand's grandmother standing proudly beside him at his graduation from high school.

The grandchildren thought it was the funniest thing ever. His long hair and slender build. And there on the mantelpiece was a more recent picture of the whole family, including Reine-Marie and himself.

The thought that an intruder had stood there and seen what was most private, most precious, outraged Armand, though outwardly he remained calm. His rational mind, his inspector's mind, took in the fact that there was nothing there that screamed, shouted, or even whispered that this was the home of a senior Sûreté officer.

So what did the thief see that gave it away?

"No bugs, *patron*," reported one of his agents, breaking into his thoughts. "And no cameras. We swept the place twice."

"*Bon, merci.*" Gamache couldn't conceal his relief. The agent saw this and smiled, pleased to bring his boss good news.

They drove back to the office. After a few minutes of silence, Jean-Guy Beauvoir turned to Gamache. "You're going, aren't you."

The Chief nodded.

# CHAPTER 6

⁓

I t was five to four.

Gamache sat in the car on rue Saint-Viateur and stared at the green awnings of Open Da Night. He hadn't had time for lunch, and now, as he watched customers on the terrasse enjoying Italian pastries, Armand realized how hungry he was.

Beside him in the driver's seat, Jean-Guy was scanning the area to see if the man who'd delivered the package was there. Each officer had been given his photo.

Lacoste texted from inside the café. She and her team were in place.

It was, Beauvoir knew, useless to ask the Chief one more time if he was sure. He was. It was a *fait accompli*, a certainty, from the moment they'd found the note.

*Please, I need to speak to you. Meet me today. Four o'clock at Open Da Night. I'm sorry. I didn't know it was your home.*

How could Gamache not meet the fellow who'd broken into his home?

It had been equally useless to ask the Chief if maybe he should be armed, but Beauvoir did anyway, and got exactly the reply he'd expected. An almost amused look.

"Take a firearm into a crowded café, *mon ami*? *Non*. I'll leave it to you to kill any innocent bystanders."

It was as close to gallows humor as Jean-Guy had seen the Chief come.

"Those bomboloni are to die for," said Beauvoir.

"I'll get you one if you promise not to shoot. And certainly not to shoot me."

Beauvoir almost added, *Again*. But decided that was a step too far, and perhaps not something either man wanted to remember.

The fellow on the security video hadn't arrived yet. But then, he might not be the thief. This was the disconcerting part. They really had no idea who would show up. Or why.

The place was actually called Café Olimpico. It got its nickname when some letters fell off the sign and were never replaced. *Open Day and Night* became *Open Da Night*.

It was interesting, perhaps telling, that the thief knew the nickname. Not everyone did.

Was it just coincidence that the thief had chosen perhaps the one café in Montréal that Armand was most familiar with? Where he felt most comfortable, most at home. Safest?

He'd been in many times, often for espresso allongés on a Sunday morning with Reine-Marie. Early in their marriage they'd read the paper, nurse a coffee, and chat with Rocco, the original owner.

Armand looked down at the pages in his hands. The lab had finished with the notes and returned them to the Chief. Folding them up again, he put them in his breast pocket and reached for the door.

"I can come in with you," said Jean-Guy.

"Better if you're out here," said Armand.

They'd also been through this. If the thief had studied the photographs, he might recognize Jean-Guy, who was in several of them.

While the note did not say to come alone, Gamache thought it best not to advertise that the place was now throbbing with Sûreté officers.

He walked into the café and waved at Vito, one of the longtime baristas.

"*Un allongé, per favore.*"

"Already being made, Chief. I saw you coming."

It didn't matter that Vito had just announced to everyone there, a few of whom were not cops, that the Chief Inspector was in the building. It would not come as a surprise to the fellow he was meeting. Besides, Gamache was hardly incognito.

He made himself comfortable in a corner table. From there he had a good view of the whole place.

The café was noisy, with the televisions blaring, replaying classic soccer matches that Italy invariably won. Baristas shouted orders and occasionally burst into self-mocking song, and regulars howled at the screens, though everyone knew the happy outcome of the games.

In the opposite corner two elderly men played cards. They wore white tank tops stained with sweat and mud-smeared green slacks, dirty from tending the tall tomato plants in the patch of garden at the front of their row homes.

It was not a relaxing place, but it was vibrant and comfortable and familiar, and very old-world. With its stone walls and long marble bar and tin tiled ceiling, it really hadn't changed since Armand's godfather, Stephen, had taken him there when he wasn't yet shaving.

He'd had his first cappuccino over there, at the round table by the window. He'd hated the bitter taste. But then he'd also hated his first beer and first scotch and first taste of smoked salmon. Took him a while, and some perseverance, to get used to the taste of adulthood.

Now, the cannoli were a different matter. He'd liked those from the get-go.

Vito brought him his coffee and with it a pastry. Uninvited, but appreciated.

"*Grazie.*"

"*Prego.*"

"Can you bring me another cannoli, please? I'm expecting someone."

"Madame Gamache?"

"*Non.*"

It was warm and Armand was in a suit and tie. He was tempted to take off his jacket, but decided to just loosen his tie and undo the top button of his white shirt.

At seven minutes past four a man walked through the door, looked around, then, fixing on Gamache, approached.

He wore a hoodie, with the hood up, on this warm afternoon. His hands were in the bulging front pouch of the sweatshirt. He was stocky and walked with the rolling, wary gait of a boxer approaching an adversary.

This was not the man from the video. Armand felt a sudden jab of concern, bordering on fear.

Was it a setup after all?

Out of the corner of his eye he could see Lacoste get up. In a flash he took in the customers, including an elderly man and his grand-daughter, standing between Lacoste and the man, who was getting closer. They were in her line of sight. Line of fire.

Gamache gave a subtle gesture to Lacoste to hold where she was. He could see her hand on her hip, resting on the concealed weapon. Ready. The other agents had also stood up. The grandfather, sensing something, was looking around and instinctively reached for the little girl.

Agents were stepping forward, trying to get around the clog of people at the bar who were ordering coffees and pastries and just becoming aware that something unusual was happening.

Those staring at the TV and unaware burst into cheers as Italy scored a decades-old goal.

Gamache had an imperfect view of his people, which meant they had an imperfect view of him and the stranger approaching. If the man pulled a gun, they'd have no clear shot.

The grandfather placed his large hand on the girl's shoulder and guided her so that she stood behind him.

All this happened quickly, as these things did. Within a second or two.

"May I?" The man indicated the chair.

"I'm actually expecting someone," said Gamache, tense, his palms flat under the table, prepared to push it over, into the newcomer. And then leap. Perhaps avoiding a shot, perhaps not, but at least knocking the gunman to the floor and giving his agents time to swarm.

"You're expecting me." The man swept the hoodie off and sat.

His face, close-up, was ruddy, worn by the sun and wind. This man spent a lot of time outdoors. He was, Gamache estimated, in his mid- to late twenties. No piercings or tattoos that he could see. Hair cut short. His eyes alert, clear. More grey than blue, but perhaps they were the sort that changed with clothing.

"Can you place your hands on the table, please?" Gamache asked, even as he moved his own to grip the edges. To shove the table forward if . . .

The man looked a little surprised but complied. He splayed his fingers. They were strong, and oddly sensitive, Gamache thought. More those of a pianist than a boxer. While tanned, his hands were not calloused. His cuticles and nails were nibbled and torn.

With the removal of his hands, the pouch at the front of his grey sweatshirt flattened. No weapon there.

And with that, it was over. The tension drained from the room almost as quickly as it had appeared. Though the agents remained standing, staring. Their eyes in target-acquisition mode.

The grandfather was still protecting his granddaughter. He followed the stares of those around him, into the corner where a large man sat gripping the table. And then he saw the man release the table and fold his hands together in front of him.

And the elderly man's face relaxed into a smile. He lifted his protective hand from his granddaughter's thin body.

"What is it?" she asked, picking up on the tension and then the lack of it.

"*Rien*," he said with relief. Nothing. Bending down, he pointed to the man sitting at the back of the café and whispered to her. The girl turned to look, her eyes wide. The first famous person she'd ever seen.

The grandfather was now completely relaxed, believing if Chief Inspector Gamache was there, they'd be safe.

He was, as it turned out, wrong.

"You're not the same person who dropped the package at my office."

"Do I look stupid?"

No, thought Gamache. He didn't look stupid, but he did look like a man trying desperately to appear calm, in control.

"I paid some homeless guy to do it."

"And yet here you are, in full view." Armand's voice was pleasant, also trying to appear calm, while every part of him was hyperalert. "So why the game at Sûreté headquarters?"

"I wasn't sure you'd come. I didn't want to expose myself before I had to."

"You're not planning to expose yourself, are you?"

The man stared at him for a moment, then smiled. And, as with most people, the smile transformed his face. The burly man suddenly looked younger, more innocent.

"Not unless I have to."

Vito's hand appeared over the man's shoulder, and he startled, giving a quick spasm, and almost knocking the cannoli off the plate.

"I didn't order this," he snapped, embarrassed by his reaction.

"I did. *Grazie*, Vito," said Gamache. "Would you like a coffee?"

When his guest just stared, as though not understanding the question, Gamache asked Vito to bring a cappuccino. "Perhaps decaf."

"*Non*. I don't want any coffee."

Vito filled his water glass, but the man pushed it away.

When Vito left, after giving Armand a look, the man asked, "Why are you doing this?"

"Doing what?"

"You know. Buying me food."

"I thought you might be hungry. You looked thinner on the tape. And younger."

The man gave a grunt of laughter. "I have put on weight since this morning, and a few years."

"So have I." Armand also smiled, trying to keep this easy, cordial. As though he met with people who broke into his home every day.

Gamache's companion spoke with a joual accent. The old, almost ancient patois that had come over on wooden ships with Jacques Cartier and Samuel de Champlain. It had been transplanted from the slums of Paris and taken root in the New World.

It still thrived in pockets of Montréal.

Like cockney, it had evolved. Not just the odd word or phrase, but the perception. Joual had gone from the back alleys of East End Montréal, to main street and the main stage of renowned theaters. It was heard in university classrooms and boardrooms.

Armand very much liked hearing the sound, the inflections. The words. Not all of which he understood. Though "poutine" he knew. It was joual for pudding.

The language was guttural, almost harsh. If a Québec winter could speak, it would be in joual.

Hearing it now, Gamache felt a sort of affection for this stranger. It was instinctive.

That too was something to guard against, and he wondered in passing if this young man was doing it on purpose. Joual was a trigger, a code that told another Québécois that the speaker, while perhaps rough, was salt of the earth. He or she could be trusted. As you'd trust a grandparent.

Gamache glanced at the elderly man, who was now sitting at a table and gently wiping whipped cream off his granddaughter's hands. Yes, trust was a powerful instinct. And weapon.

"Do you live in the area?" Gamache asked.

"*Non*."

The man picked up the pastry and bit down. The thick whipped cream oozed out of both ends of the roll and onto his fingers.

Gamache took a sip of coffee. "I ask because not many know this place as Open Da Night."

"I must've read an article about it online. I thought you probably knew it since you live close by. I wanted a place where you'd feel comfortable."

"*Merci*. Most thoughtful." It was bullshit, Gamache knew, but was happy for now not to challenge him. "Would you like something else to eat? They make wonderful cornetti."

The man had already finished off his cannoli.

"No, thank you." Now he looked perplexed. "Aren't you mad at me?"

He sounded almost childish.

"Well, I'm not pleased. You broke into my home and stole my coat.

But you returned it, which I appreciate." Gamache leaned forward. "What's your name?"

"Charles."

"Charles what?"

"Just that."

Since "Charles" was almost certainly not his real name, Gamache didn't feel the need to press for a fake last name too.

"Why are we here, Charles?"

"I needed to talk to you."

Gamache just waited. "Charles" glanced over his shoulder into the body of the café. Gamache wondered if he realized most of the people there were Sûreté agents. If he did, it didn't seem to matter. He returned his gaze to the Chief Inspector.

"This was a mistake."

"What was?"

"Meeting you."

"Why do you say that?"

"It's just not a good idea. You're a public figure. Someone might see us together."

"Would that be a problem?"

Now "Charles" almost smiled. "Well, we probably wouldn't be mistaken for friends."

"Then why do it? What do you want to tell me?"

"Charles" leaned closer. Whipped cream still clung to his fingers, and Armand was fighting the temptation to hand him a paper napkin. Or even to wipe it off himself.

There was something about this young man. He was swinging wildly from arrogance, even belligerence, to vulnerability. It was as though he couldn't decide who he was, or which attitude to strike when faced with this famous cop.

So he tried them all, and ended up just a strange man with whipped cream and dirt on his nibbled fingers. It was somehow endearing.

The younger man was slick with perspiration now, but from the heavy sweatshirt in the heat and humidity of the close café or nerves, Gamache didn't know.

"Charles" dropped his voice to a whisper, a rasp. "Look, I really didn't know it was your place. I'd never have agreed if I'd known."

The Chief was silent. He knew this "Charles" was waiting for him to ask questions, many of which were obvious. Which was precisely why Gamache did not.

Questions could have limited use. Be limiting. The person would only answer the questions that the interrogator thought to ask. It was the questions he didn't know that would get at the truth.

And so, Chief Inspector Gamache crossed his legs, sat back in his chair, folded his hands on his lap, and waited.

"Charles" was clearly confused by the silence and the stance. "Aren't you going to ask?"

"This's your party. You invited me here, I'm assuming for a reason. You'll tell me, I'm sure. You don't need to be interrogated, do you?"

This threw him off further. It was clearly not what "Charles" was expecting from the senior Sûreté officer whose home he'd burgled.

What was he expecting, Gamache wondered. But knew the answer. "Charles" was expecting to be arrested. And that still might happen.

It was possible he was also hoping to be arrested. That thought intrigued Gamache.

What "Charles" was not expecting was to be treated to cannoli and courtesy.

As Gamache watched, "Charles" reached for the water glass, then withdrew his hand as though it had bitten him.

"Okay, here's the thing. Some guy gave me a hundred bucks to break into an apartment in Outremont. He gave me a key and the address and told me to go right away. He said no one would be at home, and not to take anything, just go in, then lock up again and leave."

"He gave you a key to the place?" This was disconcerting, if true.

"*Oui.* I threw it into some dump truck."

"How did the man contact you?"

"He came to the shelter I was in. Asked if I wanted to make some quick cash."

"Why you?"

"How the fuck should I know?"

"When was this?"

"About ten yesterday morning. When I unlocked the door and recognized you in the pictures, I panicked. I grabbed the coat, then got the hell out."

Gamache paused, playing with the handle of his coffee mug. "Why take the coat?"

"Charles" shifted. "Winter's coming. I know it seems a long way off to you. It's only August. But if you've lived rough in Montréal . . ." His voice trailed off, and both men saw the snowdrifts, the bundles of ice-encrusted clothing lying curled over a Métro vent. The man or woman in the fetal position. The same position they had when entering the world.

Yes, winter was something to fear, and to prepare for. Even those with homes and warm clothing knew that.

"When I saw the coat, I grabbed it, thinking it would keep me warm and dry at least through the fall." He was staring at Gamache, trying to read the Chief Inspector. But Gamache's expression was noncommittal. Mostly because he didn't yet know what to believe.

He had a lot of questions, but those would wait. For now he wanted to know the answers to questions he didn't know to ask.

And so he lapsed into silence again and just watched the man across from him. His age, Gamache now realized, was hard to tell. He probably looked older than he was. Life on the street would do that.

Gamache also knew that many homeless were addicts or had psychiatric issues. Should, in fact, be getting help, be in care. Not dumped onto the streets like refuse.

How had this man ended up homeless? Or had he? Maybe it was all an act.

Gamache was frustrated with himself. He should be able to tell. But this man was confounding him. His instinct told him this "Charles" was lying, but about what? Everything? Most convincing liars started from the truth and took off from there into their own self-seeking fabrications.

If that was the case, what was "Charles" seeking? What was the purpose of all this?

Gamache pushed his untouched cannoli toward his companion.

"You don't believe me, do you," said "Charles."

"I'm reserving judgment. I think some of what you're telling me is the truth, some not so much. It doesn't help that you started off lying about your name."

"Did you expect the truth?"

Gamache was growing weary of this. It had been a long, stressful day. He wanted answers and he wanted to go home. To Reine-Marie.

He imagined her in the kitchen in Three Pines, preparing dinner. A mug of strong tea on the counter. The dogs, and Gracie, underfoot.

He saw Myrna in her bookshop sorting new arrivals, and Clara in her studio, a brush stuck behind her ear, staring at her latest work, part of a series she was calling *Just before something happens . . .*

The works ached of anxiety and excitement. Of potential and promise and peril. Of hope, but also dread. Anything might happen . . .

Gabri would be changing the beds at their B&B. With that thought came the memory of the stranger he'd passed the day before. The elderly man who'd looked vaguely familiar.

Then Armand's mind moved on, to Olivier in the bistro, who'd be putting mixed nuts in bowls for customers. With the nights closing in, he might lay a fire in the huge stone hearths at either end of the room. Lit more for cheer than warmth.

Yes, Armand wanted to get up and go home.

Instead, he leaned forward, keeping his voice steady. "You said you needed to speak to me. So speak, and make it the truth, otherwise I'm leaving."

Reine-Marie's phone rang. She grabbed it, thinking it was Armand, but it was another familiar voice.

"I'm experimenting with a new cocktail. Want to come over?" asked Olivier.

"Absolutely," said Reine-Marie.

The other guinea pigs were gathered in the bistro on the large sofa and in armchairs around the laid, but unlit, fire. It was a warm afternoon, but when the sun went down, so would the temperature.

"You never told us who that call yesterday morning was from," said Ruth.

Reine-Marie cut off a tranche of Bleu Bénédictin, made by the monks in the nearby abbey of Saint-Benoît-du-Lac, and placed it on a slice of baguette from Sarah's Boulangerie. Then she took one of the experimental cocktails and sniffed. It was green and smelled of turf.

It also tasted like turf. She winced and put it down again. "What's it called?"

"The Last Word," said Olivier.

Everyone else took a sip and made the same face.

"Is the last word 'yech'?" asked Myrna.

"Fucking hell." Ruth moved her tongue around in her mouth, trying to get rid of the taste. "That's awful. Are you trying to poison us?" Still, she downed the drink and reached for Clara's, who did not defend it.

"Gin," shouted Clara. "Stat!"

"Don't think our near-death experience just now has made us forget the question," said Ruth, though the others looked perplexed, having forgotten the question. "Who was on the phone yesterday morning?"

The call was private and none of their business. But Reine-Marie had trusted these people with her life. She could trust them with this. Or at least a carefully curated version.

"It was from some woman Armand used to know—"

"Ahhh," said Ruth, nodding. "I was 'some woman' once . . ."

The others grimaced. Even Rosa. But then, ducks often did.

"Not like that," Reine-Marie hurriedly said before Rosa could speak. "At all."

They leaned forward, knowing they were about to get the good stuff. Something was about to happen.

# CHAPTER 7

—

Will you arrest me?"

"Do you want to be arrested?" asked Gamache. "Because it seems like you do. But arrested for what? You entered my home uninvited, but you broke nothing and only took an old coat, which you returned. A charge might stick, but you'd get a suspended sentence. I have better things to do, more important things to do, than play games with you."

This clearly shocked "Charles." He looked around, then leaned closer.

"Look, I think I'm being set up. I think something's happening and they want me to be blamed. That's why I wanted to talk to you. To ask for help. For protection."

"From whom?"

"I don't know."

The man's voice had risen to a whine, and his joual was stronger now, the accent broad. If the language was indeed winter, Armand was in a sudden squall, in danger of losing his way.

"Why would someone hire me to break into your home and tell me not to take anything? It doesn't make sense."

"*Non*. What doesn't make sense is what you're saying," snapped Gamache. And he didn't mean just the accent.

Once again, "Charles" looked around. It was becoming almost

comical, certainly clichéd. He was the very image of a nervous man afraid he was being watched by the "bad guys."

And yet, thought Gamache with annoyance, cliché or no, it could be true. He could really be afraid. Or not.

Gamache had rarely felt so lost when faced with a suspect. Though there was nothing "suspect" about "Charles." He was guilty. But the question Armand needed answering was who'd put him up to it. Because someone had.

"You might not have known it was my home, but the guy who hired you almost certainly did. Who was it?"

"I don't know."

With that, Gamache made to get up.

"No, wait," said "Charles," reaching out to grab Gamache's sleeve.

Armand pulled it away, then leaned back in the chair, staring, daring this strange man to tell another lie.

"He was wearing a leather jacket and clean shirt." "Charles's" voice was now eager. "Good shoes. I notice shoes. Yours are good too. Not cheap shit that'll fall apart in the first rain."

This seemed a tangent, and yet it fed into the man's story that he lived for the most part on the streets. Where being able to tell good footwear from flimsy became vital to survival.

"I'm not interested in his clothing. Describe the man."

"I dunno, a guy."

"Old, young? French? Tall, short? Come on."

"He was French. Older than me but not as old as you." Clearly, to him, Gamache seemed ancient. "About my height, with dark hair. He looked fit. Like he worked out."

Either "Charles" paid much more attention than he claimed, or he was making it all up. Armand was leaning heavily toward the latter.

"Did he tell you why you were to go into the apartment?"

"Just that it was a bet. But I didn't really ask. I just wanted the money."

"A bet? Didn't that strike you as strange?"

"What the fuck, man." The belligerent, defensive "Charles" had returned. "I'm starving and some guy offers me money? I'd have blown him for less. So no, I don't even know why he told me that much. I didn't ask."

"Why you?"

"Probably because I looked the most likely to be able to do it without totally fucking up."

"And the most willing?"

"*Oui*. And why not? *Tabernak*, who wouldn't?"

Gamache did not need to say that he would not. But was that even true? If things had been different after his parents were killed in that accident? If he'd had no grandmother to raise him? No Stephen? If he'd found himself in foster care, then on the streets and starving? With holes in his shoes and thin clothing and a subway grate for a home? Who knew what he would become? What he would do?

"How did he pay you?"

"I take credit. How the fuck do you think he paid. Cash."

"Before or after?"

"Before."

"I see."

"Charles" knew he'd made a mistake, knew Gamache could see it. And the fact that the Chief Inspector didn't follow up was even more disconcerting.

"Describe the apartment."

"*Pardon?*"

"My apartment. Describe it."

There was a pause. Was this even the man who'd gone in? How much, Gamache wondered, was he being played?

"There're posters. I recognized the Jazz Festival one. There's a fireplace, and that's where I saw you, in a photograph. Magazines and books were everywhere. That's all I remember. It was . . ."

Gamache waited.

". . . nice. Comfortable."

There was a wistfulness to his voice. A longing that could not be hidden. And that Gamache did not think was feigned. An unintended truth.

"Which shelter are you in?"

"The Mission, in Old Montréal."

Gamache knew it. It would be checked.

They would also, thanks to the coffee mug, have this man's fingerprints.

Armand reached into his jacket pocket, brought out a notebook, and slid it across the table.

"I'd like you to write, 'Please, I need to speak to you.'"

He handed "Charles" a pen. The man looked at Gamache, perplexed at first, and then he understood.

"You are not a trusting man," he said as he wrote.

"Would you trust you?"

"Charles" gave one snort of near amusement, then pushed the paper back. "There. Satisfied?"

"Can you tell me why I asked you to do that?"

"Because that's in the note I wrote you. That note, right?" "Charles" pointed to the paper the Chief Inspector now held.

Unfolding it, Gamache compared the writing. They were the same.

"Where was it put?" Gamache asked.

"Fuck, man, you really do have trust issues. I put it in the jacket pocket." "Charles" mimicked placing a hand in the correct place.

"And this?" Gamache opened up the other piece of paper. The list of herbs and spices.

Reine-Marie took a deep breath, gathered her thoughts, and plunged ahead.

"Armand hasn't heard from her in years. Last time she called she wanted a favor."

Rosa nodded knowingly, as though this was familiar territory for a duck.

"What did she want?" Gabri asked, reaching for the Saint André and bread.

"Back then? She was the executive assistant to a member of Parliament. A newly elected backbencher from a rural riding outside Québec City. The MP's daughter had been in an accident. The assistant asked Armand to meet with her, and he did."

"Her the MP or her the assistant?" asked Myrna.

"The assistant. She wanted the MP to have deniability."

They leaned closer. Deniability. This was getting better and better.

"Why?" asked Clara. "What had happened?"

"The daughter was coming home from a bar. She was underage, drunk, and only had a learner's permit. She hit a cyclist. Instead of stopping to help, she took off. The Sûreté tracked her down and took her in for questioning."

"The cyclist?" asked Clara.

"A young man. Bagged groceries at the local shop. He was on his way home. The coroner said if she'd stopped to help, he might have survived. As it was, he died alone in a ditch."

There was a sigh and silence. It was no longer "better and better." It had suddenly gotten worse. And worse.

"The assistant wanted it hushed up," said Reine-Marie. "All charges dropped. Wanted the Sûreté to list it as an accident. The young man hit a pothole and was propelled off his bike into a tree."

"But surely the injuries . . . ," began Olivier.

Reine-Marie shrugged. "You'd think it couldn't be done, but anything can, with enough clout, enough influence."

"And the MP had that," said Ruth.

"So did Armand," said Clara. "He had the power to make it go away."

"*Oui*," said Reine-Marie, remembering his face when he'd gotten home that evening.

Sitting here, in this comfortable, familiar place, surrounded by good, decent people, it all seemed so simple. So obvious. The right thing to do. And Armand had done it. The charges were not dropped. Though neither he nor Reine-Marie appreciated the lengths the MP and his executive assistant would go to, to avenge that.

Years later, in their peaceful garden, Reine-Marie saw Armand was still reeling from the clout.

# CHAPTER 8

⁓

"Charles" stared at the paper with the list of herbs, then at Gamache. "I have no idea what that is."

"Why did you put it in my coat?"

"I didn't." He seemed genuinely astonished. "Can I see it?"

Gamache handed it to him.

"What's the mystery? It's a shopping list." He turned it over and his brows rose, then he handed it back. "Must've been in your coat already."

"It was not. Which means someone put it there. If not you, then who?"

Armand watched a drop of perspiration slowly make its way down "Charles's" face.

If it hadn't been involuntary, Gamache would have suspected the sweat was part of the act.

"I don't know."

Gamache stared at "Charles" so long that the perspiration had time to make its slow way to his jawline. And then the drop dropped. *Splat.* Onto the wooden table.

"How was your employer supposed to prove he'd been in the apartment?"

"What?"

"You said it was a bet, so he'd have to prove he'd succeeded. If you weren't to steal something personal, then what proof would he have?"

"I was told to take a photograph."

"Let me see." Gamache held out his hand.

"I erased it. Didn't want any evidence."

"But you must have sent it to the guy who hired you. I want to see your emails."

His hand was still out.

"I don't have a phone."

"Come on, you can do better than that," said Gamache, exasperated. "How did you take the photo? How did you send it? Do I need to teach you how to lie?"

"The guy gave me his phone."

"You're not even trying to make this believable."

Over "Charles's" shoulder, Gamache could see Lacoste watching this. He was wearing a wire, of course. She and Beauvoir would be listening in. Recording this on audio and video. Jean-Guy would have already put this man's photo into the system.

Gamache lowered his hand to the table. It was now clear that this was all bullshit. Except, perhaps, for the sweat. The drops plump with deceit.

The man knew he was cornered. And not only by Chief Inspector Gamache. There was someone else. Someone he feared more than Gamache. Actually, it was clear to the Chief Inspector that this "Charles" did not fear him at all. The opposite seemed to be true. He viewed Gamache as the lifeguard. The one swimming out to save him.

And yet, despite the fact he'd invited Gamache here for that reason, despite Gamache's entreaties, this man seemed reluctant to accept the help.

For his part, Armand Gamache was keenly aware that a drowning man could take them both down.

"Tell me." His voice was soft now, not confronting but compelling.

"Charles" took a deep breath. A decision would have to be made. Sink or swim? Clearly the truth was dangerous. But surely it had gone far too far now. What was this man's hesitation?

"All right, I'll tell you."

Gamache knew that whatever was said next would be a demi-truth.

Not a whole lie, not the entire truth. They were coming to the end-game. And that was always the most dangerous.

He was suddenly very glad Beauvoir had pretty much emptied Sûreté headquarters into Open Da Night. Though he did briefly wonder how he'd explain to accounting all the caffè cremas and bomboloni.

"Charles" had said that this meeting had been a mistake. Armand now wondered if he had made the same blunder.

His eyes traveled over to where the grandfather and little girl had been sitting and was relieved to see the seats were empty. A table had opened up on the terrasse and they'd grabbed it. If something happened, they were more likely to be out of it.

"I was told to go in and take the jacket. As proof. But not to take anything else. I thought it was a joke. I really didn't know it was your place."

"Enough," said Gamache, eyes sharp on the man across from him, but alert to all movement around them. "I have no idea if you knew, and right now it doesn't matter. But I want you to think, to really think. You were told to break into the home of the head of homicide. A senior Sûreté officer. There's a reason for it, something that goes far beyond a jacket and a joke." He looked around, then his eyes swung back to "Charles." "What's going to happen here?"

"What do you mean?"

"You were told to put the note in my jacket, the one saying you wanted to meet me here. Now. Why? To what purpose?"

"Charles" was silent.

"*Bon*," said Gamache, standing up. "I've had enough. You're on your own. Good luck."

"No, wait." "Charles's" hand shot out and grabbed Gamache's wrist, tight.

"For what?" demanded Gamache, breaking the grip. "Are you expecting someone?"

"No. I don't know. Maybe."

"Who?"

"Look, sit. Please."

"Charles" seemed genuinely desperate.

Gamache sat. "You have two minutes, then I'm leaving. The truth. Who are you?"

"Okay. I don't live at The Mission, not anymore. I got into cocaine, then fentanyl. But I got my shit together when I got clean. I volunteer there now. I was approached by someone to do this job. He gave me a thousand, half before, half after. I was to drop the coat off on a peg at The Mission and that would be that."

This, at least, was beginning to make sense. Gamache knew this "Charles" had lied when he said he'd been paid up front. And "Charles" had realized he'd made a mistake, which partly explained the wild swings from anger to pleading. He was off-balance, and he wanted to throw Gamache off too.

"Do you know the man?"

"Not his name, but I'd seen him around. He seemed a sort of assistant. He'd shown up at The Mission when there was an official tour."

"What sort of tour?"

"You know, politicians. They're photographed handing out meals to the great unwashed. I was once served by the Premier."

Gamache grew very still before asking the next question. "Was the person who contacted you with the Premier? Could he have been part of his security detail?"

Guarding the Premier was the responsibility of the Sûreté since the Premier was the head of the provincial government. If the fellow who'd approached "Charles" was on that detail, then—

"I don't know."

"Think," snapped Gamache, then reined himself in. He continued, his voice gentle now, coaxing. "Did you see him there when the Premier wasn't around?"

"Charles" thought. And nodded. "Yes. A few times, on other tours."

"All provincial politicians, or others?"

"I don't know." "Charles" sounded annoyed by what must've seemed a trivial question.

But Gamache knew it was anything but that.

"Please. Think."

And to Armand's astonishment, "Charles" did.

"There was a tour of federal politicians including the minister of something. Someone important. High up. The guy was there then."

"And no provincial politician was present? Not the Québec Premier or anyone else?"

"Not that I know of, but I don't know all of them."

It wasn't conclusive, but it helped. Gamache brought a hand up to his mouth, thinking. His mind working quickly.

"Do you know the dates?"

"Of the tours when the guy was there?" asked "Charles." "Are you kidding? I barely know today's date."

"When do you volunteer?" probed Gamache. "Specific days?"

"Yes. Every second Sunday."

That was something at least. A place to start.

The Mission had cameras up. He'd get those tapes and review them for tours when this "Charles" was also there. Have him identify the man who approached him. It should not be difficult.

"The coat," Gamache began, working his way forward slowly. "You were told to take it."

"*Oui.*"

"You put one note in the pocket, but not the other. So someone else put this one in." Gamache placed his hand on the list of herbs and spices.

And now "Charles" colored. "I lied. I did. I put both in. I was told to."

"That's a lie. I saw your face when I handed you this second note. You were surprised. You need to tell me the truth. That's why you wanted to see me, *non*? You're afraid, and I think you're right to be. You asked to see me. Why? What do you want to tell me?"

Gamache reached for his glass of water, but before he could get there, "Charles" also reached for it, knocking it over. Gamache reacted quickly, grabbing the paper off the table before the wave of water soaked it.

"Why did you just do that?"

"What? It was an accident."

"It was not. You did it on purpose. You wanted to destroy the paper. Why?"

Now "Charles" smiled. "You think water will destroy that? Believe what you want, but actually, you're partway there."

"What's that supposed to mean?"

"Charles's" lips pressed together, as though he'd said too much already.

Then Gamache had it. He'd been wrong. Very wrong. This whole thing was a lie. And it started with the note.

*Please, I need to speak to you. Meet me today. Four o'clock at Open Da Night. I'm sorry. I didn't know it was your home.*

"How did you know what the man was going to do with my coat?"

"I didn't."

"But you put the note in the pocket. You must've known the coat was going to be returned to me."

And there it was. They were finally at the center of the labyrinth Armand had been wandering in since opening the package that morning.

Now he saw his companion for who he really was. Not some ruined creature chosen at random and being set up. This man was at the center of it all. He knew everything.

The man smiled and nodded. His demeanor, his posture, his face, his entire being transformed into someone else.

"You might not believe it, Monsieur Gamache, but I am trying to help." Even his voice had changed. The joual gone.

"Then why these lies? Why not just tell me? What's going on? What's going to happen?"

"Not 'going to,'" said "Charles." "Is happening. And has been for a while."

"What?" demanded Gamache. "For Chrissake, out with it."

"To be honest, I don't know the full extent, but the person I work for does, though I'm beginning to wonder which side he's on. And until just now, I didn't know which side you were on."

This shocked Gamache. "Why would you have any doubts about me?"

"I just need to be careful."

"Who told you to break into my home? Who are you working for? A name, man."

"Look, I asked to meet you in person to look you in the eye, to see if you really could be trusted. The fact you kept pushing, the fact you stayed even when you were faced with a pile of bullshit, even when you suspected this might be a setup, told me you will see this through."

"See what through? Come on, enough of the games."

The man stared at Gamache. "This's no game. You have no idea how deep this goes."

"Of course I don't. You haven't told me anything."

"And yet you have suspicions."

Gamache's eyes widened and his voice rose in frustration. "I don't know what you think I know, but I have nothing."

"But you do." The man looked around. "We should go. I've been here too long." Seeing the look on Gamache's face, he smiled. "No. Nothing's going to happen here. This meeting was just to make sure I could trust you."

"And the other note? The list? The one you tried to spill water all over. What does it mean? Why was it given to me?"

For the first time since admitting who he was, the man looked concerned. "I actually don't know. I've never seen it. I don't know why it was put in your coat."

"You didn't put it there?"

"No."

"Then who did? Who had access to the coat once you stole it?"

"My boss. I gave it to him."

"Did you know your boss planned to send the coat back to me?"

"I did. That's why I put my message in the pocket."

"Didn't you wonder why he had it stolen, only to send it right back?"

"He said it was to get your attention."

"And you believed him?"

"Well, it worked." The man almost smiled. Gamache did not.

"Come on, man," said Gamache. "Think. Simply sending my own

coat back, without anything else, would've been strange, but it would not get my attention. The notes did. Your note, but also his. You must've known there'd be more to it."

Then Gamache had it. "You wanted to tell me something, but you also want me to tell you something. What?"

And he had. He'd shown this "Charles" the other note. Had that been the blunder?

"I knew there was more," admitted "Charles." "But I didn't know why my boss was trying to get your attention. That list means nothing to me, but the paper does."

"In what way? What does it tell you?"

"The same thing it tells you. I know I've lied my way through this meeting, and you have no reason at all to trust me. Maybe one day you will. But the only thing I really needed out of this was to know if I could trust you. And I do."

Gamache's face told him that his trust was of no concern to him.

"I'll tell you something for free," said Gamache, getting up and putting cash on the table with a large tip. He caught the eye of an agent standing behind "Charles" and glanced down at the coffee mug. "Unless your boss is a complete fool, he found your note and knows about this meeting."

"Charles" grew very still. This was clearly a new and disconcerting thought.

"You need to tell me who he is."

"Charles" shook his head. "Not until I know if he can be trusted. I owe him that much. He's either incredibly brave or . . ."

*Or*, thought Gamache. He'd met his share of the "ors." But he'd also met his share of incredibly brave people. He thought, despite the lying, that he might be in the company of one at that moment.

# CHAPTER 9

The meeting was over.

After half an hour together, Gamache had gotten almost nothing out of this "Charles," except some vague allusions to something larger in the works.

No facts, no evidence, no names. Not even this stranger's name.

As he followed "Charles" to the door, Gamache was troubled and frustrated. And felt he had not done a very good job.

Since he had no facts or evidence, he had to rely on his instincts. Oddly enough, though Gamache fought against it, his instincts told him "Charles" had been sincere when he'd said he was trying to help. Though the young man was clearly deeply conflicted. And he hadn't actually been any help. In fact, quite the opposite. He'd created a house of specters, of partly seen, insubstantial threats, and then thrown Gamache into it.

Once outside, they paused on the sidewalk.

"Why did you wonder if you could trust me?" Gamache asked.

He was squinting into the sun and moved slightly. From that angle he could see Beauvoir standing across the street, and behind him an SUV parked half a block away. Probably an unmarked Sûreté vehicle.

Lacoste was just coming out of Open Da Night, followed closely by a woman who glanced around, looking for someone or for an empty table on the packed terrasse.

"Charles" hadn't answered his question. Instead, he continued to stare at him. And Armand understood.

"You're afraid the Sûreté is compromised."

"I'm sure of it. And yes, Chief Inspector, I'm afraid."

"Who? Who in the Sûreté?"

"Charles" shook his head. "I don't know. And that's the least of it."

"The least of what?" demanded Gamache, his patience far exceeded.

"Charles" thought for a moment, considering and weighing his answer. "I gave up drugs and booze, and now everyone is telling me that to be healthy I should drink more water, but you know, I don't think that's true."

He stared at Gamache as though expecting the Chief Inspector to understand.

"Come on, son. I need more."

Armand didn't know why he just called this young man "son," except that he wasn't that far off Daniel's age. In fact, "Charles" and Daniel had a lot in common. Not least of all drug use. And managing to claw back their lives.

Out of the corner of his eye, Gamache saw the woman behind Lacoste raise her hand and wave cheerily toward the SUV. It began moving to pick her up.

Instead of answering Gamache's question, "Charles" said, "I'll be in touch."

"You've given me nothing!"

"I've given you more than I meant to. More than was wise. I need to find something out. I'll let you know. I promise."

"I'll leave my coat by the door."

"Charles" laughed and turned away. But Gamache had one more question.

"What's your name?"

The man turned back and smiled. "Actually, it really is Charles."

A movement over Charles's shoulder caught Gamache's eye.

The SUV was moving toward Open Da Night. But instead of

slowing down to pick up the woman, it was gathering speed, accelerating toward them. Aiming for the sidewalk. The terrasse. Them. And anyone in between.

Gamache's eyes widened. Seeing this, Charles began to turn, to look behind him. But there was no time.

Between them and the SUV sat the man and his granddaughter. The girl was coloring in a book, and he was reading the newspaper. Oblivious.

It all happened so fast, and yet in slow motion. The SUV was so close now Gamache locked eyes with the driver.

And then . . .

Too late, Jean-Guy Beauvoir saw what was happening, though he could never have done anything anyway.

His first, and only, warning was the look on Gamache's face. His surprise. His body tensing. Preparing.

And then the flash of black across Beauvoir's vision as the vehicle sped by.

Isabelle Lacoste had just left the café and was checking her messages to see if there were any updates. Her earpiece was still in, picking up the last of the conversation between the Chief and this man. Whose name—she smiled—turned out to be Charles after all.

She could just imagine Gamache shaking his head in self-deprecating exasperation.

But the smile froze when she heard a gasp. His gasp. A half shout. She looked up just as there was a terrible sound.

Jean-Guy ran toward the sudden chaos. Of chairs and tables overturned.

Of bodies on the ground.

There had been silence, for a moment, after the initial rending crash. As though life and death were suspended. All mashed up. Fate trying to decide.

And then the screaming started. The vehicle had plowed into the terrasse, into the people, then sped off. Rounding the corner and disappearing onto avenue Fairmount.

Tires screeched and sirens wailed, joining the screaming on the terrasse, as Sûreté vehicles took off after the SUV.

Beauvoir raced over just as Gamache shoved the heavy table off himself. He was protecting the child with his body, while bracing on the pavement. Her eyes were wide. There was blood on her face and in her hair. The girl and the Chief Inspector stared at each other for a moment.

And then she started crying. Huge, gusty wails. The cries of a terrified but healthy child. It was the best sound ever. Armand pushed himself to his knees and ran expert eyes over her thin body. It wasn't broken. He checked her head. She had a scrape, nothing more.

"*Patron?*" shouted Beauvoir, clearing off more debris.

Gamache looked around, spotting the grandfather just sitting up, dazed. The elderly man screamed, "Patricia!" His voice high with panic. Then, seeing his granddaughter, he reached for her, wincing as he did.

"Ambulances."

"On it, *patron*," said Lacoste, who'd run over.

"Look after them," Gamache commanded as he stumbled, scrambling, half crawling, half tripping over the debris, to the body in the middle of the road.

Dropping to his knees, Armand whispered, "Charles?"

Others were crowding around now. He half heard Lacoste shouting into her phone for paramedics. But his attention was focused on the broken man sprawled unnaturally on the asphalt.

Charles was lying on his side, and Gamache didn't dare turn him. Not for fear of doing more damage—it was clear the man was either dead or dying—but if he was still alive, Gamache did not want to inflict even more pain.

He laid himself down on his side so that his body was within inches of the other man's. Charles's grey eyes were glassy, staring. Blood bubbled on his lips. He was breathing. Barely.

Gamache reached for his hand and held it.

"Charles," he said softly. "Charles."

He repeated the name, hoping it would comfort the dying man to know he was not alone. For just an instant, the eyes focused. And the lips moved.

Gamache inched closer. He could smell the hot tar of the road and the slight scent of sweet whipped cream on Charles's weak breath. He felt the asphalt warm beneath him and the late-afternoon sun on his face.

And he knew he had to do it. He had to ask one more, one last, time.

"A name. Give me a name, son."

"Family," whispered Charles.

"I will," said Armand. "I'll tell your family. I promise." He felt Charles squeeze his hand and saw, just for an instant, panic in those eyes.

Then the panic left. Everything left.

And Charles was gone. And everything he knew was gone.

*P*atron, are you all right?"

It was Lacoste's voice. She was kneeling beside him, her hand on his shoulder.

"Sir, are you all right?" Now it was the voice of a paramedic, and Gamache realized he was lying in the road, giving every impression of being far from "all right."

He struggled to his feet. After giving him a quick once-over, including shining a light into his eyes to see if there was a concussion, the paramedic's firm hand moved him aside to better examine the man who would not get up.

Lacoste was saying something. There were screams and shouts from the sidewalk.

Gamache realized that the ambulance must have already been waiting. He wondered whether it was Lacoste or Beauvoir who'd thought to order one out. Just in case . . .

"He's dead," snapped the paramedic and, leaving the body, she rushed to others who could be helped.

Gamache looked around. Men and women were just beginning to

sit up, some staggering to their feet, holding parts of their body that were in pain.

The attack had happened, what? A minute earlier? Only that. If that.

The SUV was gone. The wailing of the police sirens receding.

"Did you get it?" He turned to Lacoste.

"On video, yes." She followed him as he walked quickly, limping slightly, into the chaos.

"Our people took off after him, and the Montréal cops are alerted. We'll get him."

Onlookers were already taking out their phones to record and post. Some no doubt live-streaming on the internet. Gamache was tempted to go over and unload his rage on them. Instead, he pointed at one of his agents.

"You there. Stand in front of them. Try to block their view of the body."

"*Oui, patron.*"

"Here." Gamache took off his jacket and was a little surprised to see it torn. "Put it over him. Wait."

Taking the jacket back, Armand removed what was in the pockets, including the two notes. "Now, go. Stand guard over the body."

"Yessir."

"His name is Charles," Gamache called after the agent. It seemed important that she know.

The agent ran over, spread the coat. Then she opened her arms to make herself as big as possible. To hide the broken man, Charles, from this final assault.

*Family*, thought Gamache.

How horrific if they found out by seeing it online. Those filming had a right, though perhaps not a perfect right, to video, but Gamache wondered if they realized that with every second they posted, they lost pieces of their humanity.

*Family*, Charles had muttered. Just that. His last thought was, as Armand knew his would have been, had been, for his family. A few years earlier, as he lay on the factory floor bleeding and dying, Armand

61

had whispered to Isabelle Lacoste what they both believed would be his last words.

*Reine-Marie.*

He'd placed all his love into Lacoste, trusting it would be delivered.

He had not, of course, died. But that moment had bound him to Lacoste. Just as Charles's last moment bound him to Gamache. There was now an agreement, a contract, between the living man and the newly dead.

Gamache could have saved Charles, but had let him die. Choosing instead to knock the child out of the way. And now he had to go and tell Charles's family. Was he married? Did he have a young daughter? Son?

And yet something was off. When he'd assured Charles that he'd speak to his family, he hadn't looked relieved. Just the opposite. He'd looked panicked.

Armand had thought it was that last desperate awareness that he really was going to die. But the head of homicide had seen enough people die, had held them. Reassured them in their final moments that they were not alone.

He'd said the rosary over some, those he knew it would comfort. Seen broken lips move with his. Held those hands, held their eyes, until the light left. He'd absorbed their pain, their fear, their sorrow. Their love.

He'd never ever seen that exact look.

"For what it's worth, we have the license plate." Lacoste was following Gamache, the two of them helping people to their feet. Comforting. Assessing injuries. "It'll be stolen, of course. I sent the video to our people."

"*Bon.*" But even as he said that, Gamache realized he no longer knew for sure who their "people" were. Not after what Charles had said. A thought sped across his mind as he reached out to help a woman to her feet—

"Are you hurt?"

Had that been the true purpose of this meeting? To sow doubt in the Chief Inspector's mind?

"My arm, but it's okay. Just a bruise, I think."

"Stay here." Gamache righted a chair and patted the seat. "A medic will come by."

Was he close to something in one of his investigations? Too close?

"I'm a doctor, Monsieur Gamache."

Had someone wanted to undermine his investigation by sending this young man to him? Making him doubt his colleagues? Was that what Charles was supposed to do?

Did do? Did Charles know, or was he being used?

"I can help," she said.

Why kill him, then? But the Chief Inspector had the answer.

"Are you sure you're all right?"

They'd do it to drive home the point. That Charles was telling the truth. They'd do it so that Gamache would believe that he could not trust his colleagues in the Sûreté. So that he would believe the lie.

"Absolutely." The doctor pushed past him, not waiting for permission that was not his to give anyway.

Dear God, thought the Chief. What was worse? That Charles was lying, and they were dealing with people who would murder their own? Or that Charles was telling the truth?

"Because of the angle, we don't have the driver's face," said Lacoste.

"*Pardon?*" said the man she was helping.

"Not talking to you. Are you okay?"

"You asking me?" the man said.

She nodded and so did he. "I'm okay, I guess."

"I saw him," said Gamache.

"You did?" She stood up and stared at the Chief Inspector.

His greying hair was disheveled, as were his clothes. His white shirt untucked and smeared with blood. His tie was loose and off to one side. The knees were torn from his slacks and slightly bloody. His right hand was bleeding from scrapes on his palm where he'd braced for the impact. He was clearly not seriously hurt. Not what it could have been. What she'd thought it would be, in that terrible instant.

"Can you describe him?" she asked.

"I can do better, Isabelle. I can show you a photo. It was the man who dropped off the package this morning. I'm sure of it."

*Dear God, was it only this morning?*

It took her just a beat to understand what he was saying.

"Shit." She scrolled through her images, found the photo, and sent it out. There was no clear shot of the man's face, but it gave an impression.

"There was a woman on the terrasse," said Armand as he helped someone else. "You might not have seen her. She came out behind you and waved at the vehicle. She must've signaled it." He scanned the scene. "I can't see her now."

"We had cameras outside," said Lacoste. "I'll find her."

Gamache assessed the situation. The chaos had settled down. Beauvoir had gotten it under control quickly and was organizing the medical efforts. More ambulances and paramedics were arriving.

The damage was not as bad as it looked, not as bad as it could have been. Most of the injuries had happened when people fell off their chairs, knocking the heavy tables over on top of themselves as they scrambled out of the way of the vehicle. People had cuts and bruises and were more shocked than hurt.

Though shock was itself an injury.

"I have some photos," said Lacoste.

Gamache swiped through them quickly. "That's her."

Lacoste got the picture out with a message to pick the woman up but approach with caution, while Gamache made his way back to the man and his granddaughter.

Paramedics had put a bandage on the girl's head and were now working on the grandfather.

She was just a little older than Armand's own granddaughter Florence.

He knelt, placing himself so that he blocked her view of the lump lying in the street, though of course she'd already seen it. Him. Only Charles's twisted legs were visible, sprawling out from under Gamache's suit jacket. Charles's shoes had been knocked off in the impact and were lying on the road.

The girl had stopped crying and was looking, in some amazement, at the scene around her.

"Is your name Patricia?" Armand asked.

She nodded.

"You are very brave."

She nodded again, agreeing with him. He took out his clean handkerchief and licked it, making it moist so that he could wash the tears and congealing blood off her face.

Her deep blue eyes were watching him. Then they dropped, and she smiled.

He followed her gaze and noticed a smear of whipped cream sticking to the back of his hand. He stared at it, then looked over at Charles lying in a heap, alone in the street. It must have come from his hand, as he'd held it.

The paramedics had left Charles where he'd landed, quite reasonably choosing to leave the dead and look after the living. As Gamache had made his choice, to save the girl and not the young man. As the SUV plowed by, Armand had felt it graze his leg. It had been that close.

But he was alive, and Charles was dead. Killed by the SUV driver, and Armand's choice.

Using his handkerchief, stained with the little girl's blood, Armand carefully wiped the whipped cream off his hand.

# CHAPTER 10

⁓

Reine-Marie sat in the study, staring at the blank screen. Knowing she should look. But putting it off.

Armand had called to tell her he'd gone to the rendezvous, and what had happened.

"There's video. It's going to be all over the internet and on the news."

"Are you all right?" That was really all she cared about.

"Yes." She heard the hubbub behind him, of shouting and sirens.

"Are you coming home?"

"Not just yet. But I'll be home tonight. Not for dinner, but later."

He was tempted to say, *Don't wait up.* But he knew she would.

That had been an hour ago.

Clara sat in Myrna's loft above the bookstore, a glass of beer partway to her lips.

On the sofa, facing the television, Myrna and Billy Williams also watched as the CBC anchor announced the lead story of the six o'clock news. And the video began.

Billy reached out to take Myrna's hand. And Myrna reached for Clara.

Gabri stood in the laundry room off the kitchen of the B&B, shoving bedding and towels into the washing machine. Their guest had checked out, and this needed doing before he could sit down with a cocktail. But not the one the elderly man had suggested. That had been vile.

The television was on in the living room, tuned to the French Radio-Canada television news. At the mention of Chief Inspector Gamache of the Sûreté du Québec, Gabri stopped what he was doing and poked his head around the corner.

Then, a towel still in his hand, he walked into the room and dropped onto the sofa. His eyes wide, his mouth partly open, he twisted the towel as the video played.

Oh, fuck," muttered Ruth.

"Fuck, fuck, fuck," agreed Rosa. A contrary fowl who rarely agreed with anything, this time there was no argument and no other word for it.

Before the story was even over, Ruth scooped up Rosa and headed for the door.

Bonjour?"

Reine-Marie turned to see Clara in the doorway of the study. Then Gabri and Olivier appeared. Then Myrna. And finally, though out of sight, Reine-Marie heard, "Fuck, fuck, fuck."

"We let ourselves in," said Olivier, as though it were unusual and needed to be said.

"Are you okay?" Clara asked.

"Have you seen it?" asked Myrna.

"Armand called and told me, but I haven't yet." Reine-Marie looked at the clock on the bookcase and was surprised to see it was ten past six. "It's all over the news?"

"*Oui*," said Gabri.

"All you need to know is that Armand and Jean-Guy are all right," said Olivier.

"She needs to know more than that." Ruth's querulous voice entered the room, followed by the rest of the old poet. Her rheumy blue eyes held Reine-Marie's. "You need to see it. So your imagination won't make it worse than it already is."

And Reine-Marie knew two things.

The demented old woman was right. And that was why they were there. So that she wouldn't be alone when she watched.

The curtains at the window billowed softly, like a breath, as fresh air wafted in from the village green. It brought with it the scent of grass, and the sound of children playing, and the soft murmur of bees bumbling in the intertwined honeysuckle and sweet pea growing up the trellis.

How nice it was, how peaceful, thought Reine-Marie, to live in a place where bumbling was a virtue. Even a necessity. And where lives were intertwined.

Then, as Clara took the chair beside her and held her hand, Reine-Marie watched.

Armand went back to their city apartment, where he showered and changed into a light blue shirt, a summer sweater, and slacks.

When he'd undressed, he was not surprised to see scrapes and bruises. Welts. Most not actually painful. What hurt the most was his left foot. It was swollen and bruised.

Armand put antiseptic on the cuts and scrapes.

The clothes he'd been in lay in a lump in the corner of the bedroom. They'd have to be thrown out. They were torn, and stained with dirt and blood. Beyond repair.

Beauvoir had found and given him the shoe that had flown off, and now Armand put it on, since he didn't have another pair in that apartment.

He'd tried to clean it with a washcloth but couldn't get the deep scuffing off.

It was the least of his concerns. That thought brought back what Charles had said. He'd made it clear that the Sûreté being compromised was the least of it.

But he hadn't said what "it" was.

They now knew that his full name was Charles Langlois. He lived on rue Versailles, in the Petite-Bourgogne *quartier* of Montréal. They got that much from the wallet they'd found on his body. There was also a house key and phone, but nothing else.

Gamache had gone directly from the crime scene to that address, not stopping to clean up or change. He needed to get to Charles's family quickly, before they saw the video.

So far, a search of the database had not shown anything for a Charles Langlois. He had no police record. While Beauvoir drove, Gamache took a call from Chief Superintendent Toussaint.

"I'm watching a video, Armand. Is there something you'd like to tell me?"

"I was just about to call you."

Beauvoir shot him a look and wondered how truthful that was.

Gamache told the Chief Superintendent what had happened, albeit a carefully curated version.

"You say this man, the dead man, asked to meet you? So this wasn't a random act."

"Definitely targeted."

"You're sure? There's no further risk to the public?"

"Not from the SUV, *non*."

If the Superintendent heard the implication, she did not follow up.

"The Mayor of Montréal will be holding a news conference. She wants us both there. The video's already all over the internet."

He muttered under his breath, and the Chief Super did not ask him to repeat it.

"Are you sure it wasn't a terror attack?"

"Absolutely."

"Are you sure you were not the target, Armand?"

He saw once again the face, the eyes, of the driver. Locking on him for an instant. Before shifting to Charles. "Absolutely sure."

"You need to tell me everything you know, Chief Inspector. I'll be in my office."

"Understood."

What he understood was that he was in for a dressing-down.

Chief Superintendent Toussaint was younger than him by ten

years. She'd come up through Cybercrimes and the Anti-Terror unit. While some grumbled that she'd been appointed simply because she was a Black woman, Gamache knew different. He'd been one of her professors at the academy, back in the day. And several years ago, after he was demoted, he'd put her name forward to replace him as Chief Superintendent of the Sûreté du Québec, though that was confidential, and he doubted she knew.

It was, after all, irrelevant.

The Chief Superintendent had earned her place at the top. And, Gamache knew, he'd earned whatever consequences were coming his way. For not foreseeing what would happen. For not preventing it.

"I'm on my way to speak to the dead man's family."

"Get here as soon as you can. I'll be waiting," she snapped. Then her voice softened. "Are you sure you're all right, Armand?"

"I'm fine, Madeleine. *Merci*."

As he hung up, he could feel the doubt, planted by Charles, spreading. Could he really trust Toussaint? He'd helped put her in place, but things happened to people in power. And she had more power than most.

As they drove to Charles's home, Gamache tucked in his shirt and tried to at least clean up his hands and face and smooth his hair so that he was more presentable. When the body had been removed, he'd taken back his suit jacket and put it on, to cover the all-too-obvious blood on his white shirt. Now he wondered if that had been a mistake. The jacket was torn, and there was blood on it too.

Leave it on, or take it off? What would be less horrific for Charles's family?

There seemed no good choice. Just degrees of bad.

Beauvoir drove, silent in the car, trying to find the words to apologize.

As they stopped at a traffic light, Armand turned to his son-in-law. Knowing what he was thinking. Feeling.

"The vehicle was electric. It made no sound. You were focused on the café, and rightly so. I saw it parked there and said nothing. I could have signaled you, Jean-Guy, but didn't."

70

"Because you trusted me to have checked it out." Jean-Guy's hands were tight on the wheel. His eyes forward.

He wondered how long it would be before he stopped seeing the Chief's face, and the streak of black.

"I should have."

"And I should have understood the danger sooner. And Charles Langlois should have met me in my office and not a public place."

Armand wondered how long it would be before he stopped seeing Charles's face, when he knew he was dying. He was twenty-seven years old and lying broken on the road. Some stranger holding his sticky hand.

"There's enough blame to go around, Jean-Guy, there always is. We need to set that aside and figure out who did this and why."

And what was going to happen next. Because there was a next. Something was about to happen.

"*Oui.*"

Both were lost in their own thoughts for the rest of the journey.

"You're that cop." The downstairs neighbor had come out onto her landing when she heard the knocking on her neighbor's door. She eyed the larger, the older, of the two men, bloody and disheveled. "From the video."

Gamache sighed. Were they too late to get to the family?

The neighbor's eyes widened as she looked at the door, then back at them. "Was that him? The guy who was killed?"

"Does Charles Langlois live here?" When she nodded, Gamache added, "Alone?"

"*Oui.* Never seen or heard anyone up there with him. God, that's awful. Terrorists, do you think? That's what they're saying."

"*Non*, not terrorists. How long's he been here?"

The woman thought. "Less than a year, I'd say. The landlord'll know more."

"We'll need the landlord's name and number," said Beauvoir. "And yours."

Gamache knocked, then knocked again, before using the key they'd found on Charles's body. They walked in. And stopped.

The single room was a shambles. Books splayed on the floor. The cushions of the sofa bed ripped. The mattress tipped over.

The drawers of the old desk in the corner were pulled out and contents dumped.

"I'll get forensics," said Beauvoir.

"And find out if the other neighbors saw or heard anything."

While Beauvoir did that, Gamache stood in the small studio apartment, surveying the mess. Then he walked slowly around. Not touching anything.

There was no computer. No papers or notebooks that he could see. It had all been scooped. Gamache walked over to the wall where he could see staples with scraps of paper trapped under them. Whatever had been up there had been ripped off, leaving just the corners.

But he recognized those scraps, and so did Jean-Guy when he returned.

"Map," he said, joining Gamache. "Charles had a huge map stapled up."

"The neighbors?"

Beauvoir shook his head. "The woman downstairs is the only one in right now, but she said she was out most of the afternoon. Didn't hear or see anyone."

Clothes were scattered on the floor, pockets turned inside out.

"Look at this." Gamache was kneeling over a sweater. On it was a pin with a symbol. "Recognize it?"

It was the yin-and-yang symbol, half in blue, half green. With a leaping fish in the middle.

"*Non,*" said Jean-Guy.

Gamache struggled a little to stand up, the bruising and stiffness setting in. Beauvoir reached out to steady him. "We'll have to get a hoist soon, *patron.*"

Gamache smiled. "I can still take you." Though both knew that had stopped being true a few years earlier.

"Someone obviously did this while he was at Open Da Night," said Beauvoir. "So they must've known about the rendezvous."

Gamache nodded.

"But why not kill him before you met, if they knew about it and were so afraid of what he'd say to you?"

Gamache stood looking out the window, his hands clasped behind his back, and considered the question.

"Maybe they didn't know about our meeting." His warm breath clouded the windowpane. "It's possible they were following him, and when they saw him talking to a Sûreté officer, they panicked. Throwing something together at the last minute. Sending someone here to rifle his place, then running him over in broad daylight. It doesn't seem like a well-thought-out plan."

"They must be shitting themselves," said Beauvoir. "They don't know what he told you, and now you'd have told others. They couldn't contain it."

"The problem is, he didn't tell me anything."

*You know*, Charles had said. *Or at least you suspect.*

Gamache sighed in frustration. Charles had been wrong. He neither knew nor suspected.

Beauvoir's phone buzzed with a text from Lacoste. "Shit. They found the SUV in Terrebonne, the Lachenaie landfill. And the driver."

Gamache turned from the window. "Dead?"

"One shot in the head. No ID. She's sending photos."

Gamache had often wondered if it was intentional, or unintentionally ironic, that the place the city had chosen to dump all its garbage was called Terrebonne. Good earth.

And not just garbage. It was a favorite dumping ground for the Montréal mafia. More than a few bodies had been found there.

Gamache gave a curt nod. "Did you get a photo of that pin?"

"*Oui.* I'll send it into the system."

"No," said Gamache abruptly. "Keep it between us. Show Isabelle, but no one else."

"You believed him about the Sûreté? That there's someone on the inside?"

"I don't know, but we have to assume."

Did Charles know he was being more than just set up? That he was targeted? Is that why he wanted to meet away from the Sûreté?

And yet he'd chosen to meet the most recognizable cop in Québec, in a public place. If he suspected he was being watched, then he
wanted them to be seen together. That's why the popular café. That's
why he'd even paused on the sidewalk.

Far from wanting to hide, he wanted to be seen, and seen with
Chief Inspector Gamache. Charles must have thought that would
guarantee his safety. No use killing him if he'd already spilled everything, and to a senior Sûreté officer.

But he was wrong. And that meant there was even more, much
more, at stake than even Charles Langlois realized.

"Jean-Guy?"

"*Oui?*"

"If you knew you were being watched, and you had evidence that
could damage some very nasty and desperate people, what would
you do?"

Beauvoir thought. "If I was that afraid? I'd broadcast it. Send it to
the cops. So that it wouldn't do any good to kill me for it. The information was already out there."

"But if you couldn't do that? If you still had to sort out the innocent
from the guilty?"

"Weellll." Jean-Guy thought. "I guess I'd hide it until I knew."

"That's what I'd do too."

Gamache looked over to the desk. Was it possible the laptop and
papers and whatever was on the wall hadn't been stolen but hidden?

"Got it, *patron*. The symbol on the pin." Beauvoir held out his phone.
"It's for a group called Action Québec Bleu. Some environmental organization." He hit the small phone icon and put it on speaker.

"Action Québec Bleu," said the cheerful young voice.

"*Bonjour*," said Gamache. "I'm calling to find out if you know a
Charles Langlois."

"Well, yes," said the woman. "He works here, but he's not in today.
Can I take a message?"

"*Non, merci.* I might drop by, can you give me your address please?"

She did. He wrote it down and thanked her before hanging up.

"Isabelle's traced his phone calls. Looks like it was a burner phone. New. Only one call made from it."

Armand's plan had been to send Beauvoir to Action Québec Bleu, while he went back to the city apartment, showered, changed, then met the Chief Super. But the next call he made, the last one Charles Langlois had made, changed that. A man answered. Yes, he knew him.

"He's our son. Why're you asking?"

While Beauvoir went to Action Québec Bleu, Armand made his way to Charles's parents' place. The home was small, neat, almost painfully clean. "*Propre*" was the word that came to Armand's mind. Not just clean, but immaculate.

At the door Madame Langlois had, quite reasonably, asked to see his ID. Gamache showed them, painfully aware of the state of his clothes. The state of him.

Before leaving Charles's building, Armand had asked the downstairs neighbor if he could use her bathroom, to wash up. When he'd emerged, after washing his hands and face and wiping down his clothes as best he could, she'd studied him and nodded.

"Better."

Though better was a sliding scale, and he was at the very low end. Still, it was better.

Madame and Monsieur Langlois invited him in. They were about Gamache's age, and while guarded, they obviously had not seen the video or heard from family or friends.

He broke the news to them as gently as he could, but also clearly. There could be no doubt, no way for delusion and wishful thinking to find purchase. That would not be a kindness.

He looked at Madame Langlois as he spoke the final words. He expected to see, in those eyes so like her son's, a death there too. As the light drained away. With his words, which allowed no escape, he would end their lives as they'd known them, and send them off into a netherworld. Of perpetual twilight. Time would stop and be remeasured from this moment forward.

But Madame Langlois did not actually register surprise. And neither did Charles's father.

They told him then that they hadn't heard from their son in almost a year. They'd banned him from their home, from their lives, when his addictions took over. When he'd stolen from them. Over and over. When he'd threatened his mother with a knife if she didn't give him more money.

They lived in fear that he'd return. And had accepted that one day someone would knock on the door and tell them he was dead.

Gamache was that someone. This was the day.

Madame and Monsieur Langlois seemed almost relieved. The worst had happened. Now they could stop waiting for the nightmare. They had grieved for their lost little boy for so long, now they finally had a body to bury.

It was horrific, tragic, but it was not a surprise.

"Do you know anything about his life now?" Gamache asked.

They shook their heads.

"The last call he made was to you, this morning."

"*Oui*. I know," said his mother. "We didn't answer, and he didn't leave a message."

She did not seem to regret that. In fact, she seemed defiant, challenging Gamache to challenge her. It wasn't, Gamache thought, because she didn't care, but because her love for their son was buried beneath so much hurt and pain that she could not yet retrieve it.

He thought of his own son, Daniel, and their struggles with him when he'd been in his late teens. How horrific it had been, trying to reach a young man who was out of control. Out of reach. How wide the crevasse between them and their son, their child, had become. How deep the wound. A hurt, Armand knew, he had made far worse.

How close it had come to Reine-Marie and him sitting where the Langlois were now. Listening to some poor officer giving them the bad, the worst, news.

Thankfully it never came to that. To this.

Even now, Armand could not think of those days, those months and even years, without feeling sick.

Both Daniel and Charles had finally gotten straight. Daniel had come back to them. Slowly, tentatively. Like some wounded animal approaching the hunter for help.

And Charles might have returned to his family had he been given more time.

Armand didn't know if what he was about to say would make it worse, or better, but he felt the need to say it.

"Your son was, from what I could see, straight and sober. His last thought was of you." Armand looked from father to mother. Settling on Madame Langlois. "He was a brave man."

Armand warned them about the video and advised them not to watch. As he left, Monsieur Langlois showed him to the door. Just before it closed behind him, Charles's father looked him in the eye and said, "I can see he has you fooled too."

The door swung shut, and Armand walked, limping, to his car. And drove home.

He stood under the hot water for a long time, tilting his head, so that the stream hit his face. His eyes closed, he tried to clear his mind. But Monsieur Langlois's parting words would not be washed away with the blood and dirt circling the drain.

*I can see he has you fooled too.*

Though it was the look in Madame Langlois's eyes that followed him, haunted him. Exactly the same look her son had had, when he knew he was dying. It wasn't sorrow. It wasn't pain. Madame Langlois was panicked.

# CHAPTER 11

—⁓—

"What are you saying?"

The woman, introduced to Beauvoir as Margaux Chalifoux, the Executive Director of Action Québec Bleu, was staring at him across her desk.

"I'm not sure how to put it more clearly, Madame. I'm afraid Charles Langlois is dead. He was killed by a car this afternoon."

He watched closely for her reaction. One of the last things Langlois had said was that he didn't know if his boss was involved in whatever was happening.

She was his boss.

And yet Charles had said "he" when talking about the boss. Was that a lie? Or did Charles not consider this woman his boss? There must be, might be, someone else.

Madame Chalifoux tilted her head. She was middle-aged, with thinning hair and a slight mustache, and a full face that now registered understanding, if not sorrow. "That's terrible. He was a nice young man." She paused. "Which department of the Sûreté are you with?"

"Homicide."

She closed her eyes for a long moment. When they opened again, her gaze was sharp, intelligent. No-nonsense. "You think he was murdered."

"I know it. I was there."

"Someone actually wanted to kill him? On purpose? But why

Charles?" Then she shook her head. "I'm sorry. Stupid question. That's what you're trying to find out."

"What did he do?"

"He was one of our biologists." On seeing his surprise, she said, "What exactly do you know about Charles?"

"Nothing," admitted Beauvoir. He took a seat without being asked. "Tell me."

It was clear to Chief Inspector Gamache, as he walked through the corridors of Sûreté headquarters, that most of his colleagues had seen the video. Some stopped to ask if he was all right, others just smiled and nodded in a show of commiseration.

Though with each nod, each smile, he wondered how sincere these colleagues were.

With every step down the long corridor of SQ headquarters, he felt his left shoe pinching his bruised foot. When he made it to the elevator and the doors closed, he leaned against the wall, heaved a sigh, and lifted his foot.

"Come in, Chief Inspector," said Madeleine Toussaint a minute or so later, when her assistant announced him. "Sit. Coffee?"

"*Non, merci.*"

Toussaint came around her desk and sat in the chair beside him. "Tell me everything you know, Armand."

Charles Langlois is, was, a marine biologist," said Madame Chalifoux.

"Marine? So he specialized in oceans? Salt water?"

"Well, yes, but when he came to us, it was to study the situation with fresh water." On seeing his puzzled expression, she smiled. "The truth is, Inspector, as you can probably see, we're a shoestring operation. We take what and who we can get. Charles needed a job, and we needed a biologist."

"What 'situation' exactly was he working on?"

"What we are all working on. Water security."

He sat forward. "Did Charles think someone was threatening our water supply?"

"Well, yes, Inspector."

Beauvoir sat very still. He wondered if he was about to hear what Langlois could not tell Gamache.

"We're all threatening our drinking water, with development, pollutants, climate change, with unchecked industry. I can't imagine his work had anything to do with his death." She paused. "I hate to bring it up, but you're aware of his past?"

"We're looking into that too. But my questions right now are for you. I'd like to see anything he was working on."

Beauvoir followed her into the large open space. The eight other workers stared at them. It was clear they'd just found out what had happened. Some of the faces were blotchy from crying. Others looked stoic, stone-faced.

"This is Inspector Beauvoir. He's with the Sûreté. He has some questions for us."

"*Merci*," he said. "But first I want to look at Monsieur Langlois's desk."

Jean-Guy put on gloves and spent a few minutes going over the papers on top of and inside Langlois's desk.

"There's not much here. Would you expect more? Don't touch."

Madame Chalifoux withdrew her hand and just looked, her brows drawing together.

"He must've taken his laptop home. I'd have expected notebooks, but those might be at his place too."

"Did anyone else come by here today, asking about him?"

Everyone shook their heads.

"Do you know which project he was working on specifically?"

"He was working mostly in the northern and central lakes. Testing for pollution." This from a young woman.

"Was he working alone?"

She nodded.

"Did he have a supervisor?" A man, thought Beauvoir. The "he" whom Charles had referred to.

"Margaux," said the young woman, nodding toward Madame Chalifoux.

"No one else?" They shook their heads. "Could Charles have found something in his testing that was dangerous?"

"Well, even up there, there's a lot of pollution that hurts biodiversity," an older man said. "Acid rain, PCBs. Mercury stirred up by the hydrodams. If even the algae is affected then—"

At the word "algae," Beauvoir lost interest. There was only so much he could care about, and that did not make the list.

"I meant for Monsieur Langlois, not pond scum." They shook their heads and stared at him as though he were a caveman. "How did Langlois come to work for you?"

"He walked in one day and offered his services," said Madame Chalifoux. "He started as a volunteer. When we got some money, I hired him."

"Did he say how he came to hear of you?"

"*Non*, and I didn't ask. We're just grateful for the help. We're a small organization, as you can see. We function mostly on goodwill. No one works full-time, everyone's paid minimum wage, and most donate at least some of their earnings back to the organization."

Beauvoir looked at those in the room. Men and women, young and old, from different cultural groups. "You must be very dedicated."

"Maybe even fanatical," said an elderly woman. "We do this for our grandchildren."

"Was Monsieur Langlois a fanatic?"

"No, that implies a sort of crazy." Madame Chalifoux shot a warning look to the others. "But he was dedicated. He understood that fresh water was soon going to become more and more scarce as the climate changed. We all understand that."

Beauvoir didn't. As a father, he was very worried what sort of world his children would inherit. The shifting food supply. Forest fires, disease, famines, catastrophic floods. The wars that scarcity provoked. Those were the effects of climate change that kept him awake at night.

Water, so abundant in Canada, wasn't one of them.

"Margaux," said a young woman, whose face was blotchy and streaked with tears.

"Yes, Debs?"

"There's a video . . ."

It was a risk, but Gamache had calculated it. How much to tell the Chief Superintendent. How to tell her. Armand watched closely, trying to read Toussaint's expression.

"A collaborator?" she said when he stopped. She'd skipped right over the part about the break-in at his home and landed on the most important point for her. "You really think that's what the young man was trying to tell you?"

"Not trying, he did."

"Who?"

Armand raised his brows in some amusement. "Don't you think I'd have led with that, if I knew?"

But his expression was such that the head of the Sûreté stared at him. Unsure.

And that's what Gamache wanted.

Madeleine Toussaint, the Chief Superintendent, was nobody's fool. Which was, maddeningly, why he'd backed her to take over the top job. She was whip-smart, a good administrator, an inspired leader. Both rational and intuitive, she'd be able to spot a fraud. She'd be able to tell if he was lying.

It didn't help that she knew him well. But he also knew her.

He needed her off-balance. He needed this perceptive leader to believe him when he said he didn't know. But also to have a sneaking suspicion that he did.

He also needed her to think that was the only reason Langlois had needed to speak to him. Nothing else.

"And who is this collaborator supposedly collaborating with?"

"I don't know." That at least was the truth.

He secretly, privately feared the Sûreté collaborator was the woman sitting across from him now.

Beauvoir had heard that a video had been posted and gone viral, but this was the first time he'd seen it.

It surprised him how upsetting it was. He'd been there, after all. Had seen it in person. But this was a different angle. Much more intimate.

He watched as the SUV grazed Armand, twisting him slightly as it raced by. He hadn't realized how close it came. Within centimeters . . .

So close that Armand's shoe had been torn from his foot.

Langlois's body landed with a thud. Not even a bounce. Just like a sack of sand. His shoes had also come off on impact and tumbled along the road, finally coming to rest.

Somehow the sight of empty shoes lying on the ground seemed almost worse than the body. It often happened in explosions, and sometimes when people were shot by an especially high-caliber gun. They were blown off their feet and out of their shoes.

Very few survived to put them back on.

When the video ended, there was silence. It had cut off before the part where Jean-Guy picked up Armand's shoe and handed it back to him.

Jean-Guy finally broke the silence in the room. "Did any of you ever visit Charles's apartment?"

They shook their heads. Except . . .

Jean-Guy looked at the young woman named Debs, who was more distressed than the others.

"Did you?" he asked her softly. And she nodded.

Everyone looked at her, surprised.

"We went out a few times."

"And you went back to his place?" When she nodded, he asked, "Can you tell me what he had on his walls?"

"Walls?"

Beauvoir waited.

She was thinking. "A map of Québec."

"Did he say why?"

"We weren't actually interested in the map."

"We all take work home, Inspector," said an older woman. "I suspect most of us have maps on our walls."

She looked around and others nodded in agreement.

83

"Did Charles take his laptop home at night?"

Debs nodded.

"We can't find it or any notebooks. Any idea where they might've gone?"

They shook their heads.

"Does this look familiar?" Beauvoir brought up a photo on his phone and they crowded around. And saw a list of herbs and spices.

"Are these plants, herbs, of particular concern to the environment?" he asked.

"Angelica stems? Nutmeg? If they are, it's not our environment. And not our mandate," said Madame Chalifoux.

"That's not even his handwriting," said Debs.

"No," said Beauvoir, slipping his phone back into his pocket. "Do you recognize it?"

Again, they all shook their heads.

He had not shown them the other side of the list, where the word *Water* was written.

Before he left, Beauvoir got Langlois's schedule. When and where he had traveled.

Once back in his car, Jean-Guy applied for a search warrant for Action Québec Bleu and the home of its Executive Director. Langlois's boss. Although in the meeting with Gamache the young man had described his boss as a man, that almost guaranteed it was a woman.

A news conference had been called by the Mayor to reassure the population of Montréal that there was no threat. This was a random act by a madman, not a terrorist attack.

And the murderer had been found dead. Shot. Not by police.

The implication being it was suicide.

Gamache looked into the bright lights of the cameras. His body was aching from the scrapes and bruises, especially his foot.

He knew that most of the journalists, most of the cameras, were trained on him, and he was not going to show any discomfort.

After the Mayor, the Chief Superintendent spoke. She made a brief statement, again reassuring the public, and then it was Gamache's turn. He'd been given a prepared statement, which he needed to read. But they could not dictate or control his pauses, his tone. His facial expression. Or his answers to questions.

Whoever had ordered the hit at the café would be watching.

When it came time for reporters' questions, they were hurled at him and only him.

*Describe what happened, Chief Inspector.*

*How did it feel?*

*You and the dead man were seen together in the café. Do you know him?*

*Why were you meeting?*

*Who was the driver? Why did he run his vehicle into that café? Did he have a grudge against you? Against the café?*

*What did Charles Langlois say to you as he was dying?*

Armand answered all the questions as truthfully as he could.

He was interviewing Monsieur Langlois in connection with (pause) a possible crime. One he could not discuss. *Non*, Charles Langlois was not a suspect in that crime.

In terms of what Langlois had said when he lay dying on the road— Gamache looked into the cameras—that was (pause) private.

An online vlogger stood up and asked if Langlois had been the target.

Gamache turned to her. He knew her well. She had pretty much devoted her site to tearing down the Sûreté in general and Gamache in particular. And now she had him in the crosshairs.

"We're looking into that possibility," said Gamache.

"But it seems obvious it was either him or you."

"Do you have a question?"

"He must've been important, to bring you out."

It was not said with respect. But Gamache hadn't expected it to be. Though he also had not expected her to be at this hastily called news conference. But there she was.

"Again, do you have a question?"

"We've all seen the video, Monsieur Gamache. It's clear that you saw the vehicle approaching before anyone else. You could've saved Monsieur Langlois, but you chose to save yourself. Why is that?"

Gamache was silent, and into that beat, she demanded, "How can the public feel safe when the Sûreté protects itself first?"

While the word "coward" was not actually said, not yet anyway, it hung in the air.

The seasoned journalists looked from the Chief Inspector to the vlogger and back.

Gamache stared at her, assessing. Not an answer, but a sudden thought. An idea.

He opened his mouth to answer, but the Chief Superintendent stepped in front of the microphone.

Madeleine Toussaint launched into a blistering defense of her head of homicide, pointing out that he'd saved two people, at considerable risk to himself. That was clear to anyone who watched that video.

"It might've been clear to you," said the vlogger. "But I saw a man who saved himself and just happened to fall into an elderly man and a little girl. Injuring them in the process. I saw no evidence it was a deliberate act to save them."

It was difficult to shock seasoned journalists, many of whom had been on the crime beat for years, but this very personal attack on Gamache did.

Most in the room knew him well. They'd all watched the video, over and over. It was clear that the Chief Inspector had made a choice and, yes, managed to save himself, but that hadn't been the goal. His only aim had been to push the child out of the way of the speeding vehicle.

"Chief Inspector Gamache faced a split-second decision," said Toussaint, her voice glacial. "I hope I'd have made the same one." She stared at the vlogger. "Or would you have let the child die?"

The vlogger colored and glared at the two of them. Trapped without an answer.

Standing beside Toussaint, Armand muttered, "*Merci.*" And felt a slight pang of guilt that he had suspected her of betraying not just the Sûreté, but also the citizens of Québec. And him.

But he also knew that if the Chief Superintendent was the collaborator, she'd have done exactly what she just did. And his racing mind went one step further.

Toussaint might have even set up the question, or at the very least predicted it. She might have made sure this vlogger was invited to the news conference, knowing she would attack Gamache. Because she always did.

And that would give Toussaint the opportunity to defend him. Reassuring Gamache that she was on his side.

It was, he recognized, a catch-22. Toussaint was damned if she defended him, damned if she did not. But he didn't care. He just wanted to get at the truth.

# CHAPTER 12

⁓

I 'll be there in a few minutes," Jean-Guy replied.

Gamache had texted both Beauvoir and Lacoste to meet him at Chez Mère Grand, a hole-in-the-wall diner in the old port area of Montréal, not far from Champ-de-Mars. It was conveniently, and not coincidently, on the way from Sûreté headquarters to their next stop.

Grandma's was not a place frequented by Sûreté officers, most of whom preferred darkened bars even during the day. Which was one of the reasons the Chief Inspector had chosen it.

It didn't hurt that the place, and the young owners, were cheerful and the food homemade and delicious.

Normally Armand would have walked there, to get some fresh air and clear his mind on this fine summer evening. But the damaged shoe was biting into his bruised foot, and the cobbled streets of the old city would make walking even more difficult. So he'd grabbed a taxi.

Isabelle was already there when he arrived. Armand ordered grilled cheese sandwiches for the table, bulging with melted Gruyère and blue cheese, with chutney oozing out. He added an éclair for Isabelle, a mille-feuille for Jean-Guy, and a slice of tall, wobbly lemon meringue pie for himself.

While they waited for Jean-Guy, Armand described for Isabelle the search of Charles's apartment, and the missing computer, notes, and map.

"He got too close to something," she said. "We recorded your conversation, of course. I've been over it again, and two things stand out. One"—she raised a finger—"he was sure there was someone in the Sûreté working with whoever's behind this. Two"—another finger—"he wasn't sure about his boss. He must have meant the head of that environmental organization."

"Who's a woman, but that means nothing. The other thing that was clear was that he was afraid, but I don't think he really grasped how much danger he was in. Or couldn't bring himself to believe it."

Most decent people could not fully see, or believe, the size of the monster.

Just then, Jean-Guy breezed in. He went up to the counter, spoke to the owner, waited, then came to the table, handing something to Armand.

"It's an ice pack, *patron*. And—" He held out a large bag.

Gamache opened it and smiled. Inside was a cardboard box. With new shoes. Soft-sided.

"*Merci.*" He held Jean-Guy's eyes. "*Beaucoup.*"

When, Armand wondered as he took off the offending shoe and laid the ice pack across his swollen and bruised foot, had things changed? When did Jean-Guy begin to look after him, when it had long been the other way around?

But as the pain eased, Armand realized it had always been mutual. They'd guarded and protected each other from the moment they'd met, lifetimes ago.

"What did you find out at Action Québec Bleu?"

"Not much." As he ate the sandwich, Jean-Guy gave his report.

Armand sat back and listened. Watching them.

He felt enormous pride in his people, and none more than these two, who shared second-in-command duties.

His entire department had been handpicked, not from the top of the heap but from the bottom. To his colleagues' amusement, Chief Inspector Gamache had, in effect, gone dumpster diving for his agents. Chosen men and women on the verge of being tossed out.

The homicide department of the Sûreté, made up of agents no one else wanted, was the most successful in the country. Because Armand Gamache knew something his colleagues did not. That given direction, clear expectations, and encouragement, given a second chance, people could flourish.

Armand Gamache had pulled them back from the edge, then sent them out across Québec to find those who had fallen.

"What do you think, Jean-Guy?" he asked when the younger man had finished.

"The fact Langlois was investigating pollution in lakes in central and northern Québec, and not just his notes but his map are missing, points to something really shitty. It's gotta be a toxic waste spill, probably from one of the major pulp mills or mines in the area."

"Companies pollute all the time," said Lacoste, "and don't murder to cover it up."

"Unless it's huge, ongoing, and involves high-ranking politicians in a cover-up," said Beauvoir.

It was possible, thought Gamache. Certainly the most likely scenario. Though there was another possibility. One he wouldn't mention just yet. He needed to think.

"If made public, this would not just shut down their operations and cost hundreds of millions in cleanup and fines," said Beauvoir. "But they could end up in jail."

"It would cost politicians their jobs and maybe even cost the government the next election," said Lacoste.

They looked at Gamache, who'd been listening. Now he spoke. "What you describe is what should happen, not what actually does. How many heads of corporations end up in prison for pollution? How many governments are toppled?"

They were silent.

"Exactly. I'm not convinced the consequences are all that great that CEOs would resort to murder."

"What do you think?" asked Lacoste.

Instead of answering, he asked Jean-Guy, "What was your impression of Langlois's boss?"

Beauvoir considered. He'd known he'd be asked this question. "I got the impression that she and her people were sincere. Though I guess anyone can be bought off. A few million would shut most people up."

"But when she found out that Langlois was murdered, wouldn't she say something?" asked Lacoste.

"Would you?" asked Beauvoir. "If the last person who did was killed?"

Whipped cream squeezed out from between the layers of the mille-feuille as Jean-Guy took a big bite.

"It seems obvious that Charles was doing his own investigation," said Gamache. "He must've realized he'd tripped up and told someone he shouldn't have."

"And who would he tell? His boss," said Lacoste. "But wait a minute. This doesn't track. Why break into your home? Why take the jacket? If he'd found something, why not just tell you? Why all this sneaking around?"

"About the jacket, I have no idea. But he said the Sûreté is compromised. He needed to meet me away from headquarters."

"But why someplace so public? And why didn't he tell you what he'd found?" said Lacoste. "That was one frustrating conversation. He kept hinting, coming close, but not actually telling you anything. Even when he was dying."

"He said he needed to make sure I could be trusted, and to confirm that his boss was not part of the conspiracy."

"I have a search warrant for AQB and Madame Chalifoux's home."

"Good," said Gamache. "Very good. We need to get a list of all major industries, mostly pulp and paper and mining, that have plants on lakes in the central and northern parts of the province, in case a huge spill is it. And we need to speak to another environmentalist to find out what they know about those specific multinationals."

"I have a biologist friend," said Lacoste. "He can be trusted."

Gamache dug into his pocket and brought out the list that had been left in his jacket.

"What're you thinking, *patron*?" asked Beauvoir. "You think Langlois did put it there?"

"*Non.* He was genuinely surprised by this." Gamache tapped his finger on it. "But someone gave it to me to find. It means something."

Nutmeg, thyme . . . All fairly common household ingredients. Except.

"What's that?" He pointed to the last word on the list. "I've never heard of angelica stems."

Beauvoir brought his phone out. "Got it. It's known as archang— . . . whatever."

"Archangelica," said Lacoste, reading off his screen. "Archangel."

"It grows in Russia." Beauvoir caught the Chief's eye, then went back to the page. "It's used in vermouth, Chartreuse, Bénédictine. But, get this, it's often mistaken for a poisonous species."

Gamache had his hand up to his face, thinking. Poison.

"What is it, *patron*?" said Beauvoir. He knew Gamache better than almost anyone.

Gamache brought out his phone and, tapping on the secure-communication app, he paused.

"*Patron?*" asked Isabelle.

"Give me a moment, please."

He needed to think. Gamache stared out the window. It was almost dark. Not many more minutes before the sun set completely. But what Armand saw weren't the buildings warmed in the last glow of a spent day in Old Montréal, it was a list of names scrolling by in his mind.

Men and women he'd met in his years of policing. Trusted allies, colleagues, friends.

He needed to choose one, just one. And it needed to be the right one. Rarely had one of his decisions had such consequence.

The scroll stopped on one name. While Jean-Guy and Isabelle watched, Armand stared at the name and considered, examining that person from every angle.

Then he sent off a terse message and placed his phone on the table.

"What was that about?" asked Jean-Guy. The look on Gamache's face was scaring him.

"It's probably a toxic spill into one of the lakes," he said. And paused before he went on. "I hope it is."

"Oh, God," said Beauvoir. "What're you thinking? What would be worse?"

Armand turned to Lacoste. "You said you watched our meeting several times. Did you notice the water?"

"When he spilled your glass? Yes. You think it was to try to destroy the list? You said so at the time."

"But he pointed out a little water wouldn't do that. No. I think there was another reason. He also refused water himself and made some cryptic remark about water not being all that healthy to drink."

Gamache was looking down at the list still on the table. "When I showed this to him, he said it meant nothing to him. But he said that the paper did. I had no idea what he meant, and we went on to other things. But now I think . . ." Armand turned the paper over.

"Water," said Jean-Guy. His brow furrowed, trying to put it all together.

"After 9/11, multinational, multidisciplinary anti-terrorist task forces were formed," said Armand. "Their job was to not just look at possible threats, but targets."

"Go on."

"I got a seat on one when I took over the Sûreté. Most of the focus was on hijackings, bombs. Assassinations. But some had a different concern."

"What?" said Lacoste, her face growing paler.

"Water security."

"That's what Action Québec Bleu studies," said Beauvoir. "Pollution. Weren't we just talking about that? That Langlois discovered a toxic spill."

"*Non.* Not a spill in a remote lake. The attack these strategists are looking at, are afraid of, is against drinking water."

"What do you mean?" asked Lacoste, though by her face it seemed she knew exactly what the Chief meant. She just refused to see the size of the monster he'd conjured.

"I mean a deliberate attack by terrorists, foreign or domestic, on the water supply of a major city."

Jean-Guy and Isabelle looked at each other.

"God," she said. "Is that possible?"

"Possible, yes. Probable?" He shrugged.

"It would be wholesale murder of civilians," said Isabelle. "Children."

"How?" Beauvoir asked.

"If we're talking about chemical or biological weapons, neurotoxins—"

"And it looks like we are," said Lacoste.

"—then the list of threats is unfortunately long. Most are airborne, but anthrax, ricin, plague, Q fever are stable and lethal in water."

"How do we begin to guard against that?" demanded Isabelle. She put down her water glass.

Armand sent off another message to his contact, including a photo of the strange list. Then he slid his phone into his pocket.

The alarms in his head were turning into sirens, though he also knew this was all speculation. They needed facts.

"If it's terrorists, why choose us?" asked Isabelle. "Why Québec?"

"Why not?" asked Beauvoir.

"Well, for one thing, we're hardly the epicenter of world power. If terrorists were going to go to that much trouble, you'd expect them to hit the US or the UK, or, if Canada, it would be Toronto or Ottawa, the nation's capital. Attacking us is horrific, for us. But there are much bigger, more effective targets."

"Maybe they're planning multiple attacks," suggested Beauvoir. "Hoping one or more actually hit. Like with 9/11."

"*Voyons*. We're way out beyond our facts. This"—Gamache tapped the paper on the table beside his untouched lemon meringue pie—"might be someone's shopping list. We know nothing. Let's just take it one step at a time."

And yet both could see he was rattled.

*That's the least of it.*

Charles Langlois's words came back to Gamache. If the Sûreté being compromised was the least of their problems, what was the worst?

This was.

"It's curious that while we were together, he never mentioned his job at Action Québec Bleu," said Armand.

"He did mention his boss," Jean-Guy pointed out.

"True. And he talked repeatedly about The Mission. That was where he met his contact."

As he spoke, Isabelle Lacoste looked from one to the other. How often, she wondered, had the three of them sat like this, discussing murder? In crappy hotel rooms, in shacks in the middle of nowhere that doubled as incident rooms. On boats. Once in a canoe in Northern Québec. In tents, as they'd camped out, searching the dense bush for a killer on the run.

Jean-Guy loved to tell her about the two-holer outhouse he and the Chief had once used as headquarters. She doubted it was true, though she enjoyed the story and was grateful she hadn't been on that case.

But her favorite was when the trail of a killer took them to Gamache's own village of Three Pines. They'd confer in the Old Train Station, set up as an incident room, or in the bistro. And sometimes in the Chief's own home. At the worn pine table in his kitchen. Drinking coffee, or iced tea, or beer, or that delicious vibrant pink lemonade the Chief claimed to make for Florence and Zora.

They'd eat sandwiches, or burgers, or grilled salmon, and go over notes. Feeding the log fire on bitterly cold winter nights and hearing the crickets through the screen doors on steamy summer days.

While Isabelle Lacoste hated murder, she loved this process. She loved these people.

She realized the two men were looking at her. "*Pardon?*"

"The woman who signaled the SUV," said Jean-Guy. "Any news?"

"None yet." It was her turn to report. "We have her photo on the wire. I went to the landfill to check out the body of the driver. We still don't have an ID, and it's not our case, as you know. It's Montréal homicide, but I know the investigating officer and he's happy to co-operate."

"Security video?" asked Beauvoir.

"Cameras down."

Gamache narrowed his eyes, taking this in. "The security guard?"

"Had left before her shift was over. We're trying to track her down."

"Garbage collection and the landfill are both run by the mob in Montréal," said Beauvoir. "Could they be behind this?"

"We've gone from an environmental group, to international terrorists, to the Montréal mafia," said Gamache. "What next? The National Hockey League? Let's just regroup. The mob is not interested in contaminating the water supply, or working with terrorists. It has its own agenda. It wants to hook the population on fentanyl, not kill us all off. I want to know how Charles Langlois fits into this. Whose side was he on? Was he trying to help, or was he sent to confuse?"

The voice of Charles's father drifted across Gamache's mind.

*I can see he has you fooled too.*

Beauvoir heaved an exasperated sigh. "Shit. Why didn't he tell us more?"

"Maybe he did," said Lacoste. "He sure seemed to think he'd told us enough."

"If he thought he was in danger, he might've hidden his notes, right?" said Beauvoir. "Maybe that's why he kept mentioning The Mission."

Gamache raised his brows. That had not occurred to him.

"*Bon,*" he said, leaning down to put on his new shoes. The ice pack had done its job. His foot no longer hurt, and the swelling was going down. "There's one way to find out."

As he got up, he noticed a smear of whipped cream on Beauvoir's fingers. To Jean-Guy and Isabelle's surprise, the Chief Inspector took a paper napkin and wiped it off.

Then he walked, without a limp, to the door.

# CHAPTER 13

⁓

"Fucking hell."

Those were the first words out of the mouth of the first person they met at the entrance to The Mission. In a crescendo of irony, the founders had chosen to place the homeless shelter in an abandoned distillery in the old port.

"*Pardon?*" said Gamache, staring at the tiny woman blocking their way.

"Saw the video. Poor Charles. Talks to you and dies." She looked around as though expecting a vehicle to come crashing through the entrance.

"We're with the Sûreté."

"I know."

"Armand Gamache. And these are—"

"I don't care."

The woman's grey hair was shooting off in all directions, including from her chin and upper lip. Her head looked like a Russian satellite. Her face, crisscrossed with deep lines like the earth after a drought, had a homemade tattoo between her eyes. A cross. Or an *X*. It was the sort made in prison.

She wore a sagging tracksuit over her thin frame.

"We're here to see the Executive Director, Monsieur Gagnon."

Armand stepped to his left to get around her, but she stepped to her right, and again they were face-to-face. Or face-to-chest.

"Is he here?" Gamache looked around, his view slightly obscured by her cloud of hair, to see if he could spot the Exec, or any employee. Anyone at all who could rescue them. But it was past dinnertime, and there was no one else around.

"I can take you to the office."

Her voice was slightly slurred, and when she turned around, she walked with a shuffle. Wet brain, Gamache thought, as they followed her. Or perhaps a stroke.

"Ruth's sister?" whispered Jean-Guy.

"I don't have a fucking sister."

"Could've fooled me," muttered Jean-Guy.

"Can't imagine that's difficult, Mrs. Fletcher."

"What's your name?" he asked, stepping forward to walk beside her.

"Claudine."

"You knew Charles Langlois?"

"We all did. Nice kid. He lived here for a while. We used to eat together. On spaghetti nights."

"I believe once he left he came back as a volunteer," volunteered Gamache.

"Is that so?" Somehow Gamache had the impression she was mocking him.

They passed a few people, all residents it seemed. Men and women off the streets who came to The Mission for a hot meal and a bed. A shower. Clean clothes. Someplace safe. Then left in the morning. But always returned. Or almost always. Some never quite made it back.

Claudine was clearly a regular. As she passed, everyone nodded at her and glared at the other three, so clearly cops.

"There," she said, indicating the office. "You can wait. The Exec will join you soon. Just making sure there're no knife fights over the last sausage."

She shuffled away.

"My money's on her starting that knife fight," said Beauvoir.

"And getting the last sausage," said Lacoste.

The cramped office seemed more like a storeroom. Clothing, dishes, cardboard boxes were piled high. The whole place smelled of mashed potatoes. Jean-Guy had expected something far worse.

Armand had been to The Mission a few times, and he and Reine-Marie made regular donations. Ever since Daniel . . . But he hadn't been back since the pandemic.

Claudine reappeared. "All good. No blood in the vegetables."

Which was not, Beauvoir thought, the same as no blood anywhere.

"Did you get the last sausage?" he asked.

"What's that to you, numbnuts?"

Lacoste couldn't quite stifle a snort and looked at the elderly woman as though in love.

Claudine took the seat behind the desk. "How can I help?"

Gamache winced and could have kicked himself. "You're the Exec?"

"I am. Sit."

There was only one chair, and she clearly meant the Chief Inspector. After his inexcusable gaffe, he did not feel like disobeying her.

Removing a pile of neatly folded white T-shirts from the chair, he sat. "What happened to Monsieur Gagnon?"

"It's complicated."

"Try me. Let's see if I can grasp it."

"The fucker took off during the pandemic. Never came back."

"Got it." Gagnon wasn't the only administrator to abandon vulnerable people during the lockdown. "You took over?"

"Someone had to. The board wanted to replace me when they realized the inmates were running the asylum, but then they couldn't find anyone crazy enough to want the job."

Gamache shot Beauvoir a warning look before turning back to Claudine.

"And Gagnon?"

"Given a nice pension, I heard." She didn't seem angry. "That's life. Worse things happen. Like being mowed down and dying in the middle of the road just when you've gotten your life together. I saw what you did."

Gamache thought she, like the vlogger, was about to accuse him of saving himself.

"You held his hand." Claudine held his eyes. "We all want that, don't we? At the end."

Gamache didn't turn to look at Lacoste, but he felt again her hand holding his, and knew Claudine was right. He also suspected that when her time came, she'd be surrounded by people who cared for her, as she cared for them.

"How can I help?" she asked.

"We don't have a warrant—"

"Now you're just being insulting," she snapped. "You think we'd only help if we had no choice?"

"I'm sorry," said Gamache. "I didn't mean that."

"Are you so sure?"

"We think Charles might've hidden something here."

"Étoile!" she shouted so suddenly even Gamache jumped. "I know you're listening, you little shit. Get in here."

A young man, or woman, appeared at the door. They were clearly in transition.

"Show these cops whatever they want to see. Let them search anywhere they want."

"Yes, Auntie."

Lacoste and Beauvoir followed them out of the office while Gamache, not given permission to leave, stayed glued to his chair.

"They call me Auntie, for some reason."

"What's your full name?"

"Just Claudine will do."

"I'm afraid it won't."

They stared at each other for a moment.

"McGregor."

"*Merci.*"

It had not gone unnoticed that if Charles volunteered here, then Claudine McGregor could also be considered his boss. And while unlikely, she might have been the one he meant when he said he had to make sure he could trust his boss.

Claudine McGregor seemed the sort to notice a lot. To hear a lot.

And, as he himself had shamefully demonstrated, to be vastly under-estimated. A lot.

These were powerful assets if you were planning something hor-rific.

"Charles mentioned the tours you sometimes give to politicians."

"True. They like to be seen around the great unwashed. They seem to think it makes them look like they care. Like they're almost human. Dumbasses don't realize those shots of them in hairnets, scooping out soggy carrots for the homeless, just makes 'em look patronizing. I love giving them tours if only for that reason."

Her voice was getting more and more slurred, and Gamache real-ized it was late. She had probably been there since the morning and must be hungry and tired. But he needed to press on, and so did she.

"I'd like to see video of those tours," he said.

"All of them?"

"*Non.* Just the ones where Charles was present."

She reached for her agenda and flipped through it, making notes.

Lacoste and Beauvoir returned. "We searched his locker and the storeroom. Nothing, *patron.* But the place is huge, we'll need more help."

"What're you looking for?"

Gamache hesitated for a moment. Then made up his mind. "Charles's laptop and notebooks. And a map."

"Really? Well, that's easy. He kept them in my office for a while."

"He did?" Gamache's hopes were raised but muted by the "for a while."

"But he took them away a week ago or so."

The cops exchanged glances. While not ideal, this was neverthe-less good news. It probably meant the people who'd ransacked his apartment didn't have them. Charles must've hidden them someplace no one would think to look. But that meant Gamache and his people probably wouldn't think of it either.

"He didn't say where he was taking them?" asked Beauvoir as they followed her out of the cramped office.

"Right. He said if anyone wants to know where I'm hiding this stuff, just tell them." She muttered, "Shit for brains."

"If you had to guess, where would you say he took them?"

"I don't know. Home, I guess. Where else?"

Madame McGregor took a few more steps. Then, without turning to Gamache, she said, "He volunteered every second Sunday."

Gamache was about to say, *Yes, I know.* But stopped himself. He wasn't going to underestimate her again. So he waited. And was rewarded.

"But he came here almost every night." She looked at him now. "He worked in my office. I promised I wouldn't tell. But . . ."

*But he's dead.*

"*Merci*," said Gamache, recognizing that it still felt to Madame McGregor like violating Charles's trust. "Did he ever have any visitors?"

"Not that I know of. He came late at night and was gone by morning."

"Is there anything else you need to tell us?"

They were at a door marked *Security*.

"When I said he probably took the stuff home, it wasn't a wild guess. He told me that's what he was going to do."

Gamache stared at her. "He told you?"

"*Oui*."

Gamache absorbed this. If true, it meant whoever broke into Charles's home had found what they were looking for.

But why would he do that? Why hide them here, then take them to the first place anyone would look? And why tell Madame McGregor where they were?

Was it possible he wanted her to be able to tell whoever came looking for them that he'd taken them to his home? While he hid them someplace else?

Gamache tiptoed from supposition to supposition, like someone fording a rushing river, from one stepstone to the next. Hoping not to slip. To slip up.

Which meant—Gamache took the next step—Charles must've known someone would come looking. Which meant the young man knew he was in danger. And if someone was asking, it meant something terrible had happened to him.

How frightened Charles must have been. And yet he'd kept up the investigation. He could have stopped. Could have handed over his files to the conspirators in hopes they'd leave him alone.

But instead, Charles Langlois, just emerging from the nightmare of addiction and homelessness, had entered another nightmare.

How terrible his secret must have been.

Why, why, why hadn't Charles told him? Just a name. As he lay dying, just a name. Something. Anything.

But now the one person who could tell them was gone, taking all he knew with him. And their only real hope was that Charles had once again lied, and had not taken his files home.

"If anyone else comes asking about Charles and his notebooks, let me know." He gave her his card.

Once the security videos were teed up, they went through them at double speed. Stopping now and then, slowing down occasionally.

There was the Premier of Québec, smiling and looking silly in his hairnet. Gamache knew him to be a decent individual, though they did not share the same politics.

They skipped ahead to other visits. Gamache recognized a number of provincial cabinet ministers, whose protection was part of the Sûreté mandate, and lower-level federal, provincial, and municipal politicians.

The hairnets the pols were given never quite fit. They were either too tight, so they looked like they'd just come out of unsuccessful brain surgery, or much, much too large, so they looked like mushrooms.

Gamache suspected that was not an accident.

Then he tipped forward in his chair as though about to dive through the screen. He hit pause. Not tapped but slammed his finger down on it.

"It's Langlois," said Lacoste, leaning in.

Gamache sat very, very still. As though afraid to alert the people on the screen to his presence.

Charles Langlois stood in the background as some almost maniacally cheerful member of Parliament, whose hairnet made him look like a big toe, tried to make small talk with a homeless man who just wanted a slice of bacon.

Charles was talking to a woman. They clearly knew each other. This was no meet-and-greet casual chat. There was an urgency about their conversation.

The homeless man had raised his head and was looking at them. The date on the tape was the Sunday before last.

Beauvoir looked at the frozen image, then at Gamache. "What is it?"

The Chief zoomed in for a closer look.

The woman was older than when he'd last seen her. Her clothes were much more elegant, her hair perfectly coiffed. But there was no mistaking her.

It was the woman who'd called him, shattering the peace of their Sunday morning.

It was the one he'd told to go to hell.

"Christ." And with the word came a breath from deep down inside the Chief Inspector. One he'd held for decades.

# CHAPTER 14

It was almost midnight by the time Armand stepped onto the veranda of their home in Three Pines.

The fieldstone, clapboard, and brick homes around the village green were in darkness, but visible against the splash of stars in the night sky. The only light in the village came from his home, like a beacon. He stood on the porch and watched the fireflies lighting up here and there. At random. Impossible to predict where the next one might appear.

The bulb on the porch was attracting moths. They flapped around, bumping into it. Repeatedly.

Armand often wondered what they hoped would happen after that first bump. Why keep trying?

Though he understood the compulsion. He sometimes felt like a moth. Butting his head against something that looked promising but was an illusion. Even a delusion.

The door opened before he reached it, and Henri bounded out, curling around Armand's legs. He'd have tripped had he not been prepared for it.

Reine-Marie was just a step behind the shepherd and had Armand in her arms before he'd made it across the threshold. She hugged him tight, and he buried his face in her sweater, smelling the scent of old garden rose.

And she inhaled the scent of sandalwood. Then she held him at arm's length to study his face. "Are you all right?"

"I am. Now."

She smiled and in her best Clouseau said, "You have a 'bimp,' *monsieur*." Bending his head down, she kissed the bruise on his forehead.

He laughed. And just like that, his headache disappeared.

"Better?"

"Always."

They sat on the two-seater porch swing, rocking gently, back and forth, back and forth. Henri, Fred, and little Gracie asleep at their feet.

There had been no question that Armand would tell Reine-Marie everything. And he had, to the accompaniment of the crickets and frogs and the far-off howl of a wolf, down from the mountains to hunt.

The night was cool, verging on cold, but they were warm under the striped Hudson's Bay blanket across their knees. Reine-Marie brewed a pot of tea while Armand got into fresh flannel pajamas. He didn't often wear them in summer, but he felt the need for the comfort they provided. Besides, Reine-Marie was in hers.

It was, as he sat beside her and sipped the tea, possible to forget for a moment, a blessed moment, his suspicions. His fears. The size of the monster he suspected was there.

He felt Reine-Marie's hand in his, her thumb softly, softly caressing the back of his hand, where Charles's whipped cream had been. As though it were still there. Always there.

And then, not looking at her but staring up at the night sky, he'd begun.

When he finished, he looked at her. They had turned the porch light off, and her face was lit softly by the light from their living room. She looked tired. Drained. Older than her fifty-seven years. Older than she'd looked just minutes earlier. Before he told her.

And he suspected he looked ancient.

How different their lives might have been had he become a professor or lawyer. Carpenter or farmer. Had he studied anything else besides the ways and whys people killed each other.

But then they'd never have found this village. These friends. This rambling old home. Their daughter, Annie, would not have met and married Jean-Guy and had Honoré and Idola.

Was it a fair trade? After days like this, on nights like this when his job weighed heavy on them both, Armand was far from sure.

"It might be a toxic spill," she said. "Up north."

"True."

She was quiet for a minute or so. "But you don't think so?"

"A toxic spill is an accident. Whatever is happening has been planned."

"You really think this is an attack on our drinking water."

He nodded. "I'm afraid that's what it is. We're looking into pollution by some mining or paper company, but the scope of this is too big. The planning too complete."

"But that would harm thousands," she said.

He wondered how far he should go, but realized she needed to hear the truth.

"They'd probably use a nerve agent, a neurotoxin. The anti-terrorist task forces have run the scenarios. Tens of thousands dead is on the conservative side."

"Oh, dear God." She clutched his arm. "You have to warn people."

"I can't. Not until I'm sure."

"People have a right to know. You need to give them a chance to get out, to defend themselves. Their children . . ."

"You're right, but if we do, the terrorists will know we're on to them, and they'll move up the attack."

"Or stop it. Decide not to do it." Her eyes were wide, imploring him to see reason. To see what she saw.

"That would be worse."

"How?"

"This has been years in the planning. Too many people are involved, compromised. Too much money. If I'm right, probably hundreds of millions have gone into it. They won't stop the attack, they'll postpone it. Move it to another time, another place. One we can't predict. *Non*, we got lucky, and have this warning. It won't happen again. Our only hope is to catch them."

He could see Reine-Marie's mind working fast, twisting, sliding, trying to find an argument that would see him issue a public alert. But finally she closed her eyes.

He waited.

When she opened them again, she nodded.

"We're on well water. I'll call Annie and Daniel first thing in the morning and have them come down with the children."

"But you can't tell them why. This needs to stay between us. And we can't warn anyone else."

"The LaPierres?" He shook his head. "Your agents? Armand, the men and women in your department."

Armand felt sick. All the way down he'd wrestled with this. Like a moth, he kept bumping into the light, knowing all the time that it was hopeless. And worrying it wasn't a light but a flame.

"*Non.* Just the children." He felt a lump fizz in his throat. He understood the terrible thing he was doing. Saving his own family, and leaving the rest behind.

Reine-Marie was about to argue, but seeing his face, she stopped herself. Together they sat on the porch, the swing now still, and stared at the stars.

"Can you maybe issue an alert to not drink tap water?" she finally said. "Just drink bottled water? Say there's *E. coli* or something. It happens."

Reine-Marie was traveling down the same route he'd taken, desperately examining all the options. But again, they were illusions, delusions. There were no options.

"That would also alert the terrorists. I'm sorry, but they have to believe that Langlois told me nothing. That at worst we think it's a toxic spill in some northern lake. There is one more thing."

Putting down his mug, Armand turned to her fully. In the demi-light, he saw Reine-Marie's eyes widen, then narrow as she steeled herself.

Armand hated, hated, hated having to do this. And he despised the person who'd made it necessary.

"I think Jeanne Caron might be behind this."

Of all the things Reine-Marie expected to hear, that was not one.

"Caron?" Her voice was high. Not loud, but the voice of someone trying to tamp down panic. Henri raised his head, his gigantic ears swiveling toward her. "What makes you think that?"

Armand told her about the video from The Mission. Jeanne Caron deep in conversation with Charles Langlois.

"What does this mean, Armand?"

He sighed. "I don't know."

"Will you meet her now? Ask her?"

"Not before I have more information. I can't walk in there unprepared."

As he had the last time, the only time, he'd met with Caron. Both he and Reine-Marie knew what had happened then. To Armand, yes, but mostly to Daniel.

Reine-Marie's mind was whirring, racing. "Is she still the Chief of Staff to That Politician?"

Reine-Marie knew his name, would never forget it. But she could not bring herself to say it. He was simply That Politician. The one who'd gone after her husband and teenage son years ago, when Armand had refused to drop vehicular homicide charges against The Daughter.

Of course That Politician had stayed out of it and made Jeanne Caron do the dirty work. Something she was only too happy to do. And did well. But there was no doubt who was directing it. Directing her.

That Politician had been a lowly backbencher at the time, but a clever and ambitious one. Armand had managed to fight off most of the attacks, but not all. Daniel still bore the scars. And still blamed his father.

And rightly so, Armand knew.

Reine-Marie had followed That Politician's career over the years. Always hoping that fate or karma or any higher power floating around would intervene. But it had not. At least not in any way she recognized or approved of.

Instead of losing the next election and sinking back into his cesspool, That Politician had flourished, always being reelected and going from strength to strength within the party. Until he'd landed a federal cabinet post. And even then, his star had continued to rise.

"Jeanne Caron is still his Chief of Staff," said Armand. "And he's the Deputy Prime Minister."

"Dear God." Reine-Marie sighed. "I knew he was the Environment minister, but Deputy Prime Minister? How stupid is the PM to have elevated that vile man?"

Armand had wondered the same thing.

"It gets worse. He's just been handed another portfolio. He's now in charge of the Global Affairs Canada."

"I don't understand how that can be bad."

"GAC is the federal department that looks after foreign affairs and international trade, but it's also in charge of investigating domestic and international terrorism."

Had Reine-Marie been standing, she'd have sat down. As it was, she just stared at her husband.

"The Prime Minister did that? He handed both Environment and Terrorism to that man? Is he crazy? Has he lost his mind?" She continued to stare at her husband, then her mouth dropped open and she whispered, "My God, Armand. You think the PM is involved."

"*Non.* I don't. But I am worried."

"Why would any politician want to poison tens of thousands of their own citizens?" She shook her head. "I voted for the Prime Minister. Twice."

That was only, Armand knew, because the other candidate was even worse. A far-right lunatic. But now their centrist leader, a man elected on a platform of sober second thought and sanity, looked like the madman.

"If Jeanne Caron was at The Mission talking with Langlois," said Reine-Marie, "that must mean she was sent there by That Politician."

"Probably."

"Do you think he was the boss that Charles mentioned?"

"Could be."

"So whose side was Charles on?"

"That's a good question. I think he was being used, and when he realized what was going on, he started his own investigation."

"Then contacted you. But why break into our home? Why take your jacket?"

"I don't know yet. If only we'd found his laptop and notes."

"You will."

He smiled his thanks for that optimism. It helped, in the dark and cold. When they could hear the far-off howling of a wolf in pursuit.

Armand was woken up from a deep sleep by the sound of his phone ringing.

He struggled to the surface, fighting the sheets to get his hand clear.

"*Oui, allô?*" he said, groggily, though his mind was quickly engaging.

It was still dark, and he looked at the clock on the bedside table as he shoved himself into a semi-sitting position. It was 3:42.

Reine-Marie turned the lamp on and was staring at him. Her eyes wide.

Had it happened? Were they too late?

"It's Jean-Guy," he whispered. "Everything's all right. But he found something."

Reine-Marie got up and went into the bathroom.

"I'm at The Mission," said Jean-Guy. "I couldn't sleep and wanted to look at the other security tapes."

"What other ones?"

"From the overnights. Took me a while, but I finally found it."

"What?"

"Proof. That same woman came here at least three times. Well past lights-out and after the doors were locked. Langlois let her in. She was dressed down and wore a hoodie, but it's her, I'm sure of it."

Jeanne Caron. Now Armand was fully awake, as though someone had slapped him hard across the face.

"They went down the hall, toward the Exec's office. There's no camera there, so we can't see what they did."

"Well done," said Gamache. "Make a copy of those tapes and send them to me on my private account."

"Copies already made. I've just hit send."

Reine-Marie was in the kitchen making coffee when he came back from walking the confused dogs around the dark village green.

A mist was rising from the Rivière Bella Bella as the cool morning air hit the warmer water.

Armand had woken up stiff, with aches and pains. But after a warm shower and walk around the village green, he'd loosened up.

"Three hours' sleep," she said, carrying their mugs to the far end of the kitchen. "You going into Montréal?"

He was already dressed for work, in a suit and tie.

"In a few hours. I need to go over some things."

They sat with their coffees in the armchairs on either side of the woodstove, and he told her what Jean-Guy had said.

"So Jeanne Caron must be the 'boss' Charles was talking about." Reine-Marie paused. "But he seemed to think she might be on his side. Is that possible?"

"I suppose it is."

"But you doubt it."

He thought for a moment before answering. "I think the Jeanne Caron we met years ago was a chrysalis. Practicing, training, learning. Just beginning to turn into the person she's become."

"If that was the larva, what is she now?"

"I think we both know the answer to that."

"And Charles Langlois didn't see it?"

"He was beginning to. And she probably realized that. On the tape from The Mission, it looks like Caron and Langlois weren't so much talking as arguing. We can't blame Langlois for being taken in by her. She's a master manipulator. And I'm no better than him. Worse, in fact. Charles told me the Sûreté is compromised, and I have no idea who he means, and I work with them every day. Have for years."

That was one of the most terrifying things about what was happening. The fact he could not see the threats that must be so close.

Disguised as colleagues, allies, friends. The fact he could no longer trust people he'd trusted for years.

"I'm sorry. I've been so wrapped up in what happened that I haven't asked you about your day."

"Let's see. My Montréal home needed new locks because it was broken into, then my husband was almost killed, and finally I learned about a plot to murder the entire population. As though that wasn't bad enough, Olivier almost poisoned us all."

"Huh? What do you mean?" He sat forward. "Food poisoning? Are you all right?"

Could he really have been so distracted that he hadn't seen that she was ill?

"No. A drink, if you can believe it. Disgusting. Some guest at the B&B gave him the recipe for a cocktail and a bottle of booze to make it with. Ruth pounded back two before she realized how awful they were. It's a miracle she didn't die."

"Well, miracle is one way of looking at it. But you weren't really sick, were you?"

"No, but close. It was vile. Even looked it. Green." She made a face. "The name alone should've warned us."

"Was it called Don't Drink This?"

She laughed. "Or maybe Poison?"

"Did the bottle have a skull and crossbones?"

"Should have. The cocktail was called something like Famous Last Words. What?"

# CHAPTER 15

⁓

"Holy shit, Armand, you scared the life outta me."
Olivier had opened his eyes to see a man's face, in the dark, within inches of his own. He'd bolted upright so quickly they'd almost banged heads.

"What're you doing here? What's happened?"

"We need to talk."

"Now?" Olivier put on his glasses. "It's four thirty in the morning. I'm in bed, for Chrissake." Seeing Armand's face, he gave in, grudgingly. "Oh, okay."

Beside him, Gabri was snoring, and smiling.

"He smiles in his sleep?" asked Armand as Olivier threw on a bathrobe and slippers.

"And sometimes he laughs. What I wouldn't give to spend just five minutes in his head. I think it must smell of fresh baking in there."

Despite himself Armand laughed, and tried to think what the inside of Reine-Marie's head would smell like. Roses, probably. The garden on a warm summer morning. And perhaps just a hint of dusty documents.

He knew Jean-Guy's must smell like bacon.

Clara's would smell of oil paints and overripe banana. Myrna's of books and strong tea. Olivier's of money. Billy Williams of the musky forest. Ruth's? Well, they all knew what that would smell like.

And his own? He hoped it would smell of lemon meringue pie with a soupçon of damp dog, but he had his doubts.

He followed Olivier down the stairs of the bed and breakfast. On the outside, the building looked like what it was. A centuries-old former coaching inn. A brief rest stop on the road between New York and Montréal. Many stopped, few stayed.

But the inside had been redone by the two men when they'd bought it more than a decade ago. Far from the overstuffed chintz furniture and lace curtains one might have expected, the walls were a soothing blue grey. Floor-to-ceiling bookcases, painted white, were in practically every room, overflowing with volumes actually read, jigsaw puzzles, board games. A fireplace in the living room faced the original leaded glass windows that looked out over the wide veranda and the village green beyond. From there, the men could see their bistro.

The flooring was worn wide plank, with oriental carpets scattered about.

It was comfortable and comforting. A relaxed marriage of the traditional and contemporary. Much like Olivier and Gabri themselves.

Going downstairs, Olivier, fully awake now, asked how Armand was, without mentioning the hit-and-run.

"I'm fine."

"'Fine' as in Fucked-up. Insecure. Neurotic. And Egotistical?"

"Exactly. I have a question."

"That couldn't wait."

"*Non.*"

As they passed the front door, Olivier said, "We have to remember to lock it. We do when there're guests, but not when it's just us. We never thought anyone would be rude enough to come right into our bedroom." He gave Armand the stink eye. "Ruth sometimes comes in at night and takes booze and food. We thought it was a mouse at first, but then a bottle of scotch disappeared. We now leave dinner out on the counter."

"Like Santa Claus."

"If he was a lunatic, yes. But even she hasn't gotten as far as the bedroom."

"Though if that was where you kept the alcohol . . ."

Armand followed Olivier into the large country kitchen, where he was waved onto a stool. He watched while Olivier made them cappuccinos and put warmed almond croissants on plates for them both.

"What do you want, Armand?"

"You made a cocktail yesterday afternoon."

Olivier's brows shot up. "Don't tell me you woke me up in the middle of the night because you want one. I wouldn't advise it."

"*Non,*" Armand said with a smile. "What was it called?"

"Called? You're kidding, right?" When Armand just waited, Olivier paused to think. "The Last Word. Yes, that was it."

Armand was quiet for a moment. "Where did you get the recipe?"

"From our guest."

"I take it he's no longer here?"

"No. Stayed one night. Left yesterday afternoon."

Armand thought of the older man he and Reine-Marie had passed two days earlier. Both men had turned and caught each other's eye. It was just an instant, before the contact was broken, though enough for Armand to feel the man looked vaguely familiar.

"What was his name?"

"Monsieur Gilbert. Can't remember his first name, but it'll be in our reservations."

Armand felt a vague stirring. As though someone had just ruffled the air around him. It was not an alarming feeling. In fact, it was somehow comforting. Like the hint of a scent from a pleasant experience.

"Was the recipe he had from a newspaper clipping?" Armand had his phone out. He'd already looked up the photo.

"Yes. And he'd brought the bottle that was the main ingredient. Not many places carry it anymore. It was a gift, he said."

"Do you still have the clipping?"

"No. After a couple of sips, and when even Ruth gagged, I threw it into the fire."

That, thought Armand, was a shame. He'd have liked to see it.

Armand turned his phone around. Olivier saw the photograph of a page from *Le Journal de Montréal*. On it was the picture of a drink and the recipe for the Last Word. Across the top of the photo was neatly printed, *Chief Inspector Gamache. This might interest you.*

"Yup, that's it."

Armand clicked off his phone and put it on the kitchen island. "When was the last time you heard of this cocktail?"

"Never. Never heard of it. And no one's ever asked for one. And I can't remember the last time I was asked for anything with Chartreuse in it."

"It had Chartreuse?" Armand hadn't actually read the recipe—why would he? It had seemed unimportant. But now he opened his phone again and enlarged the newspaper article. Sure enough, the green liqueur was the main ingredient.

Now another presence stirred the air. One a lot less friendly than the first. And still, Armand could not quite grasp it.

"*Oui.*"

"What was he like?"

"Older. I'd say in his early seventies. Slender. But his clothes . . ."

"Yes?" Even in his brief glimpse of the man on the village green, his clothing had struck Armand. And his hat. It was like something he saw in old photos of his father. No one wore hats like that anymore.

"They were in good condition," said Olivier. "But out of date by about fifty years. Wide lapels. Fat tie. And his slacks and jacket didn't quite fit him."

Armand had noticed that too.

"It was like he got them from a secondhand store or the Salvation Army," said Olivier.

Or, thought Armand, from the back room of a mission for the homeless. Or maybe from a prison locker, left there when convicted and picked up decades later when released.

Was Monsieur Gilbert someone he'd arrested for murder? But it could not have been fifty years ago. Armand would have been a boy. Precocious, for sure, but not to that extent.

"And his personality?"

Olivier dragged a stool around and sat across from Armand. He took a sip of his cappuccino and considered.

"Very polite. Soft-spoken. But he had a presence. A nice one. Calming. He asked questions and actually listened to the answers."

"What sort of questions?"

"Oh, just about the village. How old it was. Why we chose to live here. He'd been up to St. Thomas's. Called it a sanctuary."

Armand smiled. It was the word that came to his mind too, when thinking of the tiny chapel.

It overlooked the village and smelled of the balance of time. Of weddings and baptisms and funerals. Of gatherings in the basement, where villagers brought deviled eggs and cucumber sandwiches without crusts, and brownies with marshmallows on top. Mostly they brought companionship, in celebrations and in grief.

But the overpowering presence in St. Thomas's was that of three brothers, boys really, depicted in the stained-glass window. Marching to their fate in the Great War. Never to return home. And yet always there.

There was, in the little chapel, the stench of shame and the overpowering fragrance of forgiveness for the unforgivable.

"Did you find out anything about him?"

"Monsieur Gilbert? I asked what he did, but he was vague. I can't actually remember what he said."

Which probably meant, Armand thought, that Olivier wasn't interested in the answer.

"I asked what brought him to Three Pines."

"And?"

"He just said he'd heard about it from someone. I asked who, but he didn't seem to remember."

"Did he ask about me?"

"You? No. Why would he?"

"His accent?"

"Québécois. Educated. But there was a slight twang in certain words. You know?"

Armand nodded. People often tried to hide their upbringing, but it was like caging an animal. It might not be free, but it was still there.

"Tell me you didn't wake me up at four thirty in the morning just to ask about our guest and some horrible drink he had us make."

"Actually, I did. Can you show me Monsieur Gilbert's reservation?"

"Well, I can, but it doesn't say much. He called, and I took down the information. He didn't do it online. Here."

Olivier opened the calendar on his phone. He wasn't wrong. The reservation simply said, *P. Gilbert. Montréal.* There was a phone number and the date he'd be staying. No address.

Armand took down the information. "When did he make the reservation?"

"A few days earlier. Not long."

"How did he pay?"

"Now that was a little strange. He paid cash. Almost no one does these days."

Armand took a sip of the strong, smooth coffee, and considered. Maybe the appearance of the Last Word on the bundle sent to the office and the recipe from the B&B guest was just a coincidence. It often happened that obscure things appeared in clusters. Unrelated. Then disappeared just as suddenly.

"There's a party and I wasn't invited?"

They turned to find Gabri in his huge pink frilly dressing gown and bunny slippers.

"Ladies and gentlemen," said Olivier. "My husband."

"What's going on?"

"Armand came by to ask about that cocktail."

"At this hour? And here we thought Ruth was the one with the problem. It's all right, Armand, you're among friends."

When Armand just smiled, Gabri went on, in a more serious tone. "Didn't Reine-Marie tell you how awful it was? Blech. Even Ruth couldn't drink it, and she drinks from the toilet bowl."

"I don't think that's true," said Olivier.

"I saw her once."

While the two argued, Armand stood up. "Thanks for the coffee and croissant."

"You didn't touch it. Take it home for Reine-Marie."

"*Merci.* I will." He wrapped it in a napkin and put it in his pocket. "I imagine you've already cleaned his room."

"Whose?" asked Gabri.

"Monsieur Gilbert's."

"Yes. You're interested in him? He was such a nice man. Beautiful singing voice."

"How do you know that?"

"I heard him. He was in his room singing, softly. Couldn't make out the words and I didn't recognize the tune, but it was calming."

There was that word again, thought Armand. "Do you mind showing me his room?"

"Now you ask permission to go into a bedroom?" said Olivier, getting off his stool. "You have a strange idea of appropriate behavior."

The room Monsieur Gilbert had was simply and tastefully furnished, with a queen bed covered in a rose silk eiderdown. There was a comfortable armchair by an ornamental fireplace. The window looked out onto the village green, just becoming visible through the early-morning light struggling through the mist.

"He actually booked a smaller room," said Olivier.

"The smallest," added Gabri. "But since no one was here, we upgraded him."

"For free." Olivier's tone held a note of regret, if not resentment.

The two men watched as Armand poked around but found nothing. "*Merci.*"

As they made for the front door, Gabri said, "I heard you talk about the church. When I went up there last night to clean up after the Sunday service—"

"What is it you do in those services?" Armand asked. "How do you make a mess?"

"Well, you know, chicken blood . . . ," Gabri said, to Armand's laugh. "I found an envelope with your name on it. I meant to bring it with me but forgot it up there."

The hairs on Armand's neck went up.

A heavy mist, almost drizzle, now hung over the village, draining it of color so that everything appeared to be shades of grey. By the time they arrived at St. Thomas's, their clothing was damp, but not actually wet.

The church was unlocked, as usual.

Gabri turned on the overhead light, illuminating the few rows of gleaming wooden pews and the simple altar at the front.

The stained-glass brothers glowed red and green and the softest of blues.

"There." Gabri pointed to the white envelope. It was leaning against the top of the brass plaque under the window. The plaque had the names of those from the area who went to war and never returned. Names like Billy and Tommy, Gabrielle and P'tit Marcel.

Beneath the list was written, *They were our children.*

Gabri reached for the envelope, but Armand stopped him.

"When you found it yesterday, did you touch it?"

"Me? *Non.*"

Armand approached. Sure enough, in a fine clear hand, was written, *Armand Gamache.*

It was not, he could see, the same hand that had written on the newspaper.

He took a photo of it, then brought out a handkerchief and picked it up. The envelope was unsealed.

Sitting in the pew, enveloped by dull light from the brittle boys, he opened it and took out a piece of paper. And grew very quiet.

"What is it?" asked Olivier. The two men edged closer and leaned in as Armand unfolded the paper.

"Herbs?" said Olivier. "And spices. A recipe?"

"God," said Gabri. "Not another cocktail."

The top of the page was feathered, where it had been torn, and Armand was just able to make out two words, ripped in half.

*Angelica stems.*

He turned the page over. Someone had written:

*Some malady . . .*

# CHAPTER 16

⁓

The paper sat on the gleaming pew beside Armand.

*Some malady* was looking up at him.

He'd asked Olivier and Gabri to leave him alone in the chapel so he could think.

Gabri had been about to ask a question, or ten, but stopped himself. He could see that Armand wasn't just surprised, he was dumbstruck. Thunderstruck. And needed space and time and peace and quiet. To find some answers.

What he didn't need were more questions.

They left. And Armand stared ahead. Trying to see his way clear. The fog was getting thicker. Settling around him. He felt he was well and truly lost. Wandering in circles. And if that was the case, the only thing to do was to stand still. And think. Assess. Think some more.

Deep breath in. Deep breath out.

He had to tell himself not to race ahead. Not to leap from uncertain conclusion to uncertain conclusion. Until he leaped right over the edge.

Now was the time for clarity, not speed.

But still, his mind sped. Then, with effort, it slowed, and slowed. And landed on the one certainty.

Armand Gamache knew who that man was. The one he'd passed on the village green. The one he'd recognized, but not recognized. The one who'd given his name as Monsieur Gilbert.

Armand almost smiled at that. Perhaps he should have twigged then, when Olivier said it. But he hadn't. It was just too unlikely.

Monsieur Gilbert, who'd sung softly alone in his room at the B&B. Armand would bet good money that it had been just as the sun set when Gabri had heard that beautiful voice behind the door.

Monsieur Gilbert, who'd worn baggy old clothes and spent time in the church, and left a note here, for Armand to find. The other half of which had been placed in the coat stolen from his home. For Armand to find.

Placed there by a very different hand. Who had written on the reverse side a single word.

*Water.*

What was the connection? For there was one. A very strong one. Two halves of a note. Two halves of a whole. Were the people who'd possessed the document that too?

Did the one know about the other? Know what the other had done with their half? Know that Armand now possessed both halves? The whole?

But the whole of what?

Armand looked down at the piece of paper, sitting like a companion beside him on the pew in the peaceful little chapel.

*Some malady* . . . It sounded like a threat, and might be one. But it was also a quote. One he knew, and one Monsieur Gilbert knew he'd recognize.

*Some malady is coming upon us. We wait. We wait.*

It was from the T. S. Eliot play *Murder in the Cathedral*. About the brutal murder of Thomas à Becket by assassins, after the king had muttered, "Who will rid me of this meddlesome priest?"

Given all the people, all the churchmen, who'd abandoned the Archbishop of Canterbury, only one had stood by him. Stood up for him. At great peril to himself. An unlikely hero.

Saint Gilbert. Though he wasn't a saint at the time. That came later, for reasons that were unclear since the man had done nothing to distinguish himself except that one glorious, courageous, unlikely act. He'd stood up and, in the face of great peril, had defended his archbishop.

And now Monsieur Gilbert had visited Three Pines. And brought with him some malady.

What malady? Though Armand feared he knew.

He sat there in the uncertain light of the chapel and waited. And waited. For his mind to calm, and for the answer to come. Though, to be honest, he'd known as soon as he'd seen those two words. A threat maybe. More likely a warning.

Placed together, the two halves read, *Some malady . . . water*.

And on the other side of the paper were the words both halves shared. *Angelica stems*. Was it just coincidence that the paper had been torn just there? But Armand was beginning to think few things about these events had been left to chance.

Like a competitor in a race to solve the Rubik's Cube, everything had twisted and clicked into place.

The soft singing.

The baggy clothing.

The vague recognition.

The sense of calm he'd had as he'd locked eyes with the older man.

The name the man had given to Olivier and Gabri. Monsieur P. Gilbert.

And now, the quote. That was the clincher. It put it beyond doubt.

What remained unclear was the purpose of the note someone, two someones, had wanted him to have. A list of herbs and spices. And the scribbled words on the back.

And what about the cocktail? The Last Word?

Armand closed his eyes and tipped his face to the cathedral ceiling. There was something someone had said yesterday. Isabelle? Reine-Marie?

It was Jean-Guy. Opening his eyes, Armand brought from his breast pocket the other half of the note. He reread the list of herbs. Until he came to the demi-words, the last words, clinging to the bottom of the page. *Angelica stems*.

Named after an archangel. The obscure herb often mistaken for its poisonous look-alike. It was used to make, among other things, the liqueur Chartreuse. And Chartreuse was the main ingredient in the cocktail. The Last Word.

Armand lowered his hand slowly, until it rested on the pew, the one page sitting beside the other. Reunited. The page made whole.

He knew now what that list was. It was part of the recipe for the liqueur Chartreuse.

And the elderly man who'd come to Three Pines and left it for him? Armand had met him a few years ago.

Dom Philippe, the Abbot of the remote monastery Saint-Gilbert-Entre-les-Loups. P. Gilbert.

And now Armand felt sure that the other half of the recipe had come from the Abbot's opposite number. Charles Langlois had given his jacket to his boss, and she'd returned it to Armand.

That horror, Jeanne Caron, had slipped it into his jacket. Two halves of a whole. Heaven and Hell.

Armand was still sitting there when he heard the door to the chapel open, and footsteps down the aisle.

He'd been so lost in thought that the drumming of rain, heavy now against the windows and on the roof, came as a surprise. But the voice that greeted him did not.

"Olivier said you'd be here." Jean-Guy slipped in beside him. "Annie and I brought the kids down. Daniel and Roz have just arrived with Florence and Zora. Your home sounds like a day care. Are you claiming sanctuary here? Can I come too?"

Armand gave a grunt of laughter. He could almost hear the ear-splitting shrieks of the grandchildren playing together, to be followed by wailing as one or the other, or all four youngsters, either fell or suffered hurt feelings. Both events were inevitable.

"I saw the security video you sent," Armand said.

"It's the same woman, isn't it? Jeanne Caron. The Chief of Staff to the Deputy Prime Minister of Canada."

Armand nodded.

"Fucking hell."

Gamache didn't disagree.

"And she's involved?"

"Up to her neck," said Gamache.

"You obviously know her."

Armand knew this would come up and had weighed what he would say. It wasn't that he didn't trust Jean-Guy with the truth. He trusted him with his life. But the truth involved Daniel, and that was the problem. He'd betrayed his son once, and Daniel would see this, rightly so, as yet another.

Before he could say anything, the door opened again. Both men turned around to see Isabelle Lacoste shaking water off her coat. Her hair was plastered to her skull, and strands, whipped by the wind, stuck to her cheeks.

"Jesus, Chief. Couldn't you have been in the bistro?"

The little chapel had become damp and chilly, and even with the overhead light on, it was dark. And now smelled of wet wool.

Isabelle sat in the pew in front of them and leaned over the back to talk.

"Thank you for inviting my family down," she said. "We've checked into the B&B."

"I'm sorry there isn't room in the house," said Gamache.

"The kids think staying in a hotel is pretty cool. Their first time." She and her husband had not, of course, told them why they'd suddenly decamped to the countryside. To a village with well water and a spring-fed stream running through it.

It was still far from certain that there was a threat to the drinking water, but Armand wanted to be safe. Just in case . . .

Though he wondered if this was how Noah had felt as he stood on the deck of the ark and stared at those left behind.

"They're over at your place now. I would not advise returning any time soon unless you want Play-Doh to the side of the head." She lifted her hand and removed a bright green glob from her wet hair. "Your house is insured, right?"

"*Oui.*" But his marriage was not. He thought he really should go home and rescue Reine-Marie. Soon . . .

Isabelle turned to Jean-Guy. "I saw the video you sent. So it's confirmed. Jeanne Caron was Charles Langlois's contact and probably the boss he talked about. She's Chief of Staff to the Deputy PM. Does that mean he's behind this?"

"Not just him," said Jean-Guy. "If the PM gave him the counter-terrorism dossier, does that mean he's involved too?"

They were staring at the Chief.

"I think we have to assume the worst." It was, he knew, part of his job. To assume and prepare for the worst. To try to see it coming.

And what he now saw coming blotted out the sun.

"There's something you need to know," said Gamache. "Madame Caron called me on Sunday morning. She wanted to meet. I told her to go to hell."

"Why would you do that?" asked Lacoste.

"And why would she call you?" asked Beauvoir.

"I don't know what she wanted, but you need to know that we have a history. Years ago, when she was a young executive assistant and her boss was a newly elected member of Parliament, they asked me for a favor. To get his daughter off a manslaughter charge. I refused."

"What happened?"

"Despite overwhelming evidence, she was acquitted. Then they came after me. But not just me. They found out about Daniel's drug use." As he spoke, Armand's hands slowly closed. Clenched. "He was in court-ordered rehab, as part of his plea bargain. They had it reversed. Had him charged with trafficking. He never trafficked."

Armand could feel his face growing hot, and his anger rising. Taking over. He paused and took a deep breath before continuing.

"He was sent to prison, where he relapsed. His lawyers and I fought the new charge, and he was eventually released, the charge expunged, and he was sent back to rehab. It took many months, and a suicide attempt." Armand steadied himself, and exhaled deeply, before he was able to go on. "But he got clean. Has been clean ever since. He blamed me for many years. We've come a long way, but I think it's a wound that will never completely heal."

Beauvoir's eyes were closed. He'd been down the same road. Been addicted to painkillers, then worse. Had done untold damage to those he loved. Including this man. But had finally gotten clean.

He'd known there was something between Daniel and his father, but he hadn't known what. Something that had been resolved in Paris a year or so earlier.

But now he saw that the hurt, the rage, still existed. Probably in both men. Certainly in Daniel's father.

Jeanne Caron and her boss had almost succeeded in killing Daniel Gamache. Armand would never, could never, forgive that.

Was that why he'd often find his father-in-law sitting in this seat in this tiny church? Was he drawn to the three boys, who seemed to have forgiven far worse?

They were quiet for a moment, giving him time to recover. Armand wiped his face with his hand, as though to erase the worst of the memory.

"I have no idea why she wanted to meet," he finally said.

"Well, we'll find out soon enough. We need to question her," said Beauvoir.

"Not yet," said Armand. "We don't have enough evidence. And something else has come up. On Sunday afternoon, just as Reine-Marie and I were walking to our car to drive into Montréal, we passed an older man. A guest who'd just arrived at the B&B. He left an envelope for me here, in the church." Gamache continued to hold Beauvoir's puzzled gaze. "This was inside. Careful, we need to fingerprint it."

Beauvoir used a tissue to pick up the torn paper. Then he looked down at the other half, still sitting on the pew. The one left in Gamache's jacket.

Beauvoir turned the page in his hand around. "What does *Some malady* mean?"

"It's a quote from a play. I think it's both a warning, and a way for me to identify him. He knew I'd recognize it. That paper isn't the only thing he left behind. He gave Olivier a bottle of Chartreuse and a recipe for a cocktail called the Last Word."

Isabelle Lacoste tilted her head. "That's the same cocktail that's in the newspaper your coat was wrapped in."

"*Oui.*"

"Wait a minute," said Beauvoir. "The videos confirm Jeanne Caron was Charles's boss. She got him to break into your home, *patron*, and take your coat. And she had your coat sent back to you, wrapped in the newspaper with the recipe and the list in one of the pockets."

"And then she called you," said Lacoste.

"No. The call came first," said Armand. "The break-in happened later that morning."

"Are they connected?" asked Lacoste. "Did she want to warn you? But that doesn't make sense. Why would the person ordering the break-in also try to stop it?"

"And she didn't want to warn me, she wanted to meet me."

"True."

"And then that man comes here with the same cocktail," said Beauvoir. "Does this mean they're in it together? The B&B guest you recognized and Jeanne Caron?"

"They must be," said Lacoste. "Who is he? You know, don't you."

Gamache once again looked at Beauvoir, who was now troubled by that gaze.

"He gave his name to Olivier and Gabri as Monsieur Gilbert. P. Gilbert. I'd met him before. So have you."

Beauvoir cocked his head, his brow furrowed. "A criminal? A killer? Who?"

"It was Dom Philippe." Gamache watched Jean-Guy as he said the name.

It took Jean-Guy a moment or two to cast his mind back, but he finally got there. To that charred spot in both their lives. When the two men had stepped off a boat onto the rocky shore, to investigate a murder. They'd looked up at the remote monastery on some God-forsaken lake. Though not completely forsaken.

Many times a day, at matins and lauds, at compline and vespers, the voices of the monks rose from the abbey to join the old-growth forest, and the wildflowers, and wild animals, the fresh water and fish and fowl. The men, the monks, sang ancient Gregorian chants. The word of God, in the voice of God. And with those chants they became one with each other. One with nature. One with the universe. One with God.

All led by their Abbot, Dom Philippe. The spiritual leader of Saint-Gilbert-Entre-les-Loups. The all but forgotten, and forsaken, abbey in the wilderness.

By the time they'd left there, Armand and Jean-Guy's relationship was in ruins. A terrible chapter in their lives had begun at the monastery of Saint Gilbert Between the Wolves.

That was now in their past, was history. Though like all history, it had left its mark.

But clearly something else had happened at Saint-Gilbert. Something recent that had propelled the gentle Abbot from his cloistered existence into the world. Into Three Pines. From one forgotten place to another.

He'd put on the clothes he'd been wearing fifty years earlier, when he'd entered Saint-Gilbert as a young man and, placing a grey hat on grey head, he'd left.

Armand wondered why, if the Abbot had traveled all that way to give him a message, had even recognized him as they'd passed, he hadn't stopped him. Hadn't handed him the note in person, hadn't sat down and explained instead of leaving the envelope propped against the chapel wall.

Was it because Dom Philippe did not want to answer the inevitable questions? Did not want to provide an explanation? Which could mean either Dom Philippe or someone he cared about was involved.

"I know what those notes, when put together, make," he said. "It's a recipe, or at least part of one. I think it's for Chartreuse."

Beauvoir and Lacoste stared at him.

"The drink?" said Lacoste. "What my grandmother used to have on special occasions?"

"The drink."

They brought out their phones, and while Gamache stared at the stained-glass window, they looked up the liqueur.

Then all three Sûreté officers sat in the weak light and, as the three boys looked on, they talked about murder and monks and how a remote monastery and an obscure recipe for a little-used liqueur could possibly have anything to do with the killing of Charles Langlois. A biologist who might, or might not, have stumbled onto a plan to poison Montréal's drinking water.

# CHAPTER 17

~

"Oh God, oh God, oh shit."

Armand felt the grip tighten on his forearm and placed his large hand over Jean-Guy's claw.

"It's all right. We'll be fine."

"We're fucked."

Armand did not completely disagree. And he suspected the insincerity of his reassurance was obvious, in the tremble in his own voice. And the fact it was about an octave higher than usual.

Even seeing that SUV heading toward him hadn't scared him this much. Probably because he hadn't had time.

Now he had time. To see the crash. To wonder how much it was going to hurt.

The tiny single-engine float plane was not so much floating as being flung. They were flying through, or trying to, battering wind and torrential rain. And now there was a huge flash of light and an explosion.

For an instant, Gamache thought the plane had blown apart. Hit by lightning. But the flash had been off to their left. And now there was another, to their right. They were in the middle of a thunderstorm. It was like tines of a gigantic fork trying to skewer a pea.

They were the pea.

They should never have taken off, but the pilot had assured them there was a break in the weather and he could quickly get above it.

"How far above?" Jean-Guy had shouted over the noise. "Did he mean Heaven? Oh God, oh God, oh shit."

The plane dropped several hundred feet, the pilot fighting for control and height.

"Hang on," he yelled as the plane plunged sideways, almost flipping over.

*Ooooh*, thought Armand, as he splayed his hand on the ceiling to keep from hitting it. *Ooooh, God. Not like this. Please let us be found. Let our bodies be found. Reine-Marie, I'm sorry . . .*

The grey waves rushed up at them, so close now he could see the frothing white caps. Hitting the water at this speed would be like hitting concrete. He braced himself and held his breath, while Jean-Guy gripped his hand. And he held Jean-Guy's.

Then the engine roared and they gained height, zooming up. Into the clouds. Into the storm.

"We need to turn around," Gamache yelled at the pilot over the noise.

"Too late."

"What do you mean, 'too late'?"

"We've gone too far. We have to keep going. We'll be out of the weather soon."

That would have been reassuring had it not been for the blind panic in the pilot's voice and another crackling, then bang of thunder so loud the small craft shook.

Gamache thrust himself back against the seat and continued to brace as the craft and their bodies were flung to the left and right, up and down. This was a Sûreté plane and a pilot he'd used many times before, including on his recent trips to Les Îles de la Madeleine and the Saguenay, to investigate what still seemed to him to be mob executions.

He'd contacted his investigators on site that morning when he'd arrived at Sûreté headquarters, having gone straight there from Three Pines.

Ruth had gone over to their home and relieved Reine-Marie and

Annie and the others of the need to babysit. Somehow the mad old poet cast a spell over children and they behaved with her.

Armand tried not to think of what had happened to Hansel and Gretel.

He'd last seen Reine-Marie and the others in the bistro, staring wide-eyed into the mumbling fire. Gripping mugs of coffee and recovering their wits.

He now thought they'd probably been muttering, *Oh God, oh God, oh shit.*

Armand, Jean-Guy, and Isabelle had split up when they'd arrived at the Sûreté. Beauvoir to take the envelope and note to forensics and get an update, while Lacoste called the phone number Dom Philippe had put on his B&B reservation.

Armand sat at his desk and made some calls, including to the Sûreté hanger at the airport, while he looked out at the rain streaming down his window. Then he used a secure app to send a message.

*Can we meet?*

*Yes. When? Where?*

*Ninety minutes. Broken Kettle in Vankleek Hill.*

There was no reply and none needed.

Before heading out, Armand called his officers investigating the murders on Les Îles de la Madeleine, and in the Saguenay region.

"Sorry, *patron*, no progress yet," said the senior investigator. "No connection between the murders, and nothing I can find to link the dead guy here to the mob. But we'll keep looking."

He got virtually the same report from his lead investigator in the other execution-style killing, this one in Chicoutimi, in the Saguenay area north of Québec City. No leads. No apparent connection to the other murder, or the mob.

"Talk to her colleagues again. Someone knows something."

On his way out, he dropped in on Evelyn Tardiff, who ran the Organized Crime division.

"Anything?"

"Nothing, Armand. None of my informants report hit men traveling to either area. Doesn't mean there weren't any."

"The killings are too similar, Evelyn. Hands zip-tied. Shot to the base of the skull. Same caliber, though not the same weapon. Neat, efficient, effective. These were executions."

"Let's not get ahead of ourselves. I can't find any evidence of a mob hit."

"No evidence? It has all the hallmarks."

"Okay, if it was, what did these two do to make them targets of the mob?" She sat back and stared at him.

"We can't find any reason they'd be hit," he admitted. "And there's no connection to the mob, or between them, that we can see. But there's something there, Evelyn. And I think you agree."

"You hear agreement in this conversation? What must disagreement sound like to you? Look, what would the mob be doing with two middle-aged people who have led blameless lives? Doesn't make sense. Besides, there's nothing up in the Saguenay but lakes and trees."

"There's aluminum."

Tardiff laughed. "You think the Sixth Family is now trafficking in tin foil?"

She'd used the nickname for the Moretti family. After the five leading mob families in the US, this Montréal mafia family was considered the sixth. Powerful and ruthless, it had consolidated its hold on territory after the paterfamilias had died.

Armand managed a smile. "It seems unlikely, I agree."

He decided not to pursue it. As he left, he wondered why Tardiff was being so obtuse. Almost defensive. As he pressed the down button, he wondered if she was telling him everything.

As he walked out of the elevator, he wondered why he was wondering when he knew the answer to that. It was no. She was not telling him everything.

And now he wondered why.

David."

"Armand."

Gamache stood up to greet his friend and colleague from the RCMP. "Thank you for meeting me. Coffee?"

"I'll get it."

He came back to the small table shoved against the brick wall with a mug and a blueberry muffin. Sitting down, he stared at Gamache.

"I got your text yesterday."

"But you didn't reply."

He fiddled with the handle of his chipped mug. "It's delicate."

"To say the least, yes."

"I needed to do some research."

Gamache waited.

"Your message didn't have any information," said Commissioner Lavigne. "No context."

"True. Do you need it?"

"I think what we need is an exchange of information."

They were sitting at the back of the small restaurant, invisible to anyone walking by.

Vankleek Hill was a village in Ontario, almost exactly halfway between Ottawa and Montréal. An hour's drive for each of them. It was outside Sûreté jurisdiction. He would not run into anyone who worked with him.

David Lavigne wasn't just a colleague in law enforcement, he was the assistant commissioner of the RCMP. And a friend. His specialty, over twenty-five years, was domestic and international terrorism.

"You asked about recent movement in the biological or chemical weapons sector."

"And?"

He sat back and considered for a moment. "There're rumblings out of Rome and Paris, about something, some target in North America. We're trying to get a handle on it. It's vague. Our informants are scampering for cover."

"Which means it's big."

"Or at least different. Anything outside the regular playbook gets people nervous. And not just us, also the terrorists." He smiled. "When terrorists get scared, we get terrified. Do you have information?"

"I don't honestly know. Is it possible it's a biological weapon?"

"Could be. Might be chemical. Even nuclear. Might be nothing."

"Never nothing," he said.

Both veterans knew that, at any given moment, hundreds of plots by international and domestic terrorists were at various stages of gestation.

"Is there a reason you mention bioweapons, Armand?"

Instead of answering, he said, "I hear there's a new boss at GAC."

"You've heard?" he said. "Of course you've heard. Hasn't been announced yet, but yes, Marcus Lauzon has been given that portfolio by the PM. He's been acting head for almost a year now."

"What do you think of that?" He tried to keep his tone neutral.

"I think it's both worrisome and good, like most things politicians do. Worrisome because I think Monsieur Lauzon is an opportunist, and doesn't give a shit about the Canadian people, or even his party."

"He's already the Deputy PM," said Gamache. "And holds Environment. Now, with this new responsibility—"

"His power is almost limitless."

"And the good?"

"Well, when power's concentrated in one hand, it's easier to monitor for abuse. But also, on a more macro front, the environment and foreign affairs are becoming more closely aligned. It's quite a strategic move on the part of a Prime Minister elected to act on climate change."

"But why would the PM give it to Lauzon?" asked Gamache. The *of all people* was implied.

"I learned early on not to try to figure out why politicians do anything. Circles within circles. Their logic, such as it is, is tortured. You know that."

"What worries me is the other part of the portfolio. International trade is more and more connected to international terrorism. And domestic too, for that matter. A way to funnel money from one country to another. From one entity to another."

"Very true, Chief Inspector. I see you've been reading your briefing notes."

"I keep them in the bathroom. Money laundering, getting funds to where they need to be through legitimate businesses. A complex international organization, with ambitions to disrupt, needs a lot of money. Lauzon is now in charge of monitoring, even policing, that flow of money."

Gamache raised his brows and waited for his companion to say something.

Lavigne pushed his muffin aside and leaned across the table.

"You knew all this before coming here. That's not why you wanted to meet. Come on, Armand, I haven't got all day. Tell me." He paused and studied him, then threw himself back in the chair. "My God. You're trying to decide if you trust me. Twenty years we've worked together. You invited me here and now suddenly you're not sure?"

He was right.

This was the moment for his *beau risque*. The leap of faith. Armand Gamache knew he and his core group of trusted officers couldn't investigate on their own. At the very least, after seeing Jeanne Caron on the tape, he knew he needed someone on the federal side. If a player as powerful as the Deputy PM was involved, he needed powerful help.

He needed David Lavigne, the leading expert on domestic and international terrorism, who also had a seat on the GAC committee.

But the same thing that made him a perfect choice to help in the investigation also made him the perfect choice to be recruited by whoever was behind this. Caron? Lauzon?

Was this man in one of those circles? Was he part of the inner circle?

Could he be turned? Could he be trusted?

All the way up in the car, Gamache had agonized over this. Hoping he'd know when he saw him. Spoke to him. Hoping some instinct would kick in. So far, he'd met with two senior cops, top Sûreté officers, and dismissed them both as suspicious. How would he feel about Lavigne?

"Do you remember when Idola was born?" he said.

"Your granddaughter. Of course I do." He was clearly puzzled by this aside.

"You sent a gift and wrote a note for Annie and Jean-Guy. You described how your wife's sister, Charlene, has Down, and that you can't imagine life without her."

"Yes, so?"

"So, I trust you."

"Because my sister-in-law also has Down syndrome? I'm not saying you're wrong to trust me, but that reasoning seems pretty flimsy, Armand, even for you."

Gamache gave a small grunt of amusement. "I trust you because of that kindness to my daughter and Jean-Guy. You could not be that empathetic and be party to a mass murder that would include children."

"Mass murder?" His voice had risen, then suddenly dropped to a hoarse whisper. "What do you know, Armand? You have to tell me."

He took a breath, then took the leap. He told the assistant commissioner of the RCMP everything. There was no going back now. When he finished, there was a long, long silence.

"I think you're wrong. It must be the toxic spills." Despite his denial, he'd become very still. The way a hunted animal became when it senses a predator. "Doesn't that seem much more likely? I mean, really, Armand. Why poison Montréal's drinking water?"

There was a plea now, in his voice. He was begging Gamache to agree with him.

"Let me ask you a question," said Armand. "What happens if the drinking water is poisoned? Not the deaths, I know about those, but the political fallout."

"What happened when the FLQ kidnapped and killed a politician, and set off bombs in Montréal back in 1970?"

He was referring, of course, to the October Crisis. It was a rhetorical question since both knew the answer. But still, he said it.

"The Prime Minister invoked the War Measures Act."

"*Oui.* And this PM would too. Would have to."

"Civil liberties would be suspended," said Gamache. "The Charter of Rights and Freedoms frozen. Québec, all of Canada, would become a police state."

"The federal government would have unlimited power."

"Unbridled power," said Gamache. "A *coup de grâce* followed by a *coup d'état.*"

"Are you really saying"—Lavigne lowered his voice—"that the PM is behind this? I'm not a huge fan, but even I stop at thinking he's a tyrant willing to kill thousands to make himself dictator."

When Gamache just stared at him, he shook his head and grinned.

"Sorry, that was naïve. Just look at world leaders today. Insanity rules. Would this PM do it? I don't know. Maybe. But still, I can't believe it. I think you're wrong."

Lavigne reached into his pocket and brought out a small bottle of extra-strength aspirin. "You've given me a headache." He tipped it toward Armand, who shook his head and watched his companion down two.

"I hope to God I'm wrong, but you might want to keep that bottle close. David, you've run the scenarios. How easy would it be to poison our drinking water?"

"It's one of our top concerns. It wouldn't be easy, but it could be done. My God, Armand, if you're right—" His eyes widened. "Montréal? That would mean—"

"*Oui.*"

The shock was wearing off. Lavigne's mind was engaging.

"We can't issue a warning to the population," he said, ticking through the options. "Certainly not until we're sure. And if it's true, a civil warning would also warn whoever is behind this. They'd either move up their plans or put them on hold and go to ground."

He looked at Gamache, who nodded but remained quiet.

"Our only hope is to catch them. Rip it out, root and branch. Jesus, Armand, how deep are the roots? How high up does it go?"

Now it was Armand's turn to lean across the table. "That's what you need to find out."

"And you?"

"I need to find the Abbot."

"Really? That's your first move? Find some old monk with a partial recipe for an obscure liqueur? Don't you think there're more promising leads?"

"My people are looking into others, and you're right, had it been just Dom Philippe and a ripped piece of paper, I wouldn't have given him a second thought, but it isn't. Not when the other part of that paper was sent to me by Jeanne Caron."

Lavigne nodded. "That's a good point. Somehow the two are related."

"I don't know how, but I think Dom Philippe found out about this and is afraid."

"Or involved."

"*Non*." Armand shook his head. "I know the man. He couldn't be."

"And yet, by your reckoning, he knows about an imminent attack that could kill tens of thousands and he doesn't say anything. Is that the act of a decent man?"

"I'll find out soon enough. I'm heading to the monastery. I think he's gone back there."

"Won't he know you'll come looking?"

"Maybe that's what he wants. It's where he feels safest, in control. There's something else," said Armand. "Two others I need to know about. I can't do it, for reasons that will be obvious. One is Evelyn Tardiff—"

"The head of your Organized Crime division?" said David, not hiding his surprise. "You think she's involved?"

"And Madeleine Toussaint."

"Are you shitting me?" He dropped his voice and all but rasped, "The head of the Sûreté? Jesus Christ. If those two are involved, then who's flying your plane?"

David Lavigne meant it figuratively, but at that moment Armand had the same question, only his was real and urgent.

Who was flying the plane? The tiny single-engine craft bobbed and tossed and dropped and jerked. It shuddered and twisted, and Armand expected to see parts flying off. Was the pilot in control, functioning or panicking? Was he even still conscious?

At that moment there was a shout, at least confirming the pilot was alive, if not in control. There were no words, no instructions. Just a sort of cry from the cockpit.

Jean-Guy, never happy in confined spaces anyway, was almost comatose.

Armand, never happy with heights, was not much better.

This was never going to be a fun flight. Add in the fact they were almost certainly about to die, and neither man was functioning all that highly.

Armand was afraid to open his mouth now, in case he threw up. He swallowed hard and tasted bile and a burning in his throat. He looked over at Jean-Guy, who was pale, almost green. His face glistened with sweat. His eyes were wide and staring straight ahead. Helping the pilot fly the plane. Afraid to break focus, in case only his hypervigilance was keeping them aloft.

They'd both been in terrible, life-threatening situations. Shootouts. Firefights. But always with the ability to do something. To fight back. Even to run away. By now they were powerless. Strapped into the rear seat of a prop plane. With nothing to do. Except wait.

*We wait. We wait.*

Armand had taken his phone out and managed to type a message to Reine-Marie, just saying, *I love you. I'm sorry.* But he didn't send it. He didn't want to scare her. But now his finger hovered over the send icon.

The plane banked suddenly, lunging onto its side, throwing Armand against the window. His phone flew out of his hand and his cheek squished against the glass. He was forced, like it or not, to look down. There he saw not water but forest. A thick canopy of evergreens and then, below them, shrouded in mist, a familiar building came into sight.

Armand placed his hands on either side of his head and tried to push away from the window, but the force was too great. Jean-Guy's body was pressing into his, trapping him.

Out the steamy window Armand could just make out the four wings of the monastery.

The plane was on its side, descending. The wings of the plane getting closer and closer to the wings of the building.

He wanted to shut his eyes, but did not. More than hiding from what seemed inevitable, Armand wanted to see as much of this world as possible, before . . .

The plane gave another mighty convulsion and flipped over to the other side. Armand's body smashed against Jean-Guy's. He put his hands out to brace himself against the fuselage and push away from Beauvoir.

Then the plane lurched again and, in the chaos and confusion, Armand was no longer certain if it had righted itself or if they were now upside down. Then he saw the whitecaps just feet away and threw his arm across Jean-Guy's chest. As one would a child's, anticipating a sudden stop. It was useless but instinctive.

The pilot screamed, "Look out!"

There was a violent thud and the rending of metal. Jean-Guy and the pilot shouted as they were all thrown forward. Armand thought he shouted too. A sort of cry.

And he waited. Numb now.

Nothing.

Opening his eyes, he could see water all around. But the plane bobbed on top of it, on its pontoons, not in the water, sinking.

"Oh shit," exhaled Jean-Guy. "Oh, God."

Up front, the pilot seemed to be weeping.

Armand blinked a few times and caught his breath. If he was ever going to have a heart attack, this would be it. He waited. But his heart, thudding in his chest, began to calm.

"You okay?" he asked the other two, and got silent, stunned nods.

Wiping his sleeve across the window to clear away the vapor and the smudge from his face-plant, he saw two monks standing on the shore, like apparitions. In unison they made the sign of the cross.

*Dear God*, thought Armand.

# CHAPTER 18

⁓

Isabelle Lacoste knew, of course, why she hadn't been assigned to go along with the Chief and Beauvoir. A woman would not be allowed into any cloistered monastery, and certainly not Saint-Gilbert-Entre-les-Loups.

There was a good chance Gamache and Beauvoir would not be allowed in either. No one crossed that threshold. The only reason the Chief and Beauvoir had been admitted last time was because of the body. Murder, it seemed, was a skeleton key.

Besides, there was a lot to do back in Montréal.

The first thing Lacoste did was call the number Dom Philippe had given Olivier when making the reservations at the B&B. It was answered by a man who said he'd never heard of Dom Philippe or Monsieur Gilbert.

He was home sick from work, with a cold. A summer cold.

The man was clearly about to go into detail, but Lacoste thanked him and hung up.

It seemed to Lacoste fairly telling that the Abbot had given a false number. Which, in Lacoste's experience, spoke of guilt. Or at the very least, something to hide.

She also wondered if this Dom Philippe, whom she'd never met and so had no preconceptions, was really the decent man the Chief seemed to think. Decent people did not, generally, have so many secrets. And so much to hide.

The next thing she did was go to the morgue.

"No ID?" she asked, standing with Dr. Harris over the remains of the man who'd murdered Charles Langlois, then been murdered himself.

"No. Shot in the head, once. His clothes are with forensics, but there was nothing in his pockets. We might be able to ID him through dental records. You have his prints and DNA."

"Nothing there," said Lacoste. "Not in the Québec system, or nationally. I'm going to send them to the Americans and Interpol. What else can you tell me about him?"

"Pretty much what you see. Male, Caucasian," said Dr. Harris. "Between twenty-five and thirty years old. His last meal was a burger and fries, two hours before he was killed. Oh, he also has alcohol in his system. Not enough to get drunk, but enough to take the edge off."

Lacoste stared down at the slender body. "Getting up courage, maybe."

She looked over at the other body, covered in a sheet. Charles Langlois. Murdered and murderer, side by side.

They moved over to Charles's body. The autopsy had already been done on him.

"We know his name and age," said Dr. Harris. "And what killed him. I can tell you that he has all the signs of a very serious addiction that's damaged part of his brain and some internal organs. But nothing recent. I'd say he was clean, and had been for at least a year, maybe two."

"Brain damage? How severe? Could it cause delusions? Paranoia?"

"For sure, but only if he was using. He wasn't so far gone that he'd hallucinate while straight. No—" She looked down at Charles. "Here's a now healthy young man."

"Can you tell where he'd been recently?"

"I've taken swabs of his hands, face, and feet, in case there's residue, but there's nothing obvious. Maybe on his clothing."

"*Merci.*"

Beauvoir, before leaving, had sent out the report from forensics.

Langlois's clothes were newly washed. There was nothing on or in them to say where he'd last been.

After that, Isabelle Lacoste collected a team and headed out to execute the search warrants for Action Québec Bleu and the home of its Executive Director, Margaux Chalifoux.

Chief Inspector Gamache had called from the airport just before they'd taken off, telling her to lead the search herself of Madame Chalifoux's place, figuring if there was anything to hide, it would most likely be there. Besides, the Exec would be occupied with the Sûreté search at the office. Lacoste and her team could work without being disturbed or distracted.

The small home in East End Montréal was, on first entering, a shambles.

"Great," said the head of the forensics team. "Another hoarder."

But a few minutes in and it became apparent Madame Chalifoux was anything but. Hoarders tended to collect items at random. Their homes were filthy and neglected and piled high with junk and mummified cats.

Here there was actually order. What appeared a jumble was in fact a collection of boxes from different investigations. All orderly. All apparently in the fight to protect fresh water in Québec.

"We have plenty of water," said one of the Sûreté agents, going through the boxes. "Why does it need protecting? Just a bunch of left-wing alarmists."

"It's a crazy world, with crazy people," said another agent. "Nothing is safe."

Lacoste had also gained access to Madame Chalifoux's bank records. She had $49 there. And $1,456 in credit card debt. Her last purchase was T-shirts, made from bamboo. To promote AQB.

"She used her own money," said Lacoste, to the senior agent.

"A fanatic," he replied.

The two of them were standing in the basement on the only square feet of carpet that were clear of clutter. They were looking at a map stapled to the wall.

It was of Québec, with little flags of different colors stuck into various lakes and rivers.

"I started with the Sûreté in the Abitibi," said the agent, taking a step closer and pointing at the map. "Some of those flags are in the smelters and the pulp mills up there."

"Get photos. I want to know what those flags mean."

"All of them? There must be hundreds."

"All of them. And I want a list of any pollutants."

"Well, I can tell you that the copper smelters emit arsenic."

"Christ," muttered Lacoste as she took a photo of the entire map and emailed it to Gamache and Beauvoir.

Two hours later the searches of the offices and home were complete, and Lacoste was sitting with Margaux Chalifoux in her kitchen, having had the Executive Director of Action Québec Bleu brought home.

The search of their offices had revealed nothing.

Her home was another matter.

"Tell me about arsenic."

Chalifoux knew she was in trouble. Not from the tone of the woman sitting across the table from her. The senior homicide investigator's voice actually sounded calm, even kind.

No, it was the familiar file folder in front of Inspector Lacoste.

"I wasn't going to do anything."

"The documents we found say different." Lacoste laid her hand on the manila file.

Chalifoux took a deep breath, as though to speak, then thought better of it. After a few moments of silence, Lacoste got up.

"I saw a bottle of rye somewhere. I think you could use a drink."

She pulled out the Canadian Club rye whiskey, then found a glass and some ice and, mixing the rye with Canada Dry ginger ale, she handed the stiff drink to Chalifoux.

"Why're you being nice?"

"Why not?" Though Lacoste wondered the same thing, and realized that she had some sympathy, even respect, for this woman. Not, perhaps, her methods, but her goals.

"It's not what you think."

"It never is. Besides, you don't know what I think."

"You think I sent those letters." Chalifoux nodded toward the file.

"Didn't you?"

"No. I was never going to. They're ravings, that's all. I was angry and frustrated and scared and broke. And drunk. And it seemed like a good idea at two in the morning. At seven in the morning it seemed insane."

"And yet you kept the letters."

Chalifoux colored. "You have to understand, Action Québec Bleu was, is, about to close. The fucking government cut our funding. This"—she looked around—"has become a community kitchen. We all pitch in, bring what food we can. Most from food banks. Some come and live with me when they've been evicted. It's a shambles. We do good work, important work. But no one's listening."

She put her head in her hands, her fingers gripping her scalp. Speaking to the vinyl floor, she said, "I was desperate." She lifted her head and jerked her chin toward the file. "So I wrote those."

Lacoste read from the top printout.

"*Dear Shit-Faces. Unless you give Action Québec Bleu ten million dollars, we will poison the drinking water with arsenic. The arsenic you produce, you asshole fucks.*"

"Acch," said Chalifoux, rolling her eyes. "I can't believe I wrote that. It's the childish ravings of a desperate person. If I was really going to threaten them, it wouldn't be with a letter like that. No one's going to take that"—again the chin jut—"seriously. I was venting, nothing more. I never sent it. You can ask the companies."

"That doesn't mean you weren't planning to do it."

"Put arsenic in the drinking water?" Chalifoux's face had opened up in a look of incredulity.

"Did Charles find out about this?" Lacoste tapped the file. "Did he come to you demanding answers?"

"And then what?" demanded Chalifoux, regaining some equilibrium. "I had him killed? Are you insane?"

*Are you?* Lacoste almost asked, but decided not to.

She knew that people who were monomaniacal often became maniacs, losing all sense of proportion, all sense of right and wrong, in pursuit of what they convinced themselves was a righteous cause.

What would an unbalanced person not do if they felt that all life on earth was in the balance?

Industry had untold resources in money and lobbyists and power. So environmentalists were often driven to guerilla tactics. The more radical among them to radical acts of ecoterrorism.

Yes, Isabelle Lacoste, the mother of two young children, could sympathize. But not support, not condone, mass murder in the name of the greater good.

She left the kitchen and spoke to her team leader.

"Did you find any arsenic?"

"*Non, chef.*"

"Anything that could be considered a poison?"

"No. We found a lot of references to poisons, but those were in their investigations into polluters. Did you know that the pulp and paper industry—"

"Yes," she said wearily. "I know. Wrap it up. Bring any suspicious files with you. And I want that map from her basement. With the pins still in it."

"*D'accord, chef.*" He went away, trying to figure out how to remove the map without the flags falling out.

# CHAPTER 19

~

The first thing Beauvoir did when he'd scrambled out of the plane and was standing on a pontoon, lifting and dropping, lifting and dropping in the waves, was throw up.

The storm, like some cosmic joke, had blown itself out as soon as they'd landed. But the wind was still strong, churning up the water and their stomachs.

They'd managed to motor over to the dock, and soon all three stood on the wharf, their legs weak, their heads still spinning.

The fresh air was bracing and reviving. Armand closed his eyes for a moment and turned his face into the wind. He took a deep breath and smelled pine. It smelled of home.

The next thing Jean-Guy Beauvoir did, once his brain focused, was attack the pilot.

"You fucker." Beauvoir lunged at the man. "You almost got us killed."

Gamache just managed to grab Beauvoir, dropping the phone he'd been clutching.

"Stop it!" he yelled, stepping between the two men.

"I saved us, you moron," shouted the pilot. "Without me you'd be dead."

"Without you I'd be safe at home. You took off when you shouldn't have." He was glaring over Gamache's shoulder and almost weeping now. "I have two children. A wife. I can't . . . I can't . . ." He pulled himself together and stood straight, gathering himself. "I'm not getting back in that thing." He threw his arm out toward the plane. "It's a death trap. It's falling apart."

The pilot flung his own arm out toward the craft. "It held together, which is more than I can say for you."

Beauvoir lunged forward again, but again Gamache, predicting it, held him back.

"Enough! Inspector Beauvoir is right. We should never have taken off. But I'm as responsible as the pilot. I agreed. But we're here now. We have a job to do. We can't turn on each other."

Gamache glared from one to the other, and waited for each to nod. Then he stepped closer to Beauvoir, looking the younger man in the eyes. He saw fury in them. And something else. Some other strong emotion. No, thought Gamache. A strong memory, provoking this outburst.

And he knew what it was. It was the same memory he'd been struggling with. One that had come on him suddenly, the moment they'd stepped onto the dock. As they'd listened to the waves lapping, and the pontoon bumping up against the fenders, and the birds shrieking, and the wind through the forest and flapping their clothing.

They were both recalling, reliving, the last time they'd stood on this dock. On this very spot. When Dom Philippe had told him about the grey wolf, and Jean-Guy had made a choice.

What Armand saw in those familiar, those beloved eyes was shame.

"It's okay. We're okay," he said quietly to Jean-Guy. He smiled, and saw his second-in-command, his son-in-law, relax.

Jean-Guy took a deep breath and smiled too. "*Oui.*" He looked over Gamache's shoulder to the pilot. "*Désolé.* I was just . . ."

"So was I," the pilot admitted. "I'm sorry too." Then he turned to Gamache. "I'll get the plane ready for the return flight, *patron.*"

"*Bon, merci.*"

Armand bent down and picked his phone off the wharf. Wiping the moisture off on his slacks, he looked at its face, hoping, in all the jostling and dropping, the message hadn't been sent to Reine-Marie.

He scrolled and searched with increasing anxiety but couldn't find it. That meant it had either been erased or . . .

"Oh no," he mumbled. "Oh no, oh no, no, no."

Now he really needed to get a message to her.

*All's well. Arrived safely*, he wrote and hit send. Not expecting it to, and it did not. There was no service there. Or at least it was intermittent.

"Can you get anything?" He raised his phone to Jean-Guy and the pilot, who shook their heads.

"Nothing," said Jean-Guy. "I just tried texting Annie."

"Can you send a message from the plane?"

"No," said the pilot. "I can set off the emergency beacon, but that probably won't get far enough, and if it does . . ."

Armand could imagine the reaction back in Montréal if they picked up an emergency beacon, normally sent by a plane that had crashed. It would trigger an unnecessary search and rescue. It would also trigger a panic. If he hadn't already.

"Probably don't do that."

He took a few steps away from the others, and staring out at the vast, grey lake and the dense evergreen forest beyond, he held the phone above his head and walked around the long dock, in hopes the message he wrote might catch a single bar and fly off home.

"You expecting a call from the higher power, Chief Inspector?" came a voice behind him. "I'm afraid even the Almighty struggles with the internet here."

"Though He does like a good calling," came another voice, followed by a small chuckle.

The two monks Armand had seen standing on the rocks were now walking out of the mist and down the long wharf toward them, their hands shoved up their drooping sleeves. Their black robes flapping in the gusts of wind.

Neither man was the Abbot.

Where are they?" Reine-Marie demanded.

She was in the study at home. It was quiet. The children, and Ruth, were having naps, though the poet and her duck were more passed out than asleep. The others were in the kitchen preparing dinner.

Reine-Marie stared out the window. The storm had blown itself out, and the early-evening sky was tinged with a pretty pink. Tomorrow promised to be a lovely day.

Reine-Marie stared at the sky with loathing. The storm hadn't ended soon enough. And tomorrow held . . .

*I love you. I'm sorry.*

Reine-Marie hadn't heard from Armand since that terrifying text.

She'd tried calling. Texting. She'd tried Jean-Guy's phone. Nothing. And now she was on the line with Isabelle Lacoste. Trying to keep her mounting hysteria just below outright panic.

Reine-Marie looked at the closed door and wondered when she had to tell the others.

Armand and Jean-Guy were on a flight, through a storm. And were missing. And sorry.

"We're trying to contact the pilot," said Isabelle, struggling to keep her own alarm under control. "And the monastery. No answer yet, but we'll keep trying."

Until Reine-Marie called, she'd had no idea the Chief and Beauvoir were missing. She'd checked her messages a few times, but when there was nothing, she hadn't been worried.

"There's almost no signal up there," Isabelle said.

"I know that," snapped Reine-Marie, then took a breath, a beat. "I'm sorry. It just, his last message . . ."

She'd forwarded it to Isabelle, who looked at it again and felt her own heart contract.

*I love you. I'm sorry.*

She hated, hated, hated to admit that it was the sort of message a person who knows they're about to die would send. Coupled with the silence, it was ominous.

"I'll send searchers to the lake."

"Tonight? Now?"

"If possible, yes." Though both knew, with approaching nightfall, it was not going to be possible. "We'll find them."

Bells sounded. Tolling out from the monastery and joining the far-off call of a loon. Both haunting. All the more so for the mist that clung in wisps to the forest.

The monks turned and, without a word, followed the sound of the bells. Beauvoir and the pilot looked at the Chief Inspector, who signaled them to follow.

At the huge wooden doors that guarded Saint-Gilbert-Entre-les-Loups, the monks stopped.

One of them picked up an iron rod and pounded. Behind them, from the lake, Gamache heard the flutter and splashing as ducks, startled by the unfamiliar sound, took off.

A small slit appeared, followed by bright blue eyes. Then the slit slammed shut and there was a grinding of old metal against old metal. And the thick door slowly swung open.

Not a word was exchanged. These were monks who had taken a vow of silence. And yet had become, in an act of grand irony, world-famous for their voices. The Gregorian chants they'd recorded as a modest fundraiser to repair the monastery roof had become a global hit. A phenomenon. A miracle, some thought. But one that had plunged the quiet order into chaos.

A chaos that had culminated in murder and brought Gamache and Beauvoir to this place years earlier.

"There's no way I'm getting in that plane again," said Jean-Guy.

He glanced at the pilot, who was staring wide-eyed at his surroundings.

Like the rest of Québec, he'd heard of these cloistered monks who never let anyone past that thick door. But somehow, he'd gotten in. Thanks to the setting sun.

So there they were. Admitted to the inadmissible.

The pilot looked around, his mouth dropping open. Even in the weakening light, the place was magical. From the outside it looked frightening, foreboding. But inside? It was glorious.

The windows, high up in the long, long corridor, captured every last ray available in the dying light and magnified it, brought it to life. The stone hallway was giddy with the evening sun.

Everything about this building, every stone, every sound, every ray of light, every movement, every moment of the monastic day and night, was symbolic. Multilayered. Planned. With purpose.

"Just so you know, *patron*," Jean-Guy said. "I'm signing up. Taking the vow."

"I'll break the news to Annie."

"He did hit a perfect high C," one of the monks said to the other.

"Yes. We could use a boy soprano."

Jean-Guy's eyes narrowed as he glared at the backs of the two monks. The thick doors had been shut and locked behind them. The world was kept out, and they were now kept in.

When the monks had first appeared, Gamache had asked to see the Abbot.

"Please follow us, Chief Inspector," said the older of the Gilbertine brothers. One he recognized as Frère Auguste. And who clearly recognized him.

And now, finally, he was about to get answers from Dom Philippe.

At the end of the corridor they stepped into a vast open space. The chapel, the heart of Saint-Gilbert.

It was stark, austere in the fading light. Just a few rows of wooden pews on the flagstone floor. And at the front, two rows of benches faced each other.

No art. No altar. No ornamentation. No crucifix. No lights. The sun had finally set, and what had been giddy light had descended into gloom that was fast becoming complete darkness.

As Beauvoir watched, Armand made a tiny dip, then an almost unnoticeable sweep of his right hand. Jean-Guy did not.

"What's that?" demanded the pilot, now spooked. His voice bounced off the stone walls and echoed. Until that too faded, as though swallowed by the void. The peace he'd felt moments earlier had also descended into gloom.

A weak glow was visible off to their left, and they could hear a faint sound, a kind of moan that joined with the deep tolling of the bell.

Backing up a pace, the pilot stepped right into the Chief Inspector. And gave a little yelp.

"Steady," whispered Gamache. "It's all right."

The pilot, taking no chances, crossed himself.

They stood in complete darkness now except for the glow, which was getting brighter.

Closer.

Then a single monk, hood up, appeared. He brought with him a candle and a low, rhythmic chant.

Then another voice, another monk, another steady light. And another, and another. Until the empty space was filled with their clear voices, and the darkness was broken.

The bells stopped, but the chanting continued, prayers sung by men who believed with all their heart and soul that what they did was divine.

And it was hard to disagree. Even the pilot, frightened moments earlier, seemed overcome. His eyes caught the candlelight and glistened as he watched the solemn, simple procession.

The monks, in single file, walked across the stone floor and took their places at the front, facing each other.

The singing ended. They sat. And silence descended.

The only light came from the candles that wavered and flickered.

Armand, Jean-Guy, and the pilot sat on the hard benches and watched as the monks of Saint-Gilbert-Entre-les-Loups held vespers, one of the canonical hours of the monastic day. "Vespers" translated literally as "shadows." It signaled the end of day. When light became shadow, and shadow became night.

One of the lights rose, and the silence was broken by a single voice, pure and strong. Lifting and falling, it was joyful and mesmerizing and hypnotic. Then the others stood as one and joined in as one. At once. Filling the huge space with song. With prayer that swooped and swirled and rode on robust notes. It whirled around the men, the monks and those watching. It entered them, embraced them, filled them. Kept them company so that they knew they were not, were never, alone.

Armand glanced at Jean-Guy and saw that his eyes were closed and his face tipped slightly back, as the younger man let the words, the music, the peace wash over him.

But the Chief Inspector's eyes were wide open, taking it all in. What he saw was less important than what he did not see.

Dom Philippe was not there.

Maman, what is it?" asked Annie.

She was making a potato salad, while Daniel and Roslyn shucked corn on the cob and Isabelle's husband shaped burgers for the barbecue.

Reine-Marie could wait no longer. Annie and Daniel had a right to know. They'd be furious if they found out that their mother was keeping this information about Annie's husband and their father from them.

Still, she'd waited. Staying in, hiding in, the study. Staring out the window, then checking her phone. Then staring again. Until the shadows lengthened in the little village and twilight became night and she was standing in complete darkness. Except for the light that came from her phone when she checked. And rechecked. And checked again.

Nothing.

Before leaving the study, she'd called Isabelle, who confirmed there was no news.

"I was just about to call you. It's too dark to send search planes and there's a heavy fog. The local Sûreté commander said he would organize boats to go look at first light, along with the search planes. There was no emergency beacon, so that's a good sign. And we know where they were headed. If they landed on the water, well, it's a float plane. There's every reason to hope."

"*Oui.* Are you coming down?"

"No. I'm staying here. I want to go up at first light with the planes."

Reine-Marie hung up and turned once again to the window, staring at the village. At the three soaring pines. She tried to sense it. Armand alive. She could not. But neither did she feel he was dead. She thought she'd know. Surely she'd know. Wouldn't she?

Finally, she knew it was time.

*Reason to hope, reason to hope,* she repeated as she walked slowly toward the kitchen, where she could hear Annie and Daniel teasing each other.

"Maman?" said Daniel, who spotted her first and saw his mother's face.

Then Annie spoke—"Maman?"—putting down the knife and stepping toward the door.

Just then, there was a small sound. A ding.

Reine-Marie looked down at her phone.

*All's well. Arrived safely.*

She looked at Annie and Daniel, then turned and walked quickly back to the study, where, her back against the closed door, she slid to the floor. And wept.

# CHAPTER 20

⁓

The last notes of vespers, reluctant to leave, drifted down the long corridors to the far reaches of the monastery before fading into the walls. As though the abbey of Saint-Gilbert-Entre-les-Loups were made not of stone but of notes, of neumes.

"I heard the plane overhead," the monk who'd led the service said as he approached the three visitors, "and sent Brothers Auguste and Patel out to make sure you were all right. I'm glad you're safe, Chief Inspector. For a few moments there . . ." He lifted one slender hand, palm up, in an eloquent gesture.

"*Oui*," agreed Gamache. "Us too, for a while there."

The monk turned to Jean-Guy. "Inspector Beauvoir. Welcome back." Then he returned to Gamache. "I don't know if you remember me. Frère Simon."

"Yes, I remember. You're the Abbot's secretary. I'd like to speak with Dom Philippe," said Gamache. "I didn't see him at vespers."

"You wouldn't. He's not here."

Gamache stopped and stared at the monk. "Where is he?"

Now Simon looked uncomfortable. "We don't really know. He left me in charge."

"You and I need to talk, *mon frère*."

"Agreed, but not right now. Come. You must be hungry."

Jean-Guy realized he was. Having lost his lunch, he was now looking forward to dinner. Beside him, the pilot's eyes had widened in happy anticipation.

"They're vegetarians," Beauvoir warned as they followed the monk down another corridor. Jean-Guy was pleased to burst that carnivore's bubble.

The dinner turned out to be delicious, starting with squash and wild garlic soup, followed by a casserole of baked ratatouille and goat's cheese.

Baskets of warm fresh-baked bread were passed around, along with churned butter and wooden boards filled with various cheeses. The meal concluded with an apple crisp and thick cream.

All the food was grown, or foraged, by the monks.

"Where're the blueberries?" Jean-Guy asked the young monk beside him, who just shrugged. Then looked around and whispered, "Too early."

"Shame," said Jean-Guy. The tiny chocolate-covered wild berries were a specialty of Saint-Gilbert-Entre-les-Loups.

The meal was eaten, like all else in the abbey, in silence, except for the prayers that began and ended it.

Armand had arrived late, having convinced Brother Simon that he needed to use the phone. The request had a dual purpose. He knew that the only telephone in the abbey, one connected to a not-very-reliable satellite dish for emergencies, was in the Abbot's office. It would allow him to try to get through to Reine-Marie. And also to do a quick search of the offices.

"I know the way," said Armand.

"I'm sure you do, Chief Inspector, but I'll still come with you. The monastery at night can be a confusing place. We've lost several postulants." He shook his head sadly, then smiled at Armand.

"Well, perhaps we'll find them," said Armand.

"At this stage, I hope not."

Gamache was no longer completely sure it was a joke.

The phone line turned out to be dead, and there was no way to do anything other than glance at the papers on Dom Philippe's desk, since the only light in the room was from the candle Frère Simon held.

"The clothing you're wearing when you arrive," he said to the monk as they left the office. "What happens to it?"

"We put it in boxes in the basement, in case we leave."

"Leave? Don't you wear your robes if you leave?"

"Not if we quit the order. It's never happened, but we keep the clothing in case. When a monk dies, we donate his belongings."

"Can you show me the Abbot's?"

Minutes later they were staring into a box labeled *Frère Philippe*. It contained mothballs. But nothing else.

"Huh." Though Simon sounded puzzled, he looked worried. "He must've taken them with him. Now why would he do that?"

Gamache knew the answer, but said nothing.

Before he went in to dinner, Armand checked his messages.

"What is it?" asked Frère Simon. "Everything all right?"

The monk, ever watchful, had noticed the change in Gamache's body, and heard the slight moan, almost a sob.

"Very," said Armand.

His second message to Reine-Marie, saying all was well, had found some fragile connection and gone out. And she had replied.

When he arrived at the dining hall, he leaned over Jean-Guy and said, "They know we're safe."

Jean-Guy closed his eyes, lowered his head, and gave a sigh so long and strong the candles flickered. All the monks turned to see what had caused it. And to a man, they smiled on seeing Jean-Guy's happy face.

When the meal was over, Gamache, along with Beauvoir and Brother Simon, returned to the Abbot's rooms, while the pilot was shown to a bedroom, which they called a cell. He was given a candle and asked to stay put.

He did not need to be told twice.

What happened?" Gamache asked.

"Happened?"

"Please, *mon frère*, don't be obtuse. You know what I'm asking."

The Chief Inspector's patience, normally one of his strengths, was at an end.

They'd been given candles in holders, which they placed on tables around the Abbot's small but comfortable office.

Brother Simon took a deep breath. "A lot has changed since you were last here."

Jean-Guy raised his brows. It seemed to him very little, if anything, had changed. Beyond the disappearance of the Abbot. But he also suspected that, in a closed, hermetic community, getting different soap would be seismic.

"After you left, the Abbot needed a new Prior. His second-in-command, if you will. To everyone's surprise he chose Frère Sébastien."

"Sébastien," said Gamache, sitting forward and placing his elbows on his knees. His face was mostly in shadow now. "The monk who was sent by the Vatican to investigate the Gilbertines? He's not even a member of your order."

"*Non*. He's a Dominican." His smile was indulgent but not exactly warm. "Frère Sébastien agreed to become a Gilbertine. Though once a Hound of the Lord . . ."

Again, the monk raised his hand.

"What does that mean?" asked Beauvoir.

"Dominican. Domini Canis," said Simon. "Hound of the Lord. They were the Inquisition."

Now it came back to Jean-Guy. "The young monk."

"He had a fine singing voice, from what I remember," said Gamache.

"Yes," agreed Simon.

Both investigators, used to listening closely, heard in that other fine voice the minor key of resentment.

"And where is Brother Sébastien?" asked Gamache. "I didn't see him either."

"He got a message from a colleague in the Vatican, an American, I think, and left for Rome."

"How long ago was this?"

Frère Simon considered. "It was after the Nativity of Saint John the Baptist."

"Saint-Jean-Baptiste Day," said Jean-Guy. "Late June."

"How long after?" asked Gamache.

Frère Simon looked apologetic. "I'm sorry, I don't know. Time is measured differently here."

"Did he say why he was going?"

"If he did, he only told Dom Philippe, and the Abbot didn't share it with us. Then the Abbot received a letter from Frère Sébastien, and he left. Left me in charge."

He did not look happy.

"And said nothing to you?" said Gamache, astonished.

"He said he'd be back. But . . ." The monk looked around the office and through the door into the small neat room that served as the Abbot's bedroom.

Frère Simon, stoic until now, pressed his lips together so firmly they disappeared, as his chin dimpled.

Leaving the monk to his thoughts, and feelings, the Sûreté officers began their search of the office and bedroom.

Once recovered, Frère Simon joined Gamache, who was looking through the desk. "We've looked. I've looked. Almost every day I come in here and search again, thinking he must have left a note behind. Some explanation. He wouldn't just leave us. Would he?"

There was yearning in the man's voice and desperation in his eyes.

"*Non*," said Gamache. "I don't think he would."

He brought a sheet of paper from his breast pocket and handed it to the monk. "Do you know what that is?"

Jean-Guy had joined them and shook his head, indicating he'd found nothing.

"A list of herbs," said Simon. "Why are you showing me this?"

"Dom Philippe gave it to me."

"You saw him? When?" Frère Simon was suddenly animated.

"He came to visit me a couple days ago."

"What did he say? How did he look? Was he all right?"

"We didn't actually meet, but he left that. And"—Armand took out the other page—"this was also sent to me, by someone else."

Frère Simon took it and leaned so close to the open flame Jean-Guy was worried it would catch fire. He stepped forward, ready to snatch the evidence away if necessary.

The monk stared at the page. Then, picking up the first sheet, he held the two together.

"Like I said, it's just a list of herbs and spices."

"Do you know why Dom Philippe would have it?"

Simon handed the sheets back to Gamache. "No. Most of those aren't in our gardens, and the Abbot wasn't the head gardener anyway."

Gamache replaced the paper in his pocket. "I think it's far more than a list of herbs and spices. It's part of a recipe. For Chartreuse."

Now the acting Abbot made a noise that sounded like a raspberry. Then he looked at the two Sûreté officers. "You're serious? How much of our cider did you drink?"

"Why would it be so unbelievable?" asked Beauvoir.

It was the monk's turn to stare. "Now who's being obtuse? I think you know."

Gamache gave a thin smile and said, "Please just answer the question."

The monk sighed, resigned.

"As you know"—clearly he could not resist a dig—"Chartreuse, the real Chartreuse, is made in only one place. By the Carthusian brothers in France. Only two monks at any one time know the recipe. It's been a tightly guarded secret for centuries. When one brother dies, his recipe is passed to another."

"Like a torch," said Beauvoir.

Frère Simon smiled, clearly liking the analogy. "Yes. It's been like that since the beginning."

"And they've managed to keep the recipe secret all this time? Even now?" Beauvoir had read all this, having done research, but he still barely believed it.

"*Oui.* The Church is very good at keeping secrets and holding on to its mysteries. There have been imitators, but no one has cracked the actual recipe."

"Why keep it a secret?"

"Because with secrets comes power. And this was no ordinary secret. It was first given to a monk back in 1605, by an alchemist. He said it was an elixir."

Frère Simon was now warming to his subject. For a man who'd taken a vow of silence, this monk liked the sound of his own voice. As Gamache listened, he tried to work out what was slightly odd about that voice. It was beautiful, mellifluous. But there was something else.

Then he had it.

Frère Simon's words were spoken with a sort of lilt. Almost sung. It gave what he said a resonance. Made it all the more captivating. And what he was saying was already compelling.

"It wasn't just medicinal," Frère Simon continued. "The concoction the Carthusians had been given was said to be the secret to a long life. Many still consider it that. People would travel hundreds of miles, thousands of miles, to drink it." Now the monk allowed himself a smile. "Clearly, if you drank enough, your pain and worries would disappear."

"To be replaced by others," said Jean-Guy.

"True. May I see the list again?"

Gamache handed him the torn pages.

"We know a few things about the ingredients," said the monk, scanning the list. "There are one hundred and thirty herbs and spices. We can name some, but what we don't have are the measurements. Or the process. This"—he put the two pages together—"mentions angelica stems. A rare herb. We know that's one of the main ingredients. Combined with the others, it seems obvious." Now he studied the cops. "How did you know?"

Beauvoir looked at the Chief Inspector, who just gave a tight smile. Jean-Guy knew the answer. It was because of the bottle of Chartreuse Dom Philippe had left in Three Pines. And the repetition of the cocktail whose main ingredient was Chartreuse.

The Last Word.

And angelica stems, which no one had heard of, but which were a major ingredient in the liqueur. Alone these factors told the investigators nothing. Put together, it seemed, as the monk said, obvious.

But clearly Gamache was not going to tell this monk, with the shrewd eyes and hypnotic voice, all this.

The homicide department of the Sûreté had something in common with the monks. It too guarded its secrets.

Through the window they could hear crickets and a distant splash as either a waterfowl landed on the now calm lake, or a large fish jumped.

"Why would Dom Philippe leave me part of that recipe?"

Brother Simon shook his head. "I honestly have no idea."

"Is there another significance to it? A code maybe?" Even as he said it, Gamache felt foolish. Speaking of codes. Though the Catholic Church, like most religions, was rife with them. Hidden meanings. Shorthand only the faithful and the chosen would know.

"You said Dom Philippe received a letter from Frère Sébastien, who'd returned to Rome. It seems reasonable to assume that that"—Gamache gestured toward the papers—"was in the letter. Either all of it or half."

"It would have to be whole, *non*?" said Beauvoir. "For the Abbot to know what it was? Half wouldn't be enough."

He looked from Gamache to the acting Abbot, who nodded. "I think you're right. Half wouldn't tell him anything."

"So you think Dom Philippe tore it in two?" asked Gamache.

"I think it's possible," said the monk, slowly.

"Why?" asked Beauvoir.

"Perhaps to continue to protect the secret," said Simon.

There was, Gamache knew, another possibility. That Sébastien himself had torn the page, sending half to the Abbot and half to someone else. Someone he trusted. And in his letter to Dom Philippe, he'd told him what it was, and why.

Told him to find the person with the other half. That it would be someone he could trust. But again, why use some obscure recipe for an obscure drink as a code?

"That obviously isn't the original recipe," Gamache said. "It was written recently. Is that Sébastien's handwriting?"

"I don't know."

"Can we find out? Are there samples? Perhaps in his cell?"

"When he left, he took everything with him. His cell was completely empty. In fact, I've put you into it for the night."

"Is it the Abbot's handwriting?" Gamache asked.

"No."

"Is"—Gamache turned over one of the pages—"this?"

"*Some malady.*" Simon read and nodded. "*Oui.* But why would he write that?"

"I think it was so that I'd know who'd left it," said Gamache. "He knew I'd recognize the quote and remember our conversation here."

"It's from *Murder in the Cathedral*," said the acting Abbot. "*Some malady is coming upon us. We wait. We wait.* But for what? What are we waiting for?"

"For the malady," said Jean-Guy. For, he knew but did not say, someone to poison the drinking water and kill thousands.

A plot it now seemed the head of an obscure monastic order in the wilderness of Québec had stumbled upon. Or been told about. By a Hound of the Lord.

Charles Langlois had also found out. And Langlois was dead. And now the Abbot had disappeared. Had some malady found him?

"How about this word?" Gamache turned the other paper around.

"*Water,*" read Simon. "It might be the Abbot's, but it's kinda scrawled, and his writing is very neat. Is it at all useful for me to ask what it means?"

"Probably not," said Gamache.

"Has anyone else come here?" asked Beauvoir.

"No. And even if they did, we don't let anyone in. You're the exception."

"Yes, I realize that, but was a young biologist in the area? Perhaps testing the lake water?"

"Not that I know of, and even if he was testing the water, why would he come to this end of the lake? And even if he had, as I said, he wouldn't be admitted. You can ask the Keeper of the Keys, though."

"The one who unlocks the door?"

"He mostly locks it," said Frère Simon.

Gamache thought for a moment, then asked, "Is there a file on Dom Philippe? Something that tells us about his family, his upbringing and background?"

Simon cocked his head and stared. "We don't keep files on each other, Chief Inspector."

"You know what I'm asking. Not some deep state spying, just records. Perhaps from when he, when you all, apply to join the church. Before a postulant is accepted here, the Abbot must go over his personal information. There must be something."

"There is. We fill out questionnaires and are interviewed. There's rigorous psychological testing too. Especially now."

That last comment did not need explanation.

"And?" Gamache glanced around. "Where's that information kept?"

"It's burned."

"*Pardon?*"

"In a ceremony, when a postulant is accepted as a full brother in the Gilbertines. We build a bonfire on the shore and burn the file. His past no longer matters. He has a new life, a new family. A new Father and Mother. And Brothers."

It seemed to Jean-Guy almost pagan. But it also made more sense to him than some of the other rituals he'd grown up with. Incense, for instance, and the host.

The fire represented a fresh start. They'd been given a new life, got to choose a new name. Who knew if "Philippe" was even the Abbot's birth name?

If only, Beauvoir thought, it were that simple. To reinvent yourself. To leave the past behind. If only it were possible.

"Did Dom Philippe tell you anything at all about his family?" asked Gamache. "His background?"

"No."

"How did you know the letter to Dom Philippe was from Frère Sébastien?" he asked, and immediately knew he'd found a crack in the calm veneer.

The monk looked uncomfortable. Just a little. But for men who did not do a lot of talking, their faces, their bodies, spoke for them. An eye roll became an assault, a turned back a declaration of war. A smile was an invitation.

A "little" uncomfortable was akin to hysteria.

"I collect the mail and provisions from a boat that comes once a week. I saw the envelope. It had the crest of the Vatican."

"But so did the one to Frère Sébastien a few months earlier," said Beauvoir, seeing where Gamache was going with this line of questioning. "So why did you think the one to the Abbot was from Sébastien and not whoever sent the first? Or anyone else at the Vatican?"

The monk was silent, but his cheeks betrayed him.

"Did you open it?" asked Gamache.

Silence.

"And how did you know what that first letter to Frère Sébastien contained? And that it was from an American?"

Once again, the bells began tolling. The acting Abbot, as though an automaton, turned and made for the door.

"I asked you a question, Frère Simon," Gamache called after the receding figure, then strode down the long corridor after him. "Answer me. Did you open the mail?"

He almost reached out to grab the monk but stopped himself. He watched as Frère Simon was enveloped by the shadows, until the monk became just a glowing silhouette filled with darkness.

The bells were summoning the monks. It was compline, Gamache knew. The final service of the day. Before the Great Silence.

The Chief turned. "Follow me." They headed back to Dom Philippe's office.

At the end of the hallway, Frère Simon looked back. He'd heard, between the peals of the bells, the sound of the Chief Inspector's feet on the flagstones, quickly approaching him. Which was disconcerting. Then he'd heard those feet stop. And recede. Getting farther away. Which was even more disconcerting.

Why did you ask about the Abbot's family?" asked Jean-Guy, once they were back in the office.

"Because there's more than a month unaccounted for. What did Dom Philippe do when he left here? Where did he go? He can't have had much money."

"You think he went to family?"

"Or friends." Gamache was opening and closing drawers. Previously, he'd been looking for a note from the Abbot explaining why he'd left. Now he was looking for personnel files. Or anything personal. Letters perhaps, from those left behind when he'd taken vows.

"The Abbot left here weeks ago and showed up in Three Pines days ago. What was he doing in the meantime?"

"There's something else, *patron*. If we're right, Dom Philippe tore the recipe and gave the other half to someone else. I don't think he'd give it to Jeanne Caron, do you?"

"*Non.*" Gamache's reply was categorical.

"So how did she get it?"

The Chief stopped what he was doing and looked at Beauvoir. "That, my son, is a very good question."

Jean-Guy, who'd been lying on his side on the stone floor shining his phone flashlight under Dom Philippe's desk, got to his feet.

"Caron must've taken it from someone," he said, brushing dirt from his clothes. "From whoever the Abbot sent it to."

"Though Sébastien himself might have sent the other half to someone."

"Either way, Caron ended up with it. But why does that page matter? It's not even the full recipe for Chartreuse. And honestly, even if it was, who really cares? What does this have to do with a plan to poison the water?"

And since there was no answer to that yet, he said, "Whoever was sent the other half must be dead. Otherwise, Caron wouldn't have it. I think that's a safe assumption."

Gamache did not disagree.

"We should look for another body," said Beauvoir.

Or perhaps, thought Gamache, they'd already found it. Hands tied behind their back. Bullet to the base of the skull. The Saguenay region, where the woman was murdered execution-style, was not all that far from where they were.

Was Jeanne Caron behind that murder? Those murders? Had the other half of the recipe been given to that woman in the Saguenay? Or that man on the Magdalen Islands?

If so, who were they?

How would Caron know the woman, or man, had it? And, to Beauvoir's point, how could that recipe matter? He looked down at the two pieces of paper that he now possessed. Had two people, maybe more, been murdered for them?

And why, if she'd killed to possess the torn page, would Jeanne Caron then send it to him? What was he missing? A lot, it seemed.

"We need to get information on Dom Philippe," he said. "His background."

"We don't even know if 'Philippe' is his real name," said Jean-Guy.

"*C'est vrai*." Gamache rubbed his face and felt stubble. He was, he suspected, in very real danger of turning into a fantasist. Imagining events that never happened. Seeing relationships and connections that might not exist. And wasting time pursuing them.

It was one of the great dangers for an investigator. Turning guesses into fact. Interpreting slim evidence to fit a convenient theory.

They needed to trust their instincts, but rely on proof. So far they had precious little evidence. Of anything. Even the plot to poison the water was constructed of guesses.

Still, he reminded himself, something was happening.

Charles Langlois had been murdered.

Charles Langlois probably worked for Jeanne Caron.

Charles Langlois had obviously found something out. Something so dangerous he had to be killed.

Charles Langlois studied water security. And what needed to be more secure than drinking water? Ergo . . .

These were not unreasonable leaps. This was not complete fantasy.

Armand looked over and saw Jean-Guy going through the contents of a basket.

"Those are just the architectural drawings for the abbey," said Gamache. He knew that from the first time they visited Saint-Gilbert-Entre-les-Loups. "Leave them."

Still, Beauvoir unrolled a couple of scrolls, and sure enough, there were drawings, made centuries ago in a careful hand. They weren't just plans, they were works of art.

"*Patron*."

Gamache, knowing that tone, stopped his own search and looked over.

Jean-Guy was holding a scroll. It was paper, not vellum. Both investigators recognized the type of paper. There were similar ones on the walls of their homicide department, and in every incident room when investigating a murder. The Sûreté du Québec ordered them by the truckload.

"It was rolled up inside an old scroll."

There, on the Abbot's tilted worktable, was a large map of Québec. It had creases in it, as though it had at one time been folded.

This map was stamped *Ministère de l'Environnement du Québec*. And on it were handwritten notes in red ink.

Chief Inspector Gamache put on his reading glasses, and both he and Beauvoir brought their phone flashlights close.

The corners of the map were torn, where it had been ripped in haste off a wall. They were pretty sure where those corners could be found.

Gamache's index finger hovered above the paper as he traced an invisible line from Montréal, up, up. Past the deep green of forests and white of human settlement. He went along the blue of snaking rivers and over lakes. Until he stopped.

The monastery was not shown, but Gamache knew that where his finger hovered was exactly where they stood.

And right there, over what would be the monastery of Saint-Gilbert-Entre-les-Loups, was an asterisk. In bright red ink, like a splotch of blood.

The two officers stared at each other. Both knew what this find meant. But barely dared believe it.

"He was here," said Jean-Guy, in a whisper. "Charles Langlois was here. He brought this map with him. To hide it."

Gamache nodded. It seemed a reasonable leap, onto fairly solid ground.

This, finally, was evidence. Of what, he wasn't yet sure. But they'd find out. And if Langlois brought this map, what else had he given the Abbot for safekeeping?

Soft voices, deep and rhythmic, drifted through the open door and filled the air around them so that it felt as though they were breathing in the prayers of the monks.

Armand inhaled deeply. He'd need all the help, all the prayers, he could get.

# CHAPTER 21

Compline was long over and the Great Silence had descended on the abbey of Saint-Gilbert-Entre-les-Loups, broken only by the far-off cry of a loon and the whispered conversation of two homicide investigators.

Armand and Jean-Guy sat on the narrow cot in Armand's cell, backs against the stone wall, knees up, stocking feet lifted off the cold stone floor and resting on the rough blanket. A board of cheeses and sliced apples Jean-Guy had pilfered from the kitchen was on the bed between them.

"There's no way Frère Simon could know that the letter to Sébastien was from an American, or the one to the Abbot was from Sébastien, unless he read them," said Armand.

"He opened the mail."

"I think he probably made a habit of it. In a closed community secrets are powerful. He said it himself."

"You think he used what he found in the letters against the others?"

"I'm not sure. How does he strike you?"

Jean-Guy chose a piece of crumbly blue cheese and considered the question.

"I want to say he seems sly, but I actually don't think he is. I think if he lived anywhere else but here he probably wouldn't sneak around reading mail. Wouldn't need to. Maybe he's just hungry for anything new. For news. So he opens the mail. Not to manipulate, maybe not even for power, but really just curiosity about the outside world. I'd probably do the same, eventually."

Armand nodded. He could see the circumstances where he might be driven to it too. Desperate for anything that could stimulate the mind. These monks were supposed to be beyond that, but were, finally, human.

"What could've been in that first letter to get Sébastien to leave?" asked Jean-Guy. "And what could he have written to Dom Philippe to get the Abbot to go?"

Armand took a piece of soft cheese and placed it on a wedge of sweet apple. This was just about his favorite part of any investigation. Tossing around ideas. Building on each other's thoughts.

"It was from an American monk or priest," said Armand. "Now assigned to the Vatican."

"There must be lots."

"Probably, but I expect this one would be a Dominican. Probably someone Sébastien knew from his own time there. So that narrows it down. We need to find Sébastien."

"Right. I'll do that."

Beauvoir was feeling better. There was finally a clear path forward. Something concrete to do. Find this Frère Sébastien, the Hound of the Lord, and most of their questions would be answered.

"If Charles Langlois brought the map here," he said, "then he probably also brought his notes and laptop. To hide."

"I think so too. But the monastery is far too big for us to search the whole place ourselves. And even if we could, we need to get back to Montréal to continue the investigation."

He could feel the tension rise in him. Time was draining away.

"So what do we do? Get a warrant and call in a team?"

"We'll have to. If Brother Simon is holding out on us and knows where the items are, then maybe the threat of an all-out search by police will be enough for him to hand them over. If not, we take him with us."

"You'd arrest him?"

"For obstructing our investigation. Charge won't stick, but he has information we need."

Jean-Guy slid a look at the Chief Inspector. What he saw was a determined, and very worried, man.

"But why wouldn't he just give us the stuff?"

"I don't know. You asked him if anyone else had been here, and he said no. It looks like someone had."

Gamache nodded toward the map, now spread on the stone floor and held in place by a shoe on each corner.

The notes Langlois had scribbled on it made no sense to either of them. A marine biologist could probably decipher them, but homicide investigators could not.

Jean-Guy had sent off photos of the map to Lacoste. Or at least tried. The email and attachments were in limbo.

"Langlois wasn't necessarily here," said Gamache. "He might have mailed the map to the Abbot."

"Along with his notes and laptop?"

It seemed unlikely. The most likely was that the young biologist had come to the monastery and given the map and notes to the Abbot, for safekeeping. Dom Philippe had rolled the map up inside an older scroll no one had looked at in centuries.

Which meant the map was important. Vital even.

It was maddening. To know they were almost certainly staring at the answer. But without knowing the question.

And where were the laptop and notebooks?

"There must be a reason Langlois would come here, of all places," said Beauvoir. "He must've known the Abbot, and known he'd help. There's some connection."

There was that word again. *Connection.*

It felt to Gamache as though they were caught in a web of invisible threads. And getting all tangled up.

"But Langlois knew Jeanne Caron," said Beauvoir. "Does that mean the Abbot does too?"

"Not necessarily." But . . . it was possible.

"You have to admit," said Jean-Guy, looking around. "It's a pretty damned good hiding place. It's like a fortress, and there's no way anyone's getting in without the monks' permission. And they never give that."

It was true. Almost.

"We got in. And they'd have to let in a team with a search warrant. Jesus." Armand stared at Beauvoir. "I was actually considering doing that. What was I thinking? I can't order a search of the place."

It took Jean-Guy a moment to understand what Gamache was saying. "Shit. If there are collaborators high up in the Sûreté, this would play right into their hands. We'd give them the key to the monastery, and practically hand them the laptop and notebooks. So what do we do?"

"Do we trust the monks?"

Jean-Guy knew what the Chief was proposing. And he knew how much might be riding on his answer.

"Yes. I trust them. Even Simon. He has his faults, but then, so do you."

Armand gave one burst of laughter at that unexpected, but quite accurate, dig. His amusement was absorbed by the walls, to join the centuries of notes and neumes. To become part of the abbey of Saint-Gilbert-Entre-les-Loups.

"We get the monks to search," said Jean-Guy.

"Exactly. I wish we knew when Langlois was here."

"Wait a minute." Beauvoir reached for his phone. "I got Langlois's travel schedule from AQB. I doubt he'd put down that he'd come to the monastery, but . . ."

His voice petered out as he read the document he'd downloaded. Then he got off the bed and knelt beside the map.

"These are dates, *patron*. He wrote other stuff too, but some are the dates when he visited certain sites. Look."

He handed his phone to the Chief, who compared the travel schedule with the notes on the map. The reason they hadn't immediately realized they were dates was because Langlois had written them in a strange way. Instead of putting slashes or even dots between day, month, year, he'd just written down the numbers without a divide.

Once Jean-Guy had seen it, they were able to correlate. Dates and locations. There was no date attached to the lake with the monastery, and it was not on the research schedule he'd submitted to AQB.

"Look here, *patron*. The most recent date was last week. Just days before he was killed."

Gamache bent over the map to study the lake. It was unremarkable. Nothing on it except the monastery. No other settlement. No industry. He wondered what could have taken Langlois there.

"There're more numbers and letters," said Jean-Guy, also leaning close to the map and looking at the notes Charles had written.

"Maybe the results of his water tests," said Gamache, getting up from crouching with a slight groan. "We need sleep. It'll be an early morning. Leave that." He stopped Beauvoir from rolling up the map. "It's fine where it is."

They put Bibles on the corners vacated by Jean-Guy's shoes, and the younger man left. With the cheese.

Armand blew out his candle and lay down on the surprisingly comfortable bed. There were no outlets in their cells, so no way to charge their phones or laptops.

His phone was down to 32 percent. Each use must be not just important, but vital. Armand wrote *Bonne nuit. Je t'aime* to Reine-Marie and sent it into limbo with a heart attached.

Then, by the glow of the phone, he did one more vital thing. He reread her message. The one that had come in after she'd received his, reassuring her that they were safe.

*Oh, thank God* was followed by a heart and *Je t'aime*.

Clicking the phone off, the small room descended into complete darkness.

Into the Great Silence he whispered, "*Je t'aime*."

The next morning, as day broke, Jean-Guy and Armand stood on the shores of the lake and watched the pilot checking out the plane. It wasn't yet light enough to fly, but he was clearly anxious to get away.

"He'd better not leave without us."

"I thought you were taking the vow," said Armand.

"If they'd had those little chocolate-covered blueberries, absolutely. But since they don't . . ."

Armand smiled.

As so often happened after a fierce storm, the new day was calm, the lake a mirror. There was, at that early hour, the softest mauve in the east. The lake was disturbed here and there by fish just breaking the surface to grab insects.

The air smelled fresh and clean and slightly musky from the mud of the shore, and the damp moss, and the pine needles.

Lauds, the office of the monastic day that signaled dawn, had just begun.

Standing on the shore, it was possible for Armand to believe that it was not just a new day, but that the world itself was young. Unspoiled. That nothing bad, nothing terrible, nothing catastrophic was planned.

That it did not fall to him to stop it.

Jean-Guy bent down and carefully selected a stone; then, as he tossed it, he counted. Five skips disturbed the calm lake. "Tell me about the wolf."

The wolf.

Armand barely slept that night. His cell was chilly, and he found himself curled into a tight ball, clutching the thin blanket to conserve body heat. He looked over at his jacket on the chair but couldn't bring himself to get up and get it to spread it on top of him. He fell into a fitful sleep and awoke after a few hours. Lying in the darkness for a couple of minutes, he finally surrendered to the inevitable and got up.

After taking a lukewarm shower, he dressed quickly, grateful for the heavy sweater Reine-Marie had stuffed into his satchel at the last minute. He turned on his flashlight and stared down at the map that all but covered the stone floor of his cell, in the hopes that some inspiration would strike him. It did not.

Turning off the light, he placed the now rolled-up map behind his satchel under the bed. A not-very-effective hiding place, but the only one available. Which was exactly what made it not a hiding place at all.

Heaving himself to his feet with the help of a hand on the bed and a muffled groan, he left the cell. After a few steps down the dark corridor, he returned to his room, grabbed the map, and took it with him. He also put the two halves of the Chartreuse recipe in his pocket.

As he walked, Armand dragged his hand along the rough stone wall. For equilibrium. It was disorienting to be in complete darkness and utter silence.

Instead of turning on his phone flashlight, he allowed his eyes to adjust. It was, he thought, a sort of metaphor. How easily humans could adjust to darkness. To dark thoughts and darker deeds. Until, finally, the darkness became normal. And they no longer missed, or looked for, or trusted, the light.

It was a survival instinct, but not always one of the more laudable.

Even this place was not immune. The specter of the Inquisition haunted Saint-Gilbert. If so-called men of God could turn a blind eye to those atrocities, and so much more, then anything could be done, by anyone.

Including poisoning drinking water, murdering tens of thousands.

"*Some malady is coming upon us,*" Armand muttered, as he walked. "*We wait. We wait.*"

He was pretty sure the wait was almost over.

He wasn't ready. He did not have enough answers. He could not see clearly. Armand suppressed the urge to run off in all directions. To send out half-baked orders to his team.

After getting lost once, he found the corridor that led to the huge doors. That led outside. Once there, he ran his hand over the smooth wood, then the stone on either side. Hoping to find a key hanging there.

Then he looked over at the small opening in the stone wall where there was a desk, a narrow bed, and a sleeping monk.

The Keeper of the Keys.

Gamache decided to risk it. Turning on his phone flashlight, he stepped over to the opening and shone it on the wall, where he thought the key—

"What's going on?" A voice, not as groggy as you'd expect, called out. The Keeper of the Keys sat up in bed as Armand quickly clicked off the light. "What time is it?" The monk grabbed for his glasses. "Am I late? I don't hear bells."

"*Non, non. Désolé.* It's only four in the morning. I was wondering if I could go out for a walk."

"A walk?" It was as though the man had never heard of such a thing. The Keeper struck a match and peered at the stranger. "Who are you? Wait, I remember. You're the police."

"Yes. I'd like some fresh air," said Gamache. "Do you mind?"

The Keeper of the Keys looked unsure. Clearly this was a unique, and unwelcome, request.

He lit his candle; then, getting up, he faced Gamache. The man was short and plump. His head was shaved, his face smooth, and his eyes very blue. It was difficult to tell his age, but Gamache estimated about forty, maybe fifty. Perhaps sixty.

The monk grunted and reached for a huge black wrought iron key that hung beside his bed.

As the huge door swung open, Armand paused on the threshold. "I'm wondering if a young man visited here recently."

"No."

"You get mail once a week."

"Yes."

"What do you do with it?"

"I give it to Frère Simon."

"Did the Abbot receive much mail?"

"*Non.*"

"Do you remember one, maybe more, from the Vatican?"

His brows rose. "No. Why would the Pope write us?"

"Not necessarily the Pope. Just anyone in the Vatican."

The Keeper shook his head.

"Can you remember where any of his mail came from?"

"I didn't look."

"Is that true?" Gamache asked, gently.

It seemed reasonable to think that the Keeper would at least glance at any return addresses, and certainly any intricate crests on an envelope. Surely their vows did not forbid curiosity, even if they could.

"Most don't have return addresses," the Keeper admitted. "I can't remember the Abbot's mail having any."

"And nothing from the Vatican?"

The Keeper smiled and with that smile he became fully human. "I'd have remembered."

"*Merci.*"

Armand heard the door swing shut behind him, then the key turn. He was now locked out. Or was it in? In the world. Out of the cloister.

The sun wasn't yet even a suggestion. Instead, the night sky was splayed with stars, from horizon to horizon. Armand looked up and took a deep breath of the cool fresh air, and thought of Reine-Marie and his family, asleep at home, safe at home, under the same stars.

He'd planned to sit on a large flat stone on the shore and look out at the calm lake, perhaps even dangle his bruised foot in the cold water, and think about next steps. Once back in Montréal, they'd have to move quickly and decisively.

But instead of sitting, Armand remembered the advice of Saint Augustine. *It is solved by walking.* And so, Armand Gamache went for a walk.

He took the narrow dirt path away from the lake and into the woods. It was dark, but far less disorienting than the complete silence of the abbey. It reminded him of early-morning strolls in the woods outside Three Pines with Reine-Marie and the dogs, and Gracie.

His hands behind his back holding the rolled-up map, and his head bowed slightly, Armand walked and thought. And thought. And . . .

A thought came to him.

Frère Simon had said a letter had arrived for Sébastien, from the Vatican. And then one for Dom Philippe a few weeks later from Sébastien, also on Vatican stationary. Simon was sure about that. Even if he hadn't opened the letter, the emblem on the envelope would have been unmissable.

And yet the Keeper of the Keys had said there'd been no such letters.

Which meant either the Keeper was lying, or Simon was lying, or—

There was a sound off to his right. He stopped to look but couldn't see anything.

Then he heard it again. Movement. Being used to the sounds of a forest, Armand was not alarmed. But then he heard something else that made him freeze.

A low growl.

Slowly, carefully, taking out his phone, Armand dropped the map and put on the flashlight. Two bright eyes were staring at him, not twenty meters away.

There was another, deeper, longer guttural growl.

Armand's heart leaped in his chest and sweat broke out on his forehead.

It was a wolf.

He put his arms out wide, making himself appear as big as possible. Perhaps the light from his phone would blind it. Or at least scare it away.

But the creature was made of sterner stuff.

The wolf took one slow, careful, almost delicate step forward. Then another. So close now Armand could see its raised hackles and the yellow of its bared teeth.

Their eyes locked. Do you stare into the eyes of a wild animal? Or look away? Should he growl back?

He had no idea. But he'd better decide quickly.

This would not be solved by walking. Or even running. Saint Augustine suddenly seemed not so brilliant. *Nor*, thought Armand, *am I*. If he died now, it wouldn't be the wolf's fault. He'd have been killed by stupidity.

*Idiot, idiot, idiot.* He hoped that was not going to be his last thought. *Idiot.*

Then both man and wolf turned their heads, at another sound. Something else was approaching. Something even bigger. *Oh, God*, thought Armand. *It's a bear.*

"*Patron?*"

The wolf turned back to Armand, gave another low growl, then bounded off into the thick forest.

"Armand?" said Jean-Guy, approaching through the woods. "Was that a coyote?"

"A wolf." He was panting as though he'd run a great distance and realized he'd been holding his breath.

"Fucking hell." Jean-Guy placed his hand on his holster and stared into the forest, but it was too dark to see anything. "Let's get out of here."

Gamache scooped up the map. Then they quickly retraced their steps, glancing behind them now and then.

"What're you doing out here anyway?"

"Thinking."

"Not very clearly. This is what happens when you think too much," said Jean-Guy. "I'll never be eaten by wolves."

Armand gave a small laugh, then fell silent. After a few steps Jean-Guy looked at him. "What is it?"

"I'm remembering a story Dom Philippe told me, about how the monastery got its name."

"Yes, it now seems obvious. Saint Gilbert Among the Wolves."

Jean-Guy had mistranslated the name of the monastery, Saint-Gilbert-Entre-les-Loups. A common mistake, and one Armand didn't feel the need to correct. He glanced behind them again, but there was no sign they were being followed. Hunted.

"At least it's not called Saint Gilbert Eaten by Wolves," said Jean-Guy.

Armand laughed again, though with an edge of nerves. "True. That would've been worrisome, though at least a warning."

Jean-Guy muttered something about not needing a warning.

"Before coming out, I spoke to the Keeper of the Keys," said Armand. "He insists that no letters came from the Vatican."

"But Frère Simon said—"

"Yes."

"One of them's lying."

"Or not," said Gamache.

"What do you mean?"

They were out of the woods and heading for the monastery when they heard the first deep toll.

"Damn." Gamache started toward the huge doors, but Jean-Guy got there first. Picking up the iron bar, he pounded.

Nothing. He hit it again.

"Lauds," said Gamache.

"That's not the word that comes to my mind," said Jean-Guy, dropping the iron rod.

"It's the first service. The monk must've gone to it."

"And locked us out. How long will it last?"

"Twenty minutes or so."

As the solemn bells stopped and the last toll drifted over the lake and into the dark forest, the first rays of the sun struck the monastery. Only then did they notice the pilot on the dock checking out the plane.

"He'd better not leave without us," said Jean-Guy.

As they walked toward the rocky shore, Jean-Guy made sure to place himself between Armand and the forest, in case the wolf returned.

"I thought you were taking the vow," said Armand.

"If they'd had those little chocolate-covered blueberries, absolutely. But since they don't . . ."

Jean-Guy picked up a stone, examined it, then he skipped it across the lake. "One, two . . ." He counted five skips, then turned to Gamache.

"Tell me about the wolf."

They could hear singing. Very, very softly, it drifted out of the monastery, as though the building itself were exhaling prayers.

"There's nothing to tell," said Armand. "It just appeared. It was foolish of me to walk alone in the woods at dawn."

"*Oui.* But I meant the ones in the name. You were just thinking of it. It's a strange thing to call a monastery, isn't it? After wolves. Aren't they normally called something like Saint Gilbert of the Sacred Heart? Or Saint Gilbert of Eternal Life. It's like calling it Saint Gilbert of the Disembowelment. Not very welcoming."

"It's not 'Among the Wolves.'"

"What do you mean?"

Armand picked up a pebble. He studied it for a moment, dropped it, and after choosing another, he cocked his arm and whipped it across the smooth water in a practiced movement. Plop, plop . . .

Four skips. "Not as good as you."

"Stick with me, kid. I'll teach you all I know," said Jean-Guy, with a grin. "So, if that isn't the name of this place, what is?"

"When we were here last, the Abbot told me it's actually Saint Gilbert Between the Wolves."

"Between, among, does it matter?"

"Probably not. You asked. That's the answer." He turned to look at the high thick walls of the building. "Their robes are black with a white hood, but I've only just noticed on this visit that it isn't white, it's actually a light grey."

"You didn't get much sleep, did you? You might need a nap on the plane."

Gamache smiled. "I might." He wondered if he should tell Jean-Guy the rest. Where the abbey actually got its strange name. But that would risk opening an old wound. And it probably didn't matter.

Probably.

He looked down at the map he still clasped. And thought of Charles Langlois and Dom Philippe. And nosy Frère Simon. And felt more anxious than ever to get back inside Saint Gilbert Between the Wolves.

"What did you mean when you said that it's possible neither Simon nor the Keeper of the Keys was lying about the letters from the Vatican?" said Beauvoir. "They contradicted each other. One must be."

They'd found comfortable rocks and were now sitting on the shore, watching the sky shift from mauve to a soft blue. Only the morning star remained, bright on the horizon.

"Let me ask you this," said Gamache. "If you discovered someone at work was opening and reading your mail, what would you do?"

"I'm thinking pistol-whip them isn't the answer you're looking for."

"The first thing you'd do, before anything else, is make sure it stopped."

"By—"

"No, not by pistol-whipping them. You'd tell the person collecting the mail to hand it directly to you from now on. Cut out the middle person."

"Honestly, that's not what I'd do. And neither would you. You'd discipline the person and probably transfer them out."

"Eventually, yes, but first I'd make sure that person did not have access to any more mail. Get rid of the problem first, then deal with blame." He tossed a stone into the lake and saw minnows scatter. He thought, for a moment, what that must have been like, from the minnow's point of view. To have the equivalent of a bomb drop on them.

"The Sûreté isn't a monastery," Gamache continued, and watched as one, then two minnows approached the stone and seemed to stare at it. In wonderment? In fear? Were they brave, foolhardy, curious? Had the stone become a god?

"This is a closed community." He looked at Jean-Guy. "Saint-Gilbert is essentially a lifeboat. You need to live with these people, you can't make war on other passengers in the lifeboat. Any transgression must be handled delicately."

"You think the Abbot told the Keeper to stop giving mail to Frère Simon, and to hand it out directly."

"We'll find out. Mostly we need to find out what Simon knows about the contents of those letters."

"But still, why didn't the Keeper tell you about the Abbot's directive and the Vatican letters?"

"He didn't because he didn't know about them. I think this Keeper of the Keys is new to the post. He wasn't the one on duty when Dom Philippe was here. Once the Abbot left, Simon was free to make changes. I think he put someone else at the door and went back to the old system, where all the mail went through him."

"So he could go back to reading it. This Keeper wouldn't have known about the Abbot's directive, and he wouldn't have seen the Vatican letters. They were delivered before he got the job."

"I was talking to the wrong monk."

"We need to find the previous Keeper."

"Now who's thinking?" said Gamache, as though talking to a puppy. *Who's a good boy?*

Beauvoir's face cracked into a smile. Then settled back to serious. "Knowing what he was like, and not trusting him, why would the Abbot leave Frère Simon in charge? Why not choose one of the other monks?"

Gamache had wondered the same thing, but then he remembered his talks with Dom Philippe on their first visit. The Abbot was kindly, yes. Not very worldly. But still wise. Very astute. He might not know much about the outside world, but he knew the one inside the walls very well. He might not be up on the news, but he was well-versed in human nature.

"He was depending on Simon's weakness. Dom Philippe knew I'd come looking for him. Made sure I did. And he knew that the monk I'd have most contact with would be the acting Abbot. Frère Simon."

"He wanted you to talk to him. To question him. Simon's the only person here who knew what the letters said. The Abbot wanted you to get the information out of him. But he was still reluctant. He didn't tell us everything."

"True. He was in a prickly position. He wanted to blurt out what he knew, but he also knew it would expose him."

"A rock and a hard place." Jean-Guy almost had sympathy for Simon. Almost.

"We need to find the original Keeper of the Keys and confirm all this." Armand turned to look back at the abbey. They hadn't heard singing in a few minutes. "Try the door again. Lauds must be over."

While Beauvoir did that, Gamache walked down the long wharf to the plane and the pilot.

"Look at that," said the pilot, pointing into the clear water. "What I wouldn't give for a fishing rod."

"Bass," said Gamache. Water made everything look bigger, but still what he saw swimming languidly just off the dock were plump, healthy fish.

"I wonder why the monks don't catch them."

"I think they have an aversion to killing."

"Fish?"

"Anything."

"Wasn't Christ a fisherman?"

"A fisher of men. And he didn't actually eat them."

Just then, Beauvoir shouted. The huge doors were open.

"Are we ready to go?" Gamache asked the pilot, who looked into the sky.

"*Oui, patron.* It's light enough now. Just say the word."

"Give us half an hour."

# CHAPTER 22

~

"Looking for this?"

Armand held up the map.

Frère Simon was on his stomach, on the stone floor, his body half under Gamache's bed.

The monk scrambled up, not an easy thing to do in robes, brushed himself off with as much dignity as possible, which was very little, and faced the Sûreté officer.

"So, you found it," said Frère Simon.

"We did. How did you know I had it?"

"I went to the study to make sure it was still there."

"Dom Philippe showed you?"

"He told me not to tell anyone."

Gamache suppressed a smile, thinking of the wily Abbot. Though, to be fair to Frère Simon, he hadn't yet coughed up that secret. Jean-Guy had had to find the map himself.

"I can explain."

"I think you'd better. But not here."

A few minutes later they walked into Dom Philippe's study. Frère Simon stopped at the threshold. There, in the middle of the room, was another monk. Not as old as Simon, but more grizzled, more solid. More stolid.

They looked at each other in awkward silence.

Simon nodded a greeting.

The other monk did not.

"Let me introduce Frère Roland," said Beauvoir. "He was the Keeper of the Keys under Dom Philippe. *Merci, mon frère.* I'll let you get back to your chores. He's now," Beauvoir explained to Gamache, "assigned by Frère Simon to look after the physical plant, or at least the part of it having to do with the septic system."

They turned to the acting Abbot, who had the grace to look embarrassed and step aside to let Brother Roland pass. There was a slight pause while Roland glared. And Simon dropped his eyes.

It was the monastic equivalent of a thrashing.

The day had barely begun and already it was very bad for the acting Abbot. And about, he knew, they all knew, to get worse.

When they were alone, Armand closed the door and gestured with the map toward the chairs. Then he nodded to Beauvoir to take the lead.

"Let's not waste time. We know you opened the mail. We know the Abbot found out and told Frère Roland to hand it out himself, and bypass you. He didn't explain why, but Roland guessed."

Simon sat silent. Neither protesting nor confirming.

"When the Abbot left, he put you in charge, and you replaced Roland with your own person and went back to opening all the correspondence."

The color had returned to Simon's cheeks. They could have warmed their hands by it.

Beauvoir leaned toward the monk.

"We don't care about that. In fact, for our purposes, we're very glad you did. We just need to know what those letters from the Vatican said."

There was a pause that seemed to elongate. Light was now pouring into the room, into the entire abbey. The original architect monk had positioned the windows of Saint-Gilbert just so, to capture every available ray and draw it down. So that the entire building, from the chapel to the bathrooms, was bathed in light so giddy it was almost impossible not to smile.

It was like being immersed, baptized, in brightness.

Now Frère Simon sighed, setting the dust motes dancing in the sunshine. "That first letter, from the American monk to Frère Sébastien, was vague. It said that he'd heard about a plot, something so terrible he'd traveled from his place in the States to Rome. He wanted Sébastien to join him there."

The Sûreté officers exchanged glances.

"No specifics?"

Simon shook his head.

"That would be asking a lot of Sébastien," said Beauvoir.

"So much so I dismissed it, thinking he'd never leave an abbey where he'd taken an oath to remain cloistered, to go all the way to Rome, on the vague request of another monk."

"But he did," said Beauvoir.

Simon nodded. He looked down at his long, elegant hands, then raised his eyes to the investigators. "He left the next day. The Abbot walked him to the boat and embraced him."

"Did the Abbot know what was happening?"

"How could he, when Frère Sébastien didn't even know? There are moral, ecclesiastical bonds to this place. But we're not in bondage. We're free to leave. Though I can't remember anyone ever doing it. Until now."

And now both the Prior and the Abbot of Saint-Gilbert-Entre-les-Loups had left. Those letters had been the equivalent of the stone in the calm lake. A shocking event that disturbed the tranquil lives of these monks. And sent them scattering.

"The monk who sent the first letter from the Vatican must've signed it," said Gamache.

"No, that was the other odd thing. There was no signature."

"There was no way to identify who it was from?"

"Not that I could see."

"And yet Sébastien knew," said Gamache. "He must've known the sender very well to recognize him without even a signature."

"There was one thing that I do remember. Every *B* was underlined."

"*B*?" said Beauvoir. "Bee? Like the insect or the word 'be'? Or the letter?"

"Why would there be bees in the letter?" asked Simon.

"You just said there were," snapped Beauvoir.

Now the two men stared at each other.

"I think you mean the letter *B*," said Gamache, and Simon nodded.

"What's that supposed to mean?" Beauvoir finally said.

"How should I know? I have no idea what any of this means. But I can tell you that the letterhead wasn't just the Vatican. It was from the Office of the Doctrine of the Faith."

Both Gamache and Beauvoir looked puzzled.

"It used to be known as the Inquisition."

"Ahh," said Beauvoir, sitting back in his seat. "So this American is a Dominican. That would've been helpful to know."

"No, he's not necessarily a Dominican. All orders now contribute to that department of the Curia. But I think since Sébastien was a Dominican once, it's a reasonable assumption. That must've been where they met. When both worked for the Doctrine of the Faith."

Gamache nodded. It tracked. And yet something was off.

"So Frère Sébastien left here and presumably went to Rome. A while later he writes to Dom Philippe," said Beauvoir. "What did that letter say?"

Both investigators watched the monk closely. This was the vital moment. The vital question.

"It was short. More a note. Sébastien just asked the Abbot to meet him and said he'd send the time and place in another package."

"Nothing else?" asked Gamache. "Just that?"

"Just that."

"Was the letter *B* underlined?" asked Gamache.

"No, why would it be?"

"Oh, for God's sake," said Beauvoir, then stopped when Gamache raised his hand slightly. And the small room settled into silence.

The Chief Inspector let it stretch on, an interrogation technique he preferred, since most people found silence far more threatening than shouting.

Except . . .

Gamache realized that for these people, these monks, silence was their happy place. So he broke it himself. "What was in the second letter?"

Simon lifted his hands. "If Sébastien sent the details, I never found out. It was then that the Abbot spoke to Frère Roland, and I no longer had access to the mail. If anyone knows, it's Brother Roland."

He seemed aggrieved, as though a great wrong had been done him.

Gamache turned to Beauvoir, who nodded. His eyes bright. Anxious to tell Gamache what he knew. What the original Keeper of the Keys must have told him. But they needed to speak privately, not in front of this meddlesome monk.

The thought stirred something in the Chief Inspector. It was what King Henry had said that provoked the murder of the Archbishop. The murder in the cathedral.

*Will no one rid me of this meddlesome priest?*

He looked at Frère Simon and wondered . . .

There was one more thing Gamache needed to get out of the monk. "Did you look at the map?"

Simon shrugged. No use denying it now. Bigger cats had already escaped the bag. "But it didn't tell me anything. It's just numbers on lakes."

"Do you know who gave it to the Abbot?"

Simon shook his head.

"Did Dom Philippe have a visitor?" asked Gamache, his eyes searching, penetrating.

"Not that I know. I guess someone might've come on the supply boat, but if he did, he didn't come into the monastery."

"Did the Abbot say anything about it?"

"Only that I wasn't to show it to anyone."

Gamache and Beauvoir exchanged glances. Clearly if Dom Philippe really wanted it to be a secret, he wouldn't have told anyone about it, and certainly not the blabbermouth.

"I'd never actually seen a map of Québec before," said Simon. "The thing that most struck me was water."

Gamache cocked his head, but said nothing.

"You don't realize how much there is in Québec until you see it on a map or from a plane," said the monk.

"There's also a lot of forest," said Gamache, his voice calm, even. Not giving away the importance of the question. "But you thought of water. Why?"

Simon shrugged, but then hesitated. "Actually, now that I remember, it was because the Abbot quoted the Psalms. *In a dry and parched land where there is no water.* It seemed strange, since we're not exactly a dry and parched land. But I think he might've meant allegorically. About faith."

"Did he say anything else?" asked Beauvoir.

"No."

"Did he show you anything else?" asked Beauvoir.

"Like what?"

The two investigators just stared at the monk, who stared back.

"I can get a search warrant," said Gamache. His voice was low, grave. Filled with regret and warning.

Frère Simon blanched. "You'd do that? You'd violate the monastery?"

"I won't be the one violating it," said the Chief Inspector. "You will, by refusing to cooperate. You might not be lying, but you are holding out on us. You can stop a search by telling us everything. Showing us everything."

Gamache was more and more convinced that if Langlois had given the Abbot the map to hide, then he also had given him the laptop and notebooks. How the biologist came to know the monk and the monastery remained a question to be answered. And they would. But first things first. They had to find what was hidden there.

Simon's eyes were wide with panic.

There was no doubt that this monk genuinely loved this place. And it was his job now to protect it. But instead, Frère Simon had brought this horror upon his brothers. His family.

"I don't know what you're talking about." His voice was high with alarm, a siren voice. "The Abbot didn't give me anything else. You have the map. Can't you just go? Take it. Leave us alone. Please."

Gamache studied the man, then stood up. "Right. You're coming with us. Go to your cell and pack. Take enough clothing for a few days. The rest can be sent for."

"What? Why?"

"I'm arresting you for obstruction."

"But that's absurd. I've done everything you've asked."

"You're hiding something, something vital." Gamache paused, giving the monk a chance to come clean. "Go. Pack."

Simon stared in disbelief but finally left.

When they were sure they were alone, Gamache turned to Beauvoir. "Tell me."

"I spoke to Frère Roland. He confirmed that two letters came with Vatican crests and postmarks. One for Sébastien, then, weeks later, one for the Abbot. We already knew about them. What we didn't know, and neither did Simon, is that something else arrived for the Abbot. Without a Vatican crest or postmark."

"It must've been the letter from Sébastien, telling Dom Philippe where to meet."

"Maybe, but it was big. A box. Dom Philippe left a few days later."

A box.

He looked around the tiny study. He really, really wanted to pace. To think. But the place was too small, and he sure didn't want to take another walk in the woods.

He could have gone into the Abbot's walled garden, but decided to stay where he was and let his mind run wild while he stood still. His hands grasping each other behind his back, the Chief Inspector stared out the window. The morning sun warmed his face as he closed his eyes and chased his thoughts.

Finally, he ran one to ground.

"Suppose what was in that box wasn't from the Vatican at all, but from Charles Langlois."

Beauvoir's eyes widened. "His notebooks and laptop?"

"Maybe."

"That means they are here."

"Maybe."

But there was something else. Some small thought that had brushed by Armand when they were discussing that first letter.

"The American monk said he'd discovered something so disturbing that it sent him from his community in the States to Rome."

"Yes," said Beauvoir.

"Which makes it sound as though he arrived in Rome recently."

"Probably, yes."

"Which means that Frère Sébastien and this American monk could not have met in the Curia," said Gamache. "Sébastien left Rome a couple of years ago. And the American just arrived."

"So they must have met somewhere else. We need to find out more about this Sébastien," said Jean-Guy. "But his records were burned. Simon told us that's their ritual."

"His application to the Gilbertines was burned—"

"But not necessarily his original application and records with the Dominicans." Beauvoir was smiling broadly. "I'll get on it as soon as we get back."

"Good, good. It makes sense that if there's something nasty going on, a Dominican would find it."

"Why do you say that?"

"The Inquisition. It's no longer active, but the Dominicans are clearly an order given to inquiring. Not that different from what we do."

"There's a world of difference," said Jean-Guy, flaring up. "The Inquisitors found and punished what never existed. They used the excuse of sacrilege to exact revenge and gain power. At least the Gilbertines only burned paper. The Dominicans burned people." He glared at Gamache. "And we do neither."

Armand had never asked his son-in-law why he loathed the church and now was not the time. But the time would come. And perhaps sooner rather than later.

Instead, he said, "That was hundreds of years ago."

"You're no longer a practicing Catholic, *patron*."

Gamache tilted his head, wondering about what seemed a non sequitur, but suspected it was a sequitur.

"That's true."

"You rarely go to church," Beauvoir continued. "And when you do, it's the little chapel in Three Pines, which, from what I can see, has no actual denomination."

"*Oui.*"

"And yet when you do go into a Catholic church, for a wedding or funeral, or during an investigation, you cross yourself and give a little genuflect. You even do it here." Beauvoir waved vaguely toward the chapel.

Gamache frowned. He hadn't realized that anyone had noticed. It wasn't a secret, but it was, he thought, private.

"Also true." His frown turned into a grin. "Just in case."

"You don't believe a little curtsy will get you into Heaven. It serves no purpose. But you do it anyway. You believe in God, but you don't believe that going to church, or any of its rules and rituals, brings you closer to God. And yet you still go through what you were taught." Beauvoir crossed himself and genuflected. "Just in case."

Gamache nodded, wondering where this was going.

"Do you really think, *patron*, that the Dominicans are any different? Aren't centuries of ritual, of their vocation, even more deeply ingrained in them?"

"You think the Dominicans—"

"Not just them, but the whole Office of the Protection of the Faith or whatever the hell they call it—"

"Doctrine of the Faith—"

"Doctrine, protection, comes to the same thing."

"You think it's still conducting an Inquisition?"

"Yes, I do. Just in case. It's cloaked in secrecy, hiding behind incense and chants and all sorts of magic tricks, to distract. For all we know, they're behind what's happening. Turning water into poison or power. Do you think we can really trust what these monks, once we find them, will tell us?"

Armand sighed. He did not for a moment believe the Vatican, the

Curia, was behind a plot to poison Québec's drinking water. That was absurd. He suspected the truth was far simpler, and probably much closer to home.

But he understood what Jean-Guy was saying and agreed that the Holy See did not always see clearly. And often saw what served its purposes. Still, he suspected that what these two monks had discovered had less to do with the sins of the church, and everything to do with more earthly sins. Mortal sins.

"Do we ever totally trust anyone? *Non*, we'll listen to what they say, then we'll corroborate. But I think these monks are risking a great deal. I think the American found out who's behind the plan to poison the water. He passed it on to Sébastien, who told his Abbot. Who wanted to give me the information."

"But why the games? If they knew something, why not just tell the authorities?"

"It's possible they did."

Beauvoir stared at his chief as the importance of what he said sank in.

Suppose these monks found out that there was some terrible and imminent threat to the population? Where would they go? Not to the local cop shop. They'd go to the top. To the head of the Sûreté in Québec, charged with protecting the people. And to the federal government, which had the power and resources to investigate and stop any plot. They'd go as far up the chain as they could, possibly all the way to the minister responsible for counterterrorism. The Deputy Prime Minister of Canada. Thinking the head of the Sûreté and the federal leader would stop it. Not realizing they were actually informing the very people who needed to be stopped.

"That might explain how Jeanne Caron came to have half the Chartreuse formula. They gave it to her. Not realizing . . ." Beauvoir thought for a moment. "We still don't know how Chartreuse fits into it."

"We'll find out eventually. It might be the monks' own code, using an elixir of life to stop so many deaths. But for now, we don't let anyone know we know about the monks. The Abbot. We try to look as incompetent as possible. Do you think you can manage that?"

"Which of us went for a stroll in woods thick with wolves? I think we can manage incompetence."

But it wasn't really a joke. It needed to appear, to anyone watching, as though the Chief Inspector and his team were now just bumbling along in shadow. Stuck in perpetual vespers. And it wasn't all that far from the truth.

"If Jeanne Caron somehow got the other half of that list, why did she send it to you?"

That was also worrying Gamache. He was beginning to wonder if it was a game she was playing. She'd obviously studied him. She knew about Open Da Night. She knew where he lived. She'd gotten a key to their apartment.

Was she manipulating him? Did she know him well enough to know that dangling an ancient mystery, a secret formula, right in front of him, would catch his attention, his imagination? Had it worked? Was he standing here in a remote monastery interviewing cloistered monks when he should be somewhere else?

It was ridiculous to think that an old recipe for Chartreuse, an obscure liqueur, could have anything to do with a terrorist plot to poison Québec's drinking water.

Gamache realized he might not be pretending to be incompetent. He might actually be.

And yet . . . and yet . . . Charles Langlois had been murdered, and Dom Philippe had left Gamache one of the fragments. Propelling him here. Where they'd found Langlois's map. And where there might be more hidden in this remote monastery.

Something was happening. And it was all connected.

There was still far too much they didn't know. But they knew far more than when they'd arrived, less than twenty-four hours earlier.

"Come on." The Chief Inspector made for the door.

"Are you really going to take Frère Simon with us?" Jean-Guy asked as they hurried through the pools of sunshine in the long corridor.

Saint Gilbert Between the Wolves was, Gamache knew, a place of duality. Of profound silence and the voice of God. Of light and dark. Of good and evil. Of Heaven and the Hell on earth that was coming.

"We have to," he said. "Before someone shows up here to get rid of the meddlesome monk."

"Oh, shit. You think he's next on the list?"

"I think in this case knowledge isn't power, it's a death warrant, and our curious friend knows more than he's telling."

Within minutes, the investigators were packed and standing on the dock. The monks stood shoulder to shoulder in a semicircle just outside the abbey. Not so much to say goodbye, thought Gamache, as to make sure they left.

The Chief Inspector had spoken to Frère Roland, who was now acting Abbot, and asked him to organize a search of the monastery.

"You're looking for a laptop and notebooks that belonged to a young biologist named Charles Langlois. I think the Abbot agreed to hide them here."

Frère Roland, while surprised, did not question except to ask, "And if we find them?"

"Try not to handle them. Call me. Here's my card. And *mon frère*, whatever happens, do not let anyone else into the monastery. No matter who they are."

"The Pope?"

"Not even him," said Gamache, with a smile.

"Dom Philippe?"

He thought for a moment and nodded. "Only if he's alone."

"Sébastien?"

Gamache shook his head. "No. Keep the doors closed and locked. Even if the Sûreté comes calling."

That made the monk raise his brows in what other monks would recognize as a scream.

"Are we in danger?"

"I'm not sure. Best to be careful." *Just in case*, he thought but did not say. "What is it?"

"If someone is in distress, I have to let them in." He smiled. "We

201

let you in. Casual visitors will stay outside the walls. But someone in need, we will help. We were denied sanctuary once. We would never do the same to others."

He made it sound as though it were yesterday and not centuries ago, to monks long dust. And ash. Jean-Guy was right. There was a long memory here.

"Just so you're warned."

"*Merci*. We'll do as you ask." Roland looked at Frère Simon, climbing awkwardly into the seaplane. "He's not a bad man, you know. But it's possible his place is in the world and not here. God willing, he'll discover where he belongs. It's what we all want."

As the monks watched, their hands up the drooping sleeves of their robes, the officers squeezed, albeit with a certain reluctance, into the small plane. Even the pilot seemed nervous, which did not help.

In the back seat, beside Simon, Jean-Guy was muttering.

Armand turned around from his place in the copilot seat. "Are you praying?"

"Only if there's such a person as a Saint-Merde."

"Patron saint of homicide investigators," said Armand, and heard Jean-Guy laugh.

Frère Simon only scowled, convinced now that he was indeed in the company of heathens. Beside him, Inspector Beauvoir went back to his incantations.

Armand was pretty sure he saw Jean-Guy cross himself.

They glided down the lake, gaining speed. Then the craft lifted off and left the lake and land, no longer earthbound, in an event that would have been deemed by the Inquisition proof of demonic possession. A burning offense.

As the float plane banked and headed south to Montréal, Armand forced himself to look down at the vast, seemingly endless stretches of forests and water. And once again thanked God his children and grandchildren lived in Québec, where the resources, while increasingly vulnerable, were still plentiful.

Canada might not be the most powerful nation on earth, but power was shifting from weapons to resources. And Canada was resource-rich. Which was tipping the balance of power.

Where once the population had been dismissed as hewers of wood and drawers of water, servile and menial, now, in this climate of change, that description turned out to be a very good thing. Canada had plenty of wood to hew and fresh water to draw. To drink.

They just had to do a much better job of protecting it.

What was that quote the Abbot had said as he'd hidden Langlois's map?

*In a dry and parched land where there is no water.*

There were more and more of those lands, those nations, suffering terrible droughts. And while climate change had hit Canada, especially in the form of terrible wildfires, it had been felt less forcefully than in most other areas. Even in the nation to the south, once green and fertile land had become dry and parched. Roaring rivers had withered to a trickle.

Times were becoming desperate. People were becoming desperate.

A few minutes earlier, while the pilot was preparing the plane and Simon had been saying his goodbyes, Armand and Jean-Guy had stood on the dock and stared out at the vast freshwater lake.

"I remember the last time we left," said Jean-Guy quietly.

"So do I."

"I was so angry."

Armand looked over to the rugged shoreline and the trees that clung to it, then his eyes came to rest on Jean-Guy.

"So was I."

Jean-Guy turned to him. "You were? You never told me."

Armand nodded. "When you made your choice, and I watched you leave without me, I was so angry I could barely breathe. Not at you. But at . . ." Armand didn't say the name. Didn't have to. "Dom Philippe could see my rage. That's when he explained where this place got its name."

"To distract you?"

"*Non.* To help me make my choice."

"What do you mean?"

"You were right, Saint-Gilbert-Entre-les-Loups is an unusual name for a monastery, to say the least. And it comes from an unusual, even unorthodox source.

"When the Gilbertines fled the Inquisition, they ran all the way to the New World. And still they kept going. Until they finally stopped. Here." His eyes shifted to the vast forest. "In the middle of what seemed wilderness but turned out to be much more civilized than where they'd come from. The people here, the Cree, welcomed them. Helped them."

"Bet they regretted that."

"Actually, as it turns out, it was one of the few examples of peaceful coexistence. It helped that the Gilbertines had no sense of entitlement or need to convert. After the horrors of the Inquisition, they just wanted to live in peace and be left alone. Over time the monks learned the local language. They learned the customs and beliefs of the Cree and were taught how to survive. The Abbot and the Chief discovered an unexpected friendship. One day, while visiting the monks, the Cree Chief asked why they were there. The Abbot explained that they had been chased out of their home. Some killed, burned at the stake, others tortured and imprisoned. By those meant to be their spiritual family, their fellow *frères* and *pères*. The Gilbertines who were left escaped. It was clear that the Abbot had brought his rage with him, and with each visit, as more details came out, his anger grew. His rage, while understandable, was threatening to destroy not just him but the new life they were creating. No place is safe if built on a foundation of hatred."

Listening to this, Jean-Guy became very still. He watched the Chief and could barely believe that this man had been the focus of his own hatred.

Sensing the scrutiny, Armand turned and looked at him with such tenderness it made Jean-Guy's eyes burn.

"You're not alone," said Armand quietly. "I felt the same way. As I stood on this very spot and watched you leave, I could feel hatred growing. Changing me, consuming me. Dom Philippe knew exactly what I was feeling. That's why he was telling me the story."

Armand gestured toward a point of land.

"One evening, as they sat by a fire on the shore over there, the Cree elder told the Abbot something that had happened to him when he was a child. His grandfather, the Chief at the time, told the boy that he had two wolves at war inside him, tearing at his insides. One of them, a grey wolf, wanted the old man to be strong and compassionate. Wise and courageous enough to be forgiving. The other, a black wolf, wanted him to be vengeful. To forget no wrong. To forgive no slight. To attack first. To be cruel and cunning and brutal to friends and enemies alike. To spare no one. Hearing this from his grandfather terrified the child. He ran away. It took a few days before he dared approach the old man again. When he did, he asked his grandfather, 'Which wolf will win, the grey or the black?'"

Armand was now watching Jean-Guy. It was as though they were the first, last, and only people on earth. "His grandfather said, 'The one that I feed.'"

Jean-Guy exhaled, then dropped his head, staring at the sparkling water at his feet. After taking a deep breath, he nodded and looked up at Armand.

"Saint Gilbert Between the Wolves."

"We all have them, inside. Best to acknowledge that. Only then can we choose which one we feed." Armand turned and looked out across the mirror lake. "There's a huge black wolf out there, Jean-Guy. Has been for a while. Feeding on rage, on the need for power. Spreading fear and hatred. Infecting the frightened and vulnerable. Convincing them to do the unthinkable."

"We need to find him. We need to stop him," said Jean-Guy.

"Or her," said Armand, even as he saw his own black wolf lift its head. "But there's also a grey wolf. We need to find him too."

Jean-Guy considered before saying what he was thinking. But finally, he spoke.

"Are we so sure which is which, *patron*?"

As the plane banked to make its way back to Montréal, with Jean-Guy muttering prayers and Frère Simon muttering curses in the back seat, Armand looked down at the water. But in his mind, he saw the monks of Saint-Gilbert watching them leave, their black robes fluttering lightly in the soft breeze.

# CHAPTER 23

I sabelle Lacoste met the plane and was talking even before they'd
gotten out.

"I sent the photos of the Langlois map to the biologist I know at
the Freshwater Institute in Winnipeg. I didn't want to show it to anyone here in Québec."

Gamache understood. They were in the unfortunate position of
not completely trusting anyone except each other.

"And?" he asked as he lugged his satchel out of the hatch.

But Lacoste was distracted by the presence of a man in monk's robes,
awkwardly getting out of the back seat. She looked at the Chief, who
explained.

"This is Frère Simon, from the monastery of Saint-Gilbert-Entre-
les-Loups. He's under arrest."

"On what charge?"

"Obstruction."

"I didn't obstruct anything. I answered all your questions. This's a
kidnapping."

The Chief Inspector took Lacoste aside and whispered, "Protective
custody. Make sure he's comfortable. Has anything he wants except a
cell phone."

"And freedom," said Beauvoir.

"Before you book him, have him change into civilian clothes. Give
him a false name and put him in isolation. Out of anyone's reach."

The monk wasn't wrong, thought Lacoste. This did sound more like a kidnapping than an arrest.

"You think he's in danger? He knows something?"

"He knows a lot, and I'm not convinced he's told us everything. If those involved know we have him, and suspect he knows where the laptop and notebooks are, there could be trouble. What were you saying about the map?"

They listened to Lacoste while still keeping an eye on the angry monk standing beside the plane.

"My biologist friend said some of those numbers on Langlois's map are dates."

"Yes, we figured that much out ourselves," said Beauvoir. "The most recent was just days before he was killed. But what about the other numbers?"

"Some are applications for certain companies to exceed pollution limits. And not just applications, those are approvals." She paused. "The government has given various primary industries permission to exceed their pollution limits by thirty times. Not percent, but times."

Gamache absorbed this while Beauvoir muttered words the monk should not hear. "Can he give us the names of the companies?"

"He's looking into it."

"Good. And the other numbers?"

"He needs to double-check, because he can't believe it."

"What?" said Beauvoir.

"They look like approvals—"

"Yes, you said. To pollute."

"No. These are different. They're for American companies to buy controlling interest in Canadian plants. Again, primary industries."

"But that's illegal," said Gamache.

"Exactly. The government guards Canadian ownership closely, especially in things like forestry and mining and fisheries."

"But someone's giving the shop away," said Jean-Guy.

"Not someone. He has a name," said Gamache. "Both of those

approvals would have to go through one minister. The one who controls both Environment and Industry, Trade, and Commerce."

"Marcus Lauzon. Caron's boss," said Beauvoir.

*That Politician*, thought Gamache. "Tell your friend he needs to stop digging and to keep quiet."

"I will. *Patron*, there was a map similar to Langlois's in Madame Chalifoux's basement—"

"The head of Action Québec Bleu," Beauvoir reminded Gamache. "Where Langlois worked."

"That one had pins in it where AQB had done tests, right?" said Gamache, who'd read her report.

"Yes."

"Did Langlois's map match up with Chalifoux's?" asked Beauvoir.

"Not exactly. I showed her his map. She had no idea what the numbers meant. I asked her why he'd go to those lakes and rivers. She said he was assigned to some, but not all. I made of list of the ones he went to on his own."

"He must've been sent by Caron," said Beauvoir. "His other boss. His real boss."

Gamache wasn't so sure. "It's possible he discovered something on his own. There's a mark on Langlois's map on the lake with the monastery. Did she put a pin in that lake too?"

"*Non.*"

Gamache was considering. "Why was Charles Langlois there?"

"We don't know for sure that he was," said Beauvoir. "His map ended up there, and maybe his notebooks, but you said yourself, they might've been mailed."

"Still, he knew about Saint-Gilbert and the Abbot. How?" Gamache looked into their blank faces. "Okay, let's set that aside for now. We need facts, evidence."

"We need the notebook and laptop," said Beauvoir.

"We need the missing monks." Gamache stared at Isabelle.

"Do I have spinach in my teeth?" She moved her tongue around. "I had an omelet for breakfast at the canteen."

"Do you have a valid passport?"

"Of course I do, *patron*. What?"

"Have you ever been to Rome?"

While they stood on the tarmac, Gamache handed out the assignments.

Isabelle Lacoste was to search for Frère Sébastien and the American monk in Rome.

Beauvoir's job was to find out all he could about Frère Sébastien.

"But if he's in Rome, shouldn't I be the one to go?" said Beauvoir. "I know what he looks like."

"He has a point, *patron*," said Lacoste. "Besides, would the Office of the Doctrine of the Faith really welcome a woman asking questions?"

"I doubt it would welcome anyone asking questions," said the Chief. "But you'd also be beyond suspicion. No one would think anyone in their right mind would send a woman—"

"To do a man's job?" asked Lacoste, with a wry smile. "And are you in your right mind?"

He grinned. "Perhaps not. If anyone is watching, we have to do the unexpected. Make them think we're just bumbling along. Not threats at all."

"They might not be wrong," said Beauvoir.

"There's more than enough for you to do here, Jean-Guy. Frère Sébastien knew the American well enough for the monk to turn to him for help. And for Sébastien to drop everything and go. They met somewhere. Spent time together. If you can get a name, we can feed it to Isabelle."

"A name would help," she agreed.

"If we have him, then we have what we need to stop whatever's going to happen." The Chief Inspector's voice, while steady, held an unmistakable edge of anxiety. Not panic, but getting close.

"And you, *patron*?" asked Lacoste.

"I'll look into Dom Philippe. Try to work out where the Abbot went after he left the monastery."

"He went to Rome, *non?*" said Beauvoir.

"Yes, but he couldn't just stroll onto a flight. So how did he get there?"

"He got help," said Lacoste. "From his family and friends."

"Must have. I need to find out who they are. Who he stayed with, who he spoke to. And, I hope, find the man himself. If he was in Rome, he obviously came back. He was in Three Pines just a few days ago." He rubbed his forehead. "The thing is, we can't wait much longer to sound the alarm. We're going to have to tell the mayors and Premier and those in charge of treatment plants. To warn them. It's getting far too dangerous to wait."

Isabelle and Jean-Guy exchanged looks. They didn't envy the Chief. It had been his decision to wait. And it would be his decision when to sound the alarm.

And if the terrorists struck first, it would be partly his fault if thousands were killed, without warning. By the deepening lines down his face, it was clear that he was very aware of that.

"Fortunately," said Gamache, "if one of us succeeds, we have a good chance of stopping this. Find any one of the monks, and we have our answers. Find the laptop and notebooks, and it's probably even clearer."

"*Pardon.*" They looked over and saw that Frère Simon had crept closer. Now he looked sheepish. "You were talking about Dom Philippe's family."

"Do you know anything?" asked Gamache. "You said all the records had been burned."

"True, but there was one thing."

Beauvoir looked like he was going to strangle the maddening monk. "What?"

Simon, understandably, chose to speak to Gamache. "A photograph. The Abbot kept it in his cell. He must've taken it with him when he left. It was of Dom Philippe before he joined the order. He'd have been in his early twenties. He was with a young woman and a girl. I think it was his family."

"He was married?"

"I don't know. Maybe. The young woman could've been his wife, I guess. And the girl his daughter."

"Was anything written on the back?" asked Gamache.

Simon had obviously studied the photograph, being a man given to curiosity and crossing boundaries. Gamache suspected the picture was not in full view but probably in a drawer, or the pages of a book. And Simon, snooping, found it. But that didn't matter. What mattered was that in violating trust and privacy, the monk might have inadvertently saved thousands of lives.

Simon shook his head. "No, nothing."

"Can you describe the background? Did it look at all familiar?"

"They were standing in front of what looked like a shack, built on rocks. It looked"—he hesitated to say the word—"desolate."

"And he never talked about his family? Where he was from?" pressed Gamache. "Now's the time to tell us. You're not doing him any favors by holding out. There's a good chance he's in danger. We need to find him."

"*Désolé*. I know nothing more."

Staring at this obstinate man, Gamache could understand the temptation to drag information out of suspects. To beat it out. To pistol-whip and waterboard and do anything necessary to one person, to save tens of thousands. To save his own family.

He would never do it. He thought. But Armand Gamache could understand the frustrations, the fears, the pressures that drove otherwise decent people to it. As Sister Prejean said, *No one of us is as bad as the worst thing we've done.*

Armand could see his worst approaching.

As the monk was placed in an unmarked car, Jean-Guy and Isabelle looked at each other. Finally, Jean-Guy ventured the question.

"Are you going to Ottawa?"

Gamache, reaching for the door handle, paused. He knew what Jean-Guy was asking. And he wasn't sure how to answer. He leaned on the roof and looked at them.

"You mean to talk to Jeanne Caron."

"Yes."

"I can go," said Isabelle.

"*Non*," he said, quickly, almost harshly. Then backed off. "Thank you for the offer, but it's a meeting I need to take myself. Though not just yet. I need to know more. You need to give me ammunition. Preferably a grenade."

"We know that the package with your coat was sent by Caron. Which means she was involved in the break-in at your home. Isn't that enough to at least charge her?"

"She'd be released within hours, minutes," said Gamache. "And she'd know we're onto her. As it stands, with luck, she doesn't know we've gotten this far. She has no idea, I hope, that we saw her on the Mission security camera, talking to Charles."

"I hope not," said Beauvoir.

"Isabelle," said Gamache, as a thought struck him. "If the letter *B* was underlined in a note you received, what would you think?"

Instead of laughing at this seemingly ridiculous question, she paused. In that silence, Jean-Guy began humming an old Beatles song.

"The letter *B*?" she said. "I'd think the sender was trying to tell me something."

"Yes, but what? Something to do with the Curia?"

She smiled. "Well, that wouldn't be my first guess, *patron*."

He too smiled. "Sorry. Context. The first note to Frère Sébastien was from someone working in the Curia. It had every letter *B* underlined. It seems the way he identified himself to Sébastien."

"Now that is interesting."

"When you're there, keep an eye out for something that might begin with *B*. Or someone."

"You think it's the monk's name?" asked Lacoste.

"I think it's probable."

As it turned out, Chief Inspector Gamache was wrong. Very wrong.

# CHAPTER 24

~

Isabelle Lacoste boarded the connecting flight to Rome. It wouldn't get her in until ten in the evening local time. Too late to go to the Vatican. It would have to wait until the next morning.

While she sat squeezed into a middle seat for the long flight, Jean-Guy Beauvoir stood in the records department of the main house of the Dominicans in Québec. Somewhere in their records was Frère Sébastien.

"Do many monks and priests change their names now?" he asked the registrar.

"Well, choosing a new name upon taking vows isn't as common as it once was."

"The man I'm looking for is fairly young, probably early thirties."

"His name's Sébastien, you say?"

"Well, I'm not sure whether that's the name he was born with or chose."

"'Sébastien' is one of our more common choices." He made it sound like a pair of boots, or a vacation destination. "Guys love him. He's the patron saint of soldiers and, for some reason, cyclists. Considered very manly, though he had to be rescued by a woman. Saint Irène. I think many of our Frère Sébastiens forget that part."

Now they sounded like clones.

The Dominican brought up a photo on his computer. "It's in the Louvre."

Beauvoir barely suppressed a laugh. The painting showed a man tied to a post and shot full of arrows. That was not the funny part. But the expression on his face was. Sébastien looked, in a vast understatement, slightly worried.

Jean-Guy sat down and went through the records. Not yet computerized, they were on file cards. But the job was not quite as daunting as he thought since not that many Québécois men signed up to be monks anymore, never mind Dominican monks.

Across town, Armand Gamache was at the Archdiocese of Montréal, to start his search for Dom Philippe.

"The Gilbertine?" the young priest on the front desk asked. "From the recordings?"

"*Oui*. One and the same," said Gamache, at his most affable. He added, "*Mon père*," as a sign of respect, though he was easily old enough to be the priest's *père*.

Young priests, Gamache knew, were similar to medical interns and police rookies. Treated by their elders with a strange mix of gratitude and disdain. Any sign of respect that did not come from their mothers was appreciated.

Gamache looked up at the large photo above the desk. It showed a distinguished man in a red mantle over simple black clothing and clerical collar. Gamache held the familiar eyes for a beat longer than would be considered normal, then turned back to the young priest.

"Is His Grace in? I'd like just a few minutes of his time."

"Archbishop Fleury is at a luncheon right now. He should be back in an hour, but I'm afraid he's all booked up today."

Gamache had hoped not to have to do it, but had no choice. He brought out his ID.

"I'm Chief Inspector Gamache. The head of homicide for the Sûreté. I won't take much of the Archbishop's time, but I do need to speak with him."

"I thought you looked familiar. I see you in the news." He glanced around before saying, "Has the Archbishop done something wrong?"

"*Non*, nothing. I just need some information from him about Dom Philippe, who also has done nothing wrong."

"Oh." The young man went to put Gamache's name in the book, but the Chief Inspector stopped him.

"Perhaps we can keep this between ourselves. Discretion."

"Understood. Come back at two thirty."

"*Merci.*"

Chief Inspector Gamache strolled out of the diocese building as though in no hurry. Then his arm shot up to hail a cab.

"Sûreté headquarters." After a couple of minutes, he changed his mind. "Pull over here and wait, please."

"I'll need to circle the block. I can't stop."

"Fine."

Gamache got out of the taxi and went into the Musée des beaux-arts in Montréal. From the double-height lobby, he placed a call. To London.

"Caufield, it's Gamache."

"Armand. God, I haven't heard from you since you were fired as head of the Sûreté. What do you want? I'm busy."

Sherry Caufield was the head of counterintelligence in the UK. She ran the ad hoc international committee on current threats. It amazed Gamache that she had not yet started a war.

"Sherry, have you heard any chatter about threats to Montréal's drinking water?"

There was a pause. Her tone had changed. "You've got something?"

"Nothing solid. It's vague, but . . ."

It was, of course, the "buts" that needed investigating.

"Send me what you have and I'll take a closer look. I haven't heard anything, but . . ."

"*Merci.* If this is real, how would they do it?"

"You know how, from your time on the committee."

"That was a few years ago. I remember most, but probably not all, and things might have changed, evolved. Does 'Chartreuse' mean anything to you?"

"The color?"

"Maybe, but more likely the drink."

"Only that Chartreuse would not be my poison of choice. Why?"

"It keeps coming up. I was wondering if any terrorist group was using it as a code."

"I'll look, but it doesn't sound familiar. You asked how drinking water could be contaminated."

"*Oui.*"

"It's not as easy as people think, certainly as conspiracy theorists think. An organization would have to have access to three things to even come close to success. They'd have to hack the computers and override security to bypass the filtration systems at the treatment plant. They'd need someone on the inside to physically put the contaminant into the system, and they'd need the poison. Probably in liquid form. Almost certainly in some small household container that wouldn't be questioned by security. Probably one of those pill bottles or a travel shampoo bottle, that sort of thing."

"And what would the poison be?"

"Not Chartreuse, I can tell you that much."

"Good to know."

"There's sarin gas, which is actually a liquid. It's water-soluble and has a history of use. Look at what happened in Japan. But it's unstable. The thinking now is that a bioweapon is most likely to be used in drinking water. Several have been weaponized. Anthrax. Q fever. Ricin. But if I was going to do it? I'd use botulinum."

"Botulism?"

"Right. A neurotoxin. Works on the muscles. Causes paralysis. According to the latest data, a gram can kill a million people."

Gamache walked over to a concrete block in the grand lobby of the Musée, barely making it before his legs gave way and he sat with a thump.

He stared straight ahead, absorbing what he had heard.

"And it can be put into water?" He knew that not all neurotoxins were effective in water.

"Yes. And remember, Armand, water splashes when it pours out, so the toxin would also become airborne."

He felt lightheaded but had to pull himself together. "Where would someone get botulinum?"

"It used to be called the miracle poison. That's where Botox comes from. But what we're talking about is a whole other class of toxin."

"Where, Sherry. Where would someone get enough to poison a whole city?"

There was a pause. "Well, it wouldn't take much, and—"

"Yes?"

"We don't know where it all went."

"I'm sorry, what?"

"When the Soviet Union fell, so did its bioweapons program. By the time the West thought to look, most was missing."

"Yes, I know about that. But that was decades ago. The thinking is, if any terrorist organization was going to use it, they'd have done it by now."

"There's domestic, state-sanctioned terrorism too."

Gamache, thinking about Caron and the Deputy PM, didn't respond.

"But, Armand, there's more. The West, especially the States, has its own bioweapons program. It was officially stopped as part of the UN Biological Weapons Convention, but not before there was a warehouse full of the stuff."

"But it was destroyed, right?"

"That's what they say."

Now Armand stood, so abruptly the docents at the Musée looked over at him. One began to approach but was stopped by someone who obviously recognized the senior police officer.

"What are you saying?"

"It's not official, but it's pretty common knowledge in the intelligence communities that the US has lost track of some of those weaponized toxins."

"Who would know?"

"Our mutual friend. But best not to contact him by phone. Do it over the secure texts, and then meet him in person. Can you tell me more? Who do you suspect? There is someone, isn't there."

"I can't say yet."

"That means it's someone I know. For a threat like this to get this far along without being detected, it would need someone familiar with anti-terror organizations. Someone who'd know how to hide it."

She waited for him to agree, but instead, he asked, "What's the antidote to botulinum?"

"It's called BAT. It's an antitoxin."

"Is there much?"

"Not enough."

He hung up and stared straight ahead. His face grey. Grim.

The docent who'd made to approach him now looked from Gamache to the statue across rue Sherbrooke, and saw an unsettling resemblance.

The sculpted man in tattered robes was staring straight ahead. His expression filled with despair. With horror.

Armand Gamache, in the bright lobby of the Musée, was staring straight ahead. His expression filled with horror.

There was little to distinguish the head of homicide for the Sûreté and Rodin's *Burghers of Calais*.

Both were facing the unthinkable.

# CHAPTER 25

—

Gamache was met at his office door by his assistant. "The Super wants to see you. She's pretty pissed off."

Gamache dropped his satchel and locked the map in his desk before heading up to the top level for what he knew would be another scolding. This suited him. He also wanted this meeting. It was why he'd returned to headquarters.

It was ten to two. He'd have to hurry along his thrashing if he was going to make the meeting with the Archbishop.

"Where have you been?" demanded Superintendent Toussaint.

"Chasing my tail." He dropped into a chair, as though weary. "Took a plane up to the Gilbertine monastery, but they wouldn't let us in."

"What? Why would you go there?" She seemed genuinely baffled.

"Accch, don't ask."

"Well, I am asking. You took a Sûreté plane and disappeared."

Gamache was glad he'd decided to tell at least part of the truth. The part they could verify and clearly had.

"The young biologist I met with who was killed worked for an environmental group. Action Québec Bleu." As he spoke, he studied her, though he kept his face placid, almost disinterested. "One of the lakes he'd tested was up there. I recognized it as the one with the monastery. I thought the monks might be able to help. Maybe he'd stayed there.

Told them something. But they hadn't seen him, and they sure didn't let him in."

"So you have no idea why he was at the lake?"

"He seemed to be testing lakes at random for pollution. Acid rain, mercury, that sort of thing. It was a waste of time. Apologies."

He stood up and noticed the Chief Superintendent was looking at him strangely.

"It's not like you to waste time and resources like that, Armand. Is anything wrong?"

He heaved a sigh. "Honestly? I'm at a loss why he was killed. There must be a reason. I keep thinking he must've told me something, or hinted at something. But I can't think what. I feel responsible, and I'm not sure where to turn next. Any thoughts, Madeleine?"

He looked like an older man who was perhaps slightly beyond it now. No longer the investigator he once was.

"I think you should go home, get some rest. Things will be clearer tomorrow. There's no hurry."

"I think I will. *Merci.*"

It did not escape his notice that the Chief Superintendent of the Sûreté had essentially told him to slow down his investigation. As he walked to the elevator, nodding vaguely to colleagues, Chief Inspector Gamache made sure to look just a little hangdog. Not too much, but enough so that gossip would start and spread.

Several turned and watched him go. A shadow, really, of the once authoritative officer they'd known.

Gamache closed his office door and quickly retrieved Langlois's map. It was twenty past two. He'd be late for the appointment with the Archbishop. Stuffing the map into his satchel, he strode across to the door. There he paused, then backtracked and stood in front of the huge map of Québec on his office wall.

Time was ticking, but still he took precious moments to contemplate it.

Then he snapped several photos. As he left, he glanced at the framed poster he'd hung by his office door. The last words of the poet Seamus Heaney.

*Noli timere.*

Be not afraid.

I need to get to DC, *patron*," said Beauvoir.

Gamache was driving across town to the archdiocese when the call came in.

"This isn't to avoid going back to Three Pines, is it?"

Armand had called Reine-Marie from the car, and he'd heard, in the background, screaming. The sort of eardrum-splitting shrieks only children could make.

"Why would I do that?" asked Jean-Guy. "You aren't saying six kids under the age of ten might be a problem?"

He'd also spoken to his wife, and Annie seemed on the verge of weeping.

"They found the marshmallows, Jean-Guy," she'd told him. "Ate most. The rest, somehow, have ended up stuck to the ceiling. How is that possible?" She lowered her voice. "They're monsters."

"Okay, why DC?" asked Armand.

"I think I've found our guy."

"Which one?"

"Sébastien. It's his real name, by the way. Sébastien Fontaine. He's from La Tuque. There's a photo of him from when he took his vows as a Dominican. It's a few years old, but still recognizable."

"Make sure Isabelle has it."

"I'll send his file to you both. He taught at the main seminary in Washington. I think that's where he met our other Dominican. I need to interview teachers and staff and see who Frère Sébastien hung out with. I'll focus on men whose names begin with the letter *B*."

"Excellent. While you're there, there's someone else I need you to meet. I'll set it up. It's someone who knows about missing biotoxins."

"Missing from where?"

Armand had arrived. He pulled into the parking lot of the diocese and filled Beauvoir in.

There was a pause while Beauvoir absorbed the information. "I'll get on the next flight and get back as quick as I can. I just hope by the time I get home Annie's managed to scrape all the marshmallow off the ceiling."

Armand raised his brows. This was new. But surely Jean-Guy was joking . . .

"*Patron*, doesn't it seem more likely that Charles Langlois was murdered because he found out that the Deputy PM approved not just the pollution, but the sales of Canadian primary industries to Americans? Probably for kickbacks. It would ruin him if it came out."

"It's possible, yes. We have to follow both trails."

"But . . . ?"

"But I'm thinking of a stalking horse."

"Of course you are. What in the world does that mean?"

Both he and Lacoste were used to the Chief throwing out odd phrases. And at least this one didn't rhyme. *Stalking horse / but of course.*

"It's something hunters hide behind to conceal the real purpose."

"A smoke screen or diversion?" Beauvoir considered. "It's possible."

Gamache had had time to think about it, and he knew that if domestic terrorists wanted to poison drinking water, they'd make damned sure attention was as far away as possible. Like on the illegal sale of primary industries.

"Okay, but if that's the case," said Beauvoir, "and they wanted those deals to become public to divert attention, wouldn't that fuck with Lauzon? He'd be screwed. And why kill the biologist? Wasn't he set up to be the whistleblower?"

These were valid points. Either way, Marcus Lauzon, That Politician, was vulnerable. Was it possible Caron was setting her boss up? The Deputy Prime Minister of Canada shown to be involved in illegal sales of companies for kickbacks would be one plump stalking horse.

"Let me know what you find."

He was already late for the meeting with the Archbishop, but Armand took time to send off a secure text to his Washington contact, asking him to meet with Inspector Beauvoir. Then, before going in, he placed a call to David Lavigne, the assistant commissioner of the RCMP.

"David, it's—"

"Yes, I know. I was about to call you. Just waiting for one more confirmation. Listen, Armand, that meeting I was called to with Caron? The Deputy PM has taken me off GAC. I no longer have access to the committee's information on domestic and international terrorism. I can get them through back channels, but it takes more time."

"Do you think they realize we're asking questions?"

"How could they? I think Lauzon is stacking the committee with his people. I've found something else. It looks like he made a covert trip to Ste. Émiline."

Gamache paused. This was news. "Are you saying the Deputy Prime Minister is involved with the mob?"

Ste. Émiline was in the lower Laurentians, north of Montréal, and was a known mafia town.

"Isn't that a bit on the nose?" Armand asked. "If he really is connected to organized crime, would he drop by the country home of one of the bosses?"

"These politicians are arrogant. I think he believes he can do whatever he wants."

Gamache wasn't so sure. A person, however arrogant, didn't reach the Deputy PM without also having smarts and a keen survival instinct. This would be stupid beyond measure.

Though so was approving huge excesses in industrial pollution, and the illegal sale of companies to Americans. With his own name attached to both.

Maybe Lauzon was both stupid and arrogant. The two so often went together.

"Is it possible Jeanne Caron is setting him up?" he asked. "She makes his schedule. Maybe she sent her boss there knowing he'd be clocked."

"That's possible, Armand. I'm just beginning to look into her. I don't want to trip any alarms."

That reminded Gamache of his other reason for checking in with the deputy commissioner of the RCMP.

"There are six water-treatment plants in Montréal. I need to know which one is the most likely target, and who has the ability to get into the control systems."

"Well, I can tell you that. Any good hacker could do it. If it can be designed, it can be hacked."

"Names, I need names. One more thing. Are you aware that approval has been given for the sale of some key resource-based industries in Québec to American corporations?"

"That's impossible. According to federal law, controlling interest needs to remain in Canadian hands."

"Well, I think Charles Langlois uncovered proof that some significant exceptions have been made in the last few months. Could this be done without GAC knowledge?"

There was silence down the line as David Lavigne thought.

"I guess it could. GAC's a consultative committee, not policy-making. Our main focus is anti-terrorism."

"But it would need the Deputy Prime Minister's approval."

"*Oui.*"

While Jean-Guy rushed to the airport to get on the next flight to Washington, and Lacoste was over the Atlantic, on her way to Rome, Chief Inspector Gamache once again stood before the young priest at the diocesan headquarters.

"*Désolé, mon père.* I'm a few minutes late."

"That's okay. The Archbishop is looking forward to seeing you. Did you know that you've met before?"

"Yes. I remember."

It was never far from his mind. When Archbishop Fleury had officiated at the funerals of Gamache's agents, killed in the raid on the factory.

Gamache himself had been badly wounded, and Jean-Guy even worse. Both had survived, and Armand had even managed to make the funerals. He was determined to walk at the head of the cortège as it wound in slow march through the city. He only faltered, slightly, on the last few steps up to the cathedral.

Once inside, the congregation stood with a rumble that echoed around the huge open space. And then there was silence. Complete and utter silence.

Chief Inspector Gamache, in full dress uniform, paused at the entrance, all eyes on him as he removed his hat and looked down the endless aisle. And wondered how he'd make it. But then he thought of his agents. Those dead. The suffering of the wounded. And the families.

He took a deep, ragged breath and gathered himself. His left hand clutching his hat, his right hand trembling, Armand Gamache managed a genuflect. As he did, Isabelle Lacoste moved to stand slightly behind him. At the ready.

Just in case.

Then, straightening up fully, Armand Gamache stepped forward to lead those young agents, in caskets behind him, one last time.

Yes, he remembered.

The actual meeting with the Archbishop had been brief. A handshake at the end of the funeral. But the more significant, the more intimate, had not been a meeting at all.

As Armand Gamache had started down the long. Long. Endless. Aisle. With the coffins behind him, followed by his officers in the homicide division, and behind them representatives from forces provincial, national, and international, he'd locked eyes with Archbishop Fleury. Waiting at the front. Watching.

The two men held each other's stare, and Armand had the sense that the Archbishop was willing him forward. Supporting him in that agonizing journey to the altar.

Armand did not break step, did not break that stare, until he was in his place at the front, gripping the pew for support as the flag-draped coffins with the bodies of the young agents he'd mentored, led into that factory, and held as they'd died were placed on the dais. The silence was broken then. The cathedral was filled with the sobs of their mothers and fathers, sisters and brothers. Wives and husbands and partners and children.

Only afterward, when he'd seen a photo in the newspaper, did he realize his face was wet with perspiration. Or tears.

"Chief Inspector." Archbishop Fleury's voice brought Gamache back to the present.

"Your Grace."

Gamache shook hands with the robust and jovial cleric, then followed him into his private office. Armand had wondered how he'd feel, seeing the Archbishop again. Looking into those eyes. Would it be a trigger?

But the fact was, he thought of those young agents all the time. Carried them with him, every step of every day. He did not need to be reminded.

And indeed, seeing the Archbishop now brought only a sense of calm.

The senior Sûreté officer was waved to an armchair as the senior cleric sat across from him in the comfortable, bright, somewhat chaotic office.

"Forgive the mess. I can't think if everything is too orderly. Between us, I find that intimidating. Father Thomas"—he tilted his head toward the door and the young man on the other side—"scares the hell out of me."

The Archbishop's handsome face cracked into a smile. He was, Armand knew, in his mid-seventies, and as active and engaged as people half his age.

"He tells me you were asking after Dom Philippe. How can I help?"

The smile disappeared, and those shrewd eyes remained on Armand. Thoughtful and still kindly. But there was so much more there. As there was in Armand Gamache's eyes.

"I need to know something of his background."

"Is there a reason?" The voice was no longer quite so warm.

"I just have a few questions. He's done nothing wrong, I promise you that."

"Then why don't you ask him?"

"I prefer to be discreet. I hope you understand. We both need to guard confidences, Your Grace."

The Archbishop nodded. "I'm not sure you know that Philippe and I studied together, centuries ago. In the Grand Séminaire de

Montréal. I didn't know him well, but I can tell you that his name wasn't Philippe. He took that when he took his vows."

"Can you remember his birth name?"

"No. As I say, I didn't know him well. The only reason I remember him at all is that he was a strange character even then. Eccentric. Of course, his accent didn't help."

"Accent?"

"Yes. He had a broad accent and a strange vocabulary."

"Joual?" Gamache felt a stab of excitement. Is that how Charles Langlois knew the Abbot? How he came to hide the map in the monastery? Were they related? Or perhaps from the same *quartier*? Different generations, but both growing up on the streets, speaking joual?

"*Non*, not that. I know joual. This was odder. And yet quite musical. Of course, even then he was making a name for himself for his singing voice."

"What years were you together in the seminary?"

The Archbishop told him. "Philippe was very bright. It came as a surprise when he chose the monastic life instead of the priesthood. It was even more surprising when he decided to join the Gilbertines. To be honest, most of us didn't realize that order still existed."

"Why do you think he did?"

"Where better to hide than in an all but forgotten cloistered order in the middle of nowhere."

"You think he was hiding? From what?"

"Perhaps from that voice inside most young men that whispers they're unlovable."

"Not just young, and not just men."

"True. But some, when they realize God loves us no matter what, choose to build a wall round themselves. Hiding behind it for fear if they leave, that voice will be waiting."

Gamache thought of the high, thick walls of Saint-Gilbert-Entre-les-Loups.

Armand wondered if this cleric knew more than he was letting on. But then, he did too. Yes, they were both good at keeping secrets.

"Do you have a yearbook?"

The Archbishop smiled. "No, Chief Inspector. The seminary didn't have a yearbook club. But I can put you in contact with the priest who was, if I remember correctly, Philippe's best friend. He'd know more. He's retired."

After asking Father Thomas to look up the information, the Archbishop got to his feet.

"I hope you find what you need. Go in peace, Armand."

"And you, Your Grace." Once again, he held those eyes. "*Merci.*"

# CHAPTER 26

~

As soon as the plane landed, Jean-Guy picked up the text with information on Gamache's contact.

He raised his brows when he saw the name. Then checked his watch. He had just enough time for his meeting at the Washington seminary where Brother Sébastien had taught before going to the Hay-Adams hotel bar to see the contact.

"How can I help you?"

Sister Joan was in her late thirties. Much younger than Beauvoir had expected. All the priests and nuns at his school had been, or seemed, elderly. Dried-up. Stern. Angry. Tired. Unhappy.

The head teacher, Père Pierre, had worn a long cassock, all black, except for the white priest's collar and the huge ivory cross that hung on his chest.

The big black Bible on the desk. The cross. The cane.

The very smell of the seminary was beginning to get to him. Disinfectant and chalk and sweet cloying incense. The walls here were painted the same light green as his school. A sort of faded chartreuse. The color of fear and powerlessness. Of shame and guilt and undefined but definite sin.

"I'm looking for information on one of your former teachers." Beauvoir was surprised to hear the voice of a grown man come out of his ten-year-old body. "A Brother Sébastien Fontaine. He's from Québec. A Dominican."

"Let me look." She put on glasses and went around to sit at her computer. "Yes. Here he is. You're right, he was a teacher but left the seminary."

"Really? Why would he do that?"

Taking off her glasses, the administrator met Beauvoir's gaze. "His personal information is confidential."

"I was hoping you could see your way clear—"

"To breaking our ethical agreement with students and staff, to a perfect stranger who wandered in off the street?" She smiled. "Would you?"

Despite his annoyance, Jean-Guy could see her point. He could also see that she was not Père Pierre. And this was not his school. And he was not ten years old.

"I didn't just wander in. I took a flight from Montréal to get here. I'm a homicide investigator, and my questions aren't just for fun. Do you know who his friends were? Did he hang out with other teachers?" Here Beauvoir paused, but decided to plow ahead. "I'm especially looking for another Dominican monk or priest. An American. His name begins with B."

"That's strangely specific while still managing to be vague, Inspector."

But he saw the head teacher's eyes flit over to the computer screen, then back again.

"I'm sorry. I can't answer your questions."

"Look, Sister." Even to his own ears he sounded like James Cagney. "Is there anything you can tell me about Sébastien? About his time here"

Nothing.

"About why he left?"

There. Again that very slight shifting eye to the computer. Years interrogating suspects, interviewing witnesses, had attuned Beauvoir to what would be invisible to others.

The important question wasn't about Sébastien's time at the seminary, it was why he left.

"I can tell you a couple of things, Inspector. According to his file, Brother Sébastien had two close friends here. Both teachers."

"Are they still here? Can I speak with them?"

"I'm afraid they've moved on now."

"Where to?"

"I can't tell you that. The only reason their names are noted is because of what happened."

Beauvoir didn't dare speak. He held his breath, willing her to go on.

"The three of them shared a common passion. One that finally got them into trouble, and that's what led to Brother Sébastien leaving." On seeing Beauvoir's face, Sister Joan hurried to say, "No, the passion isn't what you're thinking. In fact, it's one Brother Sébastien, if I'm right, now uses with the full blessing of the church. Though at the time it crossed what the seminary considered a line, especially for a teacher, a role model."

"And that line was?" He had to ask, though he knew she would not answer.

And he was right. So he forged ahead. "Brother Sébastien left. I'm assuming that's a euphemism for fired." When she didn't deny it, he went on. "The other two were allowed to stay."

"Yes."

"But they eventually left. Did one go to Rome too?"

Sister Joan raised her brows and Jean-Guy smiled. She was surprised he knew about Rome. She was thinking, trying to formulate a reply that didn't violate her ethics.

But he had his answer.

Armand arranged to meet Dom Philippe's best friend at a local brasserie in the town of Saint-Alphonse-de-Granby, where the priest had retired.

Armand looked around, and his eyes landed on a man sitting alone. Despite the crowd, Armand knew exactly who he was. It wasn't difficult to spot a retired cleric.

"Father David?"

"Monsieur Gamache." The older man struggled to stand in the booth.

"*S'il vous plaît.*" Armand waved him down and shook the priest's offered hand.

The man was physically frail but exuded well-being and a bonhomie that was contagious.

Armand slid into the booth. They talked about the weather and the Canadiens' draft picks until their cold drinks and sandwiches arrived.

"You mentioned Dom Philippe. As I told you on the phone, it's been years, decades, since we were in touch."

"Yes, but I'd like to know everything you remember about him from your student days."

"Is this somehow connected to the death of that young man? I saw what happened to him. To you."

"I'm not sure. Investigating can be less about discovering what's important than eliminating what's not."

While Armand took a sip of his iced tea, the priest smiled. "Not that different from what I used to do. Each day people would come to me to confess their sins and ask for absolution. Minor sins, mortal sins, cardinal sins, original sins. We have a truckload of them in the church. As a priest, I had to investigate, to ask questions. To decide on the category. Which are we talking about, Monsieur Gamache?"

"A mortal sin."

Father David put down his tuna sandwich and sat back in the banquette. "Committed by Yves?"

"Yves was his birth name?"

"*Oui.* Yves Rousseau. Did he—"

"*Non.* I believe he's trying to prevent deaths. But that's put him in danger. I need to find him. And I need to find out what he knows. I think he tried to tell me but didn't feel he could let it all out. I suspect he needed to do more investigating."

"You're worried about him."

"I am."

"You care about him."

"I do."

"So do I. I think these might help." He dug into the pocket of his cardigan and brought out some letters. "When you called and asked about him, I went looking. These were from Yves, years ago, after we'd left the Grand Séminaire but before we'd taken up our missions."

"Have you heard from him again? Recently?" Gamache watched him closely.

Dom Philippe, as Armand still thought of him, must have gone to someone when he left the monastery. He'd need help getting to Rome to meet Sébastien. Why not his former best friend?

"*Non*. If you find him, please ask him to get in touch. I've returned to my childhood home. Funny how clerics often do." His smile was almost whimsical. "We were so young, so innocent, when we left."

Armand picked up the yellowed letters. As he did, a black-and-white photo fell out.

It was of a very young man, with a young woman on one side of him and a little girl on the other. Almost certainly, Armand thought, a copy of the same photo Frère Simon had mentioned. The only personal item Dom Philippe had kept from his old life.

Armand turned it over. Nothing.

"Who are these people?"

"It's Yves with his sister and her daughter, his niece. It was taken outside their home."

The trio looked relaxed. Happy. Armand thought the little girl might've just said something funny because her uncle looked on the verge of laughing and was in the process of turning toward her when this moment was captured.

It was the image of a happy family. Though Armand knew that images could lie. And that no family was completely happy.

Frère Simon wasn't wrong when he'd described the background as desolate. It also looked vaguely familiar.

Armand opened the first letter.

*My dearest David,*
*How strange it is to call you that. I wonder how long it will be,*
*if ever, before I stop thinking of you as Jean. I've decided to take*
*the name Philippe and join the Gilbertines. What? I can hear*
*you mutter. Are you scratching that full head of hair I so envy?*

Armand looked up at the bald priest, who was watching him. Then he went back to reading.

*I haven't told the family. They'll be upset. I've tried to fight*
*it. I sit on the rock (God knows I have my choice of rocks here,*
*but I do have a favorite) and stare out at the water. In the re-*
*lentless waves I hear the voice of God. Day and night. It's a sort*
*of chant. A calming but inexorable calling. And I know I belong*
*in that monastery. In that little lost order. To spend my life*
*singing the word of God in the voice of God. To spend the rest of*
*my days, and nights, in silent contemplation. In simplicity.*
*I am not looking forward to telling Mama and Papa, never*
*mind the others. I will miss them terribly. I'll even miss the*
*rock.*
*Pray for me, as I pray for you, my dear David.*

Armand thought to ask his companion about their relationship, but realized it didn't matter. There was love there, and love was never wrong.

He looked at what did matter. The return address.

"Dom Philippe was from Blanc-Sablon?"

"*Oui.*" Now Father David laughed.

"What's so funny?"

"Yves's accent was so thick when he first arrived, his vocabulary such an odd mix of old French and old English, that few of us could understand him. But he had such a calm about him. A certainty. I was drawn to him. As the weeks went by, he adjusted his speech when around others, but in private Yves reverted."

"To who he really was."

Armand picked up the photo again and stared into the amused eyes of the young man who would come to lead the abbey of Saint-Gilbert-Entre-les-Loups. Who would become the grey wolf. Leaving his sanctuary to track down the other one.

It was as though they were talking about two different people. One Yves Rousseau, the innocent young novitiate. The other Dom Philippe, the elderly cleric, the Abbot in charge of his monastery. Trying to prevent a catastrophe.

"Tell me, Father, do you have a passport?"

"*Oui.* I go across to a seminary in Vermont from time to time. Why?"

"May I see it?"

"Well, I don't have it on me, but I can send you a photo."

"Better if we have a video call. You can show me then. Your birth name is Jean. And your family name?"

"Beauchemin."

"So the name on the passport would be Jean Beauchemin?" Gamache took it down. Then he looked the elderly priest in the eye. "Did you give your passport to Dom Philippe?"

"No, sir, I did not. But I would have, had he asked."

Gamache nodded, slowly. He'd do the same thing. Commit a victimless crime to help a friend. Would he lie about it if asked directly? Probably.

He tended to believe Father David but would still check to see if Jean Beauchemin had taken a flight recently.

"May I keep these?" At a nod from his companion, Armand picked up the letters and photo. "I'll get them back to you as soon as I can."

He knew why the background of the photo was familiar. He'd been to that tiny fishing outport at the very edge of Québec, where it joined Labrador.

Many who lived there were the descendants of survivors of shipwrecks centuries past. Fishing boats from Newfoundland that had been dashed onto the rocks in storms. Thought lost by their families back home, they had in fact made a new life on that rugged coast.

So desolate was this area that mariners six centuries earlier had called it the Land God Gave to Cain.

A gift to the firstborn. The first murderer. The first to commit a mortal sin.

Staring at the photo of the monk, born and raised in the Land God Gave to Cain, Armand remembered Jean-Guy's question as they'd left Saint-Gilbert-Entre-les-Loups.

Were they really so sure who was the grey wolf, and who was the black?

# CHAPTER 27

It took Jean-Guy a few moments for his eyes to adjust to the dim bar in the basement of the storied Hay-Adams hotel. At least, he suspected there were stories, though he himself didn't know any.

The Hay-Adams had a front-row view of the White House. It was, in theatrical and professional-wrestling terms, in the "spit zone."

The bar itself was windowless. Perhaps, Jean-Guy thought, because the men and women who frequented it would rather forget about the building looming right there. Or maybe there was a more practical reason. It was private. No one could see out, but neither could anyone see in.

There was a reason it was called Off the Record. He could see by the photos on the walls that this subterranean haunt was a discreet meeting place for Washington's political class.

It was where apparent adversaries downed stiff drinks and shared bowls of peanuts and information.

Where journalists met contacts.

Where intelligence agents met informants.

They sat in the blood red chairs, surrounded by burgundy walls, and whispered their confidences.

"I'll have a Shirley Temple, please."

The waiter, who'd clearly heard and seen it all, merely asked if Beauvoir wanted one maraschino cherry or two.

"Two please."

The waiter brought it, placing the perspiring glass on the face of the President of the United States. Beauvoir picked up the coasters strewn on the wooden table and saw that each had a caricature of a famous politician. Most American, but some foreign. None, that he could see, Canadian. Since Canada, as far as America's political elite knew, did not really exist. And if it did, it was merely an inconvenient extension of their nation. A sort of annoying younger sibling that sometimes tried to assert itself but could always be put in its place.

Jean-Guy was early. Which was good. He needed to send an update to Gamache. He looked up when his peripheral vision alerted him to someone approaching.

"Monsieur Beauvoir?"

Jean-Guy stood up. "*Oui*. Yes. General Whitehead?"

The two men shook hands. Whitehead's grip all but encased Jean-Guy's hand.

The handshake, like the man, was robust. But not, Beauvoir felt, designed to dominate.

Tall and solid and clean-shaven, with trim white hair, the General would have been distinguished no matter what he wore, but the fact he was in the most impressive uniform Beauvoir had ever seen made him even more so. Other patrons were looking over and, recognizing the man, were trying to catch his eye. But the General remained focused on the stranger in their midst.

Albert Whitehead had met Armand Gamache when the Chief had been, for a short but significant time, the head of the Sûreté du Québec. General Whitehead was the Chair of the Joint Chiefs of Staff for the United States. The most senior soldier in the world.

The Chief Inspector and General had formed a fast friendship that went beyond their jobs. But encompassed, like the handshake, what each did for a living.

"I won't be much use to Armand soon," said Whitehead as he took a seat. "I expect to be replaced before long. Change of government."

"You think the President will lose the upcoming election?"

"I do. Most in this room do too." He glanced around. "But a year is an eternity in politics, so who knows. That looks good." He turned to the waiter. "John, I'll have the same. Shirley Temple with two cherries."

Whitehead turned back to Jean-Guy. "I developed a taste for it when taking my grandchildren out. My grandson tells me that a Roy Rogers is the boy version, but I still prefer to ask for a Shirley Temple. Old school."

Again, he smiled in a way that was, and was meant to be, disarming. It was the secret weapon of the man who controlled so many actual weapons.

Whitehead raised his glass. "To your very good health, sir."

"And yours, sir."

"Please, call me Bert. Armand asked for this meeting but didn't say what it was about." Now the jovial man in the impressive uniform became less jovial and even more impressive, as Jean-Guy was treated to a glimpse of the force behind the smile.

Armand had advised Jean-Guy to tell Whitehead everything.

"Everything, *patron*?"

"*Oui*. If he's going to help us, he needs to know. We're asking him to give us classified information. We can't be seen to be holding back ourselves."

"*D'accord*."

And so, in the dim basement bar, as secrets floated all around them, Jean-Guy Beauvoir sipped his Shirley Temple and added to the confidences, while the Chair of the Joint Chiefs of Staff sipped his Shirley Temple and listened to a tale of impending slaughter.

Don't look up."

Reine-Marie had stepped away from their embrace and held Armand's eyes.

It was, of course, impossible now for him not to.

Raising his gaze, he saw a series of lumps stuck to the living room ceiling.

"Were those there when we bought the place?"

"Yes, Armand. Yes, they were." She was smiling as she watched her husband's brows rise, then his eyes narrow.

"How? Why?" He found it difficult to formulate a question. "What?"

"Papa." Florence had taken her grandfather's hand and was dragging him farther into the room. "That one's mine."

"No!" her little sister shouted. "It's mine. So's that." Zora pointed to one of the many marshmallows stuck to the ceiling. As though it were a trophy.

The room descended into pandemonium. Armand looked at Reine-Marie, who wore a blissful smile.

"Are you drunk?"

"I wish. I've just given up. There's a kind of freedom that comes with surrendering. I'm going to put a down payment on a home in Yukon and maybe open a bookstore there. Want to come? We can return when they're in their twenties."

"She started it," Honoré was yelling. He was pointing to Ruth, who was not denying it.

"Please don't leave me behind," Armand whispered, then looked around. "Have Annie and Daniel gone ahead?"

"The traitors jumped ship. Said they were going to the bistro and would bring back dinner. That was two hours ago."

"Well, *sauve qui peut.*"

Reine-Marie laughed. "It's good to have you home." Her face turned serious. "What can I do to help?"

Clearly, the crisis he was dealing with was far from over.

"You're going to kill me, but I need to go to the bistro. I have to look at the bottle of Chartreuse Dom Philippe left behind."

"Why?"

"I think he might've been trying to tell me something. I'll just grab it and come right back."

"Promise?"

Now Henri, who rarely barked, was barking, as was Fred. Little Gracie was on the sofa, bouncing up and down, while the children leaped on the cushions, and Ruth held little laughing Idola securely on her lap.

The sound of his flesh and blood, and some fur, shrieking and barking followed Armand across the quiet village green.

The day was cooling down, and those on the terrasse outside the bistro wore sweaters as they drank their beers and wine, and ate cheese and pâté.

Once inside, he spotted Annie and Daniel along with Roslyn, Daniel's wife, and Isabelle Lacoste's husband. They were sitting with Clara and Myrna.

Armand waved hello to Olivier behind the bar, but before heading there, he walked over to his family.

"You two deserters"—he pointed to Daniel and Annie—"will go relieve your mother." He lowered his voice. "I'll give you five dollars to do it."

They stood up.

"We were just about to go anyway," said Annie, clearly lying as she gave her father a hug. But still, she held out her hand for the money.

Daniel also stood and greeted his father. Armand hesitated, then said to him, "We need to talk. Maybe a walk after dinner?"

"Can you give me a hint?"

"I'll tell you later."

"*D'accord.* You okay?" His father looked tired. Stressed.

Armand smiled. Was a time, many years in fact, when Daniel wouldn't have noticed, and if he did, he would not have cared and certainly would not have asked after his father's well-being.

That had changed. But Armand feared it could still slide back.

"I am. Now go rescue your mother. She has marshmallow in her hair, children under her skin, and Ruth up her nose."

Daniel laughed. That full-bodied, full-throated laugh that lit up a room and always lightened his father's heart, since the moment of Daniel's first breath.

Armand walked to the bar, his eyes scanning the rows of bottles on shelves behind Olivier.

"*Salut, patron,*" he said. "I'd like to see that bottle of Chartreuse that was given to you by your guest."

"Don't have it. No room on the shelves, and honestly, no one around here drinks it anyway. I offered it to Ruth, but even she didn't want it. What?"

Armand's face registered alarm. "What did you do with it?"

"I poured the liquid out and put the bottle in recycling."

Armand's mind worked quickly. The pickup was that day. He left the bistro, got in his car, and drove to the bin, which was at the crossroads outside the village. As he leaped out, he could hear a familiar rumble. The recycling truck.

Was it coming or going?

Opening the large container for glass, Armand saw that it hadn't yet been emptied. He heaved a sigh of relief, then heaved himself over the edge. Dangling there, his body half in and half out of the smelly bin, he began digging.

It took just a minute or so. Thankfully, while some were broken, the Chartreuse bottle was intact.

Sitting in the car, he examined the label for a message from the monk. A drop of blood hit the label, and he realized the broken glass had nicked his finger. He quickly wiped it off and wrapped his handkerchief around the finger.

Putting on his glasses, he looked more closely at the bottle. Anything? Anything at all?

Nothing. Nothing at all.

He'd been so hopeful, almost convinced that Dom Philippe had left him a message. Though perhaps the message was the bottle itself.

He was just about to turn the car around and head home when he had an idea.

Jean-Guy could see why Bert Whitehead was the Chair of the Joint Chiefs.

Even being told that an attack might be imminent on the water supply of a major North American city, using a biotoxin perhaps weaponized by the United States, he was not fazed. He absorbed the news and was quickly breaking it down.

"I'll send over a list of organizations, foreign and domestic, that might be behind this. The list is, of course, not just confidential but classified. For a reason."

"I understand."

Whitehead held Beauvoir's eyes, making sure Jean-Guy did understand the risk he was taking.

"I haven't heard anything, though we're constantly stopping threats," the General continued. "More than anyone realizes. A disconcerting number of them domestic. If this is really happening, whoever's behind it isn't your garden-variety crazy. They're clever and connected. They've managed to keep it quiet for this long. Fortunately, someone's left you a mud map."

"I'm sorry, sir, but a what map?"

He could see why Whitehead and Gamache were friends.

"A mud map. Comes from when explorers or settlers would meet each other on the trail and ask directions. They'd take a stick and draw a map in the mud. Not detailed, but better than nothing."

Beauvoir nodded. It was what Dom Philippe had left Gamache. A bottle. A torn page from an old recipe. A slight shove toward Frère Simon, who opened letters and knew more than he should.

But there must be more to the map. Other signposts to get them to where they needed to go.

"I'll see what I can find out," Whitehead was saying. "The target doesn't have to be Québec, or even Canada. Though the thinking is solid. Montréal or Québec City would be a soft target, easier to achieve than New York or Washington or London, and still have a huge knock-on effect internationally."

Whitehead's mind was moving rapidly over terrain he'd studied but hoped never to have to visit. Like a vulcanologist, intimately familiar with volcanoes, who never wanted to be inside one when it erupted.

But General Whitehead could smell sulfur and feel the ground shifting beneath his feet.

"Does 'Chartreuse' mean anything to you, sir?"

The General looked at Beauvoir as though he'd lost his mind. "The drink?" His eyes shifted to the bar, where, on the shelves, there was indeed a bottle of the liqueur.

"Yes, maybe. We keep running into it."

"I'll look, but I don't know of any organization that uses it as a code name, or any slang for a poison, though it would be a good one. Have you ever tried it?"

"*Non.*"

Whitehead leaned toward Beauvoir. "I hope and pray you're wrong about the drinking water. We've gone over and over this scenario. Contaminating a city's water is one of our top fears. Just below a nuclear attack."

Beauvoir raised his brows. "Surely another 9/11 or—"

"No." Whitehead shook his head. "The thing about poisoning the drinking water isn't just the deaths, it's the knock-on effects. Hundreds of thousands would fall sick at the same time. Civilians, yes, but also essential services like police, firefighters, health care workers. Hospitals couldn't cope. Not to mention the fact that millions would be without drinking water. How long can people last without it?"

He stared at Beauvoir, who did not have the answer, but knew it wasn't long.

"Panic then spreads to other cities as they fear that their water is poisoned too. Rioting breaks out across the country to get what little bottled water, what little food is available. All authority breaks down. Businesses are vandalized. Misinformation, conspiracy theories, are everywhere, often planted by the terrorists. People don't know what to believe, what to do, who to turn to for help. Who to trust. There's chaos. Imagine a sudden, all-encompassing, catastrophic event. That we do to ourselves."

Whitehead was drawing his own mud map, leading Jean-Guy through it. But General Whitehead wasn't finished. The map just kept going.

"That's what the terrorists want. Not the deaths of a few hundred, or even a few thousand. They want us to turn on each other. To do to each other what they cannot. They want anarchy. And they'll have it."

As he spoke, Jean-Guy suddenly realized that Three Pines was not safe after all. It would be invaded by hordes of desperate people who would do anything to survive, including killing those whose offer of help would not be enough.

"Political power, as you know, Inspector, lies in trust." The General tapped the coaster in front of him, a caricature of a past president. "The only reason democracy works is that there's a contract between elected and those electing. A consent to be governed. But that contract is fragile. That consent can be withdrawn. Sophisticated terrorists know this. They hit targets that can shatter that trust. And few things are more powerful, more symbolic, more important than water security. We're already experiencing some of that fragility, that threat, with the shifting climate. Droughts, wildfires, floods. Add terrorists being able to poison what drinking water we do have, and . . ."

He lifted his hands.

Much of this Beauvoir had heard from Gamache, but even he had not gone this far, drawn so dire, so extensive a map.

"The thing is," General Whitehead continued, though now Beauvoir wished he'd stop talking, "the attack on the drinking water would not have to succeed to be catastrophic. An attack quickly contained with almost no injuries could be enough to undermine trust in our institutions. It could have significant political fallout."

"Meaning?"

"Meaning it could create a disproportionate political response."

"Such as?"

"It could be used as an excuse to declare a nationwide state of emergency. Prompt mass arrests. The shutting down of news organizations and social media. Controlling all information. Curfews. Shoot-to-kill orders. Effectively a dictatorship."

"A coup."

General Whitehead didn't respond to that, which was itself a response. "It's been done before. It would be the perfect excuse to hold on to power."

"To suspend elections? I hate to ask . . . ," said Beauvoir. The General was shaking his head, warning him not to. But he did anyway. "If the President is facing losing, could he—"

"Go no further, Inspector." The voice was sharp. Commanding.

But Jean-Guy had stared down a nun. A general was easy.

"—be behind this? Choosing a large city? Close but not American?"

"No."

"Are you sure? Who better to hide an attack than the government. The very people trusted to stop it? And who would benefit the most but a government on the verge of defeat? Wars have been started for that very reason."

General Whitehead got to his feet, as did Jean-Guy. "This meeting is over." He glared at Beauvoir, then left.

Beauvoir sat back down and finished his email to Gamache. As he hit send, he realized that everything Whitehead had said about the US President could also apply to the Canadian Prime Minister.

Armand sat in his car in the parking lot of the Société des alcools du Québec in Knowlton and stared at the bright green bottle of Chartreuse he'd just bought.

Comparing it to the one he'd dug out of the recycling bin, he saw no difference. Same emblem. Same writing. Same alcohol content.

Returning inside, he asked the manager if she could see a difference. It took her all of ten seconds.

"One has a small *E* down here." She pointed to the bottle he'd just bought. The letter was tiny. "The other doesn't."

"What does the *E* mean?"

"Export. The one we sell is for export. The other"—she handed him back the empty bottle—"is not. It must've been bought at the source, in France, and brought back in their luggage. Chief Inspector?"

He looked like he'd been flash frozen. *"Merci, merci infiniment."*

She watched as he hurried from the SAQ, clutching both bottles as though he'd just quit AA.

# CHAPTER 28

R eine-Marie was sitting in the bistro when Armand walked in.
"So much for 'I'll be right back.'"

"Sorry. But I did send your two children over to relieve you. Forgiven?"

She looked at him and saw the gleam in his eyes. "Something's happened. Something good."

He nodded but could not yet tell her that the Abbot had not been in Rome, but in France. At the monastery of Grande Chartreuse. Where the liqueur was distilled. Where the bottle was from.

Why choose to meet at that particular monastery? It was Carthusian, not Dominican. But that meant anyone searching for the monks would not think to look in the remote French monastery, hidden in the mountains.

But the real question now was whether Sébastien and the American monk were still there.

Did Dom Philippe want him to go to Grande Chartreuse? It seemed so. But time was too short, and there was too much to do here, and it was too far to go. And he might be wrong. And even if he was right, he might've been too slow off the mark, and Sébastien and the American might have already left Grande Chartreuse.

But he had no choice. He had to try.

Once back in Three Pines, the bottles beside him on the passenger's seat, he'd sent a message to Isabelle Lacoste telling her if neither monk was in the Curia, she needed to get to Grande Chartreuse.

Gamache then pondered his next move. The problem was, Lacoste did not have authority in France. If the monks were there and refused to cooperate, he'd need someone who did.

He looked at his watch, then placed a call. "Claude? Did I wake you?"

"Not quite. Is everything all right?"

Claude Dussault was the former head of the Paris police. He'd retired as Prefect and was now living with his wife in a village in the south of France.

"Do you know the monastery of Grande Chartreuse?"

"Now, of all the things I thought you might call about in the middle of the night, that was not one. Yes, I know it. Well, I know of it. Never been."

"Would you like to go?"

"Not really. I'm afraid to ask, but would you like me to go?"

"Maybe. I need to find two monks who might be hiding there."

"There are probably quite a few monks hiding there. I can't say I blame them. And who are they hiding from? You?"

"I can't tell you more except to say, as far as I know, neither has done anything wrong. I need to interview them. One's a Gilbertine."

Armand could see Reine-Marie in the bistro chatting with Clara and Myrna. Gabri had joined them.

"A Gilbertine? Is there such a thing? And you do know that the monastery is Carthusian."

"Yes. The other's"—Armand grimaced, anticipating Claude's reaction—"a Dominican."

"Jesus, Armand. Are there any actual Carthusians in Grande Chartreuse? I'll go if you want, but there's no way they'll let me in. I doubt they even let those two in. *Ces religieux* there aren't just cloistered, they're hermetic. Only Carthusians are allowed through the gates, and for good reason. The order has been persecuted and expelled over and over in their thousand years, including as recently as 1903."

"Still, I'm sending one of my most senior investigators there. If she—"

"She?" There was a laugh. "God, Armand, you really do live in a fantasy world. If they won't let a 'he' in, there's no way a 'she' will get through that gate."

"We'll see. Inspector Lacoste is quite resourceful."

"Can she drive a bulldozer? That might work."

Armand laughed. "I wouldn't put it past her. If she can't get in, we'll need a warrant. That's where you come in."

"Tell me you're not actually going to serve a warrant on Grande Chartreuse."

"Not me. You."

"I have no more authority than you do. I'm retired. Remember?"

"But you know people who can get one."

There was a heaved sigh. "I do. This must be important."

"Beyond that, *mon ami*."

"*Bon*. Give me the names of the monks you need to find." Armand could hear Claude making notes as he told him. "So we have Frère Sébastien, a Gilbertine. Who's the other? The Dominican."

"I don't know."

"You really don't make this easy, do you."

"I'm hoping Inspector Lacoste will find out who this mystery monk is, and with luck find him still in Rome. I'll connect you two. Claude, I think they stumbled onto something terrible. I need to find them before someone else does."

"I'll do what I can. Though I'll probably be excommunicated."

"Tell them to do it to me instead."

"I don't think it works that way."

"Honestly, I don't think it works at all."

"That's the spirit. One thing to keep in mind, Grande Chartreuse is a five-hour drive for me, so I'll need warning."

"I'll let Isabelle Lacoste know. *Merci*, Claude."

After hanging up, Armand shot off another message to Isabelle. She'd arrived in Rome and had checked into her hotel close to the

Vatican. He updated her on Claude Dussault and sent his contact information. Then he sat in his car and took out the two pieces of paper.

Dom Philippe had left one part for him, along with the bottle, to make sure he knew about the Grande Chartreuse connection. That now seemed obvious.

But still obscure and troubling was how Jeanne Caron got her portion. And why she put it in the coat she'd had stolen from his home.

Before going into the bistro, Armand made reservations on a flight the next day to Blanc-Sablon, where he hoped to find the Abbot and some answers.

Ever the optimist, he reserved two seats for the trip back.

So the Abbot left the bottle because he wanted you to know that he'd been to Grande Chartreuse," said Reine-Marie as they walked arm in arm around the village green.

"Not just know, but to go there."

"Will you?"

"No. I'm sending Isabelle. It's possible the other two monks are still there."

The late afternoon was cooling off, but they had each other's body heat to keep them comfortable.

"What about Dom Philippe? Where's he?"

"I think he might've gone home."

"To Saint-Gilbert-Entre-les-Loups? But you were just there."

"*Non*. To Blanc-Sablon. I'm flying there tomorrow. Father David, his friend, said that when clerics retire, they often go home. Dom Philippe isn't retired, but I think he might've gone there for help. We all have a homing instinct."

Armand glanced over to their rambling white clapboard house, with its wide veranda, and double porch swing, and buttery lights in the windows. Daniel and Annie would be making dinner. The youngsters—he included Ruth in that category—would be tired out by now and sprawled in the living room, with the dogs, and duck, and Gracie, and fallen marshmallows all around them.

Home.

"Armand . . ." Reine-Marie hesitated before asking, "The drinking water? Have you told the mayors?"

When he shook his head, she stopped to look directly at him. "You have to tell someone. You have to warn people. Suppose it's tonight? Tomorrow morning? It could happen any time."

"You're right. But I can't say anything yet."

"Why not? What're you waiting for? I don't understand. You're gambling with thousands of lives. The lives of our friends. Your colleagues."

He was gambling with more than that. Like General Whitehead, Armand knew that if the terrorists were even partially successful, it would have terrifying and lasting consequences. Ones he'd be, by that time, powerless to stop.

"We don't know who's behind this," he said. "The terrorists have to have people on the inside. If I warn the mayors and those in charge of public works, there's a good chance they'll move up their attack."

"Or call it off," she said.

"Which would be as bad. They'd go to ground and wait. Or move it to another city and we'd lose track of them. I wish I could tell the Premier, the mayors, the head of the Sûreté. Then it would be their problem. I could come back here and have dinner with the family and go to bed. Sleep. But I can't. Not yet."

She picked up his hand and kneaded it. "I'm sorry."

"Honestly, I don't know if I'm making the right decision. I think I am, but . . ."

Reine-Marie unwrapped the handkerchief around his finger. "You've been dumpster diving again, haven't you."

"It's where the best clues, and birthday gifts, are found."

"Let's go inside. It's dinnertime. We can put antiseptic on that almost invisible nick."

"Nick? It's a slash, a terrible, terrible wound." He looked at his finger.

"Wrong one, Inspector," she said, with a laugh.

Home. That was home.

As they walked along the veranda, they could smell pasta and garlic bread through the screen door.

"If you received a message with every *B* underlined, what would you think?"

It had become the question du jour. A kind of party riddle without the punchline.

"The letter *B*?"

"Yes, the letter *B*."

She stopped to think. In the silence they heard a tiny, reedy voice. "Letter *B*, letter *B*, letter *B*, oh, letter *B*."

Armand and Reine-Marie looked around, then walked to the edge of the porch and leaned over the railing. There was Honoré sitting in the flower bed, hugging Henri. And singing.

"What're you doing there, little man?" Reine-Marie asked.

"Hiding."

"From?"

"Mom. It's dinnertime and there're brussels sprouts. She puts them under the spaghetti."

"You were also singing." Armand looked at their grandson's upturned filthy face. "Can you do it again?"

Sensing a deal to be made, Honoré said, "If I do, will you eat my brussels sprouts?"

"Don't you normally give them to Henri?" asked his grandfather. At the sound of his name, the shepherd's prodigious ears swung toward Armand.

"You know about that?" said Honoré. "No, I don't."

"Someone's going to have to teach that child how to lie properly," muttered Reine-Marie.

"I will eat your brussels sprouts," said Armand. "If you sing for me."

Honoré, whose voice was thin but true, sang, "Letter *B*, letter *B* . . ."

"Shouldn't that be 'Let It Be'?" asked Reine-Marie.

"Letter *B*, ohhhh, letter *B* . . ."

"The Beatles?" It was the same tune Honoré's father had hummed earlier in the day when discussing the strange code.

"*Sesame Street*." The boy couldn't believe everyone in the world, his world, didn't know that. "Letter *B*. Don't you know the alphabet?"

Armand brought his hand to his mouth and stared, while Honoré sang. Hoping to teach his poor grandfather something. And he had.

I am on the plane, *patron*. Heading back to Montréal. They're about to close the doors."

"Get off. I need you to do something."

Beauvoir stood up, grabbed his carry-on, and, after showing his not-exactly-valid-in-the-States Sûreté ID, he left the plane moments before the door closed.

"I'm off. What is it?"

"First I need you to ask Sister Joan about either 'Let It Be' or 'Letter B.'"

"You mean the Beatles or *Sesame Street*?" He'd heard that song often enough. It was a favorite of both Honoré and Idola, who loved anything her brother liked. "I don't understand."

"In the first message, the one to Sébastien from the Dominican in Rome, the letter *B* was underlined."

"Yes, I know. It's how Sébastien knew who it was from. His friend whose name starts with *B*."

"That's what we thought, but suppose we're wrong? It did tell Sébastien who the message was from, but it might not be a name. It might be the *Sesame Street* song about the alphabet. Honoré sang it for me."

Armand, in his baritone, sang the first few notes.

"But why would monks be referencing a *Sesame Street* song?"

"Why do college students watch *The Flintstones*? It's something we all do when under more pressure than usual."

"You watch *The Flintstones*?"

"*Non*. Pay attention, Barney. We find something that reminds us of a time without stress. When we were young and someone else was in charge. We reread favorite books, we listen to music we fell in love to. Neil Young. Beau Dommage. In your case, Celine. We watch shows that bring comfort. Allow us to revert to a younger, happier, simpler time. *The Flintstones*. *La Petite Vie*—"

"Oh, I love that."

"I bet you still watch it."

Armand was right. When he or Annie was particularly stressed, they'd watch an episode of *La Petite Vie* together before bed. Sometimes two. Three. And howl with laughter, even though they knew each episode by heart.

Then they'd sleep, with lighter heads and hearts.

"I think those young men in the seminary, new teachers with all that pressure, took to watching *Sesame Street*," said Armand. "It is as much a show for adults as kids."

That was true, thought Jean-Guy. No kid would get the "Let It Be" reference, which was what made the song so funny.

"Okay, suppose you're right, what good is it to us?"

Beauvoir was being shooed off the gangway so airport personnel could move it back from the plane.

"Sister Joan talked about a passion Sébastien and his friends shared."

"Right."

"One he was now putting to good use, but that back then had gotten him fired."

Beauvoir, strolling through the airport, stopped so suddenly people behind him had to twist to avoid colliding with him. At least one man gave him the finger, but Jean-Guy was uncharacteristically oblivious to the insult.

"Singing. You think that was the passion."

"I think the song 'Letter B' was a running joke among the three of them. 'Let It Be' is essentially a hymn, so monks might find the *Sesame Street* version especially funny. Underlining the *B* in the message told Sébastien who it was from. One of his two friends who shared the joke. And the fallout."

"I'll call Sister Joan."

I have an update on the driver of the SUV," said the senior agent at headquarters. "The one who was found dead in the landfill. I was just about to send it to you."

"Yes?" Gamache sat forward and grabbed a pen on his study desk.

"His name was Paolo Parisi."

"Spell it please." He jotted the name down. "How do we know that? There wasn't any ID on the body, and his DNA and fingerprints aren't on file."

"Interpol. I sent the information and they ID'd him."

"What's he wanted for?"

"Nothing."

Gamache leaned back slightly, surprised by that answer. "So?"

"He's the youngest child of a prominent Sicilian family."

"Wait. That Parisi? The olive oil?"

The Gamaches had a can of it in their kitchen. They'd probably used it for the salad dressing that night for dinner. Very fine olive oil.

"*Oui*. He entered the US as a tourist at JFK two months ago."

"When did he come to Canada?"

"Well, that we don't know. There's no record of him at Canada Customs. Looks like he snuck across the border."

They had the longest undefended border in the world. The only surprising thing was that so many used the actual checkpoints.

"Why enter the US legally and Canada illegally? He could have come across as a tourist, *non*?"

"Absolutely. Nothing to stop him. Except maybe his plan to kill someone without being detected. Just a guess."

"That could be it," said Gamache, with some amusement. "Does his family have connections to organized crime?"

"Well, that's where it gets particularly interesting, *patron*. They have very strong connections, but not what you'd think. His mother is one of the main mafia prosecutors and Signor Parisi has organized businesses to resist the payment of protection money."

"Huh."

The inspector was secretly pleased. She'd worked under the Chief for more than a decade and could count on one hand the number of times she'd actually stunned him.

"The son rebelling against the parents?" said Gamache, essentially asking himself. "Or maybe the anti-mob stance of the family is a front." Or maybe, he thought to himself, he was wrong, and there was no connection in this case to the Montréal mafia. Why would the mob want to murder an environmental activist? Maybe this Parisi was freelance and had been hired by someone else.

"Has the Parisi family been told?"

"Not yet."

"Okay. Contact the authorities in Palermo, find out what you can about the family. Quietly. Make sure that when they're told, a senior official who knows them is there. I want to know their reaction. We need to know anything the family can tell us about Paolo. His job, his friends, his movements. Anyone they might know in New York and Montréal. Did they even know he was in North America?"

"Got it."

"And contact the head of Italy's Anti-Mafia task force. Ask them about the Parisis. If there's something going on, they'd know."

"I'll forward what Interpol sent. I'm still looking for the woman at Open Da Night who signaled him and might've killed him."

"Probably did. *Bon. Merci.*"

Gamache sat in his study and went over the autopsy report on Paolo Parisi. Twenty-four. Healthy. No reason he shouldn't live to a ripe old age. But there he lay, eyes wide open.

Armand saw the young man staring at him through the windshield of the SUV. The moment was frozen, suspended, as they caught eyes and Gamache saw a single-minded intensity. Before Parisi looked away, to his target. To Charles Langlois.

Was the murder of Langlois a mafia hit? Was the hit man then hit? The landfill was run by the mob. It was one of many legitimate businesses. Canada was famously opaque, at least among criminals and lawmakers, when it came to providing detailed information on who owned what. It was a sort of bureaucratic cataract.

The regulations had, intentionally or not, created a haven for illegal activities and led to the remarkable rise of organized crime in Québec. This brought to mind the agreements Langlois had found to sell controlling interests of primary industries to Americans. Could this be where Langlois and the mafia intersected?

But as far as Gamache knew, while much of garbage collection, the trucking industry, construction, and, and . . . were controlled by the mafia, they were not into mining and forestry and huge billowing smelters.

Very few Italians in Montréal were connected to the mafia. It was a constant slur on the community. But those who were were powerful and remorseless.

Gamache tapped his pen on his notebook and stared at his laptop. He considered sending the information on Paolo Parisi to Chief Inspector Tardiff, who ran the Sûreté's Organized Crime division.

Just then, Honoré and Florence burst into the study. Their grandfather quickly closed the computer and looked into their eyes, to make sure they hadn't seen the autopsy photo. But the children were too intent on hiding from Zora, who found them easily a moment later.

"Too obvious," said Zora. "They always come to you. Can we play cribbage?"

"One game, then bed." Armand took them out of his study, then cheated his way to victory, to the screams of mock protest from the kids, who'd come to expect it.

But his mind was only partly on the game. The rest was on the report. The one he hadn't sent to Tardiff.

While the children were bathed and put to bed, Armand was on the phone with Jean-Guy.

"Sister Joan admits that the issue was singing. But she still refuses to tell me the names of the other two monks."

"But how could singing get them into trouble?"

"Clearly they weren't singing in the seminary glee club. So it must've been some songs that the seminary would consider inappropriate, especially for teachers."

"The Beatles? 'Let It Be'? How could that be offensive enough to get one of them fired?" He thought for a moment. "If it wasn't what they were singing, maybe it was where."

"Bars? Strip joints?"

"Maybe, but I doubt they'd be that foolish."

"Karaoke bars. In civilian clothing."

"*Non.* In their robes. That would definitely cross a line."

"I'm on it."

Armand hung up and looked at Daniel, standing in the doorway.

It was time.

# CHAPTER 29

⁓

"Why didn't you tell me sooner about the call from Jeanne Caron?" They'd decided to go to the bistro so as not to disturb the household. Father and son now sat by the dying fire, the logs embers now.

It was closing time and the bistro was empty. Gabri had drifted over with the intention of asking them to leave, but on seeing their intensity, he did an about-face. Dropping the keys noisily on the bar, he left.

"I needed to find out what she wanted first." Armand twisted in his seat to look at Daniel full-on. "No. That's not true." He was as surprised as Daniel by the statement. "The truth is, I wanted to pretend that my telling her to go to hell would put an end to it."

"It didn't."

"Not by a long shot."

"What did she want?"

Armand could see Daniel bracing himself for the answer.

"She wanted to meet, but I hung up, so I don't actually know what she wanted."

"So call her back. Find out. Dad, she's fucked with us before." He stared into his father's eyes. "You think she's going to again. Was she involved in that hit-and-run?"

"I'm trying to find out."

"She might have been?" Daniel's eyes were wide. "She's the Chief of Staff to the man who might be the next PM, and you think she's involved in murder? What's going on? I was a kid the first time around. I'm a grown man now, with my own family to protect. You have to tell me." When his father hesitated, Daniel glared. "You don't trust me enough to tell me what's going on?"

The tone, the look, were all too familiar.

Armand could see that telling Daniel this much might have been a mistake. He hadn't wanted him to find out about Caron from someone else. But instead of warning Daniel, all he'd managed to do was panic him. And open an old wound.

He was so tempted to tell his son about the threat to the drinking water, it actually hurt. But could Daniel really keep it to himself and not warn his friends in Montréal who had their own young families? Perhaps. Probably. But Armand could not risk it.

"I'm sorry."

Daniel stared at his father, gave a brisk nod, then got up. And left.

Armand closed his eyes and lowered his head. Then he felt someone sit down beside him on the sofa.

"I'm scared," said Daniel quietly. "Not for myself. For Florence and Zora. I don't understand what you're doing, or why. I don't know what's happening, and that just makes it worse. But I do know that I trust you, more than you trust me."

"I can't—" Armand began, but Daniel held up his hand.

"It's okay. I know there's more at stake than just me. Maybe one day you'll trust me as much as you trust Mom. As much as you trust Jean-Guy. I want to help, Dad, and if helping means doing nothing, then that's what I'll do."

Armand reached out and placed his hand on Daniel's cheek. "Thank you."

*It ends now*, thought Armand as they walked home in silence. One way or another, Caron would never again threaten his family.

It was four in the morning in Three Pines and ten a.m. in Rome when Isabelle Lacoste walked quickly across Saint Peter's Square. The Vatican offices had just opened.

She paused to shoot a quick glance up to the famous balcony, to see if the Pope was standing there.

He was not.

The guard had called ahead, then pointed her to the Curia offices across the square. As she approached the curved wall, which acted as a sort of embrace of Saint Peter's, a door swung open to reveal a nun, all in white. A Dominican. And not just a sister, but the Mother Superior.

"Signora Lacoste?"

"*Sì.*"

"*Sono Madre Beatrice. Benvenuto—*"

"I'm sorry. I don't speak Italian," Isabelle said in English, assuming that was a language they'd both have at least passing knowledge of.

She was wrong.

"*Español?*" the nun asked.

"*Nein,*" Isabelle said before realizing that was German.

"*Latine?*" Mother Beatrice actually smiled as she asked what they both knew was a ludicrous question. And got a ludicrous answer.

"*Nyet.*"

"*Français?*"

"*Oui. Vous?*"

Mother Beatrice shook her head, and they both wondered why the Mother Superior had bothered asking.

The nun contemplated her unexpected visitor. What to do with someone who just showed up and with whom she could not communicate? The interview with this Canadian journalist seemed doomed. Unless . . .

She gestured, and Isabelle, with relief, followed Mother Beatrice through the door and down the long marble corridors. Like many magnificent old buildings, the guts were considerably less impressive than the skin. The deeper they went, the more like a rat's nest it became. Many they passed were not clerics but civilians, doing the work of running one of the most powerful and wealthy organizations on earth.

As she hurried to keep up with the long, hidden legs of the Mother Superior, Isabelle glanced into offices, scanning for Frère Sébastien.

There were hundreds, perhaps thousands of people working there. Unless she got lucky, she'd never just spot him. She'd need to be more direct.

The nun finally stopped and pointed Lacoste into a small, windowless room where another nun was working. Before she went in, Lacoste brought out the photo of Frère Sébastien and showed it to the Mother Superior. She looked at it and shook her head.

"Suora Irene," said Mother Beatrice, then said something in Italian that Lacoste took to be an explanation of who she was.

"I go away," said Beatrice.

"*Grazie.*" Isabelle had been a breath away from saying *danke* when the Italian sprang to mind.

"Mother Beatrice tells me you're doing an article on women's ascension in the Curia," said the nun in perfect English as she waved Isabelle to a seat. "Normally it would take weeks to get permission to get inside the building and do an interview, but the Holy Father is anxious that people know about the changes."

Like Mother Beatrice, Sister Irene was a Dominican. Not surprising since this was the Office of the Doctrine of the Faith.

"As you can see, I'm not one of those women in positions of authority. Yet."

"Do you mind if I record our conversation?"

"Not at all, though I doubt I'll say anything interesting. The only reason Mother Superior brought you to me is that I speak English. There are certainly more senior women in the Curia. There are crusts of bread here with more authority than me. I'm basically a clerk."

"A clerical cleric?" asked Lacoste and saw the sister smile again.

"Well, strictly speaking, nuns aren't considered part of the clergy. So, a distance to go yet. Still, I hope to be elected pope one day."

Lacoste laughed, then wondered if this woman, who was about her own age, early thirties, was serious. There was a spark of amusement, even silliness in her bright eyes.

"I would vote for you," said Lacoste. "Though I suppose I'd have to be a member of the College of Cardinals."

"Well, why not? Twenty years ago nuns in senior positions in the Curia would have been unthinkable. The unimaginable is happening, Ms. Lacoste. Slowly, but this is the Vatican, after all." She paused. "You're French."

"Québécoise."

Sister Irene raised her brows. "You're far from home."

"So are you. American?"

"From Cleveland."

"But you speak Italian."

"Second generation. Originally from Tuscany. Don't ask . . ." Why anyone would move from Tuscany to Cleveland.

"Do the Americans all hang out?" Isabelle asked as though this were casual, polite conversation and not the opening she was hoping for.

"Like Harry's Bar?" Sister Irene smiled. "Some do, but most learn quickly that they need to guard their secrets, their territory, and fraternizing is dangerous."

"Dangerous?"

"Not physically, but professionally. Fortunately my territory does not need guarding."

"Sounds lonely."

Sister Irene seemed struck by that. She paused before saying, "The Curia can be lonely. I miss my friends."

Isabelle pointed to a chair. "May I?"

"Yes, yes," said the nun eagerly. "Please do."

"Are there many Americans here?"

"Not many. You'd think we'd get together, even at Thanksgiving. And maybe they do."

"You haven't been here for a Thanksgiving?"

"No. This's my first year."

"Just out of curiosity, are there any priests or monks here from Québec?"

"There are hundreds of priests and monks here and I don't know all of them. I'm not clear what your article's about. I thought it was women in the Curia."

Isabelle realized she'd have to be more careful. She also realized she needed someone who'd been in the Office of the Doctrine of the Faith much longer. Who would have known Brother Sébastien when he worked there. And would know if he'd returned.

"I'm thinking it might be a good idea to take you up on your offer. Can I speak to one of the senior women?"

"Let me make a call." When she hung up, Sister Irene said, "Come with me."

As they walked through the warren of corridors, Lacoste continued to look into offices, in case she spotted Brother Sébastien.

"Where did you study to be a nun?" Looking into more offices.

"At the Motherhouse in Amityville. New York."

"What did you do before coming here?"

"I was a teacher."

Lacoste's pace slowed. "Where?"

"The seminary in Washington."

Lacoste stopped, and Sister Irene, after taking a few steps, turned back.

"DC?"

"Yes. What? Do you need help? Water?"

Sister Irene was staring at Lacoste. Concerned.

"Do you know a Frère Sébastien?" Lacoste fumbled to get the photo out. "He was a Dominican, but is now a Gilbert—"

Now it was Isabelle's turn to be concerned. The nun looked like she'd been struck. Hard. Across the face.

"No."

We were wrong, *patron*."

Armand was walking to his car through a light drizzle, more a heavy morning mist, when his phone rang.

Lacoste's voice, while a whisper, was urgent, packed with excitement.

"Not a monk, a nun! One of Sébastien's friends at the seminary was a nun. Sister Irene."

The satchel slipped from Armand's shoulder and dropped onto the wet grass. Reine-Marie, who was walking with him, stopped. Stooped. And picked it up.

"What?" she mouthed. Armand's grip on his phone had tightened, and he was staring, unseeing, past her and into the dark forest.

"How do you know?"

"I'm with her now."

On seeing the nun's face when she'd asked the question about Sébastien, and hearing what was clearly a lie, Lacoste had pushed the nun into a nearby bathroom and locked the door.

"She works at the Office of the Doctrine of the Faith. She refuses to speak, but by her reaction, she obviously knows Sébastien. She won't tell me where he is, or admit she even knows him, but she must be the one who wrote asking him to come here."

Isabelle was leaning against the locked door while Sister Irene leaned against a porcelain urinal.

"You need to ask her what the threat is," said Gamache.

He listened as Isabelle spoke to the nun. "We need to know what's about to happen so we can stop it. It's something to do with water, we know that. Are they planning to poison drinking water?"

There was silence.

"Is it Montréal?" Lacoste demanded. "Montréal's drinking water? For God's sake, we need to know."

Armand stared at the forest, trying to make out the trees, and willed the nun to answer.

"She's shaking her head. She either doesn't know or won't say. She looks terrified, as though I'm about to hurt her."

"Tell her we know about Grande Chartreuse."

"What do we know, *patron*?"

"Nothing, but I bet she does."

Armand heard Isabelle say, "Grande Chartreuse." Her voice was echoey. Gamache could not figure out where they might be in the Vatican. The Sistine Chapel perhaps?

"Nothing."

"Damn." He paused. "Can you sing?"

"I'm sorry?"

"Sing. Do you know 'Let It Be'?"

"Are you all right?"

"Please, just answer the question."

"Yes."

"*Bon.* Now, I want you to sing the chorus, but replace the words 'let it be' with 'letter *B*.'"

Lacoste's brow furrowed. Was the Chief losing his mind? Still, she lowered the phone and sang.

Beauvoir was trying to get through, but the Chief's line was busy. Busy.

So he called Annie.

"Jean-Guy—"

"Get me your father, fast."

Annie was already up and partly dressed. Throwing on a dressing gown, she ran around the house looking for her father.

"What is it?" asked Daniel, coming out of his bedroom.

"I need to find Dad."

"He's outside by the car."

Annie ran down the stairs and out the door in her slippers, holding the phone in front of her. "Dad! Jean-Guy needs to speak to you. It's urgent."

Armand heard a flushing sound twenty seconds into Lacoste singing "Letter B."

Probably not the Sistine Chapel.

"She looks like I slapped her," said Isabelle.

So shocked was Sister Irene by the song that she'd put out her hand for balance and ended up flushing the urinal.

"What does the song mean?" asked Lacoste.

"It means she knows far more than she's saying. Hold on." Armand spoke into the phone Annie gave him. "What is it?"

"The karaoke bars were closed last night by the time I got there, but I went out early this morning, in case the cleaning staff was in. I went to a few—"

"Jean-Guy!"

"Okay. We were right. Three of them sang karaoke every Tuesday night, in their robes. They'd become a sensation. The local newspaper did a story on them. It's tacked to the wall here, with a photo of them. I think that's how the seminary found out. And why they were punished."

"But only Frère Sébastien was kicked out," said Gamache. "Not the other two. What does the article say?"

"I'm looking at it now. I'll send a scan. *Patron*, one of them's a nun. A Dominican. A Sister Irene."

"I know. I have Lacoste on the line from the Vatican. She's with her now. The third one?"

"A Brother Robert. But get this. He's not a Dominican. He's a Carthusian."

Armand tipped his head back and exhaled.

That was it. An answer to one of their big questions. Why Grande Chartreuse? This was why.

He brought his own phone back up. "Isabelle, did you hear?"

"*Non*. What?"

"The third one is a Brother Robert. And he's a Carthusian. He must be the one they were meeting at Grande Chartreuse. Contact Claude Dussault. Tell him to meet you there. Take Sister Irene with you."

"Right."

Though she had no idea how she was going to get the nun out of the bathroom, never mind the Curia, never mind from Italy to France and the mountain stronghold of the Carthusians.

"What about Sébastien?" she asked.

"Forget about him. It's the other monk we need. He's the one who knows what's happening."

"Why do you say that?"

"Because Brother Robert's the one in hiding. He's the one the Abbot went to see. You have to find him."

Lacoste looked at the nun, who was now standing tall, glaring at her. She suddenly seemed almost formidable. Daring her unexpected visitor to do her worst. As maddening as it was, Lacoste could not help but admire Irene. The woman must be terrified, thinking she was trapped in a bathroom with the very thing they were hiding from.

Not a born martyr, Sister Irene was still willing to face whatever was coming, to protect what she knew. To protect her friends. Though she must hope this was not the time, and the men's bathroom in the Vatican was not the place.

But there was another problem.

"*Patron*, I looked it up. It takes ten hours to drive to Grande Chartreuse from here."

"You need to fly."

"But how? I don't see how I'd get her onto a commercial flight."

"When you call Claude Dussault, ask him to arrange a helicopter."

"On the Sûreté?"

"No. I'll send you my personal bank card. Use it. Do not use your Sûreté account."

He felt a hand on his arm. It was Reine-Marie. "I'll call the bank and increase our limit."

"Substantially," said Armand.

"Dad?" Armand hadn't noticed that Daniel had joined them. "This might help."

In his hand was an AmEx card.

Armand hesitated for a moment, then took it. "*Merci.*"

Annie had disappeared into the house and now returned, holding out a five-dollar bill.

"Your bribe yesterday, to rescue Mom. You might need it. And this." She handed him her Visa card.

Armand smiled. And took both. "Isabelle?"

"Here, *patron*."

"I'll send you the payment information."

After hanging up, he turned back to Annie's phone. "Jean-Guy, you need to get to Sister Joan. Tell her what you found out. If she realizes you already know that much, she might be willing to give you more."

"I also want to know if anyone else has gone to the seminary asking for them," said Beauvoir.

"Good idea. Then get home."

"As fast as I can. You?"

"I'm going to Blanc-Sablon to find Dom Philippe."

But before he left, Gamache shot off a message. An invitation for breakfast in Montréal, to someone who'd be only slightly more surprised to receive it than he was to send it.

He doubted the person would reply. Or show up.

He doubted what he'd just done was wise.

It was becoming more and more difficult to tell the wise from the foolhardy.

# CHAPTER 30

A fter hanging up, Lacoste called Claude Dussault and asked the retired Prefect of the Paris police to organize a helicopter.

He was not surprised. "I've already looked into it. You can pick me up on the way. I'll send you the details."

Lacoste turned back to the immediate problem. The nun.

"My chief has instructed me to go to Grande Chartreuse and to take you."

Irene took a step back. Lacoste took a step forward.

"I'll scream."

"Interesting that you haven't already. Look, sister." Like Jean-Guy earlier, she realized she sounded like a gangster. If there had been a half grapefruit handy, she might've shoved it into Irene's face. "We need to know exactly what's going to happen."

"I don't know."

Now Lacoste was angry. "For God's sake, don't mess with me. I'm tired and frightened, and you, who should be helping, are not." Then she stopped and stared at Sister Irene. And for the first time, Isabelle Lacoste thought that maybe, maybe Sister Irene really didn't know.

"Brother Robert," said Lacoste. "He knows. That's why he's hiding. That's why you have to protect him. He's the only one of you who knows what's going to happen, and who's behind this."

Now, Sister Irene closed her eyes and raised her hand to the cross on her white robe. And prayed. Again. Prayed harder.

The time had come. The thing she'd dreaded was upon her, in the form of a young Québécoise who looked so sincere. But then, wasn't that the guise evil always took?

Isabelle Lacoste whispered, "I think you know."

Irene's eyes remained closed. "I don't know anything."

"You do. You know everything that matters. I were."

Isabelle touched her cross. Sister Irene opened her eyes, staring into Isabelle's, just inches away.

"You know that I'm the help you've been praying for."

His guest was already there when Gamache arrived at Chez Mama.

"Monsieur Gamache."

"Madame Dorion." The woman did not stand up to greet him, and he did not offer a handshake.

She never, ever called him by his Sûreté rank. It was a minor insult, meant to graze, to annoy. To belittle.

She was barely twenty-three and unmarried, but he'd given her what was considered the honorific of "Madame," not "Mademoiselle," which tended to diminish a grown woman.

Shona Dorion looked younger than her years. She dressed younger too, like a schoolgirl. Though it was a "look," a role. Dressing like a child was a challenge to those around her. Her veneer, her public face, was meant to be ironic. A finger to those who'd dismiss her for being young and Black and female.

This was the vlogger of the hostile questions. Made, and meant to be, all the more shocking for apparently coming from a schoolchild.

They were almost always directed at Gamache. If he didn't know why she targeted him, had made it her professional *raison d'être* to take him down, he would never have asked her here.

But he knew. And he had. And she'd accepted.

She'd already ordered breakfast and a huge pile of pancakes arrived along with maple-smoked bacon and a sticky jug of syrup with an ant stuck to the base.

"I'm glad you came."

"Almost didn't, but I was curious. And who could turn down breakfast on the Sûreté at such a great place?" She looked around. "Bring your wife here, do you?"

Gamache bristled at the mention of his wife, but didn't show it. He'd chosen this dive not far from The Mission for the very reason that no one he knew would voluntarily come here. Indeed, the place was completely empty, except for the server making her slow way over, her feet making a Velcro sound as she walked across the linoleum.

"What do you want?" the server asked.

"*Café, s'il vous plaît.*"

"That's it?"

"And a croissant."

"Fine."

When it came, he pushed the pastry away. He could see bits of green mold on some of the flakes, and what looked like nibble marks on one end. He also decided not to drink the coffee. He was hungry and badly needed caffeine. And was deeply regretting his choice of restaurant.

"Why're we here? Are you going to threaten me?" Shona looked at him with undisguised scorn.

Gamache glanced at the phone on the table and knew they were being recorded.

"*Non.* And I never have."

"You arrested my mother. She was put in prison, where she hanged herself. You don't think that was threatening? I was eight years old."

"*Oui.*"

It was the part of his job he hated and would have to face one day, when he retired. The damage his investigations did to innocent people. They were lined up behind him, along with the ghosts. Ready for a "chat." But it would have to wait.

He'd first looked into Shona's eyes when he'd knocked at their door, a warrant in hand. The girl was clinging to her mother and staring at him. Not in anger or fear, but in curiosity. Then, on hearing his words, he could see in the child a growing realization that people could be mean. And adults could be wrong.

Shona was raised in a crack house. Her mother was an addict and prostitute. But also a loving and protective mother. She'd poured all her goodness, all her considerable love, into the child.

She'd shielded her daughter from an often cruel world.

But the world had knocked on their door that day in the form of Armand Gamache, and had removed the only love the child knew.

Shona never saw her mother again.

He tried to justify the damage by saying he was not the one who did it. Shona's mother had, when she'd killed her dealer. But she was herself so badly damaged, she was not responsible either.

"I need your help."

Those same eyes stared at him now. Well, almost. Now the wonderment was gone, contempt in its place.

"I'm going to tell you something," he said. "I have, in a safe in the basement of my home, files on people I've investigated."

He saw her eyes light up, and she moved her phone closer to him. But like any good investigator, she did not interrupt. She let him talk.

And he did. Slowly, clearly. Without ambiguity. For the recording. For the record.

"These are people who were witnesses, some suspects, but found to be not responsible for the crime we were investigating. Mostly murders, of course. Before you ask, I don't have a file on you."

She did not look convinced.

He couldn't blame her.

She was so attached to the narrative that Chief Inspector Gamache was a horrific human being, misusing his considerable power, that she could not see beyond it.

"The files contain things people have told me over the years, and sometimes things we found out in the course of our investigation. Things that turned out not to have a bearing on the murder itself. Some petty crimes. Shoplifting. Some drug offenses. Mostly, though, they were mistakes, lapses in judgment. Acts and events they were ashamed of. Bullying. Affairs. Lies. Acts of moral or physical cowardice. But still, things that could do considerable damage to their personal and professional lives."

Gamache looked down at his hands, then up into those gleaming brown eyes.

"A few people know about those files, but not many. These're not classified. They're not illegal. Though a case could be made that a senior officer keeping files at home on individual citizens is not only unethical, but frightening. A case could be made by you."

He held her eyes. She looked, in that moment, like the wolf in the woods at the monastery. Preparing to rip his throat out.

"If the public finds out and it's spun a certain way, I'll be fired and probably sued. The case would not stand up, but I would be ruined."

He took a deep breath. There was no going back now. He could see she was excited by this, but also perplexed. Why had he just handed her weapons-grade information?

"If they're so dangerous, why do you have them?"

"Well, another question could be, why files on those particular people and not others?"

"Okay, if you prefer, that question."

"These are people who, while not guilty of the crime we were investigating, are far from innocent. I think, I believe, I feel they'll do something terrible one day. Perhaps already have. I saw it in them."

"You're compiling information on innocent citizens to use as blackmail."

"*Non.* Not blackmail. Evidence. Insight. That's the point. I have no files on those who really are innocent."

"In your opinion."

"In my judgment, yes. If I'm wrong, they'll never be used." He leaned toward her. His hands rested for a moment on the table before he quickly raised them when they stuck. "If I'm right, then when they do commit a crime, we'll have a huge advantage. I'd be a fool not to keep that information."

"You're a fool to tell me all this. You know I'm recording what you say."

"*Oui.* I presumed."

"Then why are you doing it?"

"So that we're even. In doing my job, I altered your life, hurt you deeply. Now, in doing your job, you can do the same to me."

"Right, but why give me that ability?"

"So that you know that what I'm about to ask is important, vital. It's worth my career. Perhaps more."

She sat back and considered him.

She'd tried many times to ruin Gamache, but despite all her efforts to find something on him, and, when that failed, to belittle, mock, insult him in public, he'd remained unmoved. Even courteous in her company. Which had enraged her even further and made her redouble her efforts.

But, finally, now she had what she needed.

"You're giving me this information as a kind of mortgage. I own your ass."

"More than just my ass, but yes." She reached for the croissant. "I wouldn't eat that. I need someone on the outside to ask questions, to quietly dig."

"Outside the Sûreté?" Her eyes were bright with the implication. "Why me?"

"Why do you think?"

It didn't take much thought. "Because I so clearly hate you. No one would think we were working together."

"And because you're very good at what you do."

She turned her phone off and placed it in her pocket, then pulled out a notebook and a pen. "Okay, Gamache. Tell me."

"The federal government has given a waiver to various companies in Québec, perhaps elsewhere in Canada, to exceed the pollution limits by up to thirty times."

"Percent?"

"Times."

"Shit."

"On top of that, the federal government has agreed to sell controlling interest in certain resource-based companies to Americans."

Instead of pointing out that it was illegal, which she clearly knew, she just shook her head and continued to take notes.

"I'll need names."

"I can get you that."

"Jesus, someone's on the take." She sat back and considered him. "How does this interest the head of homicide for the Sûreté?"

"Charles Langlois, the young man killed in the hit-and-run, was a biologist at an environmental agency called Action Québec Bleu. He was visiting lakes that would be affected. I think he found out about this, and that was one of the reasons he was killed."

"One of the reasons?"

"We're looking into others, but that's the one I'm asking you to pursue."

As he looked beyond Shona to the thin, bone-weary server, he wanted to shout, *Leave. Take those you love and get out of the city. Something awful's about to happen here.*

He'd thought that as he had driven into Montréal, passing schools and hospitals, men and women flooding out of the Métro stations on their way to work. Mothers and fathers holding the hands of their children at corners, waiting to cross.

He thought about the LaPierres and their other close friends.

*Leave. Leave! For God's sake, get out of this city, before . . .*

But he said nothing. He'd stayed silent and drove deeper into the city, pursued by the words of Dr. King: *In the end, we will remember not the words of our enemies, but the silence of our friends.*

Though, of course, they would not remember his silence. They would be dead. Because he'd said nothing.

*Please God, let this work.*

"I want you to find out who's behind it. What the endgame is."

"Profit, what else?"

"Perhaps."

She looked down at her notes, then up at him. Her focus was no longer on Gamache, but on the assignment. And with that switch came a realization.

"Wait a minute. Both these events, loosening the federal environmental limits and the sale of companies, are controlled by the same man. Marcus Lauzon. The Deputy Prime Minister."

"*Oui.*"

He watched her take a deep breath. Her exhale fluttered the paper napkin stuck to the tabletop.

"You think the Deputy Prime Minister, maybe even the PM, are up to something."

"If they are, we need to know, and we need to know quickly. But remember, if I'm right, then this is dangerous. At least one person who found out has been killed."

"Can't be more dangerous than eating here."

"Consider this boot camp. And that's"—he pointed to the croissant—"a live grenade."

He smiled at her.

She looked at him in amazement and realized she'd never seen Gamache smile. When scrummed by reporters, it was always to talk about a terrible crime. Or, in her case, to absorb the abuse she was hurling at him.

As he smiled, the lines of his face deepened. And she knew if she followed them, she'd come to his most private place. His home. His heart. But Shona didn't want to see that. Not yet. She wasn't ready to stop thinking of him as heartless.

"You can refuse," Gamache said. "You have what you've wanted since you were a child. Enough to ruin me. You can take that recording and go. I won't stop you."

"*Non.* I'm in. Plenty of time to ruin you later."

He got up. "One more question. Who invited you to the news conference?"

"No reason you shouldn't know. It was your boss."

"Chief Superintendent Toussaint?"

"Got it in one. You have lots of friends, Monsieur Gamache," she said as she packed up. "But turns out you have a lot of enemies too. Powerful ones."

"Including you, Madame Dorion." He offered his hand. It hovered in the air between them.

"We're not there."

He nodded and walked to the till where the server was waiting.

Armand didn't dare use his credit card, knowing every dollar was needed to pay Lacoste's expenses. Instead, he brought out cash. Holding the five-dollar bill, he stared at it, then returned it to his pocket.

"Would you like me to pay?" asked Shona.

He expected to see her laughing at him. Instead, as he turned, he saw she was serious.

"*Non, merci*. Next time."

"Yeah, right. If there is a next time, it won't be in this shithole. And you're still paying, cheap bastard."

What're you doing here?"

Sister Joan had arrived for work at the seminary in DC to find Jean-Guy Beauvoir sitting on the hard bench in the hallway.

"Waiting for you." He stood and swung his backpack over his shoulder. "I'm on my way to the airport, but I needed to speak to you first."

"I have nothing more to say to you." She unlocked her door.

"Brother Robert. Sister Irene."

"What about them?"

"They're the other two, in the trio of singers." He held out the newspaper clipping.

"I've seen it. And now you know everything I do."

"Is lying a sin?"

She turned and looked at him.

"My colleague from the Sûreté has found Sister Irene, in the Curia. But it's Brother Robert we need to talk to."

Sister Joan sat behind her desk and stared at Jean-Guy Beauvoir. At his weary, anxious face.

"I don't know how to contact him. All I know is that he left here to take up a position in Rome."

"Were you surprised?"

"A little. He seemed happy here."

"So, you were here then."

Now she looked embarrassed. "Yes. But I never met the other one. Brother Sébastien. The one you were asking about yesterday."

"And Sister Irene? You must've known her."

"Yes. She left soon after Brother Robert."

"What's his background? Where's he from? I know he's a Carthusian."

"I can't give you his personal information."

"Can you at least tell me what he taught? That can't be a secret."

"Chemistry and biology. He also, of course, has a degree in theology."

"Of course." There was another person Jean-Guy hoped never to sit beside at a dinner party. "And Sister Irene? What did she teach?"

"History."

"They must've been good friends to have gone along with the idea of singing karaoke in a bar in their robes. They must've known it was not the best idea."

She shrugged. "That was years ago. They were young. We all do things we regret."

Jean-Guy was tempted to ask about her regrets, but instead said, "The seminary found out because of the article?"

"I wasn't here then, but yes, I think that's a good bet."

"Then all three must've been disciplined, but only Sébastien was fired. Why only him?"

"I can't tell you that. I can say it has no bearing on your investigation."

Now he cocked his head. "How do you know that? I haven't told you what it is."

"True. But you said it was extremely serious. I'm guessing you aren't looking into an old episode where two monks and a nun took to singing in a bar."

It sounded like a bad joke.

"Am I the only one who's asked about them?"

"Yes." She stood up and offered him her hand. "Good luck. I wish I could help you."

And this time Jean-Guy Beauvoir believed her.

# CHAPTER 31

For reasons Armand Gamache could never understand, when it rained, the entrance to Sûreté headquarters in Montréal smelled like wet dog.

They had a canine unit, but it was not kenneled in the lobby.

Gamache's shoes left wet marks on the floor, joining all the others who'd arrived for work that damp August morning.

He'd stopped at the café on the corner and picked up a fresh croissant and double-shot cappuccino, the scent of which now mixed with wet fur. As he waited for the elevator, he realized it reminded him of Henri and Fred in the bistro on rainy days.

While others wrinkled their nose in distaste, he inhaled deeply.

Once at his floor, the first thing Armand did was go to the bathroom to scrub his hands and face clean after that restaurant. As the water poured out of the tap, he took a handful and smelled it; then he dipped his tongue in. Though he knew that botulinum had no odor or taste, he still needed to do it.

Just in case.

Nothing. Yet.

Standing at the door into the open bullpen where his officers were working, he once again had the near overwhelming urge to shout, *Leave! Now. Take your families and get off the island. Run!* But instead of warning these men and women it was his duty to protect, he just stood there watching, and felt a wave of nausea so strong he had to steady himself. For a terrible moment, he wondered if it was from the tap water he'd tasted. If . . .

But no. This was a self-inflicted toxin. A guilty conscience.

He shoved it away. It did no good and only messed with his mind. He needed clarity, needed all his focus. Ironically, the only way to save his agents was to keep them there. In the dark. In danger.

It was necessary to give the impression of normalcy. After spending a few minutes discussing ongoing cases with his officers, he called into his office the Sûreté officer assigned as liaison with the Montréal cops investigating the Langlois and Parisi homicides.

He hung up his damp coat and sat behind his desk, waving the agent to a chair on the other side.

"Tell me what you have."

"The Parisi family has been told. It's all over the news in Italy and has just hit the internet. We're getting calls from journalists here and in Italy. It's a big story and getting bigger."

"What progress?" He tried not to sound impatient. The media was not his first concern.

The inspector looked down at his notes as the Chief took a long sip of coffee.

Rarely had it tasted so good.

"Parisi stayed at the Gramercy Park Hotel in New York City for five nights, then checked out. We think that's when he crossed into Québec, but we have no record from Canada Customs. And so far none of the hotels in Montréal have him registered. I have agents going around with the photos the cops in Italy sent when Parisi was alive."

"He obviously had help here."

"*Oui.* The Parisi family has been asked about Montréal connections. The only one is an importer who deals with their olive oil. The importer doesn't have any known mob connections. I've sent an agent over to interview him."

"Nothing personal? No friends here?"

"Parisi says no. The theory the Italian cops are putting out is that Paolo was targeted by the mafia as payback to his parents. The family, through their attorney, has also issued a statement to that effect."

"That's for public consumption," said Gamache. "What does the family say privately?"

"They're denying that their son had anything to do with the murder of Charles Langlois."

Gamache raised his hands. Of course they were. Even though an eyewitness was the head of homicide for the Sûreté du Québec.

"Did the head of their Anti-Mafia task force have any theories?"

"He wouldn't take my calls."

"Here." Gamache reached out. "Give me the name and number."

"I can try again, *patron*."

"*Non*. Just give it to me. It's a rank thing." And "rank," he thought, was the word for it. "Not your fault. Anything on the woman who signaled Parisi?"

"Nothing. She's vanished."

They both knew what that might mean. More landfill.

When the inspector left, Gamache placed the call.

"So sorry, Inspector, but Superintendent Genori is occupied."

The line went dead.

Gamache stared at the phone in disbelief, then placed the call again, getting through to the same officious voice.

"Inspector—"

"It's Chief Inspector, and tell him to answer my goddamned call. Tell him I'm head of homicide and the eyewitness to the Parisi murder. The one Parisi committed." Then he said more slowly, with emphasis, "The one that almost killed me. I'm sure he's seen the video."

The line went silent, but this time not dead. Twenty seconds later another voice came on the line. "My sincere apologies, Chief Inspector. Gamache, is it not?"

The words were highly accented but understandable, and Gamache appreciated that the man's English was far better than his own Italian.

"No harm done. I'll get right to the point. Does the Parisi family have ties to organized crime?"

"I think we've already answered that. Their ties are deep, but not in the way you're suggesting. Both Signore and Signora Parisi have spent much of their energy, professionally and personally, fighting the mafia. At considerable risk to themselves and, clearly, their family."

"Clearly? What's so clear?"

"The mafia murdered their son, Paolo. In your jurisdiction. Surely that's obvious."

Now the head of the task force sounded more accusatory than conciliatory.

"And the murder of Charles Langlois?"

"A terrible accident. The young man lost control of his vehicle. Probably fleeing what he recognized as those trying to do him harm. I am just grateful you yourself were not killed."

He did not sound grateful.

"You aren't telling me you believe that, Superintendent. You've seen the video, you've read the official reports, including my witness account. There is no doubt that Paolo Parisi meant to kill Charles Langlois."

"I see no such evidence. I see an honorable and beloved young man fleeing for his life and making a terrible mistake along the way. What possible motive would he have?"

Gamache pushed back from his desk in exasperation. The jolt sent his cup flying, splashing coffee over the reports he had yet to read.

He jumped up, and tried to save the now sodden papers. This small diversion gave him a beat or two to disengage from his frustration.

He had on the line the person who led the efforts to stop organized crime for all of Italy. A courageous man, surrounded by other brave men and women who risked their lives and those of their families to bring down the mob.

No one on earth was smarter, more steeped in mafia structure, strategies, members, lore, than the man on the other end of the phone. He must see what was obvious on the video. He must believe what the reports said. What the head of homicide for Québec, an eyewitness himself, said.

He must know more. But could not say. Indeed, this ridiculous denial told Gamache more than any agreement could have.

This man might not have proof, but he had his suspicions about Paolo Parisi, if not the entire Parisi family. The trick was getting him to share what he knew.

"I'm willing, because of my respect for you, to believe what you say," said Gamache slowly, sitting down again. "Can you still send me what you have on the young man?"

"Because he has never committed a crime, Chief Inspector, there isn't much, but I will get someone in my department to send what little we have."

"*Grazie*. How is the family taking it?"

"How do you expect?"

"Are they personal friends of yours?"

"Yes. The father, Alberto Parisi, and I were at school together. We watched our fathers beaten by mafia thugs for protection money. My own uncle was murdered. Signore and Signora Parisi hate the mafia as much as I do."

"*Merci*. Please send me anything useful."

There was a pause. "I will, Chief Inspector. I am sorry."

Sorry for what? Gamache wondered as he hung up. But he thought he knew. Sorry for not being able to tell the truth.

Gamache now believed that the parents had nothing to do with the mafia, indeed, that they fought it. But the son was a different matter. Children, as Gamache well knew, often rebelled, and when they did, they chose targets that would hurt their parents the most.

For the Parisis, it was the mafia.

Armand looked at the coffee-stained reports and sighed. He had to go through them. It had to appear it was business as usual in the homicide department. And there were other cases that needed attention.

He made notes on some of the files. Signed off on others.

One of the newer agents, nervous about an upcoming court appearance, knocked on his door wanting advice.

He called in another to discuss an imminent arrest.

*Leave. Get out of the city!*

"You okay, *patron*?" she asked.

"Just fine. Now, what's your plan?"

A day like any other. Nothing unusual . . . really . . . truly . . .

*Leave!*

He made a few calls to agents in the field, then got on a conference call with his inspectors investigating the unsolved murders in the Saguenay and the Magdalen Islands.

"Still no progress?" he asked, and heard their exasperation when they said, in unison, "*Non.*"

"We agree, *patron*, that the two must be connected, but we can't see how."

"The murdered woman in Chicoutimi worked for Canada Post," said Gamache. "Is it possible she saw some mail she shouldn't have? Perhaps opened something?" He was thinking of Frère Simon, the mail monk at the monastery of Saint-Gilbert-Entre-les-Loups, who'd done exactly that.

"We've checked. Nothing. She worked in the back offices, so didn't have access to the mail. Never married," Innez continued. "Friendly, but private. Belongs to a church book club. That seems to be her only outside interest."

Gamache already knew this. Had spent a few days up in the Saguenay looking into the murder. He had the file practically memorized. But still, they'd go over it, and over it, until they found whatever they were missing.

Someone went to this woman's home, a modest bungalow in a nice part of Chicoutimi, in the early evening. She'd begun to prepare dinner, a stir-fry, and had the television on. She'd left with the person. It seemed voluntary, though that was hard to tell. There was no evidence of a struggle, but then there probably wouldn't be.

Her neighbors hadn't seen anything. It had been a pleasant summer evening, and those on either side of her were in their backyards barbecuing.

It was immediately obvious to the investigators that this was no random home invasion gone sideways. Her handbag was left on the chair by the door, with money and credit cards still in it. Her home hadn't been ransacked or even, from what they could tell, searched. The killer was not looking for anything except her.

"I'm beginning to wonder if it was mistaken identity, *patron*."

It was possible. But surely the killer would have realized that by now. If this murder was a mistake, wouldn't he have corrected it? Gone after the real target.

But there had been no other murders in the Saguenay since. And it was hard to see how a quiet bureaucrat could be mistaken for anyone else. Though it was even more difficult to see why she was taken to a park, had her hands zip-tied behind her back. Her mouth covered. Pushed to her knees.

He imagined what that had been like for the poor woman. How terrified she must have been. Then she was shot in the base of the skull. Why? Why her?

It was a classic execution.

The killing of the teacher on the Magdalen Islands was just two days later.

Gamache had no doubt the two were connected. He'd considered the possibility that the real target was the schoolteacher, and somehow the Canada Post clerk got mixed up in it. But that made even less sense.

They had absolutely nothing in common and lived a thousand kilometers apart.

The teacher was days away from retirement when he'd been murdered.

Why? His widow had pleaded through sobs, alternately clinging to the Chief Inspector when he'd joined the investigation for a few days, and hitting him in the chest with her fists. As though, in a twist of logic, his failure to find the killers was somehow responsible for her husband's death.

Gamache knew that in the face of sudden, violent death, especially murder, logic was overwhelmed by grief. And one question drowned out all the rest. Not who, but . . .

Why? his grown children had demanded.

Why? the man's colleagues had asked.

Why? Gamache asked himself.

Why had a schoolteacher, beloved by pupils and coworkers, been taken to a cliff edge, where his hands had been zip-tied behind his back. His mouth covered. Pushed to his knees, he'd been shot at the base of the skull. Execution-style.

Exactly like the postal clerk. Exactly. With no effort made on the part of the murderer to disguise that fact.

There was a pause. "I'm sorry, Chief, but I can't think where else to look. I spoke to her sister again in case she'd remembered something. But nothing."

"She had a nephew, right?"

"Yes. Ferdinand. But they haven't been in touch for years. No estrangement, just grew apart. He isn't in her will. She left most everything to the church, though there wasn't much. I can't find a motive."

"Same here, Chief," said the investigator on the Magdalen Islands. "No motive. No connection to the other. Someone said they saw a boat land at one of the jetties where the victim liked to fish. It wasn't there in the morning. I'm trying to figure out why the killer didn't dump the body in the ocean. Why take him to the edge of a cliff, kill him, and not just kick the body over?"

"Well, there's one obvious reason."

"Yes, I know. The murderer wanted him to be found. But why? For the insurance? His wife is in the clear. His children live in BC and Ontario and are all doing well. I can't find a motive, or any sense to this killing, especially if it's a hit. It must be mistaken identity."

Gamache grunted. Not another one. The killer could not be a made man if he'd made two mistakes like that. If he really had, there was a pretty good chance he'd be the next victim, and not by mistake.

No, this was a professional hit. He might, *might*, have made one mistake, but not two. And despite what Chief Inspector Tardiff in Organized Crime said, these were mob executions.

If the murderer wanted his victims found, it was because he wanted no doubt that the same person had done both jobs. And that he was a pro. And that there was some connection.

"Their mouths being taped shut is an interesting detail," said one of the investigators.

"It seems unnecessary," said the other. "They were in the middle of nowhere. Even if they screamed, no one would hear."

Gamache was nodding. "If it was a mob hit, then this was part of the message. Sometimes they cut out the tongue. It means someone has broken the code of silence."

"Or it's a warning to someone not to," said one of the investigators.

"But to who?" asked the other.

Gamache wondered, in passing, if Paolo Parisi might have been responsible. Was he trying to make his bones, gaining credibility with his capo by committing these murders?

But Parisi was still in New York at the time.

Gamache also now wondered if these murders were related to the death of Charles Langlois. All three killings, it seemed, had ties to the mafia. Though those ties were mere threads, and tenuous at best.

"I'm going to switch you around. Get to Chicoutimi and take over the Saguenay investigation, and Innez, you go to the Magdalen Islands. No reflection on either of you. I just want fresh eyes on both of the cases."

It was the time-tested strategy of the desperate.

"*D'accord, patron.*"

Gamache hung up and reached for his coffee, then remembered he'd spilled it. He was tempted to get another but didn't have time.

An update from Isabelle had come in while he'd been on the phone.

Sister Irene still wouldn't tell her anything, but the nun had at least agreed to go to the monastery. Probably, Lacoste wrote, to try to warn or protect Brother Robert, but that was a problem for later. For now the immediate one was solved.

Lacoste, the nun, and Claude Dussault were heading to Grande Chartreuse.

Once again Gamache brought out the two pieces of the formula for the old liqueur. Flattening them on his desk, he slid them together and considered.

One part had been left by Dom Philippe, who Armand hoped to meet in Blanc-Sablon in a few hours. But the other was more problematic.

He was troubled by the question of why Jeanne Caron had sent it to him. It wasn't like two halves of a decoder ring, where putting them together solved everything. When these two halves formed a whole page, it still did not make a whole lot of sense. They created a single page of a recipe that must be many pages long. It was useless but not, he knew, meaningless.

The only thing he could think of was that Caron was playing with him, trying to distract him with some archaic secret formula. Maybe even daring him to come to her. For her. To step into some trap he couldn't yet see.

And soon he might have to.

Sweeping up the pages, he put them back in his pocket and drove to the airport to catch his flight to the Land God Gave to Cain.

The three passengers looked out the bubble-like glass of the helicopter as it made a pass over the monastery.

What they saw was extraordinary. Sitting in the cleft of a mountain range, holding the encroaching pine forests at bay by force of will and hard labor, was the monastery of Grande Chartreuse. As it had stood for centuries, a citadel in the wilderness.

There was a brutal beauty about it. It was a place where the fiercely independent lived in silence. A community of hermits, where few questions were asked. And where those wanting to disappear could hide.

"Are those the monks?" Isabelle asked.

A dozen men working in what looked like a huge vegetable garden in the center of the fortress held on to their straw hats and tipped their heads back to look up. At them.

"Lay monks," shouted Sister Irene over the rotors. "They do most of the physical labor, freeing up the monks to spend their days and nights in their cells, praying."

While magnificent, there was something ominous about the place. About the layers of concealment behind which these monks worshipped. First the mountain peaks, then the forest, then the high thick walls that encircled the abbey, and finally the cells, which the brothers rarely left. All served to separate them from the world.

They lived in silence and solitude. And wanted to keep it that way. No visitors were allowed inside.

No vehicles were allowed on the roads around the monastery.

Few messages traveled in and fewer still made it out. The world could end, and these Carthusian monks would never know. It had essentially ended for them already. They lived now in limbo, between this world and their reward.

Dussault brought his hand to his breast pocket. As the former head of the Paris police, few things worried Claude Dussault anymore. He'd seen the worst, and then worse still.

But now he was worried.

Violating the monastery could be, would be, a national scandal. And certainly a logistical nightmare. How to get inside and serve the search warrant without force?

Fortunately, the monks probably were not armed. But if the cops went in there, rifles raised against clerics with pitchforks and shovels, it would be worse than a scandal. It would be a disgrace.

And yet it might come to that. His hand dropped from his breast pocket.

"Armand better be right. This Brother Robert had better be in there," said Dussault.

They looked at the nun, who also looked worried.

On the flight over Sister Irene had heard the other two conferring. She was now convinced they were who they said they were. They were trying to help, at considerable risk to themselves, professionally and personally. Their sincerity, their desperation, their own commitment and possible sacrifice, were clear.

But there was a fine line between helping and unintentionally lighting a fuse that could not be stopped.

"He is."

It was the first information she'd volunteered. And it was what they needed.

Lacoste and Dussault looked at each other. Their cheeks puffed out in a long simultaneous exhale. They'll actually have to do this thing.

"I hear you can drive a bulldozer," said Dussault, in what struck Lacoste as a bizarre non sequitur.

The helicopter put down half a kilometer away, and they started walking.

Look at this."

Armand, realizing their schedules at the airport matched, met Jean-Guy's flight before heading to his own.

Jean-Guy, barely off the plane, was shoving his phone at the Chief. Armand exchanged it for the small paper bag he was carrying.

"A croissant?"

"Bought it at the café near HQ. A video?"

"Found on YouTube."

Armand hit play, and while Beauvoir devoured the croissant, the Chief watched three achingly young people, including an almost unrecognizable Frère Sébastien, sing.

Armand had expected "Let It Be," but instead, he got—

> *I'm goin' down to St. James Infirmary,*
> *See my baby there;*
> *She's stretched out on a long, white table,*
> *She's so sweet, so cold, so fair.*

It was riveting. Far from the drunken, sloppy singing usually found in karaoke bars, the two monks and the nun had beautiful voices, in perfect harmony.

> *Let her go, let her go, God bless her,*
> *Wherever she may be,*
> *She will search this wide world over,*
> *But she'll never find another sweet man like me.*

"This was posted on YouTube?" he asked.

"*Oui.* With more than a hundred thousand views. And lots of likes. Only one thumbs-down."

Armand wondered if the Pope watched YouTube videos.

*Now, when I die, bury me in my straight-leg britches,*
*Put on a box-back coat and a Stetson hat,*

They sang the old blues song slowly, their robes swaying, their eyes closed as though in a sort of ecstasy.

*An' give me six crap-shooting pall bearers,*
*Let a chorus girl sing me a song.*
*Put a red hot jazz band at the top of my head*
*So we can raise Hallelujah as we go along.*

It was beautiful, soulful, but not wise.

"I'm thinking their robes and that article in the local paper might not have been the only problems," said Gamache, handing the phone back. "It looks like Robert is the leader of the group."

"*Oui.* So I wonder why Sébastien was the one made to leave."

"So do I."

"Want me to come with you, *patron?*"

"To Blanc-Sablon? *Non, merci.* I want you to coordinate the investigation into Paolo Parisi. I'll send you what the head of the Anti-Mafia task force in Italy passes along, as soon as I get it." Though Gamache was beginning to wonder if the fellow would actually send anything. It had been a couple of hours since their conversation. "And see what you can find out about the woman who signaled Parisi at Open Da Night."

"And probably killed him. I'm on it."

They were almost at Gamache's gate. "Parisi must've had help getting across the border. Either a fake ID or . . ."

"The frontier is a federal responsibility," said Beauvoir. "Caron?"

"Maybe. I want to know his movements once he got here."

"I'll go to The Mission."

They could hear the final boarding call for Gamache's flight and picked up their pace.

"Why?"

"He had to stay somewhere. So far the hotels are a bust, so where better than a place where you don't need to register or pay, and they ask no questions. If he was working for Caron, she'd have told him to go there."

"And where her showing up wouldn't be odd." Gamache smiled. "Brilliant. Keep me informed."

"You too." Beauvoir wanted to say, *Be careful,* but stopped himself. Though as he watched the Chief scan his ticket and be waved down the gangway, he wished he had.

Armand put in his earbuds and listened to Cab Calloway as he looked down at the increasingly rugged coastline. There was a brutal beauty about it. It was a place where the fiercely independent lived. Where few questions were asked. And where those wanting to disappear could hide.

He took out the faded photograph he'd borrowed from Dom Philippe's best friend and stared at the smiling, almost laughing young woman and girl. But his eyes rested on the young man, Yves before Philippe. A man-child who so loved his home he even had a favorite rock.

The prop plane hurtled toward the fishing village, the farthest point in Québec and the limit of Armand Gamache's power.

*So we can raise Hallelujah as we go along.*

# CHAPTER 32

Isabelle Lacoste, Claude Dussault, and Sister Irene walked toward the dented and scarred oak door. The breeze made a *shhhhh*-ing sound as it moved over the open meadow. As though telling them to be quiet. *Shhhhh.*

Lacoste felt foolish. She'd been so single-minded in getting there that she hadn't really formulated a plan on how to get in.

Brother Robert had effectively locked himself inside a safety-deposit box, and Sister Irene was the only key they had. But how could a Dominican nun get them into the fortress home of cloistered Carthusian monks?

A less effective key would be difficult to imagine.

"How did you three become friends? Was it singing?"

Isabelle's hand absently brushed the tops of the yellow and blue and bright pink wildflowers. Butterflies took flight, took fright, as they passed.

"No. Sébastien and I were drawn together because of our names."

Lacoste noticed that Claude Dussault suddenly smiled.

"What's so funny?"

"Sébastien and Irene," he said. Isabelle didn't understand and didn't care.

"And Robert?" asked Isabelle casually. "How did he fit in?" That's what she really wanted to know. Something, anything, about the man barricaded behind the tall wall.

"Through Sébastien. They were best friends."

"I know about the karaoke. All three of you did it, but only Sébastien was punished. What did he do to deserve that?"

Sister Irene kept walking, her eyes fixed ahead. Lacoste felt like they were hobbits approaching Mordor. Though this was not that. The monastery was not evil. It was simply a huge impediment.

More butterflies took off, flailing about in the slight breeze.

When she got no answer, Isabelle tried another tack. "Brother Robert wrote to Sébastien in Saint-Gilbert-Entre-les-Loups, to get him to go to Rome. To tell him about what he'd discovered—"

Isabelle stopped. She could tell she'd said something wrong.

"*Non*," she said, staring at the nun. "Robert didn't write him. You did. Robert sent for you, and you sent for Sébastien. And Sébastien sent for Dom Philippe, who met you all here. Why?"

Silence.

"Because Robert had run away and was already inside Grande Chartreuse. He refused to see either of you." Lacoste answered her own question since the nun would not. "But he might agree to talk with Dom Philippe. Why?"

Silence.

Isabelle grabbed the nun's arm so they were looking at each other.

"Did Brother Robert speak to Dom Philippe? Did he tell the Abbot what he knows? Did the Abbot tell you?"

Silence.

"For God's sake, Irene. I'm begging you. I'll get on my knees if that would help. We need to know. We need to stop whatever's about to happen."

"But I don't know what it is."

"You must," said Dussault, who'd been listening. "Why did Robert send for you, if not to ask for your help? And to do that, you'd have to know what was happening."

"No, you don't understand Robert. He sent for me because his conscience got the better of him. He ran away from Washington to the Curia, but his God followed him, of course, and demanded that he do something. He had to tell someone, so he sent for me."

"So he did tell you," said Dussault.

"No. He only said that something awful was going to happen, and he was afraid for his life. They said they'd kill him if it even looked like he might talk."

"Who's 'they'?" demanded Lacoste.

"You don't think I've asked? But he wouldn't tell me anything else. I was furious. I'd given up my job and come all this way, and he chickened out. I should've known."

"Why do you say that?"

"Because Brother Robert's a coward, okay?" It was practically spat out. "Always was. He wanted to give me his burden, hand it off to me."

"But he didn't," said Dussault.

"No. So I sent for Sébastien, thinking he might tell him. But Robert left as soon as Sébastien arrived. We followed him here. When he still refused to see us, Sébastien asked Dom Philippe to come."

"Why him?" asked Dussault.

"Wait a minute," said Lacoste. "Before we get to that, let's back up. Brother Robert must've heard about whatever was planned while he was in DC. Is that right?"

Irene nodded.

"How did he hear it?"

"From a parishioner, in confession."

"But he's a monk," said Dussault. "He can't hear confessions."

"Well, he can," said Irene. "But he can't give absolution."

"So what good is it?" asked Dussault.

"Not a lot. He used to fill in at the local church when the priest on duty was too tired."

Lacoste wondered if "too tired" was a euphemism.

"No one knew it was a monk, not a priest, on the other side. It was wrong, but Robert felt he had no choice. He was always cowed by authority. If a priest told him to do it . . ."

"But that would mean Brother Robert was not bound by what he heard. Not bound by the confessional," said Dussault.

"True."

"And if the person who confessed discovered that . . ."

"Yes."

"If he wasn't bound by the confessional," said Lacoste, "why not go to the police? Why not tell someone?"

"I tried to get him to, but you'd have to know Robert. He's very smart, brilliant, but fragile. These butterflies would terrify him."

They were flitting all around them now, and Isabelle had to admit, she was finding them a little off-putting. All that movement right in her face.

Dussault coughed, having inhaled what looked like a moth.

"Is that what happened with the karaoke?" asked Lacoste.

"When we got caught, Sébastien and I thought he was going to harm himself, he was so scared. So we drew straws, left it up to God to decide which of us would speak to the Bishop. Sébastien lost."

"That's why Robert hates him," said Lacoste. "Sébastien reminds him of his own weakness."

"His cowardice and, by extension, his lack of faith. Yes."

They now stood in the shadow of the great wall.

"Why did Sébastien send for Dom Philippe?" Dussault asked again.

"Because he respects the man, and knew Brother Robert might tell the Abbot what he knows. Robert practically idolizes Dom Philippe. Besides, an abbot outranks a monk, and Robert's respect for authority meant he might confide in him."

"Did Brother Robert agree to see him?" asked Dussault.

Sister Irene nodded.

"And?"

"The Abbot said what Robert told him was private. He wouldn't tell us."

"It could've been anything, not necessarily to do with any attack."

Irene paused. "True, but Dom Philippe looked pretty upset when he came out."

"Where's he now?" Dussault asked.

"I don't know. He went back to Canada."

"And Frère Sébastien?"

Silence. Though Lacoste felt a hand touch her arm. She turned to look at Claude Dussault, who was staring at the monastery.

The huge oak door had swung open, and standing there, made miniscule by the size of the opening, was a man in burlap robes and a straw hat.

"It's one of the lay monks," said Lacoste.

He was gesturing to them to hurry. Irene took off toward the opening, her robes cutting a swath through the meadow. Lacoste and Dussault ran after her, trailing butterflies.

Once at the gate they saw it was no lay monk. It was Frère Sébastien.

They'd flown through and past the rain and landed in Blanc-Sablon in bright sunshine.

At the bottom of the stairs Gamache stepped aside to let others pass and checked his phone.

Messages were piled up. He did a quick triage, read updates from Beauvoir and Lacoste, then clicked on the email from the Italian police.

It contained Paolo Parisi's official documents. Driver's license, passport details, his income tax file number, and a photo of the smiling young man in what looked like a bar or restaurant. It was a close-up of Parisi, so it didn't even show who he was with.

Gamache realized he'd been overly optimistic, hoping the head of the Anti-Mafia task force would send something useful. He put away his phone and looked around.

Armand had been to the Lower North Shore of Québec many times and was prepared. As expected, a cool breeze, verging on a cold wind, was blowing off the Gulf of St. Lawrence. The air was fresh and clean, with a very slight undercurrent of salt and fish.

He hiked his satchel farther up over his shoulder and turned to face the breeze. Closing his eyes for a moment, he took a deep breath. The wind was just bracing enough to act as a small slap to the face. Exactly what he needed.

"*Patron.*"

He opened his eyes and smiled. There was the head of the Blanc-Sablon detachment.

"Valerie." Gamache extended his hand.

"I brought a jacket for you, but I see you dressed sensibly."

"Unlike the first time I came here. How long ago was that?"

They walked to her Sûreté pickup truck.

"I looked it up. One hundred and twenty-three years. And five months."

He laughed. "And nothing has changed."

It was almost the literal truth. Though he knew the first time he'd been to Blanc-Sablon was more like thirty years ago, the village itself looked exactly the same. Perhaps a new home here, an old one torn down, or fallen down, over there. But as for the rest, it seemed much like Three Pines, as though time had blown right by this place.

He tossed his bag into her vehicle and climbed in.

Valerie Michaud got behind the wheel and glanced at the Chief Inspector. Armand. Her eyes drifted up his familiar face, following the lines past the thoughtful brown eyes, to the scar at his temple.

This was the first time they'd met since it happened, though she'd been at the funeral for his slain agents. Had walked in the cortège. Had seen him stumble on the steps into the cathedral, but not fall.

They'd first met when both were junior agents. He'd arrived on the coast to assist his inspector in a homicide investigation. This had been her first posting. She'd risen through the ranks, achieving the position of station commander. She'd married and had children here, and while often offered promotion to other postings that would have been considered more prestigious, she'd chosen to stay there.

This was home.

Commander Michaud started the truck. "Where to? You haven't told me why you're here. I'm presuming it's not a vacation."

"*Non.* I need to find a Dom Philippe—"

"A *religieux*?"

"A monk, an abbot, yes."

"Wait a minute, is he the head of that order that did the recording of the chants?"

"*Oui.* Do you know him?"

"No, but I know his family. He's a Rousseau, right?"

"Yves Rousseau, before he took his vows and changed his name to Philippe. Can you take me to the family home?"

"No problem." She put the vehicle in gear and they headed off.

"Who else is in the family?"

"His sister, Eunice, died years ago, but he still has a brother here. Raymond. We call him Big Gars."

Big fella. It was very "coast" to have a phrase half in English, half in French.

"He's large?"

She laughed. "No, that's coast humor. He's actually quite small, slender, but he has a big personality." A few people waved as she drove by, and she waved back.

"Any nieces and nephews?"

"Niece. She's moved away. Most do. You think your fellow is here?"

"I hope so."

"I guess he could be. I haven't heard, but then I might not, especially if he didn't want anyone to know. At this point he'd just be another stranger. Is he hiding?"

"I think so."

"Well, he's found a good place for it. Can you tell me why you want him?"

"Afraid not. But I can say he isn't suspected of any crime. If anything, he might be a valuable witness."

As they bounced along the washboard dirt road, Gamache stared out the open window and once again marveled at the homes along the rocky shore. They were pastel-colored and beautifully kept up, though some were showing wear from the constant salt water splashed on them.

There wasn't a tree in sight, and never had been. Where there wasn't rock, there was scrub, all pushed in the same direction by the constant wind. As they passed the protected harbor, he saw fishing boats returning with their catch.

"You missed lobster season by ten days, *patron*," she said, noticing his almost faraway expression as he stared out to the gulf. "But if you have time, my husband and daughter have just landed with a fresh catch of scallops. We're planning a bonfire at the cove tonight."

Armand's hunger came surging back. If only . . .

"I'm afraid I'm booked on the next flight out. I seem to remember that many people here go to Florida in the winter."

"True. Especially the older ones. A generation ago that would have been unthinkable, but—"

"Is Raymond Rousseau one of the ones who goes to the States?"

She was surprised by the abrupt interruption. "Yes. We know because they inform us so we don't worry when we haven't seen them for a week or so."

Gamache had to squint against the sun glaring off the water. No huge refrigeration ships here. Just the small fishing vessels a parent passed on to a son or daughter. When he'd first arrived, decades ago, the harbor was thick with boats. Now he could count them on both hands.

He committed the sight to memory in case even those were gone next time he visited.

"Something's just occurred to me, Armand. About the Rousseaus."

"*Oui?*"

"I realize I haven't seen Raymond and Miriam in a while."

"How long?"

She thought. "Four days maybe. Less than a week."

"Is that unusual?"

"Slightly. They'd normally be at Sunday night bingo and spaghetti supper at the fishermen's hall, but they weren't."

"They didn't tell you they were going away?"

"*Non.*"

Chief Inspector Gamache no longer had a faraway look. Now he was completely focused on the road ahead.

Commander Michaud pressed a little harder on the gas.

# CHAPTER 33

⁓

Claudine McGregor stared at the photo Beauvoir had handed her and shook her head.

"Nope."

The Executive Director of The Mission gave it back and walked away.

So much for that theory, thought Jean-Guy. He put the photo of Paolo Parisi back in his pocket and watched the elderly woman with the wild hair and sagging sweats shuffle down the hall to the cafeteria.

"Wait up."

She did not.

When he caught up with her, he had to stand right in front of her to get her attention.

He'd had an idea. "Look at this."

"It's a waste of time."

He brought out his phone and clicked on a photo. This one showed Parisi dead.

Madame McGregor was fiercely protective of the residents, so wouldn't talk about one with a cop. At least not a living resident. But a dead one was another matter.

Claudine looked at the photo and drew her brows together. Not, Jean-Guy thought, in horror at seeing the face of someone clearly dead. She'd seen enough of those, on sidewalks and under bridges, on subway grates and in ditches.

It was seeing a familiar face that concerned her.

"I'm sorry," said Jean-Guy, and meant it. "You did know him."

She nodded, still staring into Parisi's wide-open eyes.

"What happened?"

"He was killed."

"I can see that. How? Why?"

"He was staying here?"

"*Oui.* For a couple of weeks. Left a few days ago and hasn't been back. I was worried . . ."

"Who is he?"

"He called himself Guido. I doubt that was his real name. He was a nice young guy. Italian, of course. Spoke a little English. Almost no French, but wanted to learn."

"Did he hang around with anyone in particular?"

"He had breakfast every morning with Big Stink. He was teaching Guido French."

"Is Stink his family name?" asked Beauvoir and saw Claudine's wrinkled face wrinkle even more.

"I believe they changed it to Stink when they immigrated. It had been Smith."

Beauvoir gave a grunt of laughter. "Can I speak to Monsieur Stink please."

"You're out of luck there too. He hasn't been back for a week. I think he wanders."

"Dementia?"

"Maybe. Not bad enough to alert the cops, for all the good that would do. But he always comes back."

"Can you call me when you see him next?"

"No."

Beauvoir sighed in exasperation. "I need to see your security video again. This time over the period when Guido was here. Did it coincide with any of the VIP visits?"

"Probably." But she didn't move. "Since when are the cops interested in the death of a homeless guy?"

Beauvoir felt his hackles rise, partly, mostly, because he knew the truth of it.

"And even I know this isn't your jurisdiction. So why're you investigating?"

"He was involved in the murder of Charles Langlois. We've taken over the investigation."

"Involved? How?"

"He drove the car."

"Impossible."

"Why?"

"He didn't have it in him. He was a homesick young guy who'd had some bad luck. Not a killer."

"And you might be right," Beauvoir lied. "I need to see the security video to help prove it, one way or another."

Madame McGregor glared at him, then shuffled back to the entrance and the small room with the security monitors.

It took Beauvoir a while, but he finally found him. There was Paolo Parisi, sitting at a long table in the cafeteria having breakfast. A man sat across from him.

Beauvoir hurried out of the room and ran down one corridor, then another, looking into rooms until he found Madame McGregor.

"Come with me." He showed her the image frozen on the screen. "Who's that?"

"I told you. Big Stink."

"That's the man teaching Pari—Guido—French?"

"*Oui*. Every morning."

Beauvoir advanced the tape. The two men were deep in conversation. It looked intense.

"Why do you call him Big Stink? Do you know his real name?"

"*Non*. We call him that because he smells."

"Of what?" Earlier, when he'd first heard the nickname, Jean-Guy had thought the homeless man must've smelled of shit or booze. But now . . .

"Mothballs. Stank to high heaven."

"Fucking hell." Beauvoir turned back to the screen and an image seven days old.

Of Dom Philippe chatting with Paolo Parisi.

Stop here."

They were twenty meters from the pastel home. Oddly, Gamache had asked her to make a quick stop at the grocery store, where he bought milk and eggs, coffee, tea, bread, and thick slices of maple-smoked bacon.

"Planning a picnic, Armand?"

Then they'd driven to the modest house on the outcropping of rock.

"How can someone get into Blanc-Sablon without being noticed?" Gamache asked while staring at the place.

"Not by plane. We know who arrives. Not to monitor them, but in a small commun—"

"Yes. But how else? There are no roads linking the town to the rest of Québec."

"True, but you can drive from Labrador. It's right there. You'd have to go through the Anse-au-Diable, then past the Anse-au-Loup."

Devil's Cove, then past Wolf Cove. To here. Seemed about right, thought Gamache.

"But the best would be by boat, from further down the coast, or even Newfoundland. There's a ferry, but you'd be seen and any stranger would be noted."

"It could be done, then, by a smaller boat."

"Quite easily, yes. Especially if they had a guide and landed at night."

"Okay. Are you armed?"

"*Oui.*"

"Good. I'm not."

"Would you like my gun?"

"*Non, merci.*" It was said as though he'd declined another cucumber sandwich. "At my signal, go around the house. Check the windows. If there's a back door, stay there."

They'd stopped just far enough away that any amateur getting off a shot would probably miss. A pro, though, would be another matter.

They got out of the truck and stepped behind it.

Valerie Michaud rested her hand on her holster. And waited. Tense. Eyes sharp.

"Monsieur Rousseau," Gamache shouted. "My name is Armand Gamache. I'm with the Sûreté du Québec."

The small home was two stories and painted a now faded periwinkle. Eerily quiet, it had about it an abandoned feel. As she waited for his signal to move, Valerie Michaud could hear the waves hitting the rocks. It had always seemed an almost calming sound.

Now, she heard the violence of it. The thrashing, which had been the last thing so many mariners had heard, drowning out their own screams for help that they knew would not arrive. It was now the sound of relentless despair.

Gamache signaled her to move. Now. As he stepped out from behind the truck, drawing attention momentarily to himself.

What the hell are you doing here?" demanded Frère Sébastien.

The flush of anger ran all the way down his neck. He'd swept off his straw hat and clutched it as he stared, glared, from the nun to the other two.

The heavy door had been closed and locked behind them, and now the three visitors, the three intruders, stood in the forecourt of the monastery. Admitted, but admittedly not welcome.

Ranged behind Sébastien, holding their pitchforks and shovels, were the other lay brothers. This was half of Claude Dussault's nightmare. The monks with pitchforks. Thankfully, the other half would not now happen. The assault team with automatic rifles would not be needed.

"It's okay, Sébastien. They're here to help," said Sister Irene.

"Help? How? How do you know who they are? And you've brought them straight to us."

"I didn't tell them anything. They already knew about you and

Robert and this place." She looked at the tall walls and fading blue of the early-evening sky. Despite the tension, Irene could feel the attraction of the place. Of the safety it offered from a not-always-kind world.

"Who are you hiding from?" Lacoste demanded.

"This is Inspector Lacoste, of the Soor . . . something, in Kwee-bec—" Sister Irene started.

"Sûreté du Québec." Lacoste stepped forward. "Isabelle Lacoste. And this is Claude Dussault, the former head of the Paris police. You met my boss when he investigated a murder in Saint-Gilbert."

"Gamache? Is he with you?"

"No. He's in Québec looking for Dom Philippe. Do you know where he is?"

"The Abbot? *Non.*"

"You know why we're here," she said. "You and your friends know something. Brother Robert certainly does. It scared him so much he barricaded himself in here."

She looked around. From the inside it didn't look so bad. There was a healthy, well-tended garden, the calming buzz of bees, and the walls were high enough not even butterflies could get in. Which was, she had to admit, a relief.

Sébastien took Sister Irene aside. "Do you trust them?"

"I didn't at first, but I do now. I really do believe they are who they say they are." She stared at him. "Since when are you a lay brother?"

"It was the only way I could get in. I wanted to be close to Robert, in case . . ."

"Has he told you anything?"

Sébastien shook his head.

"Do you think Dom Philippe knows? He said Robert didn't tell him anything, but maybe . . ."

"No, Robert told me he didn't trust the Abbot."

"What? Since when? He worshipped Dom Philippe."

"It was just a feeling he got when they met."

"Since when do we trust Robert's 'feelings'? He's afraid of the color beige, for God's sake."

"Is beige actually a color?"

"Now he's afraid of Dom Philippe?"

"What's wrong?" Lacoste, along with Dussault, had edged closer. "What're you talking about? I heard you mention Dom Philippe. Has something happened?"

# CHAPTER 34

Commander Michaud raced around the side of the house in Blanc-Sablon, glancing quickly into windows. She saw nothing. Not even a light.

She also didn't see one of the windows at the front, on the upper level, slide open.

But Gamache did. He also saw the tip of a rifle poke through the lace curtain.

His concern, since he'd heard that the Rousseaus hadn't been seen in days, was that they were either being held hostage, or were dead inside. Along with Dom Philippe.

If so, there was a chance the killer was still in there.

What was pointing at him was a .22. It was a hunting rifle for smaller game.

This was no professional hitman. This was a frightened villager.

"*S'il vous plaît*, Monsieur Rousseau. I'm here to help." Gamache considered edging back toward the protection of the pickup, but worried that any movement might prompt the person to shoot. So he stayed put.

"I met your brother, Yves, Dom Philippe, at Saint-Gilbert a few years ago." He paused. The tip of the rifle had not moved.

Armand also realized, as soon as he'd seen the small-caliber hunting rifle, that Dom Philippe could not be in the house. He'd have told his brother that the visitor wasn't a threat.

He put his disappointment aside. The brother would still have a lot to tell them. He must know something if he was so frightened he needed to point a gun at a Sûreté officer.

"I know Yves must've warned you about strangers and told you not to trust anyone. But you know Valerie Michaud. You know you can trust her, even if you don't know me." He paused. "Look, I'm not even armed."

Armand took his jacket off and dropped it on the ground.

"Turn around," the man called.

Armand sighed. No experienced cop would voluntarily turn their back on a gunman. Still, he did it. Pausing to stare at the empty vehicle, then turning back around.

"You see? No gun. Now, please. It's getting cold."

Though in fact, Gamache was perspiring. There were dark marks under his armpits and down his back.

Finally, the rifle disappeared, and a few moments later the front door opened and a wiry older man, unshaven and disheveled, came out still holding the .22.

"Raymond Rousseau, what do you think you're doing?"

The voice came from the corner of the house where Valerie Michaud stood. Her gun, Gamache saw, was still in its holster. He was grateful for that. It meant the situation would not escalate.

"You should be offering us hot tea, not threats. Where's Miriam?"

The station commander strolled forward as though she'd already been invited in for tea and cookies.

The rifle lowered. "In the basement."

"Well, get her up here. We need to talk."

"Miriam!"

Armand lowered his arms, scooped up his jacket, and just like that, it was over. Or almost.

Jean-Guy Beauvoir was so stunned it took him a full thirty seconds of staring at the paused image before he noted the time on the Mission security tape. Then he hit play again.

The video was at double speed so he could get through it quickly. He now knew what he was looking for. And who he was looking for.

And there it was. A section they'd already seen, but hadn't fully appreciated. Once again, he stopped the recording.

There was Charles Langlois in the kitchen of The Mission. He was talking with Jeanne Caron. They'd seen that part already. Thought that was the headline, and it still was. But the scene had more to tell them.

In the foreground a grinning politician heaped food onto the plate of one of the residents. The resident was wearing an old grey suit, too big for him.

Beauvoir could almost smell the mothballs.

"Shit, shit, shit," he muttered and started the tape again.

Jean-Guy's quick eyes, trained after years of scanning for threats, moved from one security camera to another, and finally found them again.

Charles Langlois was opening the locked front door late one night and admitting Jeanne Caron. But there was someone else standing in the shadows.

Enlarging, brightening, focusing the image, Jean-Guy was still unable to make out who it was, but thought it was again Dom Philippe. Watching them.

He hit play, and the scene played out. They'd already seen Langlois and Caron going into his office. They'd also seen the two of them leave a few minutes later, and had followed them to the door, where Langlois let her out and relocked it. But this time Beauvoir slowed down the tape and lingered on the office. He saw Caron and Langlois leave. And he saw something else, just as the door swung closed.

A third person had been in that meeting, and now he stood alone in the office, as though it belonged to him.

It was Dom Philippe.

"Holy shit," Beauvoir whispered and sat back in the chair, staring in disbelief. But the image was unmistakable, as was the look on the Abbot's face. He was content. Certainly satisfied.

This meant the person in the shadows by the front door hadn't been Dom Philippe. It must have been Parisi.

"What the hell's going on here?"

Where's your brother?"

They were sitting at the kitchen table, cups of strong tea in front of them.

Gamache had brought in the bags of groceries. He'd bought them suspecting the elderly couple, if still alive, might be running low on food if they hadn't left the house in days.

Raymond at first refused the offering, but Miriam brushed that aside and grabbed the bags, calling her husband an old fool. Though it was said with affection.

"We were afraid to leave," said Miriam. She was wearing a clean, crisp polka-dotted apron over her round body and was standing by the white enamel stove, shoving a pound of sizzling bacon around a cast-iron pan.

The home was soon filled with the scent of bacon and eggs. And fresh-perked coffee.

The toast popped up, and before Armand could butter it, Miriam waved the spatula at him. "Sit."

"Yves came here a month or so ago," said Raymond, wiping the toast into the yolk and bacon drippings on his plate. "Haven't seen him since. But he called a few days ago warning us that someone might be on their way here looking for him. They were dangerous, he said. Killers."

"You thought it was us," said Gamache.

"Yves told us they'd probably come as friends," said Miriam. She was eating standing up, even though there was a seat at the table.

"That's why you were going to shoot us," said Valerie.

"But you didn't," said Armand.

"To be honest, I was just about to when Mother stopped me."

"We only kill what we can eat," she explained. "And you're too big for the pot."

Armand laughed. "Thank God for éclairs." Then he grew serious. "And your brother didn't tell you who these people were."

"No."

"Why didn't you tell me?" asked Valerie, but after decades on the coast, she knew the reason. These were people who solved their own problems. It would never occur to them to go to the police. If there was trouble, the police came to them for help.

"Tell us about his visit a few weeks ago," said Armand.

"He showed up unannounced," said Miriam. "First time we'd seen him in—what, Big Gars? Forty years?"

"At least, Mother. Barely recognized him."

Armand smiled at her calling her husband Big Gars. Big Fella. He wondered how long it had been since she called him Raymond. And how long since he'd called his wife anything but Mother. Probably not since their first child was born.

"Why did he come here?" Gamache asked.

Now Big Gars and Mother looked uncomfortable. Armand decided to help them out.

"He came asking for money and to borrow your passport and probably driver's license."

Raymond nodded. If standing side by side, the brothers wouldn't look that much alike. The Abbot was taller, slightly softer in body. Big Gars was wiry, more weather-worn. Weather-beaten. But in a passport or Québec driver's license photo, Dom Philippe could pass for his brother.

And clearly did.

"We took all but fifty dollars out of our account and gave it to him," said Miriam. "Along with our credit card."

"How much cash was that?"

"Came to just under nine hundred dollars. Our card has a ten-thousand-dollar limit. He bought a round-trip ticket to Grenoble on it and rented a car."

"He also borrowed a bunch of clothes."

"Do you have any idea where he is now?"

"*Non*. His return flight was a few days later." Big Gars rested his bright blue eyes on Gamache's deep brown ones. "Is he okay?"

"I think so, but I need to find him. Is there anyone else he might go to for help? Another family member?" Just then, his phone buzzed. "Do you mind?"

They shook their heads.

Gamache walked into the neat front room.

"Jean-Guy?"

"I'm at The Mission, *patron*. I've watched the security tapes. Have you found Dom Philippe?"

"No. He's gone. He came here straight from the monastery, but—"

In a move almost unheard of, Jean-Guy interrupted Gamache.

"Listen. Dom Philippe and Paolo Parisi were here at the same time."

"At The Mission?"

"Yes. They had breakfast together every morning."

"*Quoi?*" What?

"But there's more. The Abbot also knows Langlois and Caron. He was in the meeting with them in the Exec's office. We didn't look closely enough. When those two left, you can just see Dom Philippe in the background as the door closed."

"He knows Caron?" Gamache was so stunned he felt he needed confirmation. "Jeanne Caron?"

"*Oui, oui.* More than in passing, it seems."

Gamache's mind raced.

*What does this mean, what does this mean, what could this possibly mean?* He looked out the window to the rocky shore. Where so many ships had been dashed. Where so many screams for help and prayers had gone unanswered.

He suddenly felt himself foundering.

"Did someone mention Jeanne?" Raymond Rousseau was standing a few feet into the living room. "We were just about to tell you about her."

"Hold on, Jean-Guy." Armand turned to Rousseau. "We're talking about Jeanne Caron. The Chief of Staff for the Deputy Prime Minister."

"Yes. That's the one. You asked about family members. She's the only one we could think of."

Jean-Guy's mosquito voice came through the phone. He'd obviously heard. But Gamache ignored him and was staring at Big Gars.

"She's family?"

"Our niece. Eunice's girl."

"Jeanne Caron?" Gamache repeated, barely able to grasp what he was hearing.

"Yes. I just said so. Lives in Ottawa now. She comes back every now and then, when there's some official visit, some federal announcement. But not recently."

"When was the last time?"

"Mother?"

"Two and a half years ago, when they announced the road project."

Big Gars turned back to Gamache and saw the sort of look a swimmer has when they've just inhaled a huge amount of seawater and are about to choke.

Gamache put the phone down and with it Beauvoir's increasingly insistent squeak. He patted his pockets and found the photograph the priest had given him.

"Who are these people?"

"Oh, so you have it. We've been looking for that picture," said Raymond. "That's Yves, Eunice, and Jeanne."

And from the phone a tiny "Oh, shit."

What do you mean he refuses to see me?" Lacoste demanded, though the meaning could not have been clearer.

"Did you expect anything else?"

She was standing in the large courtyard garden of Grande Chartreuse facing the head of the lay monks.

Isabelle took a deep breath. He was right, of course. It would have been a miracle if Brother Robert, afraid of beige, had agreed to meet her. Still, she was far from certain this smug young man had tried very hard, if at all.

With his long face and burlap smock and straw hat, he looked like one of those sad donkeys from *Don Quixote*. Though he'd been given just enough power, by the Abbot of this monastery, if not by God, that he managed to also be snooty. A haughty ass.

"You're the first women to cross that threshold since the monastery was built," said the lay monk. "I think you have gone far enough."

He clearly meant *too far*.

She rolled her shoulders and flexed her neck, to release the tension. Confrontation did no good and would only make this man dig his hooves in further.

"If I can't see him, can you take him a message?"

"No."

As she looked at his stubborn, mulish face, Isabelle tried to understand where he was coming from. She saw herself, saw the situation, through his eyes.

The sudden appearance of strangers, never mind two women, in their forecourt, having breached the wall, must have been a shock. His job, as head of the lay monks, was to stand between the Carthusians and the outside world.

He was just doing his job. As was she.

"What would you suggest?" She stepped back both physically and figuratively.

"That you leave."

She smiled. "Unfortunately we can't. We've come a long way, and Frère Robert has information we need to save perhaps thousands of lives."

"I can ask him to pray that your situation is resolved and those lives saved, but that's all."

"I imagine he's already praying for that."

"Then there you have it. His prayers will be answered, though the answer is not always yes."

It was the dismissive justification Isabelle had heard from clerics all her life. It covered a multitude of sins.

"Is it possible, *mon frère*, that we are the answer to his prayers?" It had worked once, why not again?

"I doubt it."

"Why?"

"Because if you were, I'd let you in."

Sister Irene rolled her eyes. She wished she'd thought of that.

"Goodbye." The lay monk held his arm out toward the gate. He held all the power and knew it. Lacoste had nothing. Except . . .

She looked at Dussault, who raised his bushy brows. Reluctantly reaching into his breast pocket, he withdrew an official-looking envelope and handed it to her.

"This might help," said Lacoste. "Maybe not you, but us. As you say, the answer to your prayers isn't always yes."

The lay monk took it and read the search warrant. Then he turned and walked away.

"Do you have a copy of that, Monsieur Dussault?" Lacoste asked.

"*Non.*"

They watched the mulish monk step through an archway; then he, and the warrant, disappeared.

Gamache got back to the airport just as the plane's door was closing. All the way back on the flight, he ignored the man next to him who was going on and on. How lucky he was that the seat had opened up. Then he segued into something about vaccinations and zombies.

"People do screwy things when they're scared. That's what the government's trying to do. Scare people. Take global warming . . ."

Gamache wasn't listening. He was looking out the window and willing the plane to get back to Montréal faster. Faster. And not just because he was seated beside an idiot.

Before they took off, Gamache had sent a quick text to Jean-Guy, telling him to have Customs and Immigration and Interpol do a search for a Raymond Rousseau. See where and when his passport had been used. And to track any charges on the credit card.

Once the plane landed, Jean-Guy was at the gate with news.

"Isabelle got into Grande Chartreuse."

"Thank God for that." The two of them were headed for the exit, Jean-Guy having to run slightly to keep up with the Chief Inspector's longer strides. "Has she spoken to Frère Robert?"

"I'm waiting for word. Frère Sébastien is also there, acting as a lay monk and sort of bodyguard slash gatekeeper, but seems Robert has refused to tell him anything. But he did meet with Dom Philippe."

"Robert did? So the Abbot knows what this is about. If we find him—"

"No, that's just it. Seems the damned monk didn't tell the Abbot everything."

"Why not?"

"He said he didn't trust him."

"Why not?"

"A feeling, apparently."

In the past Jean-Guy Beauvoir's disdain of feelings would have been obvious. But since working with the Chief, since going to rehab, since loving Annie, since having two children, he'd come to see how powerful feelings were. In many ways, in every way that mattered, feelings were more real, more powerful than thoughts. They were the engine of perception, which drove thought, which became words and prompted action.

Feelings were where it all began. For better and worse. And since they were homicide investigators, it was often the worse that they knelt beside.

Gamache tossed his bag into the car and got in the passenger's side. "Frère Robert had no actual reason to distrust him?"

"Apparently not."

They pulled out into the chaotic traffic at *l'aérogare de Montréal.*

Brother Robert was no longer alone in his doubts about the Abbot. Dom Philippe's presence at The Mission, his knowing both Parisi and Caron, was suspicious at best.

And Armand Gamache suspected they were not looking at the best.

You will not serve this warrant on us."

Standing in front of Isabelle Lacoste was a tall, powerfully built man. He wore a hood framing his face and radiated authority. He'd used the same tone as Obi-Wan Kenobi.

*These are not the droids you're looking for.*

But of course they were the droids. And Lacoste had every intention of serving the warrant. If necessary.

"I hope, *mon frère*, it won't be necessary."

He bristled at being called "*mon frère*," as though he and this young woman were equals. As though he was not the Abbot in charge of one of the most famous monasteries in the world. And she was, well, not.

Though he had to admit, it was the proper term. And he knew he should be one among equals, but still, it didn't feel right. Though there was more to take offense at than what she called him. The threat to search this most private of monasteries, for instance. To violate the sanctity of their home. Their place of worship.

It would not be the first time this had happened. And while this young woman was hardly the Inquisition come to slaughter them, the Carthusians knew that this was how bad things started. Innocently enough.

It was how defenses were breached. Not by force but by a smile. An offer to help.

The Abbot glared at Frère Sébastien, the Gilbertine. Who'd lied and entered their monastery as a lay monk. And opened the gate to these invaders. Yes, that's how defenses were breached. By friends. By the wolf in sheep's clothing.

"You wouldn't dare search the monastery."

Claude Dussault stepped forward, his face grave. "It would be a terrible thing. And I'd hate to do it. But too many lives are at stake. If we do have to serve the warrant, if I need to bring in a force, it will be on you. Not us. You have the power to stop it."

Sensing a weakening in the Abbot's defenses, Lacoste said, "We just need to speak to one monk. Twenty minutes should do it. I promise, we won't take him away. We don't even have to go inside. Just bring him to us. You can be here for the interview. Please."

The Abbot looked at the warrant in his hand, then stepped aside and spoke to two of the lay brothers, who left.

Irene and Sébastien exchanged looks, as did Claude Dussault and

Isabelle Lacoste. This did not guarantee that Brother Robert would tell them what they needed to know, but it was a huge step forward.

What can it mean that Dom Philippe and Jeanne Caron are related?" asked Beauvoir as they drove toward Montréal.

"And met recently at The Mission," said Gamache. "After you called, I told Raymond Rousseau that his brother had seen his niece. Both he and Miriam said that couldn't be true."

"Why not?"

"There'd been a falling-out. His niece had refused to see Dom Philippe, or even have his name mentioned. Seems he didn't return to Blanc-Sablon for her mother's funeral. Eunice died when Jeanne was thirteen. Drowned. Jeanne adored her uncle and begged him to come back and lead the service."

"Why didn't he?"

"I don't know. Might've taken his vows of silence and cloistered life to an extreme. He sent back a short letter of condolence and said he'd pray for Eunice's soul."

"That's cold."

"She couldn't forgive him. What made it worse was that years later, when the recording of the Gregorian chants came out, he did interviews and even personal appearances to promote it."

"He left the monastery for that, but not for her." Jean-Guy slid a glance at the Chief. "Doesn't sound like a nice man."

Gamache was silent for a few moments. "But something's changed."

"There's nothing like a common goal to patch things up," said Beauvoir.

"That being to poison the population?"

"If that's what's going on, yes. That's Old Testament shit. The Great Flood. Sodom and Gomorrah. Maybe when he finally did leave the monastery, he saw how screwed up the world is. Maybe he sees himself as some sort of messiah, an agent of God. Wouldn't be the first religious wingnut to take things into their own hands."

"Could be."

It was clear that Caron was the black wolf, or at least in league with it. And now it looked like her uncle Dom Philippe had joined the pack. But what use would a Gilbertine abbot be to terrorists?

One thing did occur to Gamache. If Caron knew that he and the Abbot had met. Had formed a mutual respect. Could she be using her unbalanced uncle to distract and mislead him?

Was it working?

"Why did Dom Philippe and Caron meet at The Mission?" asked Gamache, thinking out loud. "And with Charles Langlois? What were the three of them talking about? Is it possible that's how the map and maybe Langlois's notes got to the monastery? They weren't sent to Dom Philippe, they were sent by him."

Beauvoir considered that possibility. "But Frère Simon told us that Dom Philippe instructed him to keep the map safe."

"True. He made it sound like he'd told Simon in person. But suppose the Abbot 'told' him that in a letter and we just assumed it was face-to-face. We need to ask him."

Though at this point it didn't really matter. It was a detail for later.

"But why would they send Langlois's research to Saint-Gilbert?" asked Beauvoir as he navigated the heavy rush hour traffic. "Why try to keep it safe? If they're involved in the plot, wouldn't Caron and the Abbot want to destroy the evidence Langlois had collected?"

Gamache shook his head in frustration. "I don't get it. I just don't understand. Three people meet. At least one is deeply involved in a plot to poison Montréal's drinking water—"

"We're still not sure about that, *patron*. We suspect, but there's no proof. It might be toxic spills."

"Do you really think all this has been set up to cover up industrial waste?"

Beauvoir shook his head. No. A few days ago a disastrous toxic spill would have upset him. Now he was praying for it.

"Isabelle has to get in to see Brother Robert," said Gamache.

"And we have to find those notebooks."

"The Gilbertines have searched their abbey and so far nothing."

Once again, Gamache checked his messages. There was one from the agent investigating the murder in the Saguenay. Probably to tell him that he'd arrived. Armand marked it with a red flag, to be read later.

"That must be how Jeanne Caron got the other half of the Chartreuse recipe," Jean-Guy was saying. "Her uncle gave it to her."

"And Dom Philippe must've gotten it while at Grande Chartreuse."

"From Frère Robert? But why, and how? Don't only two monks have access to the recipe?"

"We need to get our thoughts in order. Let's go over it again. Brother Robert hears something in a confession that terrifies him. He suddenly applies for a job in the Curia, gets it, and leaves DC. But his conscience gets the better of him, and he asks Sister Irene to come to Rome, where he tells her that something horrific was going to happen, an attack that will kill thousands, but refuses to tell her more. She writes to Frère Sébastien at Saint-Gilbert-Entre-les-Loups and asks him to come to Rome and help her get the information out of their friend."

"Right. He goes, but by then Robert has taken off again, this time to Grande Chartreuse."

"Sister Irene doesn't know what spooked him, but something obviously did. Maybe he wanted to avoid seeing Sébastien. You said there'd been a falling-out."

"It seems an overreaction, doesn't it?" said Jean-Guy. "There're people I'd rather not see, but I don't barricade myself in a monastery."

"Either way, Irene and Sébastien follow him to Grande Chartreuse," said Gamache. "But Robert refuses to see them. That's when Sébastien had the idea of getting Dom Philippe over. Have you heard back from the parish priest in DC? Does he admit what happened?"

"That a monk took his place in confession? No. And he won't. Neither will he tell us who his regular parishioners are, those who go to confession."

"We need to go higher and ask the Archbishop then. Back to Dom Philippe. On Sébastien's request he leaves Saint-Gilbert-Entre-les-Loups and goes first to Blanc-Sablon. He borrows his brother's ID, credit card, and cash and heads to Grande Chartreuse, where Brother

Robert agrees to meet him. But once face-to-face, Robert apparently has misgivings about the Abbot. He told Dom Philippe something, but not everything. Dom Philippe then returns to Montréal and goes to The Mission."

"And connects up with Parisi and his niece. Was that planned? Or a coincidence? Did the Abbot see Caron at The Mission and realize she was someone he could tell about a possible attack?"

"But if her uncle tells her he knows about the attack," said Gamache, "why not just kill him too? He'd be dangerous to her. To them."

"It looks like Jeanne Caron brought him into the plot," said Beauvoir.

Armand shook his head. He just could not bring himself to see the Abbot siding with the black wolf.

But could it be what Beauvoir said? That isolation had driven Dom Philippe to the brink of madness, and when he finally left the monastery after forty years and saw the state of the world, he went over the edge? Did he now see himself as some sort of Old Testament avenging angel? Adopting muscular Christianity? Not just praying but acting.

"Is it possible," Gamache said, choosing his words carefully, picking his way forward, "that Brother Robert told the Abbot enough so that Dom Philippe realized the Deputy PM was behind it? When he saw his niece, the Chief of Staff, at The Mission, he rekindled the relationship. Hoping to get more information. Maybe even intimating that he was willing to help."

"You're thinking he was just pretending to be sympathetic to the cause? In hopes of what? Gaining their trust and stopping it?"

His boss's inability to see the Abbot as anything other than a decent man worried Jean-Guy.

"*Oui, exactement.* In hopes of finding out enough, getting enough evidence, and when he did, he'd come to me with it. He must've realized Brother Robert hadn't been completely honest with him. The Abbot is an astute observer. A keen listener. He's lived in community long enough, counseled enough monks to know when one wasn't being entirely truthful. He knew that Frère Robert had more information. That's why he pointed me there. In hopes I could get him to talk."

Gamache checked his phone. Still nothing more from Isabelle. He tapped out a quick message to her.

*You MUST get Robert to talk.*

He almost never used caps, so this would appear not just a shout, but a scream.

"He also pointed me to Jeanne Caron," he said. "When he gave her the other half of the Chartreuse recipe. He's not a co-conspirator. He's trying to expose her and her boss."

"But *patron*, that doesn't make sense. I agree, Dom Philippe must've given her the other half, but she was the one who sent it to you, not him. She wanted to get your attention, and he made it possible."

It was true. Armand Gamache felt his heart sink. Had Dom Philippe gone to Three Pines not to alert Gamache to the crisis, but to confuse him? Distract him from what was really happening? Get him to hare off in all directions?

Had Charles Langlois been sent by Caron to meet with him for the same reason? To send out vague half-truths that seemed more legitimate when the young man had been killed. Right in front of the Chief Inspector.

Was he an unwitting pawn? And maybe Langlois was too. And maybe, as he lay dying, the young man realized it.

He'd begged Charles to tell him who was behind this. To give him something. And the dying man had whispered, "Family."

And now, thunderstruck, Gamache had an idea. Could Charles Langlois have been trying to tell him who was behind it after all? And he'd missed it?

The family. Not his, but one of the crime families? Had Langlois recognized Paolo Parisi and known him to be connected to the mafia? That would explain the look of panic on Charles's face when he'd assured the dying man he'd tell his family.

Charles Langlois had gone to his grave, to his maker, to a drawer in the morgue, knowing he'd died senselessly. Because the numbskull head of homicide had made an assumption, based on his own experience when he thought he was dying.

Still, where did that get them? As hard as it was for Gamache to think that the Abbot was the black wolf, he also found it difficult to believe the mafia was involved in a plot to poison Montréal's drinking water. After all, they had no proof Parisi was mafia.

In Gamache's experience, the mob, while brutal, were also astute businesspeople who were surgical in their targets. An act of terrorism on this scale was too messy. And to what end for them?

He needed answers, not more questions. And he needed them now.

They'd come to a fork in the road, in every way. By habit Beauvoir got into the right-hand lane, which would take them into downtown Montréal and Sûreté headquarters.

"Go left."

"Left?" Beauvoir asked. The ramp was just meters away.

"Left!"

Jean-Guy yanked the wheel, and they just made the exit, to angry honking behind them.

"Where to, *patron*?"

"Ottawa."

# CHAPTER 35

⁓

Just over an hour later, Armand Gamache was staring at the famous buildings on Parliament Hill.

He'd been here many times. Sometimes for ceremonies. Often for meetings. He and Reine-Marie had brought the children here years ago.

This was the first time he'd looked at the buildings that were the symbol for, and housed the government of, Canada, and felt unease.

On the way to Ottawa, he'd written his friend and colleague David Lavigne, the assistant commissioner of the RCMP, to tell him what he was planning to do.

He had yet to reply.

"I'll come with you," said Beauvoir.

"*Merci,* but I need to do this on my own."

"Is that wise?"

"I think wise is disappearing in the rearview mirror, *mon ami.*"

"But," Beauvoir persisted, "if you confront Jeanne Caron, she could claim you attacked her. She could have you arrested. You need a witness."

"And what would stop her from saying we both attacked her? You're not just my second-in-command, you're my son-in-law. You'd be seen as a not-very-reliable witness, and a very likely accomplice. *Merci,* Jean-Guy, but I have something important for you to do."

"I didn't see a bakery on the way here."

Gamache laughed, then explained, giving Jean-Guy a sheet of paper written in his longhand. It could not be traced. No copy existed. And given the disturbing trend of schools no longer teaching cursive, it could not be read by a ten-year-old. Though Gamache doubted ten-year-olds were the problem. At least, thinking about the marshmallows, not this problem.

Jean-Guy looked at the list of names and numbers and nodded. "It'll be done, *patron*."

"Oh, one more thing. I need your gun."

Beauvoir stared at his chief.

"You know they won't let you in with it. You have no jurisdiction here."

"Worth a try."

"And if you do get in . . . ?"

But Gamache was silent, his hand out.

Beauvoir had a hundred more questions, most beginning with *Why?*—though *What?* was a close second. Instead, he handed the holster over and watched Gamache adjust his jacket as he walked up the hill. Then Jean-Guy got to work.

Jeanne Caron, *s'il vous plaît.*

"*Avez-vous un rendez-vous?*"

"No, I don't have an appointment. Can you let Madame Caron or her assistant know that Chief Inspector Gamache of the Sûreté du Québec wants to see her?"

He brought out his ID. The receptionist studied it. An RCMP officer, in full ceremonial scarlet uniform, came over and looked, then turned to Gamache and saluted.

"Monsieur Gamache."

"Do I know you?"

"Sargent Gauthier. Denis. My sister was—"

Gamache's expression softened. "Diane." He put out his hand.

"We met at the funeral. You keep in touch with the family. My parents. Her husband and children." His eyes had traveled to the deep scar by the Chief Inspector's temple before dropping again to hold Gamache's eyes. "They loved the bikes you sent with the Sûreté badge on them. They pretend they're part of the mounted division and the bikes are horses."

"Not motorcycles?"

"*Non*, thank God." The young man smiled.

"How are they?"

"Missing their mother. But Gerard talks to them about her and shows them photographs. He tells them how brave she was."

He did not yet, Gamache guessed, tell them how she'd died. Shot down, the young agent had died in her chief's arms. Staring up at him, pleading with him to save her. And God knew he'd tried. But finally, all he could do was say an improvised last rites—*God, take this child*—before he moved on. To say it again, and again. *God, take this child.*

Until he himself was shot twice. Tasting blood in his mouth, fighting for breath, he lay on the concrete floor of the factory and felt someone grab his hand. Tight. And heard the same prayer whispered over him. By Isabelle Lacoste. *God, take this child.* Before his eyes had rolled to the back of his head and he'd passed out.

"I'll take him up," said Gauthier.

"But he's not expected, he's not on the list."

"It'll be fine. I'll vouch for the Chief Inspector."

The metal detectors squealed when he went through, and Gamache apologized, taking out the handgun. His RCMP escort smiled, and instead of making him leave it behind, the young man handed it back to Gamache.

"I trust you, sir."

"*Merci.*"

As they stood in the elevator, Armand clasped his hands behind his back and felt the bulge of the holster on his belt. He watched the numbers count up and was determined that he would drag the truth from Jeanne Caron if it was the last thing he did. Before this nice young man, Diane's brother, was forced to shoot him. *God, forgive this child. Forgive me.*

Gamache followed the RCMP officer to the polished wooden door at the end of the corridor. The brass plaque said, *Jeanne Caron, Chief of Staff.*

Jean-Guy Beauvoir hung up from the Premier of Québec. The next on the list was the Mayor of Montréal. From there he'd go on to the Mayor of Québec City. The first person he'd called was the head of public works. It was vital that she be on the conference call. Not, Gamache had written and underlined, the cabinet minister in charge of public works, but the engineer who knew how the water-treatment plants actually worked.

It was time.

Jean-Guy punched in the number and waited for the Mayor to answer.

If the Chief wasn't back by the time the conference call was scheduled, he'd instructed Beauvoir to handle it himself.

Beauvoir started to make notes. How to convince men and women who didn't want to believe it that the unbelievable was about to happen. That an attack they'd supposedly prepared for was in the works. The worst-case scenario was unfolding, and they needed to put those preparedness plans in place.

Though it was clear, by his hesitation to tell them, that Gamache did not believe those plans were up-to-date or would do anything other than panic the population. But the people had a right to know. Had a right to defend themselves and their families.

As General Whitehead had predicted, the attack wouldn't even have to happen for society to fall apart. In fact, all that had to happen was that the warning be issued. Armand Gamache, in choosing to tell the leaders, who would have no choice but to make a public announcement, would effectively be doing the terrorists' work for them.

Beauvoir looked at the families streaming in and out of the Parliament buildings and realized these were probably the last few hours of normalcy in their lives.

What was Gamache doing in there? With a gun.

Just then, he heard sirens approaching.

"Oh, fuck," he whispered, just as the Mayor of Montréal answered. "*Excusez-moi?*"

We can't find him."

"What do you mean?" said the Abbot of Grande Chartreuse. "How hard could it be? He's a cloistered monk."

"Brother Robert's not in his cell," said the lay monk. "He might be in the showers or the chapel. We're looking. He might be preparing the recipe."

"The what?" asked Dussault. "Not the recipe for Chartreuse."

Lacoste pulled up the photo on her phone and shoved it in the Abbot's face. "Is this the recipe for Chartreuse?"

"How should I know? I'm not one of the holders." But the Abbot looked at it more closely. Then at her, more closely. "Where did you get this?"

"Dom Philippe."

"The Gilbertine. The one who came to see Frère Robert."

"Yes. Dom Philippe took away part of the recipe and a bottle of your privately labeled liqueur. He gave them to my chief."

"Why?"

"The Abbot wanted us to come here. To find out what Frère Robert knows about a terrorist attack."

"You got all that from two fragments of what might or might not be the recipe we've guarded for a thousand years? God help us if you ever get your hands on a scrap of the Dead Sea Scrolls."

"So Frère Robert was chosen to be one of two keepers of the Chartreuse recipe?" said Dussault, trying to catch up. "But he'd only just arrived. Why give it to him?"

"Because he's young and cowardly," said the Abbot. "One meant he could make the elixir for many years to come, the other meant he'd never leave."

"So where is he now?" demanded Frère Sébastien.

These silent monks just stared at each other, until finally the Abbot spoke.

"Find him," he said to his confrères, then turned to the three visitors. "Stay here."

Lacoste waited until all the monks, including Sébastien, had gone inside, then turned to Dussault. "Shall we?"

"You first."

"What about me?" called Sister Irene as her two companions disappeared into the main body of the monastery.

She looked around, then ran after them. A few butterflies that had become trapped in the billowing folds of her white habit came fluttering out.

Instinct told them to stay in the garden. Instinct was not always right. Within moments they were eaten by birds.

# CHAPTER 36

Y ou can leave me now," said Gamache once they'd entered the waiting room. "Thank you for your help."

"A pleasure, *patron*. I'll just wait and make sure you get in," said Sargent Gauthier.

"Not necessary."

"I know. It's the least I can do."

Gamache hoped he looked more grateful than he felt.

The receptionist's desk was empty. Gamache took a seat and waited, while the Mountie looked at the photos on the walls.

Taking in his surroundings, Gamache thought this office was a perfect reflection of Caron. Polished and impressive on the outside; shabby, dirty, broken on the inside. The desk looked like it had been found in a dumpster. The framed photos on the walls, which Gauthier was glancing at, were out of date, showing many politicians, now dead, shaking hands with other politicians, now disgraced.

Armand tried to order his thoughts, concerned that when he actually saw Jeanne Caron his mind would go blank. Taken hostage by an old and powerful grievance.

He could not let that happen. He needed a strategy. Some way to get this woman to tell him what was going on. Preferably without his having to draw his weapon.

Though he was willing to, and suspected it would be necessary. Time and events had overtaken him. Had run roughshod over and wiped out a lifetime of trying to do the right thing in the face of great temptation to do the easy thing.

This, what might be his last act, was what he'd be remembered for. His own travesty. The history he loved would judge him badly. But it didn't matter. He needed answers. Quickly.

Armand looked at his phone. Messages were pouring in. Though still nothing from Assistant Commissioner Lavigne or Lacoste.

Jean-Guy was setting up the call. Once that was made, the machinery would be set in motion, and nothing would ever be the same. He was about to pull the trigger and start the panic.

That panic would lead to chaos. And chaos would lead to the breaking down of civil society, of civility. Order would ultimately be restored, but it would be a strict, restrictive order. A new world order would be in place. Where rights were limited. Privacy was a thing of the past. Movement, travel denied. Elections suspended.

All for the public good. All with public consent. That passenger beside him babbling away on the flight was right about one thing. When scared, people would readily agree to things that hours earlier would have appalled them.

But there was one chance. If he could get Jeanne Caron to talk.

Just then, the door to Caron's private office opened. Gamache got to his feet.

A young man was standing there.

"My name is—"

"I know who you are, Monsieur Gamache. They called up from reception. I explained that Madame Caron can't see you."

He was polite but officious.

"*Merci.*" But instead of leaving, Gamache pushed past the assistant—

"Hey!"

—and into the Chief of Staff's private office.

It was empty.

"She's not here," said the smug voice behind him.

"Where is she?"

"I can't say."

"You had better, young man, or I'll charge you with obstruction of justice."

It was an empty threat and pretty soon this fellow would realize that Chief Inspector Gamache of the Sûreté du Québec had no authority there. But for now, for this split second . . .

Gamache didn't dare look at the RCMP officer, who knew full well he had no way to follow through.

"She left."

"I can see that. Where did she go?"

"I don't know."

"You must. You keep her agenda, don't you?"

"She's supposed to be in a meeting in ten minutes, but—"

"So her leaving was unexpected?"

"Yes. Some old fellow showed up an hour or so ago and she went with him. Told me she wouldn't be back today."

"Describe the man."

"Slender. Short white hair. He looked like a vagrant. Pants too short and the jacket too tight. It's like he grew a few inches overnight. Don't old people get smaller?"

He looked at the Chief Inspector as though expecting him to shrink in front of his eyes.

"Hey!" the assistant protested again as Gamache went over to the desk. "Stop him!"

But Sargent Gauthier just folded his arms across his chest and watched Gamache pull open drawers and flip through notebooks. The only thing he found was an agenda at the back of one of the drawers. It was a year old. He shoved it into his pocket, then walked up to the assistant.

"I need to see Monsieur Lauzon."

"The Deputy Prime Minister?"

"Yes. Now." Gamache softened his voice. "I'm sorry to do this to you, but this is a matter of national security. Tell me where he is. Through there?"

Gamache stepped toward what was likely a connecting door. The

COS would have offices close to, and probably connecting to, her minister.

"He's not here either. Didn't you see the news? He's in Washington for talks on a bilateral agreement on the environment."

Gamache studied the young man and realized that as soon as they left, he would contact Caron. "What's your name?"

"Frederick Castonguay."

"Well, Monsieur Castonguay, you're coming with me."

"I am not. I have dinner plans."

It was so mundane a protest it was almost laughable.

"I'll buy you dinner."

"I won't go."

"Then I'll place you under arrest."

Now Caron's assistant smiled. "You have no authority here, Chief Inspector."

"But I do," said the Mountie. "You're coming with us."

Gamache stared at the RCMP officer, Diane's older brother, in surprise. At this *beau geste*. This noble act.

At this *beau risque*. This great gamble.

"Give me your phone," Gamache said to Castonguay.

"No."

The Mountie patted him down and took it.

"Fucker."

Gauthier went to put it on the desk, but Gamache stopped him. "We need to take it with us."

"But they'll be able to trace where we are."

"Maybe. But if we leave it here, and he's gone, they'll know for sure something's happened. And we're the last ones seen with him."

The Mountie gave the phone to Gamache, and the three of them walked quickly back down the hall. When the elevator doors opened, the RCMP officer politely asked everyone to get out, and the three of them got in.

"I can't think that went to plan, *patron*," said the Mountie when the doors closed.

"*Pardon*," said Gamache, who was scanning his messages, then looked up. "*Non*. But it could have been worse. You do know your career is over. You'll be charged, along with me, with kidnapping."

"Too fucking right," said Caron's assistant.

"But at least I didn't have to shoot you. That is why you brought the gun, isn't it? To use on Caron."

"What?" demanded Castonguay.

"Don't look so surprised, Chief Inspector," said the Mountie. "It didn't take a genius to work out what you planned. Why else would you come in here armed? Diane told me you didn't wear a gun unless you thought you'd have to use it. And yet you came here, to a public building, with a weapon. And then there was the look on your face. I know that look."

Gamache studied the officer. "Is that why you came with me? To stop me?"

"No. To help. I owe Diane that. And for what it's worth, Madame Caron is so despised, I might've missed you and hit her." He smiled. "Then there was the small fact that Commissioner Lavigne told me you were headed this way. He ordered me to stay with you. To protect you. He chose me because of Diane. He knows how I feel about you."

Gamache took a deep breath and exhaled. That was one worry behind him. Lavigne was firmly on their side. Though it was the end of his career too. He was leaving quite a lot of wreckage in his wake.

"What has Caron done to make you do this?" the Mountie asked. "It must be pretty bad."

"I'll tell you when we're out of here."

Come quickly!"

Lacoste and Dussault had just turned yet another corner in the stone labyrinth that was Grande Chartreuse, when they heard the commotion.

"Hurry! Hurry!" The words bounced off the walls and floors, filling the space, making it impossible to tell where exactly they should hurry to.

"It's coming from there." Isabelle gestured down another of the long halls.

"No, no, down here." They looked behind them. Sister Irene was gesturing. "Come on."

They followed her. Footsteps, shouts for help, were all around them. Hurling, it seemed, out of the old stone.

Cries, trapped in the walls for centuries, were escaping.

The three of them ran up worn stairs. Then along more corridors, and climbed increasingly narrow and winding staircases, finally emerging at the top of a turret.

They were on a parapet high above the ground. It was dark, but they recognized the Abbot. He and two lay monks were staring over the side, their black robes flapping in the wind.

Lacoste's heart sank.

"What is it?" Frère Sébastien arrived just behind them.

Splayed at the base of the wall was a dark shape outlined by wildflowers. It was in the unmistakable shape of a body, spread-eagled. It looked, from on top of the turret, like a hatchling that had left the nest too early. Tried to fly too soon.

Or, perhaps, a dead monk.

Sister Irene sank to her knees, her forehead resting against the stone wall. Her eyes screwed shut. But it was too late. She'd seen the unthinkable, and now the Dominican nun would never stop seeing the body of her friend.

No one on the top of the wall had any doubt who was at the bottom.

"Did he fall?" asked the Abbot, shaken. "He must've fallen. It must be an accident." He looked from Lacoste to Dussault but did not get the reassurance he was searching for.

The investigators knew what the Abbot could not bring himself to believe. Someone had thrown Brother Robert from his sanctuary. His prayers, his God, his hiding place had failed him.

From the moment he'd agreed to take confession for a priest "too tired" to do his duty, Brother Robert's life was running out. He was heading to this place, this moment.

"Why was he up here?" said the Abbot. "No one ever comes here. There's no need."

"We have to go to him," said Sister Irene.

Lacoste turned to Claude Dussault. "Will you take them down?"

When they left, she sent off a quick message to Gamache.

Beauvoir saw the Chief approaching. He looked like a cabinet minister leaving Parliament. Authoritative but unremarkable. The same could not be said for the man with him.

For a terrible moment, Beauvoir thought Gamache had been arrested. Walking next to him was an RCMP officer in his impressive scarlet uniform. And between them was a young man in a sharp suit.

The officer held the man's arm in a tight grip.

Tourists were taking pictures and videos of the Mountie, excited to see the famous dress uniform. All that was missing was a horse.

There was no stopping the photos, or the fact the images would soon be posted on social media. Tomorrow all social media would probably be blacked out except for government-controlled sources. All news would be censored. Until then, images of the Mountie on Parliament Hill would be up. And with him, unintended and unmistakable, would be Chief Inspector Gamache and some strange man. For all the world, including the conspirators, to see.

Gamache got in the car, and after quickly introducing the two men who were now in the back seat, he gave Beauvoir back his gun. Jean-Guy sniffed it.

"Unused," said Armand. Then he texted David Lavigne a simple *Merci*.

The deputy commissioner had not replied to any of his recent messages. Lavigne had gone silent, gone to ground. He hoped by his own choice.

"Get across the border into Québec," said Gamache. "Quickly."

"Québec?" demanded the young man in the back seat. "Let me out."

Jean-Guy pulled into the traffic on Wellington Street as Gamache locked the doors.

Their guest was now unmistakably a hostage. And all three cops had just crossed a boundary.

# CHAPTER 37

The conference call was set up for later that evening.

"They have no idea what it's about?" Gamache asked as they headed to the border.

"None. But they got the message that it was serious."

"What is this about?" The Mountie in the back seat leaned forward.

Jeanne Caron's assistant, seated with the RCMP officer, listened as Gamache finally answered the Mountie's questions.

When Chief Inspector Gamache finished, both men were gaping at him.

"Wait a minute. My boss is planning to poison Montréal's drinking water? That's im—?"

They waited for him to say *impossible*, but instead, he fell silent. Gamache had turned in his seat and was watching the young assistant.

"Her routine has changed. She comes back after everyone else has left. Must be really late because I don't leave before eight every evening. I know she's been in by the changes on her desk next morning. Some classified files have been pulled and some have disappeared. Other executive assistants have come to me looking for them, but they're gone. I think she's also copied documents from other departments."

"What departments?"

"I can't remember them all."

"Try!" demanded Beauvoir. Gamache put his hand on Jean-Guy's arm to tell him to pull it back.

"The only one I can remember is the Auditor General. I couldn't figure out why she'd go there. When rumors started that our boss, Monsieur Lauzon, would be promoted to Deputy PM, I figured she was just familiarizing herself with the dossiers."

"But . . . ?" said Gamache, his voice steady.

"But there seemed a frenzy about it. She's normally so methodical. We call her Robo-COS. For Chief of St—"

"She wasn't consulting the files, she was cleansing them," snapped Beauvoir. "Taking out anything incriminating to her boss." He turned to Gamache. "Jesus. Including the episode with his daughter."

"What episode?" Sargent Gauthier asked but got no answer.

Privately, Gamache agreed with Jean-Guy.

After the charges of vehicular manslaughter against Lauzon's daughter were dropped, Armand had gone to the Auditor General. It was the department that oversaw ethics.

Gamache hadn't expected any action, and indeed, there was none. But he did want both the cover-up and subsequent threats placed in the record. A record that would have now been expunged. By Jeanne Caron.

That also explained why she wanted, needed, to see him. Why she'd called the other day. To issue fresh, even more serious threats. To make sure he was not tempted to go public. He could prove nothing, but an accusation against the Deputy Prime Minister might be enough.

Still, something didn't track. If Caron and the Deputy PM were that desperate, if they'd killed Langlois and Parisi and probably others, why not also kill him? Or, if they were afraid he'd left evidence with a lawyer, at least come to him with new threats. But they had not. They'd been singularly silent since those calls.

And that was frightening. It was as though some huge creature were swimming just below the surface. Biding its time.

*We wait. We wait.*

"Where to?" Beauvoir asked.

"Montréal. The Mission."

"You think Caron and Dom Philippe have gone there?" Beauvoir asked. "Why?"

"Honestly? Because I can't think where else they might've gone. If the attack is soon, within hours, maybe a day, they'll probably want to make sure everything's in order. I'm hoping they've set up a meeting with whoever has the poison and is actually going to do it. Where better than a shelter for homeless men and women? A safe place."

"A sanctuary," said Caron's assistant, sitting forward. "The old man used that word when he was convincing Madame Caron to go with him."

"He said sanctuary?" said Gamache.

"Yes. Said they'd be safe. Do you really think Monsieur Lauzon is also involved?"

"Involved?" said Beauvoir. "He's the black wolf."

"The what?"

"The one behind this. When thousands die, tens of thousands get sick, someone will have to be blamed besides the terrorists. And it won't be him."

"The Prime Minister," said the Mountie.

"Exactly. It'll be seen as his failure. There'll be a revolt against him in caucus. The Deputy PM, Lauzon, will take over. He'll declare martial law, suspend civil liberties. Political enemies will be silenced."

"A coup," said Castonguay.

"A police state," said Sargent Gauthier.

"I'll text my friend," said the assistant, "and tell her I can't make dinner. Then she won't be worried when I don't show up."

Gamache handed the phone to him, but caught the eye of the Mountie, who made sure that was what the young man really wrote.

You again." Claudine McGregor stared at the two men in front of her.

Caron's assistant and the RCMP officer had stayed in the car. A Mountie in full dress uniform tended to draw not the most welcome attention at a homeless shelter.

Gamache and Beauvoir, however, were beginning to fit right in.

Both were worn and drawn. Their clothes were rumpled and slightly soiled and not as fresh as they once were.

"Need a bed, gentlemen?" the Executive Director of The Mission asked. "And a bath?"

Gamache gave her a tight smile. "We need information. Is the man you call the Big Stink here?"

He felt ridiculous calling the Abbot that, and even more ridiculous when she corrected him.

"No 'the,' just 'Big Stink.'"

Gamache stared at her, waiting for an answer.

"I'm not going to give the cops information on any of our clients. This is a safe place for them. They need to know that."

"A sanctuary?" asked Gamache. "Did Big Stink call it that?"

"How should I know? I didn't follow him around. Tried to keep upwind of him." She held Gamache's eyes. "Okay, look, he isn't here."

"We can get a warrant," he said.

"Then get one. But you'll be wasting your time. I get the feeling you don't have much to waste. I'm telling you the truth, Chief Inspector. I really am."

Gamache gave a curt nod and made for the door. "Come on. They're not here."

"You believe her?" asked Beauvoir, following him out onto the street.

"Do you?"

Beauvoir thought. He'd actually come to respect the elderly woman, who'd stepped up when others had run away. He nodded.

"Then where are they?"

"There are two other places Dom Philippe would consider a sanctuary."

"Saint-Gilbert-Entre-les-Loups," said Beauvoir as they got into the vehicle. "And his childhood home in Blanc-Sablon."

"Exactly." Gamache slammed his door shut.

"Not there?" asked the Mountie gesturing toward The Mission.

"*Non.* So which one is it? Where'd he go?"

All three stared at the Chief Inspector, waiting for him to answer. Waiting for him to tell them what to do.

Armand brought his hands to his face. Rubbing his eyes and, as the others watched with some concern, he held his face in his hands. As though trying to shut out the world. The pressure. The pressure. The unrelenting, crushing pressure.

He had to choose. Had to answer the question. Which one?

Everything was riding on getting it right, and he'd already been wrong once. Both places were far away, there'd be no recovering from a mistake. And the conference call was fast approaching. The point of no return.

Probably not the monastery, not with Jeanne Caron, a woman, in tow. Though perhaps that was exactly why Dom Philippe would choose it.

Blanc-Sablon was remote, hard to get to, and the Abbot knew it well. Knew the hiding places, had friends and family there who'd protect them, even from the police. Especially from the police.

There was no clear answer. Maybe he should just guess. Then the scales, and his hands, dropped from his eyes and he turned to Beauvoir.

"Three Pines."

"What?"

"Dom Philippe told Olivier that the village was a sanctuary. They've gone there."

"To Three Pines?" said Beauvoir, not believing it. "Why?"

"It's close, it's essentially hidden—"

"And it's where you live, *patron*. Would a person trying to hide from you go right to where you live?"

"It's where I'd go. I'd hide in my enemy's camp. Dom Philippe might not be that cunning, but Jeanne Caron sure is."

In the rearview mirror Gamache saw the Mountie texting. Without doubt warning his family. Warning Diane's family. To get out of Montréal.

Armand didn't stop him. He owed her that.

Beauvoir pulled out and headed south toward the village. "If you're right, Annie and Reine-Marie and the family might be in danger."

"I doubt it. The Abbot and Caron would want to be as inconspicuous as possible. They'd never approach a home. They just want to lie low and wait until the worst is over. Still, I'll text them and the others, to make sure they lock their doors."

As he did that, the assistant said, "If you think Madame Caron and this Abbot are behind the plot, why would they have to hide? Who're they hiding from? Shouldn't we be the ones hiding?"

"They're hiding from us," said the Mountie. "They know we're after them."

"Come on," the assistant looked around. "If you're right, Chief Inspector, then Madame Caron has ordered at least one murder, probably more. She has killers at her disposal, and she's afraid of us?"

Beauvoir, slightly ruffled by the implication that he was not much of a threat, had to admit it was a good question. Why would Caron and the Abbot need a sanctuary?

"Oh, shit," he said, glancing at Gamache. "Maybe they're not hiding at all. You don't think they've gone to Three Pines to try to frame you? Maybe plant some of those classified documents in the village so that it looks like you're involved?"

Gamache was silent. That honestly had not occurred to him.

"Maybe they want to keep those documents safe," suggested the Mountie. "Maybe that's what 'sanctuary' meant. A safe place for the files."

"Right," said Jean-Guy, warming to the Mountie and his theory. "To be retrieved later, when the chaos settles down."

"But why?" asked the Mountie. "What's in those files?"

All three began speaking at once.

"I think they incriminate Lauzon." Gamache's quiet voice cut through the noise, and there was silence. "That's why she stole them. You might be right. It's not so much themselves they need to keep safe, but the documents. Not to incriminate me, or to protect Lauzon, but to protect themselves."

"It's insurance," said Beauvoir. "Once he's in power, he'll probably start eliminating everyone who's a danger to him. Page one of the tyrant's handbook."

"But if those documents can be insurance," said Sargent Gauthier, "they can also be a weapon. Blackmail."

"Holy shit," said Frederick Castonguay. "Lauzon might be PM, but with that evidence she, they, would hold all the power."

"If they can keep those documents safe, yes," said Gamache.

What is it?" Beauvoir asked.

They'd just turned onto the dirt road that led to Three Pines.

In the front passenger seat, the Chief had groaned. The sort of low growl or moan a person makes who's trying to suppress pain.

"An email came through an hour ago from the Chicoutimi investigation."

"The murder of that female postal employee."

"*Oui*. I'm just reading it now. I think we now know why she was murdered. She had a nephew. His name is Ferdinand, but he changed it to Robert when he became—"

"Oh, shit. A Carthusian monk."

"Yes." Gamache got on the phone to Lacoste.

"She was murdered to send a message to him," said Beauvoir as Gamache listened to the silence on the phone, waiting for it to engage. Then the line went dead.

He tried again. It could not connect. The monastery of Grande Chartreuse, like Saint-Gilbert, was too remote for reliable coverage.

"When Robert found out about his aunt's murder," Beauvoir was saying, "he took off for Grande Chartreuse. He must've been terrified. But what about the man on the Magdalen Islands? How does he fit in? It was the same hitman, wasn't it?"

"Or woman," said Gamache as he finished the quick text to Lacoste. "I think so."

Beauvoir stopped the SUV a hundred meters from the top of the hill that led down into Three Pines, and all four got out.

It was just after six o'clock. Midnight in France. He had to assume Lacoste was either speaking to Brother Robert, or would be soon.

The conference call was fast approaching. He had to get solid information before then.

On the way down, in the silent vehicle, he'd gone over where the Abbot and the Chief of Staff would lie low.

The hermit's cabin? But the Abbot almost certainly wouldn't know about that.

The B&B? The bistro? Places he'd be familiar with. Perhaps hiding in a basement. But there was no guarantee they would not be discovered.

They wouldn't dare try a private home. Or the Inn and Spa in what had been the Old Hadley House. Too many people.

Finally, all that was left was the obvious. He pointed toward St. Thomas's chapel, which had a weak glow from inside.

"Sanctuary."

He instructed Caron's assistant to stay in the car, then nodded to Beauvoir, who reluctantly gave the man the keys.

"Just in case," said Gamache, and the young man understood.

They started toward the small church, but just then, an urgent flagged message appeared. It was from Isabelle.

As Gamache read, his face grew even more stern.

"Brother Robert's dead. He fell, or more probably was thrown, from the wall of Grande Chartreuse."

"Shit. That means he can't tell us anything."

"That means the cleanup has begun," said Gamache. "And the attack is about to begin, if it hasn't already."

He began walking quickly toward the chapel, where their last hope lay.

Then broke into a run.

# CHAPTER 38

~

"There's a back door," Beauvoir instructed Sargent Gauthier. "Cover it."

The RCMP officer headed around the church, drawing his weapon as he ran.

Gamache and Beauvoir mounted the front steps, careful not to make any noise. The shadows were long, reaching out toward them from the forest. Beauvoir pulled his gun, and when Gamache nodded, he yanked open the large door and the two men went through.

"*Bonjour*, Armand."

Claude Dussault crossed himself, then slowly, methodically, moved his flashlight over and around the body of Brother Robert. Behind him the monks of Grande Chartreuse, led by the Abbot, were standing in a semicircle, chanting prayers.

There was nothing clutched in the dead man's hands. Nothing under his fingernails. No signs the monk had fought for his life.

If he was thrown from the wall—Dussault looked up and saw Lacoste looking down—then it was probably from behind. A shove. It would not take much.

There was no evidence. No reason to suspect murder. Beyond the fact the dead man was the key to stopping a terrorist attack. Which seemed enough. That and what the Abbot had said.

There was no reason to be up there. No one had been, it seemed, in decades.

Which was why it would make a perfect place for a clandestine meeting, and murder.

Isabelle Lacoste played the flashlight of her phone over the stone floor of the turret. It was thick with bird droppings and tiny skeletons of hatchlings that must have fallen out of the nest.

There were sticks and twigs and leaves that had either blown in or were brought there by brooding birds building their nests. Not realizing that it was too high. The wind too strong. Their babies too vulnerable.

Grande Chartreuse had been built when monasteries were also fortifications. From the rampart Isabelle Lacoste could see into the distant mountains. She could see an enemy coming. Though she knew she did not have to look nearly that far.

Dropping her eyes, she took a photo of the monk who had fallen from such a great height. And the monks around him praying for his soul. One of whom had fallen even further.

The friendly voice froze Armand and raised the hairs on his forearms.

He would recognize it anywhere. Anytime. Though it was more mature, more melodic, with more resonance than that first time, which was also the last time, they'd met. Years ago.

Beauvoir had his gun clasped in both hands and was pointing it at the Chief of Staff to the Deputy Prime Minister of Canada, and the Abbot of Saint-Gilbert-Entre-les-Loups. His body tense, his stare intense.

Instinctively, Jean-Guy had stepped slightly in front of the unarmed Gamache.

Armand had stopped dead in his tracks. The sound of her voice had paralyzed him, just for an instant. But for a cop, that was literally a lifetime. It was how long it took to pull a trigger. It was what he was afraid would happen. What he thought he'd prepared for. But apparently not quite enough.

He immediately felt ashamed of himself, for leaving Jean-Guy vulnerable for that split second. Then, as quickly as he'd frozen, he pulled himself together. Though he could feel the flush of cold sweat and his heart throwing itself against his rib cage, trying to get at Jeanne Caron. The unforgiven.

Caron and the Abbot stood at the front of the small chapel. As though waiting for them.

"You're under arrest," said Gamache.

"Hands out. I need to see your hands," commanded Beauvoir. When neither moved, he bellowed, "Your hands! Now!"

There was a moment when the earth stopped moving. When time was suspended. When all the ghosts who followed Armand stood staring at the scene. Wondering if another was about to join them, and if so, who would it be?

Then the Abbot's hands shot out and up. "Arrested? Why, Armand? We haven't done anything. We came here to find you. Jeanne is my niece. We're here to ask for your help."

"Help?" demanded Beauvoir. "She's behind it."

Dom Philippe turned to Jeanne Caron, then back to Beauvoir. "What're you talking about? Something terrible's about to happen. She's trying to stop it."

"That's why I was calling you," said Caron, who hadn't yet moved.

Gamache had seen Jeanne Caron often enough on the news, standing behind Lauzon, as he made some sort of announcement. He'd seen her age. And yet, in his mind, he still saw the woman in her late twenties who'd looked him in the eyes, so sure of herself, her position, her power. So sure she could bring him down. And she almost had. She'd almost ruined not just him, but young Daniel as well. His son. She'd almost killed his child.

This woman, standing once again in front of him. Slender, elegant, with hair now dyed and lines in her face almost covered by makeup. What hadn't changed were her eyes. In them he saw the same cold calculation. That certainty that she would win.

"Hands!" snapped Beauvoir.

She finally moved her arms away from her body. "I needed to see you, to warn you, Armand."

Armand. She called him Armand, as though they were friends. Still, he tried not to focus on such a trivial detail. No doubt meant to get under his skin. And, dare he admit, it had. Was he so very thin-skinned when it came to her?

"About what?" Gamache's voice was steady, his gaze unyielding.

"There's going to be an attack on Montréal's drinking water." She was pleading, almost begging. "You have to stop it."

And yet, those eyes. Those eyes as she watched for his reaction. When there wasn't any, she said, "But you already know. You followed our trail."

Caron took a step forward.

"Stop!" commanded Gamache. He'd had enough. Turning to Beauvoir, he said, "Give me the gun."

Without hesitation, he did and watched the Chief walk up to Caron and the Abbot. Dom Philippe took a step back, but Caron held her ground.

Gun in hand, Armand stood where Jean-Guy and Annie had gotten married. On the spot where his grandchildren had been baptized, Armand put a gun to Jeanne Caron's head.

The Mountie entered the chapel. She shifted her eyes to him. "For God's sake, make him stop, make him believe me."

Gauthier did not move.

"I need to know where and when and how it will happen," said Gamache.

"If I knew that, I could stop it myself, but I don't." She was cringing away now, her hands up as though in defense against a bullet.

"What do you know?" he demanded.

"I know it's soon. I know Lauzon's behind it. I know the target is one of the six treatment plants, but I don't know which one. Not for sure."

He knew she was lying, or, like most accomplished liars, she'd mixed the lie in with the truth. Gamache just hoped if he kept questioning her, some of that truth would slip out.

And that he'd recognize it.

"How did Charles Langlois fit into this?"

"I hired him to do some investigating, figuring no one would suspect him. I was wrong."

Gamache turned to the Abbot, who was watching this with wide eyes.

"And you? How did you get involved?"

"Does it matter, Armand? Please, time's short—"

"How?" Gamache all but shouted.

"My prior." Philippe took another step away from Gamache. "He wrote and asked me to go to Grande Chartreuse. There was some crisis. We had to meet in secret."

"And you went? All that way? He just had to ask?"

"Would this young man"—the Abbot pointed to Beauvoir—"have to ask twice? When I got there, one of the monks, a Brother Robert, told me what he'd heard in a confessional."

"And what was that?"

"That Montréal's water was going to be poisoned."

"That's all? No more?"

"No. And he had no proof. But he was terrified, Armand. Panicked."

"Who told him that?" demanded Beauvoir.

"I asked, but he didn't know. At least, I think he did know but wouldn't say. He begged me not to tell Sébastien, my prior, or his friend Sister Irene. He didn't want to put them in danger. I lied to them and said he hadn't told me anything."

"What did Brother Robert give you?" Gamache asked.

"You mean evidence? Nothing, I told you, he had nothing to prove any of it." The Abbot stared at Gamache, who just waited. *We wait. We wait.* And finally Dom Philippe understood. "I asked him to write out a page of the Chartreuse recipe, and to give me a bottle."

"Why?" Beauvoir seemed mesmerized by this soft-spoken man.

"If anything happened to me, I wanted those found in my possession so that whoever investigated would know I'd been to Grande Chartreuse. I'm pretty sure Brother Robert has more to say, but I couldn't get it out of him. We said a prayer together, then I left."

"You left them here for me," said Gamache. "Why?"

"I knew I couldn't stop whatever was going to happen. And neither could Jeanne. We didn't have proof. And I had to be careful. But you'd figure out who'd left them and go there. And get more out of him. You could stop it."

"*Some malady*," said Armand.

The Abbot nodded. "You obviously found them, but you're here, not there. You didn't understand."

Beauvoir was about to say that Lacoste was there, talking to Brother Robert, but some instinct told him not to.

Gamache's mind was working quickly, picking up the various shards of evidence and conjecture, examining them, then moving to the next. What the Abbot said fitted with what they'd discovered.

"You said Brother Robert told you he wanted to protect his friends—"

"*Oui.*"

"Think carefully. Did he actually say that, or was that your conclusion?"

The Abbot's eyes narrowed as he cast his mind back to that great reckoning in the small cell. Brother Robert's moment of truth.

"No. He didn't actually say that, but why else would he ask me not to tell them anything?"

Isabelle Lacoste was not afraid of heights, but still, it was difficult not to succumb to the terrible, the traitorous temptation to let herself be dragged right over the edge in a sort of hypnotic state.

Is that what had happened to Robert? Was it an accident after all? Had he arranged to meet someone up here and then been lured over the edge by his own phobia? Had his fears finally killed him?

But even so, how had Brother Robert managed to climb those steep stairs in the first place? How desperate was he that he'd agreed to a meeting in the most terrifying place in his world?

Who could possibly lure him up there?

# CHAPTER 39

⁓

Armand Gamache lowered the gun, all the better to see Jeanne Caron's face, her eyes, as he questioned her.

"As you said, there are six treatment plants, but you suspect the target is one in particular. Which one?"

"That's what I was trying to find among Lauzon's papers. When he left for DC this morning, I broke into his desk. He has a hidden drawer in an antique rolltop in his office. I found some papers. They're in there." She pointed to the satchel on the altar.

"If you knew about the threat to the water, why not alert the RCMP?" demanded Gamache. "Why not tell someone who could stop it?"

"I tried. I called you on Sunday morning."

"I'm the last person you'd turn to for help. The truth. Now!"

"That is the truth. Listen, listen." She seemed desperate now. "Years ago, when I tried to bribe you, then threatened you, then went after your son, you still charged Lauzon's daughter with manslaughter. You couldn't be corrupted, you couldn't be intimidated. You held your ground and took the hit. I came to you because you're the only one I knew for sure would never be involved."

Gamache glanced quickly at the Abbot, whose eyes were wide with anxiety.

"Look," she said. "I know my boss. Lauzon has no brakes, no moral guardrails. He'll stop at nothing to get what he wants."

"And that is?" asked Gamache.

"Power, of course. And with it wealth, and all that goes with both."

"How does poisoning the drinking water get him all that?"

She shook her head. "You know the answer, but if you want to play games, so be it. Here's what's going to happen. People turn on their taps and begin to die. All over the city. Within minutes there's complete panic. The main job of a leader is to keep the people safe. If they fail at that spectacularly, they're out. Within a week the PM is ousted. Lauzon is a Liberal, so when against all he's publicly stood for he brings in draconian measures, they're seen as necessary. *Voilà*. A coup."

"Why not just kill the Prime Minister?" Beauvoir asked. "Isn't that an easier way to become PM?"

"True, but then he wouldn't have absolute power. This way he would. He'd effectively be a dictator and a savior at the same time. I began to suspect something was going on about a year ago. I saw references to private meetings. At first, I thought Lauzon was having an affair. Then I realized he was meeting with people who were dangerous to him politically. People he should never be seen with."

"I need names."

"You need only one name." Even before she spoke, Gamache knew what she'd say. "Joseph Moretti."

It was what David Lavigne had essentially told him, without naming names. The Deputy PM had been seen visiting Ste. Émiline. The Moretti family had a second home there.

Joseph Moretti was the head of the Sixth Family. Considered as powerful as the five mafia families in the United States. From his homes in Montréal and Ste. Émiline, he controlled the drug trade, tobacco, booze, prostitution, gambling, and any number of so-called legitimate businesses across Canada.

Gamache had suspected the mob was involved, but only as hired killers, doing the hits in Chicoutimi and the Magdalen Islands. Hiring, then killing Paolo Parisi.

He never suspected it went up as high as the capomandamento. The head of the family. Joseph Moretti.

"You have proof?"

"Some. I know they met, but I don't know what they talked about.

I think what we need is in there." She again pointed to the satchel sitting on the raised wooden floor of the chapel.

"You've been by Marcus Lauzon's side since his first campaign. You've run his reelections, you've been his Chief of Staff. You've engineered his rise. He trusts you, relies on you. You're his right hand." Gamache glared at her. "You're saying he didn't bring you in on this?"

He had her. Her mask slipped and her old malevolence slithered out. Her contempt for him become visible for just an instant before being sucked back in.

Her face relaxed into a smile. "Got me, *monsieur*. I helped with some. At first. Bribes to prosecutors, to parole boards. To help move him up the ladder. I thought this was Lauzon collecting IOUs, to get to the final rung. But then I realized there were other events, meetings, agreements he hadn't told me about. I decided to try to figure out what he was up to. I kept seeing references to fresh water. Water security. Americans. But no specifics." She paused. "This goes back years."

Now she no longer looked sly. Jeanne Caron looked, and was, afraid. And for once, Gamache believed her.

He handed the gun back to Beauvoir. "What do you know about Paolo Parisi?"

"Parisi? I saw his name in one of the documents. Some minor figure Lauzon helped across the border. Why?"

Gamache turned to Dom Philippe. "And you?"

"Me?"

"You had breakfast with him every morning at The Mission."

"I did not. I had breakfast with some poor Italian boy who didn't speak French. Or English."

"Why?"

"Why? Because he was alone in a strange city. Wouldn't you try to help?"

The Abbot looked so sincere, Gamache almost believed him.

"What did he tell you?"

"Honestly, Armand, I couldn't understand what he was saying most of the time."

Gamache studied the elderly monk. There was no proof that Big

Stink and Parisi had a relationship outside of those breakfasts together. Parisi wasn't in the meeting with Caron and Langlois. In fact, he'd spied on them. It was possible the Abbot was telling the truth.

It was also possible, probable, both the Abbot and Charles Langlois were trying to stop the attack, while Caron was actually just using them. And Langlois had started to see that.

"When did you realize the plan was to poison Montréal's drinking water?" Gamache asked Caron.

"That was me," said the Abbot. "After Brother Robert told me what he knew, I went right to my niece in Ottawa, but she refused to see me."

"We were," Caron said, "estranged."

"I decided to write her a note, something that would get me in. The only paper I had was the page of the recipe Robert had given me. I tore it in half and wrote on the back, *Water*. I didn't want to say more because I didn't know who might see it."

"And a scribbled *Water* was enough?" said Gamache.

"I knew Lauzon's scheme had something to do with water, but not what," said Caron. "When I got that note, I needed to see whoever had written it. I was shocked to see Uncle Yves."

"I told her what Robert had said, about an attack on the drinking water. I could see she doubted me."

The phone in Gamache's pocket vibrated, but he ignored it.

"My uncle had just the word of a terrified monk hiding in some monastery in France. Without solid, irrefutable proof, there was no way anyone would believe the Deputy Prime Minister was plotting to poison thousands of citizens. I barely believed it. We needed hard evidence."

"That's when she approached young Langlois," said the Abbot.

Gamache was listening closely. Looking for the inevitable holes in Caron's fabrication.

"I'd met him on one of our official visits to The Mission a year or so ago," said Caron. "He'd told me his story. That he was a marine biologist who'd become an addict. Lost everything. Was estranged from his family. But he'd gotten straight. At the time, he was a resident of The Mission, and I'd only just begun to suspect Lauzon was up to something to do with water, but not what. I knew Charles could be trusted."

"Don't you mean used?" said Gamache, his voice cold.

"I used him the way you use your people, Chief Inspector. So far, I've lost one. How many have been killed under your leadership? How many have you told about this threat?"

Beauvoir took a step forward, but Gamache stopped him. He turned to Caron. "What's your relationship with Action Québec Bleu?"

"What?"

"AQB. The environmental group," said Beauvoir.

"Never heard of it."

Gamache stared at her. It seemed she was telling the truth. "Charles Langlois worked for them. They focus on water pollution."

"If he did, it wasn't through me. If the threat was from domestic terrorists imbedded in the federal government, why would I get him a job in some tiny provincial environmental organization no one's ever heard of? It doesn't make sense."

Beauvoir and Gamache looked at each other. She was right. It didn't make sense. But Langlois definitely worked for AQB.

Could he have been moonlighting? Working part-time with the environmental group? But if so, why? And why not tell Caron?

"When my uncle came to me with the story about poisoning the drinking water, we finally had a focus. The attack has to be on one of the six treatment plants. Probably on one of the two largest. I got Charles a job in the Atwater treatment plant, but he found nothing. So I had him transferred to the next likely place, the Charles-J.-Des Baillets facility in LaSalle."

"He didn't find anything there either," said Dom Philippe. "We had no idea which one would be targeted, and we were out of options. The three of us met at The Mission to discuss what we should do next. That's when Jeanne decided to try to contact you, Armand."

"Wouldn't they target more than one plant?" said Beauvoir. "Like the 9/11 bombers in New York, and the 7/7 in London. They'd increase their chances of success."

"But they'd also increase the chance of someone talking," said Gamache.

"And someone clearly did, in DC," said the Abbot. "Thank God."

"Langlois was working at the LaSalle plant when he was killed," said Beauvoir. "Isn't it fair to think he found something?"

"That's what I think too," said Caron. "It's the biggest, and the newest. The only problem is that it has the most sophisticated system to detect and treat toxins. That's why I didn't start him out there."

Gamache had done his homework on the various plants. The La-Salle one had multiple layers of treatment, finishing with sodium hypochlorite to kill all toxins, except—

"Botulinum would survive the treatment."

Caron nodded. "I was afraid you'd say that. It was my guess."

"Guess? You don't know the toxin?"

"Not for sure. I'm hoping it's in the papers I stole. I've read some but haven't had time to go through them all. And now you're wasting time. When Lauzon gets back in the morning, he'll discover the broken desk and know who did it. There's no going back now."

Gamache's jacket pocket buzzed again. This time he brought it out and glanced at the message. It was from Lacoste.

Brother Robert was dead. Almost certainly murdered. There was a photo attached.

"What is it?" Beauvoir asked.

As Gamache handed him his phone, he noticed Dom Philippe was staring into the dark corner of the small chapel.

Gamache grew very still. Beside him, Beauvoir, sensing the change in the Chief, lowered the phone.

St. Thomas's no longer felt like a sanctuary.

There was, in the shadows, the slightest glint.

Gamache just had time to turn, to try to warn the others, when the first shot was fired.

This didn't happen very long ago," said Dussault as Lacoste knelt and shone her flashlight on Brother Robert, face down in the grass.

She could see that her message to the Chief Inspector had been read, but he hadn't replied. Normally she'd at least get a *Got it.* But there was nothing.

"I've called the police in Grenoble," said Dussault. "They're sending a team."

She stood up and turned to the Abbot, interrupting their prayers. "Is anyone missing?"

He looked around. "Brother Constantine."

"The other monk who holds the recipe?" asked Dussault.

"Yes."

"We need to find him," said Lacoste. She turned to Sébastien. "Can you take me to him?"

The monks were looking at her as though she were either a saint or the devil, and they couldn't figure out which. What they did know was that before this woman had crossed their threshold, all of them were alive.

Lacoste followed Frère Sébastien into the monastery.

"I wanted to ask you something alone. Are you sure Frère Robert didn't tell you anything?"

"I'm sure. All he'd say was that something awful was about to happen. Brother Constantine's cell is over here."

"First, let's check out Robert's room."

"Right. It's this way." At the closed door, Sébastien hesitated. "It wasn't an accident, was it?"

"No."

Up until that moment the Québécois monk seemed to have managed a level of denial. But that was now gone.

"Who?"

"Who do you think?"

"I don't know. It can't be one of us."

*One of us,* thought Lacoste. There were few more dangerous phrases. Partly because it held truth. There were teams, tribes, families, companies. Friends. *Us.* But it was rarely just a description of a group. There was, about it, a distinction. "Us" implied there was a "Them."

And "Us" was better than "Them."

"Let's just for a moment say it was one of you. Who would you think?"

Sébastien seemed dumbfounded by the question. But he had an agile mind and had accepted the obvious. One of "Us" had killed Brother Robert.

"Let me think."

"While you do that, I need to look at his cell."

It turned out to be roughly the shape of a beehive. The lower floor was circular and fairly large, though spartan. There was a woodstove, a crude table with a single stool. The floor was slate, and there was a ladder leading to a cone-shaped loft with a mattress stuffed with straw.

Or had been.

It was now empty, the stuffing everywhere. Books had been splayed and thrown about. The table and stool were upended.

"Don't touch," she cautioned Sébastien, who'd instinctively reached out to pick a Bible off the stone floor. "We need to find Brother Constantine."

At the door she suddenly turned back and, walking over to the woodstove, she hovered her hand over it. It was cold.

Brother Constantine's cell was empty.

"Where else could he be?"

"The infirmary."

"Is he a doctor?"

"No, but there's a room off it where the elixir is mixed. Chartreuse itself is brewed off-site, but the formula is made here and sent to the distillery."

"It's after midnight. Would he really be making it up now?"

"He prefers to work at night," said Sébastien. "More private."

As they hurried down the hallway, Lacoste heard the thump-thump-thump of helicopter rotors. The Grenoble police had arrived.

The investigation would soon be taken out of her hands.

# CHAPTER 40

⌒

I t all happened in seconds.

*Bang! Bang, bang, bang!*

Wood exploded into splinters, people flew everywhere. The air was filled with cordite.

*Bang!* Gamache hit the floor and saw Beauvoir turn onto his back, aim his gun, and . . .

The shooting stopped.

Gamache twisted and looked in the direction of the gunfire. The RCMP officer was standing with his weapon in both hands, pointing at the floor and the body of a woman. Scrambling to his feet, Gamache ran over to the prone Beauvoir.

"Jean-Guy, are you—"

"I'm all right," he said, getting to his feet.

"Lights," said Gamache.

By the time Beauvoir hit the switch, seconds later, Gamache was already kneeling beside the motionless man splayed on the altar.

"It's all right," he was saying. His hands were pressing down on the wound on the Abbot's chest. Dom Philippe's eyes were wide, and a trickle of blood was coming out the side of his mouth.

He was dying. And knew it. With each beat of his heart, more blood was pumped from his body. Armand couldn't stop it, and even if he could, there was too much internal damage. So he stopped trying, and instead picked up Dom Philippe's cold hands and held them to his own chest.

The Abbot's blue eyes began to glaze over.

"Our Father, who art—" was as far as Armand got. Just before the Abbot's eyes emptied completely, Armand leaned forward and whispered into his ear, "God, take this child. Take Yves." Then he crossed himself.

"*Patron?*"

Gamache looked up.

"She's gone. Caron's gone."

"Dead?"

"Disappeared. And so's the satchel. But there's blood. She's wounded."

"Find her. And find that satchel."

Jean-Guy ran out the back door, while Armand walked quickly over to the RCMP officer. At Gauthier's feet was the bloody body of the woman from Open Da Night. The one they'd been trying to find.

Instead, she'd found them.

Jean-Guy reappeared. "The car's gone."

"Her assistant?"

"Gone."

"Do we know if Caron made it to the car?"

"She did. There's blood by where it was parked."

Gamache nodded, wiping his bloody hands on his slacks. "May I have your gun, please?"

It was said so mildly, so casually, Jean-Guy wasn't sure he understood until he again saw Gamache's hand out.

Beauvoir gave him the weapon, then watched in surprise as Gamache took it and in one easy movement placed it against the temple of the RCMP officer.

"Drop your weapon."

"Sir?"

"Now."

There was a pause before he released his handgun. Beauvoir grabbed it.

"*Patron?*" said Jean-Guy.

"Monsieur Gamache?" said Gauthier.

"Stay still." Without taking his eyes off his prisoner, Gamache said to Beauvoir, "You have ties?"

"*Oui.*" He took them out, and at Gamache's nod he reached for the right hand of the RCMP officer. The Mountie jerked it away.

"What the fuck? Are you insane? Are you on their side? Shit."

"Cuff him to the pew."

When the Mountie was secure, Gamache lowered the gun and searched the body of the killer. Nothing. He stood up and contemplated her. Then he looked at Gauthier.

"How did she find us?"

"She followed us. Isn't that obvious? For God's sake, Gamache. What's got into you?"

"We weren't followed," said Beauvoir.

"Someone told her where we were going," said Gamache. "I have Castonguay's phone, so it wasn't him. You were sending a message. I assumed it was to your family to warn them about the poison. Perhaps even to Commissioner Lavigne to update him." Here Gamache paused and then continued. "But you were telling the shooter where we were headed."

"That's bullshit!"

"You were guarding the back door. How did she get by you?"

"It's dark."

"Oh, for fuck's sake," murmured Beauvoir.

"Were both Caron and Dom Philippe supposed to die? And then your instructions were to kill the shooter? I imagine the satchel was an unpleasant surprise. Are you named in the papers?"

"You're insane. I saved your life. She'd have killed you too." He jabbed his free hand toward the dead woman.

Gamache held the man's eyes until the officer blinked.

"Your orders were to keep me alive at least until I could warn the politicians about the attack. They'd then sound the alarm and, in doing that, start the panic. And the attack would happen anyway." He turned to Beauvoir. "Why weren't we hit? I was closer to the shooter

than Dom Philippe or Caron. If she'd wanted us dead, we would be."
He turned back to the Mountie. "You need us alive. But this also
means the attack on the water is imminent. What do you know?"
Pause. "Tell us!"

Gauthier appealed to Beauvoir. "This's insane. You see that, right?
I didn't want to believe Diane when she told me Gamache was dangerous. Not listening to anyone. She said he'd get them all killed,
and you did." The Mountie turned back to Gamache. He'd worked
himself into a rage. "You got my sister killed."

"I don't have time for this." Gamache had given the gun back to
Beauvoir and was calling the local Sûreté detachment and the coroner.

"*Patron*, the conference call."

"Cancel it. Put out an APB on Caron and the vehicle."

Armand spread the altar cloth over Dom Philippe. As he did,
he noticed something sticking out from the Abbot's breast pocket.
Kneeling beside the man, Gamache pulled it out.

It was the photo of young Yves, his sister Eunice, and niece Jeanne.
The only thing he'd kept with him all those years in Saint Gilbert
Between the Wolves. The only thing he'd taken with him.

Armand tucked it back in.

"The killer shot Caron, so maybe she was telling the truth."

"Maybe. Or maybe the cleanup has started," said Gamache. "Maybe
Lauzon realized she was planning to blackmail him once he took
power. The evidence in the satchel might be Langlois's notes. In the
middle of an attack, when she was wounded, she stopped to pick it up.
It must be valuable."

"So she either took it to maybe stop the attack," said Beauvoir.
"Or she took it because she needs to have something to hold over
Lauzon."

Gamache nodded.

"So we know nothing."

"Perhaps not nothing."

They could hear sirens. The local police and coroner were arriving. Gamache took Beauvoir aside and whispered.

"I had breakfast today with Shona Dorion."

"The blogger? The one who hates you? Why..." As Armand watched, the light went on for his second-in-command. "For the same reason Caron came to you."

"No one would think we could be allies. I think Langlois did the same thing. I think I know where he hid his notes."

Brother Constantine was indeed in the small room behind the infirmary. Alive, well, and oblivious. The little round man was happily preparing his concoction. He looked up as they entered, clearly expecting someone else.

His expression changed when he saw Sébastien. And changed even more when he saw who was with him. A woman.

"What's going on? You shouldn't be here." He placed a pudgy hand over a huge manuscript on the table in front of him.

"Have you been here all day, *mon frère*?" Lacoste asked.

"Who are you? Why're you here? You can't be here. I'm making up the recipe. And you're a woman."

It wasn't clear which was the greater transgression, but the two together were more than the monk could immediately grasp.

"Where's Brother Robert? I expected him half an hour ago. You need to leave."

Constantine waved at them, knocking over one of the many mortars and pestles lined up on the table.

The shelves behind him were chockablock full with jars of dried herbs and nuts that no doubt produced spices.

There were so many scents it was impossible to identify any one of them. But it was pleasant. The sense Isabelle got, as she inhaled the scents, was one of comfort. As though Christmas and Easter, Thanksgiving, and the height of summer were holding a party.

She hated to break it up but had no choice. "I'm afraid Brother Robert is dead."

"Dead?" Now the monk was bewildered. "But he can't be. He's so young. What happened?"

Brother Constantine looked from one to the other. It was clear he'd grown attached to the quiet young newcomer to their community.

"Did he give you anything to keep safe?" Lacoste asked.

"Safe? Of course he kept something safe. The formula."

"No, I mean something else." She looked around. "Where did he keep his copy?"

"I'm not going to tell you."

Now the elderly monk stood up straight. He looked incredibly dignified. And very brave. Because he also looked very afraid.

"Who are you? Where are the others?"

"Please, Brother Constantine. You know me. Brother Sébastien."

"You're a lay monk. Not a brother at all."

"I came here to try to protect Brother Robert. I'm a Gilbertine."

This did nothing to allay his fears.

"And I'm a police officer."

It seemed to be getting worse, not better, for the Carthusian. "Not from here. You have a strange accent."

"I'm from Québec."

Moments ago, this happy monk had been doing something he'd done for decades. Continuing a tradition, a ritual, a scared duty that brother monks had done for centuries.

But now, a Gilbertine, and a woman. A cop. From Québec. Had invaded his safe place. Telling him the other holder of the recipe was dead.

"*Mon frère*, I have no need to see the recipe for Chartreuse. But I do need to know if there's something Brother Robert has hidden. Please. We'll stay here, but can you at least look?"

*Oui?*"

The door was closed and no doubt locked, and the voice that came from the other side tentative.

"Monsieur Langlois? It's Armand Gamache. We met when I came here to tell you about your son."

Before leaving Three Pines to head into Montréal, Armand and Jean-Guy had gone home, reassuring their family and the other villagers that they were safe. They could unlock the doors.

"So those were gunshots," said Reine-Marie as she looked at his bloody hands and the smears on his slacks. Though it was clear he and Jean-Guy were themselves unhurt.

"*Oui.*"

He told them what had happened, then went upstairs to wash up and change. Before leaving, he picked up the aspirin bottle and considered. He might need it. Slipping it into his pocket, he went downstairs and into his study, where he quickly wrote out all that he'd discovered. A light had caught his eye. Not, this time, the glint of a gun. These were fireflies, lighting up just outside his window.

Armand watched them for a moment. Losing himself, briefly, in what looked like a lighthearted dance. He tried to guess where the next one would appear, but couldn't. He wondered what part of evolution this served. Why had a fly been given the ability to light itself?

Or perhaps, he thought as he placed the paper where only Reine-Marie could find it, there was no purpose. Perhaps being a small light in the night was purpose enough. A show of defiance. These tiny creatures were the resistance against a vast darkness.

"I need to go," Armand said as he sat beside Reine-Marie and took her hand. Jean-Guy was upstairs with Annie and the sleeping children.

"Will you be all right?" Reine-Marie asked.

"Yes. I know what to do, where to go." He smiled. "*Ça va bien aller.*"

"*Fais attention, monsieur.*"

"I'll be careful. I promise, *madame*. And I'll bring Jean-Guy home."

"Did someone say my name?" asked the younger man, coming down the stairs with Annie.

"Numbnuts?"

Jean-Guy jumped, then turned to the unexpected voice. As did Armand and Reine-Marie. Ruth's head appeared from behind the sofa where she'd been napping. Or "napping."

"Jesus, you old hag," said Jean-Guy. "You almost scared me to death."

"Fuck, fuck, fuck," said the duck.

"True. We'll need to try harder."

The old poet struggled to get up. Jean-Guy held out his arms, and she gripped them as he lifted her to her feet.

She looked into his eyes. "You'd better come home."

"I will," he whispered and kissed her on both cheeks. "Thank you for looking after the family."

As the vehicle drove past the chapel, now lit up and surrounded by cop cars and ambulances, Ruth muttered, "*I just sit where I'm put, composed / of stone and wishful thinking.*" The elderly poet was quoting from one of her more obscure works. "*That the deity who kills for pleasure / will also heal.*"

"Come." Reine-Marie put a fleshy arm through Ruth's scrawny one, and with Annie on the other side, they walked back into the home, Rosa waddling behind. Silent, for once.

At the threshold, Reine-Marie looked up the hill as the car disappeared.

*. . . that in the midst of your nightmare,*
*the final one, a kind lion*
*will come with bandages in her mouth . . .*

Then her gaze dropped to the church, as the thin body of a kindly monk, covered in an altar cloth, was placed in an ambulance.

*and pick your soul up gently by the nape of the neck*
*and caress you into darkness and paradise.*

# CHAPTER 41

I'm with the Sûreté du Québec." Armand slid his ID under the door.
*We wait . . .*

He and Beauvoir exchanged glances.

"It's late. What do you want?" The voice of Charles Langlois's father was querulous, tremulous.

"I'm sorry, I can't explain from out here. Can you let us in?" The home was in darkness. But now a shaft of light appeared under the door. The ID was pushed back out.

"Come back in the morning."

Armand searched his mind for something to say, something that would get them inside.

Beauvoir had his ear to the door. "Madame Langlois is saying something. I can't hear, but they seem to be arguing."

Gamache turned back to the door. "I'm not sure if you've seen the videos posted online. I hope you haven't, but if you have, you know that I spoke to Charles. You can't hear what I said, but I was begging him to tell me what he'd found out. That's when he said 'family.' He wanted me to come here, not just to comfort you, but to find what he'd given you for safekeeping. He trusted you." Gamache paused. "He trusted me. Now you need to."

*We wait . . .*

There was a click, and the door opened.

\* \* \*

Brother Constantine put a worn leather bookmark in the huge volume and closed it with a thump. Then, clutching it to his chest, he walked to the back of the workshop.

When he returned, he still carried the manuscript, but there was something else in his hands.

*Merci.*" Gamache accepted the seat at the kitchen table and looked at the couple, whose only child had died within inches of this stranger now sitting in the heart of their home.

Beside him, Jean-Guy's knee was bobbing up and down. Time, time was slipping away from them.

"Charles gave you something to keep," said Gamache, without preamble. "His notebooks. He knew no one would come looking for them here since he'd made it known you hadn't spoken in years."

Monsieur and Madame Langlois did not react. They sat side by side, not saying a word. Vitally, what Armand did not hear was a denial.

Beauvoir's knee slowed but didn't stop completely.

"We need to see them."

Charles's parents looked at each other, then both got up and left the room. They returned less than a minute later with a canvas bag. On it was a yin-and-yang design and a leaping fish. The logo of Action Québec Bleu.

It wasn't heavy. There were just two notebooks inside.

Beauvoir took the bag while Armand thanked them. There was a clear question in Madame Langlois's expression.

"*Oui,*" said Gamache. "You've done the right thing."

Isabelle Lacoste took what Brother Constantine was offering.

Two clippings, in French, from the Québec newspaper *Le Soleil.* They were dated two days apart. One described the murder of a postal worker in Chicoutimi. The other the murder of a retired teacher on Les Îles de la Madeleine.

There were no markings on the clippings. Just creases where they'd been folded for mailing.

"Nothing else?" she asked the monk, who shook his head.

"What are they?" asked Sébastien, straining to see.

"Just a moment." She took a photo of them and sent it to Gamache and Beauvoir.

Gamache read Lacoste's email and looked at the photo.

*Any news?* she wrote.

*Found Langlois's notebooks,* he quickly replied. *More soon.*

Lacoste put away her phone. Then, holding up the clippings, she turned to Frère Sébastien. "Proof."

"Of what?"

"That the threats were real. These two"—she waved the clippings—"were killed to warn Brother Robert. One of them's his aunt."

"And the other?"

"I'm guessing a stranger, chosen at random. To make sure Robert realized who he was dealing with, in case there was any doubt, and to let him know he was responsible for two deaths."

"Responsible? How?"

"He met with Dom Philippe, despite their warnings not to tell anyone. But one thing I can't figure out is how they knew he'd met the Abbot. Can you?"

She watched as Brother Sébastien thought, then shook his head. He held Lacoste's eyes as she continued to stare at him.

Brother Constantine, sensing something had changed, gripped the manuscript tighter to his barrel chest.

Jean-Guy drove to a side street and parked. The immense Charles-J.-Des Baillets water-treatment plant was lit up in the dark and loomed a block away.

The two of them took out the notebooks, setting aside the first, where the young biologist documented his visits to central and northern lakes in Québec. It was, Gamache now recognized, just for show. Meant to mislead, misdirect anyone who came looking into thinking the biologist was investigating pollution in lakes.

The important information was in the second notebook. That one covered his time working first at the Atwater treatment plant, then, the last few pages, at the Charles-J.-Des Baillets facility.

Gamache went right to the final entry. There was no mistaking what Charles Langlois had found out. Writ large and underlined several times was:

*Botulinum. 08/25 @ 23:50*

"Jesus," said Beauvoir, turning pale. "That's today. In"—he looked at his phone—"forty-seven minutes."

Gamache was silent. Below the time, Langlois had written, *Which pump???*

"Question marks?" said Beauvoir. "Question marks? For God's sake, he wasn't sure?"

Gamache was skimming through the notebook, looking for names. He saw Caron, with question marks beside her name. He saw Lauzon, the Deputy Prime Minister.

There were others. Some with question marks, some not.

His heart sank when he saw both Madeleine Toussaint, the head of the Sûreté, and Evelyn Tardiff, the head of their Organized Crime division, on the list.

There was one name that did not surprise him.

David Lavigne. The deputy commissioner of the RCMP and his friend.

As soon as he'd realized the Mountie who'd been sent to "protect" him was working against them, he'd known Lavigne must be behind it.

"So he's not Diane's brother?"

"No. That was said so that I'd accept him without question. Someone thinks I'm far more fragile than I actually am."

But still, Jean-Guy could see that the mention of the murdered agent had found a wound that would never fully heal. The Chief had learned to live with it. As people in chronic pain do.

While Beauvoir scanned the notebook, Gamache accessed the background checks done on the employees by the Sûreté.

Charles Langlois, at least in his written records, seemed unsure who was involved in the plot. It would have to be someone who could get access to the massive pumps. Who could turn off the sophisticated levels of treatment.

One person couldn't do it. It would need to be a small team of trained terrorists, and at least some engineers familiar with the plant.

Gamache stared at the building, lit up and ominous.

If Langlois was right, they were now . . . Gamache checked his phone . . . forty-three minutes away from the attack.

The conspirators must already be in the plant. Gamache and Beauvoir could not risk warning anybody and setting it off, even if they knew who to warn. But there was something he could do.

Gamache called the agent on duty in homicide at Sûreté headquarters.

"Forrest, I need you to get a tactical squad together. Heavily armed. I can't tell you more. Be ready."

He hung up before he heard the "Yessir."

"Is there a way to shut down the plant completely?" Beauvoir asked.

Gamache shook his head. "I don't know." He thought there must be, but had no idea how. "We need help."

"But who?"

"Her."

Gamache was pointing to the name of a junior engineer.

"Why her?" asked Beauvoir.

"Because she'll know how to shut it down, and she isn't on shift. Whoever is going to poison the water would need to be on duty so no one would challenge them."

"You just chose her at random."

"Pretty much. But we have to trust someone."

# CHAPTER 42

⁓

"A re you accusing me of being part of all this?" Sébastien was star-ing at Lacoste in amazement. "Whatever 'this' is."

"I'm saying if these people"—she held up the clippings—"were murdered as a punishment and warning to Brother Robert, because he'd spoken to the Abbot, then only four people could have told the killers about that meeting. The Abbot, Brother Robert himself, Sister Irene, and you."

She held his stare. Not giving ground.

"That's insane."

"And," Lacoste continued as though he hadn't spoken, "only one of you could have thrown Robert from the tower."

Her stare turned into a glare. "I need to know what Robert told you. I need to know who in Washington confessed to him about the attack."

Sébastien's right hand, hidden by the folds of sackcloth, now ap-peared. In it was a knife he'd picked up off Brother Constantine's table. It was short, but sharp.

8G.

"You're sure about this?"

"Not at all," said Gamache.

Beauvoir made a guttural sound but said nothing, just pressed the buzzer.

Again. And again.

"Who is it?" The voice was young. And both annoyed and worried.

"My name is Armand Gamache. I'm with the Sûreté."

"It's"—there was a pause—"past eleven. What do you want? Has something happened?" Now her voice had risen into full-blown fear.

"Not to your family, no. We need your help. Please, let us in."

"Step back where I can see you."

Gamache did, looking up into the camera.

"What do you need? Why're you here?"

Time was ticking. No time now to be vague.

"There's going to be an attack on Montréal's drinking water. We need your help."

"That's ridiculous."

"Would I be here if it was?" Gamache was getting angry. "You recognize me, you know you can trust me."

"Maybe. But that fellow with you looks shifty."

Another growl. Then silence.

"I'll come down."

Manon Lagacé appeared minutes later, impossibly young in jeans and a sweatshirt that said *École Polytechnique*. There was a tiny white rose pin on it.

"Give me your phone." Gamache held out his hand.

"No. And I'm not getting into a car with you until I see your IDs and you tell me more."

"Oh, for God's sake," snapped Beauvoir. "The attack is going to happen in"—he checked his phone—"thirty-seven minutes."

"Then you'd better hurry."

Both Gamache and Beauvoir did, digging out their IDs. She took them, quickly compared the plastic to the real thing, then handed them back.

"Okay. Tell me."

"Can we at least walk toward the car?" Beauvoir asked.

"No. You're wasting your precious time. Tell me."

"In"—Gamache checked his phone—"thirty-six minutes, Montréal's water will be poisoned, from your treatment plant."

Both officers watched her closely. She seemed completely taken by surprise. "Why do you think that?"

It was a legitimate question, but he didn't have time to give a full answer.

"Charles Langlois told us." It was the shorthand and would have to do.

"The maintenance worker?"

"You knew him?"

"We talked. I'd heard he was killed in a hit-and-run." She studied Gamache. "You were there. It wasn't an accident?"

"*Non.* The poison is botulinum."

She quickly absorbed this information. "But that would kill . . ."

"Thousands," said Beauvoir. "Tens of thousands. *Patron*, we have to go, with or without her."

"He's right. Please, come with us." Gamache stared at her, and when there was no reaction, he turned and walked quickly to the car. When he heard footsteps running to catch up, he almost wept.

While Beauvoir sped through the suburb, Gamache asked, "Can the plant be shut down?"

"Yes, there's an emergency shutoff. It's in the command center on the top floor. This would be sabotage, obviously. A terrorist attack."

"Yes."

She looked around. "Then why aren't there more of you? The RCMP. A SWAT team. We must have an anti-terrorist unit. Why don't you have your Sûreté people all over it? Where are they?" Then she sat back, her face going slack. "Oh, shit. This's domestic terrorism. You don't know who to trust, do you?" When Gamache was silent, she said, "We're alone."

"We're enough," said Gamache. "Thanks to you."

"Yeah, well . . ."

Beauvoir pulled over half a block from the plant.

"If you were going to put poison into the system, how would you do it?" Gamache asked.

"I'd use one of the two main points of entry, on the lowest level and level two. I'd also place someone in the command center, to shut off the treatments and make sure no one sounded an alarm or powered down the plant. Overnight there's a smaller staff. The shift change happens at midnight, then eight a.m., and so on. Christ. That means the senior engineer on duty must be involved. I know him." She stared at Gamache, the full impact hitting home. "I need to reach my family, warn them." She grabbed for her phone, but Gamache leaned over and took it from her.

She went to strike him across the face, but he grabbed her wrist. "*Non.*" He barked. "The only way to save them now is to stop the attack."

"Shit," she said. "Fuck, fuck, fuck."

"You with us?" he demanded.

She looked at him with rage. "I'm not on duty today. They won't let me in."

"All you need to do is distract them," said Beauvoir.

It was easier than they dared hope. The head guard knew the junior engineer, and while he was unclear why she was there, he was not alarmed.

He became alarmed when Beauvoir pulled out his gun and forced him and his colleagues into a back room, put them in cuffs, and locked it. But not before disarming them.

Gamache took the guard's handgun and placed it in his belt.

"You didn't tell me you were going to do that," said Manon.

"Some of the guards will be in on it," said Gamache. "Where's the command center? We have to shut the plant down."

"But that won't work. Not right away. It'll take at least ten minutes for the circulation to stop completely. And they'll know it's shutting down. If they put the poison in then, it'll still flow through and out into the city."

Gamache paused for a moment. Thinking.

"Is there a way to close off the pumps themselves?"

"Yes, there's an emergency protocol, but it can only be done in the pump rooms."

"Then that's what we'll do. What's the protocol?"

"A code."

"Give it to me."

He wrote the five numbers and a symbol on his hand. "How will the attackers communicate? Will phones work?"

"No. Too much concrete and metal. There's a landline in every room."

"Just internal, or does it go outside?"

"You can make outside calls."

"Thank God for that," said Gamache as he met Beauvoir's eyes.

"You'll need this to get in." She handed him her ID card. "Place it against the screen on the outside of the door and it should unlock."

"Should?"

"Will."

"Will they know if a pump has been shut down?"

"Everyone in the command center will know. Red lights will start flashing."

"They must be able to restart the pump," said Beauvoir.

"True, but that takes hours."

"Where are these pump rooms exactly?"

Manon walked over to a wall in the security office. "Here's a schematic of the plant. Pump One is here." She pointed to the lowest level. It was in the center of the huge floor. "The other is two flights up, right over the first. The emergency controls to shut them down are on a board beside the turbine. There'll be workers there who'll challenge you."

"There'll be more than workers," said Beauvoir. "And they'll more than challenge. I can take the lowest level."

"*Non*. You need to go with Madame Lagacé and get control of the command center before those alarms go off."

"Let me go, *patron*. You get to the control room."

Gamache actually smiled. "And which of us is most likely to be stopped and challenged?"

While far from happy, Beauvoir knew he was right and that this was the only option.

"*Bon*," said Gamache. "When you see that Pump One is offline, give me three minutes, then shut down the plant and call Forrest. Get the tactical unit here. Once I shut down the second pump, we need to make sure the attackers don't escape. And we need to take them alive."

Beauvoir nodded. "Right."

Gamache gripped Jean-Guy's forearm. "You have to hold that command center. No matter what. You're the last line. It cannot be crossed." He held Jean-Guy's eyes. "No matter what happens."

Jean-Guy knew what Armand was saying.

Lacoste backed away from Sébastien.

"How in the world could you agree to this? The deaths of thousands, tens of thousands."

"How in the world?" demanded the monk, almost screaming. "How in the world? Have you seen the state of the world? Something had to be done to shake the leaders out of their complacency. Reason wasn't doing it. Facts weren't doing it. If even wildfires weren't doing it, what would?"

"My God, are you trying to tell me you're involved in a plot to poison Montréal's drinking water as a way to save the planet?"

"Yes! Yes. To get people to finally wake up and see the dangers. If it takes an act of ecoterrorism, then so be it."

"You're delusional. It's just plain terrorism."

"I don't care what you call it. My conscience is clear."

"What conscience? You're willing to kill thousands to get the attention of politicians?"

"Politicians? You're kidding, right? They're the ones who've allowed it to get this far. No, we're beyond that. We need one strong leader who can take control. Someone brave enough to do what's necessary."

"You're a fool. You're being used. They've turned your good intentions into something ugly. Can't you see? Murdering thousands isn't the answer."

"Then what is? We've tried everything else." He advanced on her.

That's as far as he got. Brother Constantine swung the heavy book containing the ancient recipe for Chartreuse and hit Sébastien squarely on the side of the head, knocking him senseless. As Chartreuse had done for centuries.

# CHAPTER 43

~

Chief Inspector Gamache passed two maintenance workers and someone who looked like a technician. For a moment Gamache thought he was going to be questioned. Instead of avoiding eye contact, Gamache caught and held the man's attention, and gave a brusque nod.

The technician hesitated, then nodded back. And walked on. Gamache could feel the perspiration trickling down the middle of his back.

He continued on, giving every appearance of a man with a lot on his mind. It was not an expression that invited chitchat. Or challenge.

Reaching the stairs, he slipped in, grabbed the handrail, and took the concrete steps two at a time.

I didn't know you were on duty," said the man who stopped them in the fourth-floor hallway. He was in shirtsleeves and tie with heavy black-rimmed glasses.

Manon smiled, jerked her head toward Beauvoir, and grimaced. "My brother-in-law. Visiting from Gaspé. He's leaving first thing tomorrow, thank God. I told him I'd show him where I worked." She lowered her voice. "He's a bit of an asshole."

Beauvoir looked around and said, "Is this it? Not very impressive. I expected more."

This was burning time they didn't have. If Gamache got to the pump before they got to the control room . . . and the red lights went on . . . and they saw in the monitors what was happening . . .

"Do you know who's on duty in the command center?"

"Lavoie."

"Oh, good. He might let us in." Again she lowered her voice. "I hope not. I just want to get this over with and put him on the flight back to Gaspé. It's almost shift change. You getting ready to go home?"

"Twenty minutes to go," said the man. "Then I'm off for a week."

"Have fun," said Manon, moving away.

"You too," the man said, with a sympathetic smile. "By the way, the men's toilet on the third floor is blocked."

Gamache got to the bottom of the stairs, and opening the door he came face-to-face with a guard holding an assault rifle.

Both were startled, but Gamache reacted more quickly.

The man was just swinging his rifle around when Gamache slugged him on the side of the head with his own gun. Grabbing the now unconscious man, he dragged him into the stairwell, and after quickly patting him down, he zip-tied the man's hands to the railing and picked up his assault rifle. Far from standard issue for security.

This was no guard.

He yanked the door open, expecting to meet resistance. What he met was a wall of near-deafening noise.

Water was roaring by on either side of the long, wide corridor. Great torrents from the St. Lawrence were being filtered through sand before entering the pump room and being sent into homes and hotels and offices and schools and hospitals in Montréal.

There was no place to hide now, no time to hide. As he ran, Gamache took the clip off the rifle and tossed it into one of the rushing rivers, then threw the rifle into the other.

He got to Pump One in less than twenty seconds. Not wasting time to see if anyone was descending on him, he brought out Manon Lagacé's ID card and tapped.

Nothing.

He tried again. Nothing.

It was like at the grocery store when his credit card refused to work and other patrons were staring at him. Annoyed.

But this was far more than an annoyance.

He was about to try one more time when he remembered her instructions. Place, don't tap. He pressed the card against the screen and heard a clunk.

The metal door opened.

The man dressed as a guard and standing by the door turned, stared. He reached for his holster, but by then Gamache had his gun in the man's face.

"What the fuck—"

"Drop your weapon. Hands where I can see them."

The man did.

Gamache scanned the room. Five people, all in white smocks, were turning to look. Their eyes widening. And Armand realized they must think he was the saboteur. Which meant the terrorists hadn't yet made their move. But it also meant it was impossible for him to tell who was who.

He realized it didn't matter. He had to assume they were all guilty.

"Everyone, on the floor. Phones out, slide them here. Hands on top of your heads." He patted the guard down. Nothing in his pockets, not even ID. This was a pro.

He zip-tied his hands and picked up the dropped weapon, shoving it in his belt before moving quickly to the control panel by the huge pump.

"What the hell are you doing?" one of the workers shouted. But got no answer.

Some of those on the floor were quietly weeping. At least one was praying.

Gamache ignored it all. Except.

He noticed that one of them had his hands awkwardly placed on his head.

"You." He pointed the gun at him. "Slowly lower your right hand to the floor and open it." The man hesitated. "Now!"

As he did, a small bottle rolled out and started making its way toward him across the concrete floor.

Are we close?" demanded Beauvoir as they walked quickly along the corridor. "We have to get to the command center before Gamache shuts down the pump."

"Yes, I was listening. It's just down here. I think."

"You think? You think? Wait a minute. Why did that man tell you about the blocked toilet?"

"Engineers. That's about the level of their conversation."

Beauvoir grabbed her arm and swung her around. "What's your job here?"

"I'm an engineer."

"Right, but what do you engineer?"

She paused. "Sanitation."

"The toilets?"

"All the waste." She stared at him, daring Beauvoir to say more. Which he did.

"Don't you think you could've told us that? We need to stop a terrorist attack, not unblock a toilet."

"Listen, asshole. I thought you knew what I did. And what would you have done if I'd told you? Driven to the next name on the list?" She glared at him. "You begged for my help, and instead of going back to bed, I came. Like it or not, I'm it." She looked around. "It's here somewhere."

"Are you fucking with me?"

"Oh, look, we're right in front of it." She waved at the door he was standing in front of and gave him a sardonic smile. "Now there's a piece of dumb luck."

Sure enough, a plate on the wall said *Command Center*.

"Get behind me."

This time there was no argument from Manon Lagacé.

Gamache scooped up the small bottle, examined it, then slipped it into his pocket. If he'd had time, he'd have questioned the technician who'd tried to palm the poison, but there were more pressing things right now.

At the control panel he quickly put in the code, pausing for a moment.

He hoped to God Beauvoir had secured the command center.

Then he pressed the final key.

The door was unlocked, which meant the terrorists hadn't yet made their move. Those inside were not alerted to the saboteurs in their midst.

Beauvoir brought out his gun and stepped through. Six people turned and stared at him, two of them in guard uniforms. They were reaching for their weapons when a single red light appeared on one screen.

Then the whole section of wall burst into flashing red.

"What the hell—" said the man at the console.

It was so surprising that one of the gunmen froze. The other did not. The man had pulled a Magnum. Not what guards would be issued. Bringing his weapon around, he only had time to aim before Beauvoir fired and the man dropped.

There was sudden and complete pandemonium.

For just a moment, between the gunfire and the flashing red lights and the screams, Beauvoir lost track of the second gunman.

"Get down," he shouted, afraid the gunman was about to open fire. But all he heard were the shouts of the panicked workers as they dropped to the floor.

Beauvoir saw the door slowly closing. Leaping to it, he yanked it open, but the man was nowhere in sight. Instinct told him to run after the gunman. If he got to the others, warned the others . . .

But instead, Beauvoir backed up and locked the door.

Manon was at the bank of controls. "Pump One is offline," she confirmed.

There were monitors with numbers and graphs, but others, where security cameras would be, were blank.

"Shut the place down. Now!"

"But shouldn't we wait? Gamache said—"

"Now!"

The red lights were flashing, and the people splayed on the floor were pleading. One was shouting at Manon. Demanding to know what she was doing.

"Quiet!"

They swung their eyes to Beauvoir and shut up.

"Hands on your heads. Don't move. Don't speak."

"I need to figure this out," muttered Manon. "Something isn't right."

"For God's sake, hurry."

Beauvoir went to the dead man and picked up his gun, then went through his pockets. No ID, no phone.

"You shit-head." Manon turned to the senior engineer, now lying on the floor. "You sabotaged it."

"What does that mean?" demanded Beauvoir.

"It means he threw a mathematical wrench into the works. A virus that's activated if one of the pumps is offline. It's their fail-safe. We can't shut the plant down."

Beauvoir went over to the man and placed the gun to his temple. "Fix it."

"He can't," said Manon.

"Of course he can. He put it in, he can take it out."

"No, it's a rotating code. It'll take days to get it out."

"Fuck." Beauvoir's mind raced. "Can Gamache still shut down Pump Two?"

She looked at him and shook her head. "I don't think so."

Fuck.

He needed to warn Gamache. But their phones didn't work here. Beauvoir looked at the locked door. He needed to leave. To get to Pump Two. To get to Gamache. But he couldn't. He needed to hold the command center.

There was no way to get a message to the Chief. He looked around, frantic. He needed to call Forrest and get the team there. A phone. There was a phone on a desk. A landline.

He grabbed the receiver. Dead.

"Can you get the phones working again?"

"I'll try."

He watched as she rolled the chair over to another console.

"And get the security cameras back up."

"Want me to do the windows while I'm at it?" Under her breath she muttered, "Asshole." Then, a moment later, "Oh, shit, it worked. This's actually easier than unblocking the men's toilet."

The security cameras were still down, but the phone had a dial tone.

"Forrest, it's Beauvoir."

"*Oui, patron.* We're ready."

Jean-Guy gave him his orders. They were blown anyway. No need for secrecy now. With luck they'd manage at least to catch the terrorists before they escaped. Even if it was too late to stop the poison.

"What do we do?" Manon asked, panic in her voice, her eyes wide.

"You need to find another way to shut the place down."

There was no mistaking the look on her face.

They'd failed. It seemed inconceivable but inescapable. And in minutes, if it hadn't happened already, botulinum would be headed into every home, office, school, hospital, into every tap in the city.

# CHAPTER 44

$\sim$

Gamache took the stairs two at a time. One hand holding the gun, his other resting on the plastic container in his pocket. Keeping it safe. It was as Sherry Caufield had said. The botulinum would be delivered in a small container, probably disguised as medicine or shampoo to get it by security screening.

Before leaving Pump Room One, he'd yanked the phone out of the wall, not realizing it was already dead, and shot into the control panel, locking the door as he left.

He had less than two minutes before Beauvoir and Lagacé started shutting down the plant. A move that would warn the terrorists, if they weren't already alerted, and they'd immediately put the poison into Pump Two.

He reached the second-floor landing and banged against the crash bar, bursting into another long corridor. Once again, rapids were coursing down either side, creating a deafening noise. Scanning up and down the hall, Gamache could see only one person a distance away.

He took off for the pump room, no longer caring if he was seen. Once again, he slapped Lagacé's ID on the screen and heard the clunk as the door unlocked.

He was reaching for the handle when he felt something against the back of his head. It was unmistakable.

The roar of the rushing water had masked the sound of others approaching.

"Drop your weapon, Armand."

Gamache turned and saw David Lavigne. While not a big surprise, it was still a shock. To see someone he had once completely trusted holding a gun on him.

"Don't do this."

"Drop your weapon." The demand came from one of the three men with him. Gamache recognized two of them as Moretti's soldiers. The third was a stranger. Large, confident. Silent. He looked like ex–special forces.

Armand had no choice. His gun clattered to the floor, where it was kicked aside. As he lowered his right hand, he brushed it against his pocket and felt the vial.

"You found Langlois's notebooks, didn't you. The one loose end, and you had to tug on it."

Gamache was silent.

"I guess Petrie should have killed you after all in that church. That was a tactical error on my part."

"Petrie. The Mountie?" Armand's mind was racing. He had to stall, had to give Beauvoir and Lagacé time to shut down the plant. "Not Diane's brother."

"No. But you worked that out too." Lavigne nodded to one of his people, who came forward and reached out to pat Gamache down.

Armand's arm lashed out, hitting the man squarely in the face and dropping him. Then he lunged for Lavigne, but was tackled before he got there. He twisted at the last minute, desperate not to fall on the container in his pocket and burst it open. As he hit the ground, he was lifted up again by a boot to his side.

He gasped in pain and lay still.

"On your knees," Lavigne barked. "Get on your fucking knees."

Gamache braced for another blow and moved his elbow into his side, to protect what was in his pocket.

Time, time. He needed time. Even seconds would count. He stayed limp.

*   *   *

What do we do?"

"For God's sake, figure out how to shut down the plant."

"I told you, I can't. But I think I got the security cameras up."

As Beauvoir looked at the bank of monitors, they sprang to life, the images rotating from camera to camera. No sign of Gamache.

"There must be a work-around. Something. Here." He offered her the gun he'd taken from the "guard." "Use it when the time comes."

But she held up her hands. "I'm not going to take it. I won't use a gun."

He'd noticed the white rose pin on her sweatshirt and knew what it meant. It was a symbol of the fourteen young women who'd been murdered at Montréal's École Polytechnique. The engineering school. The gunman had killed them because they were women. Because they dared believe they belonged in a "man's profession." Dared believe they were equal to men.

He'd murdered them for daring.

Canada's strict gun laws came out of that femicide. And now he was handing a gun to a young female engineer, a grad of the École, and asking her to use it.

"You must."

"I won't."

He placed it on the console. "You will when the time comes."

"Where're you going?"

He was heading for the door, to find Gamache, to get to Pump Two, but before he reached it, there was a pounding on the door. The attackers were already there. There was no way out now.

Beauvoir backed up.

Manon's eyes were wide. "The shit."

"There's more than one."

"No, no, no. Five years ago there was a major spill of waste into Lac-Saint-Louis, one of the sources of drinking water. It was a mess, an environmental—"

"What? Are you kidding me? Are we chatting now?"

His eyes went from Manon to the monitors. Still no Gamache.

"No, no. Listen. Since then they've installed emergency measures"—

she was talking quickly, her words running into each other—"to prevent a repeat. But also, unique to this plant, if the other measures
failed and a spill of wastewater was about to happen—"

"It would shut down the plant?"

"Automatically."

"You can do it?"

"Yes, at least, I think so. It means instigating a spill. But I can't do
it from here. I need to get to the wastewater room."

There was the pounding of a foot or a shoulder against the door.

"Where is it?"

"One flight down."

Beauvoir turned full circle, desperate for another way out. His eyes
landed on one. But he dismissed it. There was no way. Not possible.

There was a shot. The door buckled.

"Do you have claustrophobia?" he asked.

Just then, the monitor rotated to the camera outside Pump Room
Two. It showed a black-and-white image. Of Gamache. Lying on the
concrete. A gunman standing over him.

Hands grabbed him and lifted him off the floor, then shoved him into
a kneeling position.

He knew what that meant even before he felt the muzzle pressed
against the base of his skull.

Oh, no," said Jean-Guy. Not wanting to look, but needing to see.
"Nonono."

The camera rotated on, to another site.

"Bring it back."

"Are you sure you want—"

"Do it!"

Armand brought his elbows in, to protect what was in his pocket. If,
when, he fell . . .

"That's an odd thing to do, Armand. What do you have in there."

Lavigne nodded, and one of the men dragged the jacket off him and handed it to him.

"Cuff him."

His arms were pinned behind his back, and he felt the plastic wrist ties tighten until they cut into his skin.

Gamache's back was to Lavigne, so he couldn't see, but he heard a sound of genuine amusement and knew what he'd found.

"Oh, Armand. You've just become an accomplice."

Beauvoir shoved a chair to the wall and, climbing onto it, he yanked the cover off the vent. It was, he thought, just about large enough.

Or maybe it was just small enough so that a person would get wedged in there.

Looking from the dark tunnel, to the monitor, Jean-Guy felt a wave of panic.

Lavigne bent down until his face was right in front of his. His colleague. They'd shared a mutual trust. One Lavigne had counted on. Traded on. Weaponized.

He held up the small container. "Clever of them to put it into an aspirin bottle. Security would never question it." He handed it to one of the gunmen. "Take it inside. Give it to the head tech. She'll know what to do."

"No!" Gamache fought to get up but was kicked to the floor. "I'm begging you," he gasped. "For God's sake, David, don't do it."

He was once again shoved into a kneeling position.

"It's worse than you know, Armand. You obviously didn't realize that we could only get enough of the neurotoxin for one cylinder, so we decided to focus on Pump One. This one"—he gestured toward the partly open door—"was going to get brucellosis. Nasty stuff, but not as lethal as . . ." He looked at the container, which the man was holding away from his body as though that would protect him should it leak.

"You closed down Pump One. Clever. And even locked it so no one could get in or out. Also smart. But what wasn't so smart was bringing the botulinum with you. For safekeeping. You will go to your maker knowing instead of preventing a catastrophe, you've caused one. You brought the poison straight to us."

"Why?" said Armand. He'd given up playing for time. Time was up.

"Why would I do this? If you knew what happens next, you wouldn't need to ask." He watched as the heavy metal door to Pump Two closed behind the gunman. "Hard to believe something that small will kill so many. But then, a 9-millimeter bullet will kill a, what? Six-foot man?"

Gamache was straining to hear, not his words, which washed over him, but the sound of the turbines slowing. The sound that would tell him Beauvoir had succeeded.

But there was no change.

What do we do about them?" Manon pointed at the men and women sprawled on the floor.

At least one, maybe more, was among the plotters. They only knew about the senior engineer. Beauvoir had bound and gagged them all. In case.

"Leave them." Another blast of gunfire and the door finally gave way. With one last glance at the monitor, at Armand on his knees, Jean-Guy shouted, "Come on!"

Was Jean-Guy still alive? Armand was beginning to doubt it. If he was, the turbines would be slowing down by now.

He thought of Annie. Of Honoré and Idola. *Désolé. Désolé.*

And why hadn't they killed him yet? What were they waiting for? He had his answer within seconds.

"Where did you hide them?"

"What?"

"Langlois's notebooks," he shouted, his words rising above the roar of the water.

Armand remained silent, staring ahead. It was a shame, he thought, that the last thing he'd see were the words *Pump Two*. It was also a shame that that was one of his last thoughts.

But no. He didn't have many options left, but he did have one.

As David Lavigne shouted at him, he conjured up the backyard in early evening in the height of summer. Sitting with Reine-Marie. Listening to the rustle in the woods as a chipmunk scurried or a deer strolled by. On its own way home.

As he took Reine-Marie's hand, he heard birdsong and the unruly cicadas, their call comforting now.

And all around them fireflies danced.

How lucky he'd been. To be of a generation that believed it would last forever. The forests and clean rivers, the fresh air.

His was the last generation, as it turned out.

He was, he also knew, of the generation that was responsible for its murder.

His head was forced forward by a huge hand so that his chin was practically on his chest. And the muzzle pressed more firmly against his skull, and he felt a stab of panic. Of disbelief. He was about to die.

He took a deep breath and smelled old garden rose and the musky scent of the forest.

He thought of the woman in Chicoutimi and the man in Gaspé. And how terrified they must have been. He at least knew why he was about to be executed.

He wondered if that made it easier. Perhaps.

"It's done." The word was heavily accented. Russian. Of course they'd hire Russian mercenaries. They'd want the witnesses to testify that it was foreign terrorists who'd done this. Not domestic.

"The notebooks. Where are they?"

When he refused to talk, Lavigne leaned closer. "I will go to your peaceful little village, Armand, and tear it apart. And then I will burn it down, along with everyone in it. Starting with Reine-Marie. Then Annie. Daniel. Florence—"

With each name Armand screwed his eyes tighter shut. Trying to block out the images.

"Zora. Honoré. And what's the smallest one's name? The one with Down syndrome, like my sister-in-law?"

Gamache began thrashing. But to no effect. He was just held

tighter, his hair grabbed and head jerked up so that he was staring into Lavigne's eyes.

"Idola. They will all die unless you tell me where you put the note-books. Tell me and I'll spare them."

Armand's breathing came in short gasps.

This was the nightmare. The final one . . .

How he longed to tell him. To believe him. But he knew it was a lie. If he told him, they'd be killed anyway. And yet he wanted to, he wanted to, he wanted . . .

"Please," he sobbed. "For God's sake, don't do this. They know nothing. The notebooks aren't there."

"Then where are they? Tell me!"

He squeezed his eyes shut and shook his head. Charles's books were the only proof, the only documents outlining the plot. Naming names. They had to be kept safe. At all costs.

# CHAPTER 45

~

Two armed men broke through the door to the control room, assault rifles raised.

Except for those lying on the floor, the place was empty. The chief engineer, gagged, was trying to communicate something.

"Fuck." The leader strode over to the chair and the open vent.

He stepped onto the chair and pointed his rifle down the shaft. And fired.

"Drop them."

Beauvoir had stepped out from behind the console, gun drawn.

The gunmen turned, swinging their rifles around. They only got partway before—*Bang! Bang! Bang!*

Both dropped. Beauvoir grabbed their rifles. "Come on, come on!"

Lagacé followed Beauvoir through the door. Within a minute they were down the stairs and at the wastewater-treatment room. The three workers there were looking confused but not yet panicked.

"What's happening, Manon? Was that gunfire?"

They looked at the man with her. He was holding a gun.

"Step away," said Manon. "I need the console."

She punched in some codes and watched.

"What're you doing?" one of the men demanded.

"She's opened the doors. You're causing a spill. *Arrête!*"

"No," said the third. "She's shutting down the whole fucking place. Listen."

He was right. Beauvoir could hear it now. A very slight change in the hum, the thrum, the throb around them. It grew deeper, slower. Like a huge heart, stopping.

"It'll still take too long . . ." Manon looked at Beauvoir.

"Stay here."

Tell me where they are, Armand. They're no use to you now, but they can save your family." There was silence. "No?"

Lavigne stepped aside and nodded at the man behind Gamache.

Armand felt him tense, brace. The sort of thing a person does instinctively when about to shoot.

*God, take this child . . .*

The last thing he heard was the unmistakable sound of turbines slowing down.

He fell forward, his face hitting the concrete. He never heard the shot.

Beauvoir was at the stairwell door when he heard the gunfire.

Bursting through, he found himself in a long, wide-open corridor.

The sound of the shots were echoing, fading. Into silence. Complete and utter silence. The rivers on either side were still. Nothing moved. Nothing moved. Nothing moved.

He saw bodies sprawled on the concrete by the door to Pump Room Two.

The fireflies. They were all around him.

But they were making a strange sound. A sort of ringing. No. More like screaming.

Had the woman in Chicoutimi and the man in Gaspé seen fireflies too, just before they died? Was it some sort of illusion as the optic nerve failed?

Armand hoped they had. It was almost beautiful. Would even be peaceful, if not for the shrieking in his head. He felt numb. No pain. Not even fear. Just a sort of detachment.

*Family. Family . . .*

Jean-Guy grabbed the top two bodies, hauling them aside.

Armand was face down, blood covering the collar of his white shirt, soaking in. It was coming out of his ear and pooled in his left eye. His hands were zip-tied behind him.

"No," Jean-Guy pleaded. "Nonononono."

He put his hand against Armand's face and held it there. Afraid to turn him over. Afraid to see.

The fireflies dissipated, as though frightened away. Armand felt something on his face. A hand. Warm. Reassuring.

He couldn't see. There was something in his left eye. But still, he knew who it was. And felt a stab of joy. Jean-Guy was alive.

Out of his good right eye he saw a blurry gunman. Dead. On the ground.

And Armand knew what had happened. In the instant the man had shot, someone else had shot the gunman. The man's bullet hadn't done its job. Not entirely. Not yet.

Armand felt his hands cut free. He was being turned over. Jean-Guy was kneeling beside him. Holding his hand. Saying something.

He saw his lips move but could only hear the shrieking in his head. He tasted blood and knew he was blind in one eye. Had the bullet exited there?

He moved his lips.

Jean-Guy bent close.

"Go." Armand thought he'd spoken but couldn't hear his own voice. "Stop them."

Beauvoir looked at the open door to Pump Two. "The poison?"

"It was put in." The words, weak, came from the woman slumped against the wall, a handgun lying at her side. "I heard the gunman confirm it just before I shot them. We're too late. The senior tech in there has another poison."

Beauvoir ran to the door to Pump Two and pulled it open. There, on the floor, lay the workers. For a moment Beauvoir thought they were all dead. Then, one by one, they lifted their heads.

"Stay where you are. I'm with the Sûreté."

"She's one of them," a worker said, pointing to a woman in a white coat. "She put something into the water."

"Hands on your heads," Beauvoir commanded. "All of you."

Wide-eyed, wild-eyed, he looked for the landline. He had to call emergency measures. He ran toward it.

"No."

Beauvoir saw Gamache leaning against the door. Blood covered half his face, and his voice was unnaturally loud as though shouting over some sound.

"I have to call for help," said Beauvoir.

"Not poison. Water. Switched." His head was throbbing, and his vision blurred, and he was losing his ability to speak. His senses seemed to be abandoning him. He could feel his legs buckling. "Left poison at Pump One. Below console. You need to get it."

Beauvoir stared at Gamache. "Water?" Jean-Guy could feel himself growing giddy. "It was just water they put in?"

But the Chief was now just staring, his head lowering. His breathing coming in short gasps. He was on the verge of passing out. Beauvoir knew the bullet had grazed the Chief's head, but the explosion so close to his ear must've caused a bad concussion, maybe worse.

He moved toward him.

"Go," said Armand, shaking his head. "Secure the plant."

Before he did, Jean-Guy patted down the head technician and found another vial. He cuffed her to the pump.

"You going to be okay?" he asked Armand, who nodded.

Then Jean-Guy disappeared down the corridor. Pushing himself off the doorway, Armand stumbled back, passing the bodies of the gunmen and David Lavigne, before slumping against the wall next to the woman who'd saved his life.

Holding her in his arms, he whispered, "Jeanne?"

# CHAPTER 46

⁓

"He didn't," said Clara, laughing.

"He did, I swear it."

They were in the bistro in front of the fire, and Jean-Guy was regaling them with what had "happened" in the treatment plant. It was, Armand knew, mostly fiction.

He could have protested but was enjoying their laughter. Albeit at his expense.

"Now," Jean-Guy was saying, "you have to know that when he fell forward, he bit his lip and hit his nose on the floor."

"Klutz," said Ruth, and Rosa nodded. But then ducks often do.

The "he" was Armand. They all looked at him with amusement. It was not really funny. Certainly wasn't at the time, though somehow Jean-Guy was managing to make it funny.

Armand smiled back, though he was straining to understand what was being said. He couldn't actually hear the words, but in the weeks since the attack, he'd become very good at lipreading.

"All I could see was blood coming from his mouth and out his nose. I didn't realize he'd pretty much done it to himself. It looked far worse than it was."

Now, thought Armand, that was true. Jeanne Caron had shot the gunman at the very instant the man had pulled the trigger on Armand, jerking the gun millimeters away at the last instant so that the bullet just grazed him. But like most wounds to the head, though superficial, it had bled. A lot. He'd been stung by the bullet, but it was the explosion right next to his head that had done the damage.

The body of the gunman had propelled him forward, into the concrete floor, where he'd lain, stunned, semiconscious. Unsure what had happened. But sure he must be dying.

"So," Jean-Guy continued, "as I held him, Armand whispers, 'Tell' . . . then he coughs . . . 'that I love' . . . and he coughs again."

"Very dramatic," said Gabri, with approval. "A great death scene, only you forgot to actually die."

"I blame the writer," said Armand. His voice was unnaturally loud. He was having difficulty modulating it over the shriek of the hundreds of cicadas still nesting in his head.

Even Reine-Marie joined the laughter. Though hers was less robust than the others'.

"Because of the coughing, I couldn't hear whose name he said, but"—Jean-Guy lowered his voice to a confidential whisper—"I think his last words might've been, 'Tell Ruth I love her.'"

That was met with a roar. Armand looked from one to the other, unsure what Jean-Guy had said.

Ruth nodded approval. "Not the first time."

"Actually," said Reine-Marie, taking her husband's hand and looking at him directly, enunciating slowly and clearly, "I know what you probably said. 'Tell Gabri I love his steak frites.'"

This time he joined their laughter.

As the friends continued to talk, Armand's attention drifted. It was tiring, straining to follow conversations he couldn't actually hear.

He sipped his scotch and reached for a slice of fresh baguette, smeared thick with Saint André cheese, and looked out the window to the village green. It was twilight. The sky was tinged with red, so there was little to distinguish the sky from the forest, the red of dusk from the red of the bright autumn maple leaves. All seemed one.

He felt the hand on his arm and turned to look at Reine-Marie.

"Shall we?" she mouthed.

He nodded.

Reine-Marie, Armand, and Jean-Guy kicked the dried leaves ahead of them as they crossed the village green.

That morning, while in his study, Armand had seen Billy Williams raking them into a large, neat pile. Ruth and Rosa were on the bench. "Their" bench, as Ruth called it. Clara was walking out her front gate, through the crisp morning air, over to the bookstore to chat with Myrna. Woodsmoke was coming from the bistro chimney, as people began gathering for coffee and croissants.

An hour later, when he looked up from his reading, the leaves were scattered everywhere, thanks to the village children who'd leaped into the pile, laughing and rolling and throwing great handfuls at each other.

Florence and Zora, Honoré, and even little Idola came home for lunch with rosy cheeks and red-and-yellow and bright orange leaves stuck to their sweaters. And hair. And into their boots.

Summer vacation was over. It was back to school and back to the city for the family. But they still came out on weekends.

Armand watched Reine-Marie kick the leaves ahead of her in the twilight, as though she were ten years old. He was doing it too. As was Jean-Guy. They were kids, playing together. He couldn't hear the swish of the leaves, but he could remember it. And he could smell, more keenly than ever, their musky sweetness.

Fall had come early. The seasons were shifting, becoming unpredictable. The weather had become turbulent, unsettled. But as they walked through the dusk, past the three huge pine trees, to their home, all seemed right with the world. It might be an illusion, but Armand figured they could afford one, now and then.

When dinner was over, Armand and Reine-Marie bathed the grandchildren and read them a bedtime story.

It was difficult. The children didn't understand what was wrong with Papa. Why he didn't talk as much. Why he stared at them so intensely when they spoke. Why he didn't seem to always understand. Why he sometimes raised his voice to them.

They didn't understand why he was different.

It scared them, and he could see it. And it broke his heart. But each night he read them a story, glancing at Reine-Marie to make sure his voice wasn't too loud. Then he hugged and kissed them, and let them know he loved them.

Armand and Reine-Marie took their mugs of tea to the chairs at the bottom of the garden.

In the light from the house, he could just see her lips move. Those lips that had formed so many wonderful words over the years. Beginning with the first time he'd heard her say, "I love you."

While he'd become quite good at reading those lips, he missed hearing her voice. Missed terribly, and more and more each day, not being able to just chat. Missed the easy communication. The mundane observances.

And though she tried to hide it, Armand knew that Reine-Marie missed it too. Missed it terribly.

He still went to the bistro and to Clara and Myrna's homes with the others, for drinks or dinner. They still had informal gatherings at their home. But he sat quietly. Trying to follow. For the first few minutes they'd speak directly to him, saying the words slowly and distinctly.

But after a while they naturally lapsed into normal conversation. And he lapsed into his own world.

The funeral for Dom Philippe had been held at the monastery of Saint-Gilbert-Entre-les-Loups.

The funeral for Yves Rousseau was held in the small chapel overlooking the harbor of Blanc-Sablon. Then his ashes were spread over his favorite rock. The one jutting out into the water, where young Yves had sat and contemplated the great mystery. A mystery the elderly Yves had now solved.

Dom Philippe, Yves Rousseau, had come home.

Armand could not make either funeral. He wanted to, but his doctors said with his damaged eardrum and serious concussion, he could not fly. But Jean-Guy and Isabelle went to both, and Armand and Reine-Marie watched online as Father David spoke of his friend: "We will feel him in the rain, in the wind, in the bite of snow, in the scent of autumn leaves, and in deep and penetrating silence. We might miss him terribly but will never be away from him. Yves returns to joy. As we all will, one day."

Armand had leaned closer to the laptop and watched as Jeanne Caron limped forward and helped spread her uncle's ashes over his favorite rock and into the water, to join her mother, his sister. She said something. Armand had to ask what it was.

"I think she said, 'Forgive me,'" said Reine-Marie.

Isabelle had gone down to Three Pines to brief the Chief Inspector in person. He'd read her official report but wanted to hear the unofficial. Though they both quickly realized speech was just frustrating. So they'd sat together in the garden and texted.

It felt ridiculous at first. Cumbersome and even rude. But eventually they fell into a rhythm. Chief Inspector Gamache asking questions, Lacoste answering.

*What was Sébastien's role in this?*

*He isn't talking. As you know, the French police have him in custody, charged with the murder of Brother Robert. Canada has applied to have him extradited, but so far the French authorities are reluctant. A murder at the famous Grande Chartreuse, of one of the monks who held the recipe, has become a cause célèbre.*

Gamache nodded. Frère Sébastien's silence was inevitable if unfortunate.

*You have a theory?*

*I think this might be nuts, but I suspect he was the one in the confessional.*

Gamache raised his brows. *In DC? The confession Brother Robert took?*

*Oui. Sébastien didn't realize it was his friend on the other side of the confessional, but Robert knew who it was confessing his part in a terrorist attack. I think that's why Robert never sent for him, but asked Sister Irene to come to Rome instead. Robert only ran off to Grande Chartreuse when Sébastien arrived in Rome. He was running from Sébastien.*

Gamache nodded. That made sense.

*So he knew that Sébastien was involved in the plot. But how did Sébastien know it was Robert who'd heard his confession? Robert would never have told him.*

*I think Sister Irene did, inadvertently. She told him that Robert heard something in a confession when he'd stood in for a priest. Sébastien must've been in a panic when he realized what that meant*, wrote Isabelle.

Something had to be done to shut Robert up. Fast. So Sébastien followed him to Grande Chartreuse, acting as a lay monk, supposedly to protect Robert but really to watch him and, if necessary, kill him.

*It must've come as a terrible shock to Brother Robert, when he saw Sébastien there.*

*Oui. The one person he needed to avoid was locked in the remote monastery with him. Sébastien must've also told his co-conspirators back here, and they executed his aunt and that stranger. As a warning.*

*Then they sent the clippings to Sébastien to give to Robert. But why send for Dom Philippe?*

*I asked Irene about that. Turns out she was the one pressuring Sébastien to send for the Abbot. I think he did so partly to allay any suspicions Irene might've had, but also to find out if Robert would talk. If there was anyone he'd open up to, it would be the Abbot.*

*So the Abbot arrives,* Armand wrote, *and Robert does tell him about the terrorist plot to poison the water. But he didn't say that Sébastien was involved. He was too afraid. He made the Abbot promise not to say anything to Irene and Sébastien. The Abbot thought it was to protect his friends.*

*It was to protect himself.*

Gamache paused, his gaze drifting over to the forest behind Isabelle.

It lasted so long that Isabelle wondered if his mind had drifted off. He tended to do that these days. It worried her, though she said nothing.

Still, she also knew the man should never be underestimated. He was wily. Cunning even. In the hands of others, those qualities would be dangerous. In Gamache, they came in handy, as witnessed by his decision on the day of the attack to fill a small aspirin bottle with water. In case the opportunity came to switch.

Which it did. Gamache couldn't have known what the actual poison was put in, but he gambled that the terrorists would not know either. Just that it would be a small plastic container that would pass security at the plant.

The only ones who knew had been locked in Pump Room One.

Standing in his bathroom in Three Pines, knowing he might have the opportunity to make a switch, he'd looked at the aspirin bottle and the travel shampoo. He'd gambled and poured water into the aspirin bottle. He explained in his written report that by then he knew Commissioner Lavigne was behind the plot, and that he himself used aspirin. He'd instinctively trust it.

It gave Lacoste and Beauvoir, and everyone else familiar with what had happened, immense pleasure to know that instead of poison, the terrorists had poured pure Three Pines spring water into the system.

Sitting on the back terrasse of the home in Three Pines, Isabelle could see that Gamache was far from being able to resume his position as head of homicide. The Chief Inspector was on sick leave, at least until his hearing returned and he'd recovered from the concussion caused by the explosion right next to his head.

Armand spoke only to his doctor about his exhaustion. The shrieking cicadas in his head, caused by the damaged eardrum and not helped by the concussion, had barely diminished. It made sleep all but impossible. It also made clear thinking difficult.

When he did get to sleep, he often woke up shouting. He didn't realize he'd done it and only knew because Reine-Marie would turn on the light and grab his arm and ask if he was all right. He'd look at her, dazed. Then hug her. Tight. Sometimes she saw he'd been crying.

Though Reine-Marie asked, Armand had yet to tell her what the night terrors were about.

One day, he assured his therapist, he would. But not quite yet.

In his dreams, so vivid, he was again kneeling, the gun to his head. David Lavigne wanted to know something. Was shouting at him. It was about Charles's notebooks. He wanted to know where he'd hidden them.

In real life he hadn't told him. In his dream he did.

Armand couldn't quite figure out why telling Lavigne about the notebooks was his nightmare. Surely the images of the deputy commissioner following through with the threat to go to Three Pines and kill everyone was more nightmare-worthy.

Or putting the real poison into the system. Surely his nightmare should be seeing tens of thousands die because he'd failed.

Or actually being shot in the base of the skull and not just grazed. Yes, there were any number of nightmare scenarios.

Why would he keep dreaming about the damned notebooks?

His therapist suggested his subconscious was starting with the easiest part first. The others would follow. His nightmares would get worse.

It had not been his favorite session. He also wondered why, in real life, Lavigne hadn't asked about the laptop or the map. The only explanation was that he didn't know about them.

They hadn't yet found the laptop, but would.

"*Patron?*" Isabelle had leaned forward and touched his knee.

"I'm sorry," he said, smiling. His voice was the same as ever. Almost. There was a vagueness to it, and occasionally it was too loud. "I was just thinking."

"About?"

He got up and returned a minute or so later with two pads of paper and pens.

Handing one to her, he wrote longhand, *About the arrests. About those not arrested.*

This was obviously a "conversation" he didn't want anyone else to see. He held out his pad, and when she'd read it, she looked up.

Chief Inspector Gamache's eyes were as bright, as thoughtful, as intelligent as ever. He was still there. The same unwavering gaze in the storm.

And there was still a storm.

# CHAPTER 47

‿

The events at the LaSalle water-treatment plant had created a tsunami, with huge aftershocks.

On Jeanne Caron's testimony and the evidence she'd gathered and saved in the satchel, the Deputy Prime Minister, Marcus Lauzon, had been arrested and charged with murder and high treason. He, of course, denied everything, though the evidence was overwhelming.

An investigation was ongoing into other prominent political figures. The RCMP was in crisis and chaos, with the undeniable involvement of their now dead second-in-command in a terrorist plot to murder tens of thousands and overthrow the government.

And the Sûreté had not emerged unscathed.

While Superintendent Toussaint was quickly cleared, as was the head of the Organized Crime division, charges were laid against Chief Inspector Goudreau, the head of the Sûreté's Highways division.

It had long perplexed Gamache how an officer so ill-suited to command could be given such a hefty portfolio. It had become clear in recent weeks that the man was more than just incompetent. He was criminal.

*At least we now know that Paolo Parisi brought the botulinum across the border. With Goudreau's help.*

*It would be helpful to know what else he allowed in,* wrote Armand. *Or who else.*

*Do you want me to do my own investigation? Quietly?*

Gamache considered, then shook his head. *Early days yet. Good officers are conducting the investigation. They'll work it all out.*

*They haven't arrested Moretti*, Lacoste wrote, and saw Gamache's brows draw together.

Several aspects of the investigation troubled him and that was one. The involvement of the mob. Joseph Moretti had denied any knowledge, and his consigliere had claimed the mob soldiers had been working on their own. Besides, Monsieur Moretti had no connection to the mafia. And no mafia existed, in Montréal or elsewhere. The "Sixth Family" was a fantasy.

That was predictable, but what really troubled Gamache was how it was possible that Chief Inspector Tardiff, the head of the Sûreté's Organized Crime division, hadn't known about the plot and the mob involvement. She'd continually denied that the Montréal mafia could be active again, despite what were obvious signs.

Was Tardiff involved? Or had she simply made, as people eventually do, a terrible mistake?

How easy it was to slide into conspiracies. To mistake misjudgment for deceit.

To see treacheries and plots and sedition where none existed.

Gamache was very aware of the warning not to attribute to malice that which can be explained by stupidity. There was much more stupidity around than malice. Though both were dangerous. And he never discounted the malicious.

Evelyn Tardiff wasn't just a colleague, she was a friend. But then, so was David Lavigne.

Jeanne Caron, on the other hand, was his enemy. And had saved not just his life, but thousands of lives.

Fully recovered from her wound, she'd visited the Gamaches in Three Pines.

"I plan to see your son next," Jeanne had said. "To apologize for what I did years ago."

Reine-Marie listened to this, tight-lipped.

They were in the bistro. It was a rainy, cool early-autumn day, and Olivier had lit the fire in the huge grate. Reine-Marie, on hearing that

Madame Caron was coming to visit, had refused to allow the woman in her home.

She appreciated that Caron had saved Armand's life on that terrible day and that she should be grateful, but as she looked at Caron, all she felt was rage.

Reine-Marie had chosen to sit as far from Jeanne Caron as possible and still be in the conversation. For her part, Jeanne Caron, sensing what was obvious and awkward, tried to ingratiate herself, but it only seemed to make things worse.

Reine-Marie sat composed of stone and wishful thinking that this woman would just leave and leave them alone.

"It's not that I'm not grateful for what she did, Armand," Reine-Marie had said when he'd told her Madame Caron was coming to lunch in Three Pines. "But can't you just send a nice basket of fruit and be done with it?"

He'd smiled. He hadn't caught everything his wife had said, but he had caught the gist.

When the encounter in the bistro was over, Armand had walked Caron to her car.

"I hope Madame Gamache forgives me one day."

Armand had nodded but said nothing. Caron wasn't sure if he'd taken it in. His eyes were slightly unfocused and his expression almost blank.

It would be a while, she knew, before he could return to active duty. If ever. She looked around and knew that there were worse places, worse things, than retiring here.

She hoped he did.

Finally, he stirred. "The key. You gave Charles a key to our home. How did you get it?"

"I wondered if you'd ask. It was your cleaner." She realized she was talking to him in clear, simple statements, as though he were a child. "On the bus. I had someone lift the key and make an impression. She had no idea. But one thing still worries me. How did Parisi know Charles was meeting you in Open Da Night?"

Armand asked her to repeat it, staring intently at her mouth. Then he shrugged.

"He must've followed him there. How else could he have known?"

His voice was louder than it should have been, though he was obviously unaware of it.

"I'm not sure if you noticed, Armand, but when we spread my uncle's ashes in Blanc-Sablon, we found a small statue on his favorite rock. No one seemed to know where it came from."

Armand had smiled, in a vague manner. As though he'd only partly understood.

But he'd understood perfectly and had simply chosen not to tell her that Clara Morrow had created two sculptures at his request.

Armand had given them to Jean-Guy and asked him to place one on Yves's favorite rock in Blanc-Sablon, and the other on the peninsula at Saint-Gilbert-Entre-les-Loups, where the Cree Chief had told the first Abbot about the two wolves.

Jean-Guy took photos, which Armand kept framed on his desk. Of the grey wolf, staring out across the water. Ever watchful.

And he'd understood something else. That her question about Parisi was far more important than he let on.

That night, after lying awake for hours trying to settle the cicadas, Armand had finally given up and got up.

He made a pot of tea and lit the fire. Henri trudged downstairs and slowly crawled onto the sofa, placing his head on Armand's lap. Little by little Armand's eyelids grew heavy. He put down the mug of tea, and his head fell back as he drifted off to sleep.

He woke up with a start, to find Henri bolt upright, staring at him. He'd had another nightmare. Again, about the damned notebooks.

Lavigne threatening him with the slaughter of his family and more if he didn't give them up. It was obvious why he needed them. Charles Langlois had documented, in a way that was complete and utterly damning, the whole plot. Not by foreign terrorists at all, but domestic. By the Deputy Prime Minister.

If their scheme to put Lauzon in power was to succeed, David Lavigne needed to destroy those notebooks.

Once again, in his dream, he told Lavigne where to find them. Once again, he woke up screaming.

Armand dropped his face into his hands and rubbed. If this was the easiest of the nightmares, he was in big trouble.

He sat in the dark and peaceful living room in Three Pines and stared into the embers of the fire. And forced himself back to the treatment plant.

The gun was pressing hard to his head. He knew he was going to die. But it wasn't just his own murder he was facing. Lavigne was hissing threats. Give up the notebooks or he'd come here and . . .

And there it was. What had been bothering him.

*Notebooks.* Plural. Not just the one that documented the planned attack on Montréal's water. Lavigne wanted, demanded, needed both.

But why?

And why had Charles Langlois hidden both? Why not just the one to do with poisoning the drinking water?

Armand sat upright and shifted his stare from the fire to Henri, who'd been Clara's model for the grey wolf, and whose immense ears now moved fully forward.

They stared at each other for a moment before Armand got up and went to his study, where he sat in front of his laptop.

He'd given the notebooks to the prosecutors, but not before making copies.

He brought them up on his screen. Then, knowing it would be a long night, he made a pot of coffee, toasted some brioche, and returned to his study.

Smelly old Fred and tiny Gracie joined Henri, and the three were now curled at his feet.

Charles Langlois had two notebooks. The second chronicled what he'd found in his investigation at the LaSalle treatment plant. That was the one he and Beauvoir had focused on. The one the prosecutors were poring over. The one many of the charges were based on.

But . . .

Suppose. Suppose . . .

Suppose it was the other way around? Langlois's evidence about Montréal's drinking water was in the first notebook. Terrible, terrifying. But just the beginning. That discovery had sent the young biologist into an even deeper, darker cave.

And there he'd found something else. Something worse. Someone worse. And had chronicled it in the other notebook. That was why David Lavigne was demanding both books. It was actually the other that he most needed to destroy. The one about the lakes.

Gamache opened that file and started reading the scanned pages. It was just random words, numbers. Sketches. Partial sentences. But it was enough for Armand to get a sense of why David Lavigne was so desperate to get his hands on both books.

He sat for a long time, staring at the screen. Then he sent a private message to Jean-Guy and Isabelle.

It was 4:15 in the morning when they arrived, one after the other.

Armand had stoked the fire, and now it danced and popped in the grate. There was a pot of fresh coffee and the home smelled of warm cinnamon buns.

"What is it?" Jean-Guy asked.

Armand pointed to his laptop, now sitting on the coffee table in the living room.

The black wolf was in there. In the scribbles of a young biologist who was just beginning to understand what he had.

In focusing solely on the one attack, in allowing himself to be misled, Armand had given the creature time to grow even more malicious. Even more powerful.

Ever closer.

Isabelle and Jean-Guy sat down and read, then looked up.

"We have a problem."

# ACKNOWLEDGMENTS

I want to start by acknowledging you, my friend, for your support, your company, your patience. I took a year off between *A World of Curiosities* and this book, and you stuck with me. Thank you. I cannot imagine any writer ever had a more wonderful reader. You have been supportive in ways I will never forget that go far beyond the books. You have also been great company along the way. Warm and funny. Engaged. Kindly in pointing out any mistakes in a book (there will inevitably be some). And always cheering me, and the characters, on.

You have also been supportive of my own little village of Knowlton, Québec, which is not Three Pines and yet is very much an inspiration for the spirit of Three Pines. Inclusive, caring, there for each other. Not perfect (we need more places for breakfast!), but home. Home. That's really what the books are about. Home.

The Gamache books are proudly crime novels, as you see in *The Grey Wolf*, but at their core they are about community. Acceptance. Belonging. Courage. The books are about the triumph of love and the power of friendship. About trying to do better.

Progress, not perfection.

*The Grey Wolf* is dedicated to Rocky and Steve Gottlieb, my great friends in London. I met Rocky in an elevator . . . and by the time we got off she and I had bonded. Then I met her husband, Steve. Handsome, kind, generous, warm, and funny Steve, and I developed, dare I admit, a bit of a crush. I joined them for Sunday lunch every week. Rocky's roast chicken. Divine. Rocky and Steve reminded me of Michael and me. Of Armand and Reine-Marie. So much love, such a profound friendship.

Steve passed away in 2023, at the age of ninety-four, with Rocky holding his hand. It is a terrible loss. In *The Grey Wolf* I say that that's what Armand wants, what all of them, all of us want, in the end. Someone to be there, to hold our hand.

And now those of us who love Rocky and Steve are holding her hand, as she navigates this new life. I think you know what that feels like.

I want to thank My Assistant and great friend Lise Desrosiers, who is steadfast in her love and friendship. Lise, whom Michael and I found in our garden, literally, and who has grown into a beloved sister. Our ongoing joke is that I am always firing her, and when not being fired, Lise is quitting. None of that is true. She is not just my right hand, she will be there to hold my hand, in the end. As I will hold hers.

Thank you, Linda Lyall—aka Linda in Scotland, who manages the newsletter and helps with my social media, and answers most reader letters. And does so much more. Michael found Linda in Scotland even before the first book was published. Linda has been a vital part of the team, of our lives, of the success, of the fun, since before day one and is so much more than a colleague. We have been through thick and thin together.

Thank you to Danny and Lucy at Brome Lake Books for not just supporting the books but being family. Thank you too to all the booksellers and librarians who have embraced Armand and Three Pines. You have given me the most astonishing career.

Thank you to friends Normand and Peter and Bow, to Kirk and Walter and Dafne, to Cynthia and Finni and Sally, my old friends Linda and David Rosenblatt, Paul Workman and Mellissa Fung, to Rosemary Attenborough, to Sukie and Hillary, Bob and Rita, Bonnie and Patsy, to Ann and Allida and Judy. To Jack and Jane and Guy and

Wendy and Lois. Thank you Oscar and Brendan. Merci Jean et Pascale, for being the best possible neighbors. Indeed, thank you to all my neighbors in Knowlton, for your tolerance and support. Thank you to Alfred for being such a great Armand, and friend. Thanks and welcome to Isabelle Rosa, the newest member of the Three Pines coven. A great addition.

Thank you Don and Erin Weisberg, John and Connie Sargent, Sally Richardson. And the late, great Steve Rubin. So missed!

Thank you to my beloved Jamie Broadhurst, a longtime colleague and so much more, and Joan Westland-Eby. Such important friends, they also sit on the advisory committee for the Three Pines Foundation.

I am keenly aware that the funds we give away through the Three Pines Foundation is actually your money. When you buy the Gamache books much of that money goes into the foundation, which goes to those who need a bit of help. As we all do at times.

In the book I have scenes set in a place called The Mission. Many Montrealers will recognize that place as being inspired by The Old Brewery Mission, a remarkable place dedicated to helping the homeless and those in distress. It is close to my heart for many reasons. Though I do want to say that "my" Mission and the real thing are different. For one thing, one is fictional, the other real.

If you'd like to donate to it, you can go to missionoldbrewery.ca. I know they'd appreciate the help.

In *The Grey Wolf* there is a eulogy near the end. I did not write it. It comes from a letter the remarkable writer Richard Wagamese sent to our mutual friend Shelagh Rogers, when her dog died. He knew the love they shared and wrote the most beautify elegy. Shelagh then adapted his words and used them in a eulogy to her mother. And gave me permission to use them in the book.

Thank you dear Shelagh, and thanks to the huge heart and talent of the late Richard Wagamese.

Once again, Ruth's poetry is mostly that of Margaret Atwood. When Lise and Isabelle were having trouble getting permission to use it in *The Grey Wolf*, I wrote Margaret to ask for help. She leapt onto it right away, sending off emails to her agents and publishers, and staying with it until the issue was solved, even saying I could have it for free. I am smitten. Thank you, Peggy, and thanks to your colleagues.

I want to thank my amazing agent, David Gernert, and his team, including Rebecca Gardner, Will Roberts, and Ellen Goodson Coughtrey.

Thank you to Jo Dickinson and the team of Hodder in the UK, as well as all my foreign publishers. The Gamache books are hitting bestseller lists internationally, thanks to their efforts.

Thank you Louise Loiselle, my Québec publisher, friend, and neighbor.

This book is in your hands because of the hard work and vision of the brilliant men and women at Minotaur/St. Martin's Press. Kelley Ragland is my editor and has just this past year been promoted to publisher of Minotaur! Smart, diplomatic, insightful. Did I mention diplomatic? Kelley is a luminary. I am so fortunate to have her in my literary and personal life.

Andy Martin has been guiding the books for almost two decades. Paul Hochman and Allison Ziegler are the dazzling marketing minds who bring the Gamache books, and so much else, to your attention. It's not the easiest thing to come up with fresh new ideas nineteen books in, but they do.

Sarah Melnyk is my publicist—who also manages to come up with new ideas. And things to do. And who travels with me to make sure I show up where and when I am supposed to. I had the great pleasure of being at her wedding this past year to the magnificent Thom.

Do you like the cover? I adore it! It comes from the astonishing design mind of David Rotstein. Thank you, David.

Thank you to Jennifer Enderlin and Jon Yaged, the boss of bosses at Macmillan.

And finally, thank you to Muggins—the Divine Miss M. Who has turned my life upside down. Filled it with dander, with unexpected and admittedly unwelcome little "gifts." With smells. With cuddles, and licks, and hugs, and hilarity. She has introduced me to stain removers and to neighbors who would otherwise have remained strangers. She has snuggled with me, and fallen asleep snoring in my lap on the sofa as we watched *Slow Horses* (which is brilliant, by the way). Muggins, the golden retriever, is made up of mud and skunk poop and wonderment.

For some reason I sometimes find myself calling her Michael—baffling to us both. But love is love, as Ruth and Rosa would attest. As Rocky and Steve would attest. As you know, my friend.

OK, onto the next Gamache—if Mugs would just put down that squeaky toy . . .

**THE BLACK WOLF**
Coming 2025

# ABOUT THE AUTHOR

Mikaël Theimer

**Louise Penny** is the author of the #1 *New York Times, USA Today,* and *Globe and Mail* bestselling series of Chief Inspector Armand Gamache novels, and coauthor with Hillary Rodham Clinton of the #1 *New York Times* bestselling thriller *State of Terror.* She has won numerous awards, including a CWA Dagger and the Agatha Award (nine times), and was a finalist for the Edgar Award for Best Novel. In 2017, she received the Order of Canada for her contributions to Canadian culture. Louise lives in a small village south of Montréal.